"... it was impossible to lift one's eyes from the decks to the spacious, gleaming leagues of silent ocean, bounded by the glittering sky, and black as ink under it, though brightly reflecting the lustre of the larger stars in thin flakes of silver that seemed to be melting and slowing sinking in a thick trickle of white, burnished, molten metal, without finding one's merriment checked. The thought of the minute speck this ship made upon that boundless surface, and the littleness of the people whose world it was for a time, and the paltriness of the pastime, pathetic in its paltriness, that made them merry, became too violent for mirth when that soundless, breathing, ebony space of ocean was looked at."

It is with such magnetic, intense colour that W. Clark Russell consistently entertained his legions of readers and established a formidable reputation as a writer of the sea.

THE 'LADY MAUD'
SCHOONER YACHT

"Where are you coming? he yelled tossing his fist." - page 27

THE 'LADY MAUD'
SCHOONER YACHT

A NARRATIVE OF HER LOSS ON ONE
OF THE BAHAMA CAYS, FROM THE
ACCOUNT OF A GUEST ON BOARD

a novel by

W. CLARK RUSSELL

with eight illustrations by

A. BURNHAM SHUTE

ADELAIDE
MICHAEL WALMER
2014

The 'Lady Maud' first published 1876*
This edition published 2014

by

Michael Walmer
49 Second Street
Gawler South
South Australia 5118

ISBN 978-0-9925234-5-9 paperback
ISBN 978-0-9925234-6-6 ebook

ERRATA

This edition has been prepared utilizing a previous edition; thus errors have been reproduced. On page 33, line 29, for *mind* please read *mine*. On page 46, line 42, for *eat* please read *ate*. On page 52, line 14, for *Willaim* please read *William*. On page 53, line 9, for *away."* please read *away.* On page 73, line 7, for *The Mdge* please read *The Midge*. On page 162, line 12, for *seaman* please read *seamen*. On page 166, line 11, for *after, deck* please read *after deck*. On page 190, Chapter XI is misnamed Chapter XII; all numbering thereafter follows on. On page 269, line 5, for *others* please read *other*. On page 275, line 6, for *forthous and* please read *four thousand*. On page 289, line 18, for *woman* please read *women*. On page 293, line 15, for *acause* please read *a cause*. On page 307, line 4, for *he steward* please read *the steward*.

*This publication date is attested by one bibliographic record only, that of *The New Cambridge Bibliography of English Literature*, volume 3, 1969, edited by George Watson. No extant edition of this date has been found by the publisher in online library catalogues. The earliest edition found in those searches was published in 1882.

THE "LADY MAUD":
SCHOONER YACHT.

CHAPTER I.

THURSDAY, June such and such a date was the day fixed for the sailing of the yacht *Lady Maud* for a cruise as far as the latitudes of the West Indies. The voyage was planned on account of the health of Lady Brookes, the wife of the owner of the vessel. The doctors had discovered that one of her lungs was threatened, and urgently advised her to take a long sea trip, that for all the summer she might breathe nothing but ocean air. Her husband, who was a great lover of the sea, had only recently sold a forty-ton yawl named the *Ione*, and purchased in its room the *Lady Maud* schooner. In this vessel he thought his wife would be able to get as much sea air as she needed, and that she would enjoy home privileges beyond any a passenger ship could supply. It was therefore settled that the cruise should be made in the yacht, which was forthwith equipped and victualed for the voyage ; and among the persons invited to join Sir Mordaunt and Lady Brookes was the writer of this account of the journey, and of the lamentable shipwreck and sufferings of the people concerned in it.

I was willing to go for several reasons. First, I had been at sea for eight years in the merchant service, and had passed an examination as chief mate, when my father died, and bequeathed me a property that was an estate to a bachelor of simple tastes ; so I quitted that life, but I left my heart behind me in it, and was always glad for an excuse to get upon the sea. So as I say, this was one reason. Next, as I have told, I was a bachelor. The only relative I owned was a married sister, who lived at Bristol, many leagues out of my track, and thus my stake was too small to hinder me from going where I pleased and doing what I pleased. Add to this, I had just resolved to go abroad for some weeks, to kill the hot English months, when there comes the letter from Sir Mordaunt Brookes (whom I had known two years, and in whose yawl I had enjoyed several pleasant runs along our east coast), telling me about his wife's health, the proposed voyage, etc., and begging me to go with them. The offer was to my fancy, if I except the West India part. I thought June a queer month to choose for a voyage to the Antilles, as those islands where the dog-star always rages were called. But Sir Mordaunt wrote that if we touched at any port it would be merely to fill our fresh water casks, by which I understood that we were to keep almost entirely upon the water and among the blowing winds.

Preparing for a voyage ten times as long would have cost me small trouble. A few hours served to complete my arrangements, and punctually on the appointed day I was at Southampton, waiting for the arrival of the *Lady Maud's* boat to carry me aboard of her.

I was never at that town before, nor have I visited it since ; and nothing of it remains in my mind but a clear image of the stretch of beautiful sparkling water, with a vision of the Isle of Wight in the southward, and of green shores opposite melting upon the gleaming breast of the sea as they trended toward the Solent. Many yachts and other vessels were riding at anchor, and many more under way, with their white canvas flashing softly in the brilliant sunshine. A pleasant breeze blew from the northeast, but the sky was quite cloudless, a deep, darkly pure blue, like the heavens of the South Pacific.

I was anxious to see the vessel that was to be my home for some months, but none of the watermen I asked could tell me which was she. However, I had not long to wait, for whilst I stood admiring a very handsome, heavily sparred yawl, anchored within musket-shot of the pier, a boat pulling six oars shot from under her stern, clearly from one of the yachts lying beyond, and headed directly for the spot I occupied. The men rowed with fine precision, their oars flashed like glass, and the froth twinkled frostily at the stem. Before she was alongside I read the name *Lady Maud* on the breast of the cockswain's jersey, and went to meet him as he jumped ashore. He had been one of the *Ione's* men, and knew me ; and in a few minutes my luggage was brought from the hotel and bundled into the boat.

The moment we cleared the stern of the yawl, the cockswain,

pointed to a large schooner that lay a few fathoms astern of a small vessel similarly rigged, said that that was the *Lady Maud.* I looked at her eagerly, but the first impression was disappointing. She had a straight stem like a cutter's, an unusual thing in a craft of her rig ; and as her copper came high, starting at the bows a very few inches under the hawse-pipes, she had the look of a revenue boat about the hull. As we approached, however, some good features began to exhibit themselves. She was rather bluff about the forecastle rail, but rapidly fined down to the water's edge, and was like a knife at that point. Her run was beautiful, and a decided spring forward gave her a defiant posture upon the water. She was large for her class, nearly two hundred tons by Lloyd's measurement. Her spars were the handsomest sticks I had ever seen, and the soaring maintopmast, surmounted by an angular red flag that blew upward like a tongue of flame against the lovely sky, made the eye giddy that followed it from the low level of a boat. Unlike any of the other yachts about, she carried a topsail and topgallant yard : and, judging from the height of the foreyard from the deck, I reckoned that if Sir Mordaunt Brookes carried a square-sail, it should be big enough to hold a gale of wind.

We dashed alongside. I grasped the white man-ropes, and was received at the gangway by my friend.

"Up anchor now, Purchase, and get us away," he sung out, holding my hand in a cordial grip. "Tripshore, look after the baggage in the boat there, and have it stowed away in Mr. Walton's cabin."

So saying, he led me over to his wife, who was sitting aft under a short awning, in company with a young lady and a short dark man dressed in gray clothes. This was my first introduction to Lady Brookes, who spent the greater part of the year in the south of France, and had always been out of England when I was with her husband. She was a fine woman, about four-and-twenty years old—indeed, she and her husband had only been married three years—large black eyes, sparkling yet listless, complexion disposed to sallowness, good teeth, thick raven hair, lustrous as polished ebony ; dressed in blue serge that faultlessly fitted her figure—molded like one of Herman Melville's South Sea water goddesses.

On the other hand, her companion, a niece of Sir Mordaunt, was fair, her hair a pale gold, her eyes blue as the sky. My friend introducing me to her called her Ada Tuke. Indeed she was a very pretty girl, but I will not attempt to convey an idea of the *character* of her prettiness. Little Roman nose, arched upper lip, small head, almost straight eyebrows, darker than her hair—these are points easily named ; but what do they express on paper ? No more than my asserting that the *Lady Maud's* figure-head was a handsome device would assist your imagination in figuring the appearance of the vessel. If the prospect of the cruise was agreeable to me before, I found it quite delightful now that I knew our little company would include Ada Tuke.

The gentleman who stood near was Mr. Norie, M. D., who had been shipped by Sir Mordaunt to look after her ladyship's health. He had a smooth-shaven face and black eyes, and would have passed for an actor or a priest. The rest of the party consisted of two superb mastiffs, which lay near the mainmast in the sunshine, outside the shadow line of the awning. They were a noble pair of dogs, and they reclined with their great paws stretched along, enjoying the heat of the decks, and watching the men tumbling about, with slow-rolling eyes and an inquisitive cock of the ears.

The ladies had now to shift their seats, for their chairs were in the road of the men who had gathered aft to hoist the mainsail. I placed Lady Brookes's chair for her clear of the running rigging, and asked her how she liked the idea of the voyage.

" Not at all," said she, quickly, and yet without animation. " Nothing but my husband's anxiety could have induced me to take the trip."

" But it is sure to do you good," said I. " There is no finer medicine than the ocean air."

" Perhaps so," she answered, languidly ; " but even health may sometimes cost too much."

I turned to Miss Tuke, and asked her how *she* liked the prospect of the journey.

" Very much," she replied, removing a small opera glass from her eyes. " I am hoping we shall meet with exciting adventures."

Lady Brookes smiled, but the expression went out of her face quickly. Here Sir Mordaunt joined us, and catching hold of my arm, called my attention to the spaciousness of the *Lady Maud's* decks, and asked me what I thought of her. I told him I considered her a very beautiful vessel, and honestly meant what I said. Her decks were exceedingly roomy, in spite of a row of hencoops abreast of the foremast on either side, and a boat on chocks amidship and as white as snow, and as solid as a thousand-ton ship's. Strength, indeed, was the agreeable peculiarity I everywhere observed. Her bulwarks were tall and stout, her companions and skylights almost unnecessarily massive; but everything was plain, and, as I considered, the fitter by reason of that quality for ocean use. She was steered by a wheel, and I took notice of the strength of the tiller and wheel chains. Her rigging was handsomely set up, the masts stayed to a hair; every block worked as easily as a carriage wheel. I walked aft to remark her length, and was delighted by the fine sweep of shining deck and the bold incurving of the forecastle bulwarks, meeting at the long powerful bowsprit, that was slightly bowed under the taut bobstays.

But by this time they had got the mainsail on her, and were busy getting up the anchor. Purchase, the skipper, came and took hold of the wheel, looking up and around as he grasped the spokes, and hallooing to the men in a slightly wheezy deep-sea note. It was the hottest hour of an unusually hot day, yet this man was wrapped up like a North Sea pilot in thick rough cloth, and a blue shawl with white spots around his throat. As he was to have charge of the vessel, I examined him closely, and beheld a round face, purple at the cheek-bones; a pear-shaped, carrot-colored nose; small eyes, buried deep in wrinkles, and glowing like sparks in their well-thatched caverns; a capacious mouth almost destitute of lips; the whole surmounted by a cloth cap decorated with a broad gold band. In truth, he looked rather too nautical to please me. He had more the appearance of a Thames wherryman masquerading in a yachting skipper's clothes than a plain sailorman. He turned his little eyes upon me once or twice, as if he would like to ask why I looked at him so hard. I had no doubt that Sir Mordaunt was impressed by the man's nautical aspect, but for my part, if I had had the choosing of a captain for the *Lady Maud*, I should not have selected so highly flavored a tar as Purchase. I dare say I was prejudiced. No man who has been knocked about at sea can have a high opinion of yachtsmen as sailors. On the one side are many hardships, gales of wind, bitter cold, poor food, and the like; on the other, fine weather, plenty of lounging, clean forecastles, fresh provisions, and light work. The yachtsman has the best of it, and Jack may envy him, but he will not call him a sailor.

We carried a mate, named Ephraim Tripshore, as well as a captain, and eleven men, counting the cook and the steward. The decks looked pretty full with them and us, and I watched them as they worked, the thought coming into my head that if they were no better than the usual run of 'longshore-men, it would be a bad look out for us should sailorly qualities come to be needed.

By this time they had got the anchor off the ground, and the vessel, lying almost athwart the run of the water, with her nose pointing at Southampton, was already slipping along, but sweeping round fast to the southward. Talk as they will of the beauty of foreign ports and scenes, I never remember in all my voyages, nor in any journeys I have made since, the like of that scene of Southampton Water, and the shores on either hand, as I beheld it on that day. The yachts at anchor, with the flashing water trembling in their glossy sides ; the leaning pillars of canvas here and there shining like virgin silver in the sun ; the flags which filled the sky with spots of bright colors ; the houses ashore, looking as delicate as ivory work in the far distance ; the undulations of the coast making a soft horizon of trees and green country against the heavens ; the Isle of Wight ahead, and beyond its marble-like heights in the south-east the pale blue waters of the English Channel— combined to produce a picture of which no language at my command could express the beauty.

The anchor was catted and fished, and the vessel, with the wind broad on the beam, was slightly leaning under the huge mainsail and a couple of jibs. Her pace even under this canvas was good, she threw the water off her weather bow in a little wave that arched over like a coil of glass, the extremity of which, abreast of the fore-rigging, broke into foam and ran hissing to join the sparkling line of wake astern. It was per- haps characteristic that I should be watching the yacht and studying her qualities instead of contemplating the brilliant scene through which we were running. One picturesque sight, however, interested me greatly. It was a beautiful little steam- yacht lying at anchor, and as we approached her, Sir Mor- daunt motioned to the skipper to put the wheel over by a spoke or two, that we might close her. There was a group of ladies and gentlemen under the awning, who, when they saw the *Lady Maud* coming, rose and stood in a crowd at the steamer's side. As we went past, Lady Brookes waved her pocket-hand- kerchief, and Sir Mordaunt called out good-by. They gave us a demonstrative farewell, the ladies flourishing their parasols and the gentlemen shouting. But it was only a turn of the kaleidoscope, a brief shifting of the shining colors. We passed a succession of sparkling pictures of that kind, but all the rest of the people who looked at us were strangers, and no more farewells were exchanged.

I was struck by the expression on Lady Brookes's face after we had dropped the steamer, and the brief excitement kindled by the hurried salutations had passed from her. Dejection was never more strongly defined. I was sure she dreaded the voyage more than she had owned, and I now wonder, on looking back, that what was unquestionably a presentiment of ill in her mind did not decide her husband upon abandoning his resolution to find a cure for her in the heart of the North Atlantic. Her melancholy was strongly accentuated by the contrast of Miss Tuke's happy, cheerful face : the full spirit of the lustrous scene was reflected in the girl's soft eyes, and expressed in her lips subdued wonder and admiration. The wind stirred the curls of gold-bright hair upon her forehead, and now and again she would say something aloud—involuntarily and to herself apparently, for she addressed nobody—and follow it with a gentle laugh that mingled with the lip, lipping of the water, sounding like the tinkling of hundreds of little bells along the sweeping sides of the yacht, and the moan of the foam at the stem that fell upon the ear like the murmur of a fountain, and the voice of the warm wind overhead as it poured into and out of the glistening concavity of the great space of milk-white mainsail.

We had shifted our helm, and eased off the main-sheet to run through the Solent, and had hove up West Cowes until the houses were clearly visible to the naked eye, when Sir Mordaunt asked me to step below and look at the yacht's accommodation. I followed him down the companion steps, and found at the bottom a polished bulk-head, behind which was the pantry. The cabin stretched from this bulk-head aft, and was a spacious room considering the tonnage of the yacht. There was a handsome piano against the mainmast, and beyond the mainmast a door that led to the sleeping-berths, of which there were six—three of a side. The walls of the cabin were colored and grained in imitation of satin-wood ; green silk curtains protected the central skylight ; the ceiling was painted with floral devices ; and the great mainmast that pierced the upper deck, and that vanished through a rich

Turkey carpet, was framed with looking-glasses molded to the spar.   Green velvet cushions upon the lockers made them as luxurious as ottoman mats, and a curious character was given to the sumptuous interior by a tall polished brass rack, fixed abaft the companion steps, filled with rifles and guns of various patterns.   The sunshine that pierced the skylight in places sparkled in brilliant swinging trays and in large crystal globes filled with gold and silver fish, and here and there in diamond-shaped mirrors which were arranged around the cabin, filled the air with prismatic light.

Sir Mordaunt then conducted me to the sleeping berths, the first of which on the starboard side I judged was to be mine, by observing my baggage stowed away in a corner.   The bunk was draped fit for a prince to lie in ; every convenience that a comfortable bed-chamber should possess was here.   It was, in truth, a superbly fitted sleeping-room, and the warm wind pouring in through the open port-hole gave it a wonderful freshness and sweetness.

"Such a bedroom as this," said I, "might make even a Frenchman in love with the sea."

" A little snugger than a ship's forecastle, eh, Walton ? " said Sir Mordaunt.

" A little.   The sight of that bunk puts me in mind that somebody stole my blankets at the beginning of my first voyage, and that to keep myself warm I had to sleep in my sea-boots, and sometimes lie under my mattress."

" Yes, sailors have to rough it.   We yachting men know very little about the sea, though some of us can swagger. What think you of this cabin ? "

As he said this he threw open the door of Lady Brookes's berth.   There was a bright-eyed, smartly dressed little woman at work arranging some books upon a shelf.   Sir Mordaunt called her Carey, and I supposed her, as I afterward knew her to be, her ladyship's maid.   I stood in the doorway, looking with great admiration upon a room that was as unlike a sea cabin as the most expensive arts of the upholsterer could make it.   The hangings were of blue satin ; a brass bedstead swung within a foot of the deck floor upon strong irons hooked to stout eyes screwed into the beams ; pictures and looking-glasses covered the walls ; and I should tire your patience by cataloguing the carpets, couches, chairs, bracket-lamps, and the hundred knickknacks which embellished this exceedingly elegant apartment.

"Is there a passenger ship afloat that could have given my wife a more cozy room than this?" said Sir Mordaunt, looking around him with an air of grave satisfaction.

"I never saw anything more charming. That bed, Sir Mordaunt, is quite original!"

"It is. I had it made expressly for this cruise. You see Lady Brookes can step into it without help. The ordinary cot, even in a calm, is a troublesome contrivance, and in a seaway one must be very agile to 'fetch' it, as sailors say."

"Does Lady Brookes suffer from seasickness?"

"I am afraid so. But I console myself with reflecting that if she *is* to be sick, a five-thousand-ton ship could not save her."

He came out of the cabin, and as we walked forward said, "I wish my wife undertook the journey more light-heartedly. Her physician assured her that a sea-voyage was of the utmost importance to her health, and having full faith myself in the prescription, and knowing indeed that the journey *must* be taken, in one way or another, for her sake, I have not thought it wise to notice her reluctance and depression."

"Oh, she will recover her spirits in a day or two. We must all turn to and cheer her up; besides, the North Atlantic is a big stage, something more than mere sky and water in these days of ship-building, and plenty of things should happen to amuse her. What sort of skipper have you got?"

"A capital man," he answered, speaking with energy. "He has been a sailor all his life, and served, I believe, in every sort of craft you could name, from a full rigged ship down to a galley-punt. His last berth was as master of a Sunderland collier, but he was thrown out of work by a fall, and has been idle for a year. I got him through an advertisement. There was no use shipping a smooth water man for an Atlantic voyage, and when I saw his captain's certificate and heard his experiences, and that he was in the West India trade for some time as second mate and carpenter of a small Barbadoes brig, I engaged him, and I do not know that I could have done better."

"If he is all that he says, he should answer your purpose," said I.

"Lady Brookes thinks he drinks," he continued, smilingly, "because he has a red nose. But what looks like drink is, in my opinion, nothing but weather."

"Likely enough, Sir Mordaunt. Sailors soon lose their complexions, and it is not always fair to attribute the change to rum."

We had pushed through the pantry, and were in the kitchen —a neat little box of a place, hot as an oven, everything new in it, and the copper stuff shining like gold. The cook wore a white apron and cap—a dress I should have laughed at on a man in another vessel than a yacht—and was clearly of a sour temper, the expression of which in his long yellow face was not improved by the loss of his port eye. This imperfection he took no pains to conceal, but, on the contrary, seemed anxious that everybody should, in a sense, share his deformity with him, for I observed that whilst answering some questions put to him by Sir Mordaunt, he kept his dead eye bearing full upon the baronet. Sir Mordaunt, who was probably used to the man, talked to the eye as though it had been full of life. The skipper's and mate's berths faced the kitchen, and beyond was the forecastle bulk-head which shut off that end of the yacht from the after-part. The impression of strength conveyed by the exterior of the vessel was confirmed by her appearance below. She was undoubtedly a very noble, powerful boat, abundantly qualified to undertake, not indeed merely a summer Atlantic cruise, but a voyage to any part of the world at any time of the year.

CHAPTER II.

We had got under way shortly before three o'clock. We might have made the daylight watch us a long way down the English Channel by breaking out the anchor at dawn ; but the nights were too short to make our departure needful at an uncomfortable hour, and, moreover, we should have the moon overhead until hard upon daybreak. By this time I had inspected as much of the interior of the vessel as was open to me, and followed Sir Mordaunt on deck. I was surprised to find that we were nearly clear of the Solent. No more sail had been made on the vessel, the wind was on the starboard quarter, and the main-boom swung well forward, yet the *Lady Maud* was slipping through the water as though she had been in tow of a steamer. She made no noise ; the merest seething of foam came from the direction of the cut-water ; the pale blue surface alongside was only just blurred by the motion of the yacht ; but astern her passage was denoted by a long line of eddies and revolving bubbles, which broadened out like a fan, until the extremity resembled a faint puff of steam, amid which the heads of the little windy ripples flashed like dew upon grass over which a shred of mist is crawling.

With the land close aboard of us on either side it was difficult to realize that we had veritably started upon a long voyage, and that for weeks we should have nothing but the deep and distant waters of the North Atlantic under and around us. I loitered at the companion to look around me, and then joined Sir Mordaunt, who had crossed to his wife.

They might have passed for father and daughter; for he was fifty years old, though he could have made himself look younger had he chosen to rid himself of a great beard that fell, like a sapper's, to his waist. He was a tall man, nearly if not quite six feet ; hair slightly frosted ; eyes gentle and soft in repose, but bright and animated in conversation ; a thorough gentleman in feelings, though his manners had no special polish, and his language was formed of the first words which occurred to him. He was telling his wife that I was delighted with the yacht, and that my opinion ought to reassure her, as I was a sailor of some experience, and knew what the Atlantic was, and what was fit to meet its seas.

"Indeed," said I, seeing his wish, " I would rather be in a gale of wind in the *Lady Maud* than in a good many big ships I could name."

"Sir Mordaunt ought not to make you think I am nervous," said she. " It is the tediousness of the voyage that I shall not like."

" But you should remember, my love, our object in undertaking it," exclaimed Sir Mordaunt.

" And why must it be tedious, aunt ? " said Miss Tuke, turning her sunny face toward us " There are plenty of good novels downstairs, and a piano ; and you should be able to tell us, Mr. Walton, if we are likely to meet with any adventures."

" No, I can't tell you that," said I : " and, to speak the truth, we don't want to meet with any adventures. All that we have to do, Miss Tuke, is to run down our latitudes comfortably, and pray that the fine weather may hold."

" Precisely," cried Sir Mordaunt. " And what sort of adventures would you have, Ada ? All romance went out of the sea when steam was discovered. There are no more pirates, no more privateersmen, no more handsome, dashing tars, with their belts studded with pistols, and their holds full of plundered ingots and pieces of eight.   Even shipwreck is no longer picturesque."

"Well, I won't say that," said I.   "What with rockets and bluelights and life-boats, shipwreck is more highly colored than it was."

"Pray don't let us talk of shipwreck," said Lady Brookes, pettishly.

"No, no, don't let us talk of shipwreck," echoed Sir Mordaunt, quickly. "Walton, d'ye know the coast hereabouts?   Yonder's Warden Point I think, and that should be the Needles light."

Time was when I could have drawn from memory a chart of the English Channel coast, with every light-ship and light-house and beacon upon it or belonging to it ; but a great deal of that knowledge had slipped away from me.   Nothing, I think, goes out of the head more quickly than the things learned at sea. The names of ropes, blocks, and of the different portions of the standing rigging go first; coasts and lights follow; and then the science of the sun, moon, and stars disappears.   A sailor who quits the sea for a few years finds he has a great deal to learn over again when he returns to it.   Ought not this consideration to make the commissioners cautious in their selection of nautical assessors?

Happily the lives of the people aboard the *Lady Maud* were not in my charge, and consequently whether my marine memory was good or bad mattered nothing.   I borrowed Miss Tuke's opera glass to look at the coast : but the beautiful scene showed best when inspected with the naked eye, for then the whole expanse of it was in sight.   On the right was both the Hampshire and Dorset shore, visible from Stansore Point to beyond Christchurch Head, and I think Durlstan Point was in sight, though a mere film down in the west.   Astern of us was the Isle of Wight, whose towering terraces and gleaming heights were slowly drawing out as we rounded to the southward, bringing Node Beacon and the shining ramparts of chalk beyond it on our port quarter, and right under our bow, and running up into the silver blue sky of the horizon until it stood but a foot under our bowsprit end, was the broad, bright, lake-like English Channel. To behold that shining field of water was to feel at last that our voyage was fairly begun.   I own that my heart went out to meet it.   Of all seas, none can be so dear to an Englishman as the stretch of water that separates England from France. It is a stage full of glorious historical memories ; it is the busiest maritime highway in the world ; its margin is enriched on the

British side with spaces of exquisite scenery ; and it is conse-
crated to sailors by the memory of the scores of mariners who
have found a resting place upon its sands.

When it opened broad under both bows we all stood gazing
at it. But whatever our thoughts may have been, they were
speedily interrupted by old Purchase, who still grasped the
wheel, bawling to the men in his husky, deep-sea note to set
the gaff foresail. Yachtsmen imitate men-of-war's men in their
manner of springing about. Where the rush is finely disciplined,
it is good ; it is always finely disciplined in a man-of-war, and
though one would think sometimes that the fellows were only
trying to break their necks, yet the whole fabric of the ship is
vitalized by their method of going to work, as any man knows
who has watched a frigate—when there *were* such things—trip
her anchor and flash into a lovely cloud of canvas all at once.
Yachtsmen sprawl and tumble about as cleverly as navy men ;
but it is not only because they are seldom numerous enough as
a crew that they never produce man-of-war results. I watched
the *Lady Maud's* men making sail, and thought if they had
scrambled less they would not have done their work worse.
Some of them helped up the foresail by "riding down" the
halyards, an unseaman-like trick and very unsightly. One
after another the sails were expanded, and presently the yacht
was leaning under every stitch of fore and aft canvas that she
carried. If Sir Mordaunt's wish had been to try her speed, he
could not have had a better chance than this. The sea was
perfectly smooth, not the faintest swell disturbed the table-like
surface, and yet there was a pleasant, merry breeze that kept
the water laughing and sparkling and creaming in tiny foamy-
headed billows.

Right aft, to windward, was the best place to see the yacht.
I went there, and forking my head over the rail, had the whole
picture in my eye. The sun was veering to the westward,
but its light, as we were steering at that time, was still to windward, and the yacht's metal sheathing caught it, and gave back
a red haze like that of dull gold. Along this rich surface the
water was flying in a thin line of foam, and the rippling of the
stem sounded like the crunch of feet upon rotten leaves. From
the inclined, beautifully molded side of the vessel the shrouds
ruled the sky like bars of iron, and cast jet black tracings upon
the cotton white decks. The great spaces of canvas filled the
air overhead, and it was a delight to look up at the leaning
bright yellow masts, and mark the superb set and cut of the

sails, and the prodigious number of cloths under which the *Lady Maud* was sweeping through the calm water. It was a glorious picture, and I have it very clearly before me at this minute—the shapely fabric of white decks and gold bright sides ; the gleaming sails lifting their broad folds to the sky ; the whirling snow of the wake eddying out upon the blue water from under the stern ; the beautiful placid sea stretching for leagues ahead, and the land growing smaller and hazier upon our starboard beam and quarter.

While I stood admiring, Miss Tuke left her seat, and first of all she talked to the big mastiffs, and then came a little further aft, and took a glance aloft, and then approached the binnacle and peeped at the card. My eyes left the vessel when the girl reached the compass. She was prettier than the yacht, and could she have had her portrait taken at that moment, the picture would have been a fine one, with the sea and the huge main-boom for a background, and the deck for a platform, and old Purchase to help out the marine accessories with his strawberry-colored nose, and both great hands with fingers like bunches of carrots holding on to the wheel, and his small eyes squinting aloft.

"You can see the yacht going through the water if you'll come here," said I to her.

She came at once, and I think she had a treat. I spoke to her, but she did not answer me. The sweeping water, the sensation of *flying*, induced by the almost noiseless and quiet level passage over the clear sea, the beautiful effect of the brasslike copper against the foam, and the ocean of white canvas against the deep blue sky, acted upon her like a spell. At last she looked around, and said, "If I had been born a man, I should be a sailor."

A singular noise in Purchase's throat made me fix my eyes sternly on him ; but the old chap's face was quite wooden, and his gaze riveted upon the weather leech of the foretop-sail, for all the square canvas was upon the vessel now.

"You must not suppose," said I, "that this sort of thing is like going to sea as a sailor."

"Is a sailor's life really so hard as people say it is ? " she asked, earnestly looking at me with her intelligent, singularly clear, and winning eyes.

"Yes—that is, the life of a merchant sailor—and harder, because the people who say it is hard know very little about it. The people who *know* it is hard—I mean sailors themselves

—do not talk. It is not gales of wind, nor bitter cold, nor fiery heat that make it hard ; not even famines and shipwrecks, because they are accidents, and of no more account, so far as life at sea goes, than railway collisions and fires in churches and theaters are of account so far as life on shore goes. It's the part that's hidden that makes sailoring hard—bullying officers, leaky or overfilled ships, bad food, grinding work, broken rest, wet clothes, wretched forecastles. You might read a hundred marine novels and never get at the truth. The only way is to serve before the mast, as that fine fellow Dana did, sleep in a miserable bunk, and eat and drink with sailors. That, most fortunately, you can't do," said I, laughing ; "and why you should wish to be a man, merely that you might do it, makes me wonder."

" Perhaps if I were a man I might have different views," she said, eying me as if amused by my outbreak. "Are you still a sailor ? "

" No."

" How long were you a sailor ? " says she.

I told her.

" Beg your pardon, sir," rumbled Purchase, from the wheel, "but might you have been a merchant or a navy man ? "

" A merchantman," I answered.

" Long woyages, sir ? "

" Yes, long voyages and big ships. And you, I hear, are an old sailor ? "

He smiled slowly, as if the question amused him.

" Yes, I'm an old sailor," he answered, looking at Miss Tuke. " Fifty-three next birthday, and forty year out o' that at sea, in all sorts o' weather, and in all sorts o' wessels, from a billyboy up."

A sense of importance appeared to oppress him, and he looked away from us at the sea to leeward. Meanwhile the men had coiled the running gear away, and were grouped in the bows of the yacht, where they made a tolerable crew. Tripshore, the mate, paced the weather deck of the forecastle, and the cook, with his one eye, coming up for a breath of air, sat in the companion, talking to him as he passed to and fro.

The scene was full of beauty and quietude. Sir Mordaunt had opened a newspaper, and was reading aloud to his wife, who lay back in her comfortable invalid's chair, and was so still that she seemed sound asleep. One of the mastiffs lay with his nose between his fore-legs, and the other kept watch alongside of him, with his ears cocked at the passing water as though he should bark at it in a moment. The sun poured down upon us over our foremast-head, and I asked Miss Tuke if she was not afraid of her complexion, for she had no parasol, and the brim of her hat was narrow. No, she answered, she was not afraid; she wanted to get sunburned. I should have liked to beg her to keep her complexion, for it was a lovely thing, and warn her that fair skins don't brown, but freckle, only she was sure to know more about it than I.

"Can you realize the notion," said I, "that you are going across the Atlantic, and that you will not see land for days and days?"

"No; how should I be able to do that? The longest voyage I ever made was from Harwich to Dartmouth in the *Ione.*"

"Is this Lady Brookes's first cruise, do you know, Miss Tuke?"

"Positively the first. I hope it will do her good. Uncle Mordaunt is very anxious about her, and she was very unwilling to go."

"Well, if she doesn't love the sea naturally, as you do, she'll never love it by trying. But we must keep her spirits up, and not let sea-sickness frighten her. Since she has made a beginning, she ought to persevere. I hope she may not find the parallels we are bound to too hot."

Here Mr. Norie emerged from the cabin, and seeing Sir Mordaunt reading to his wife, came over to us. He had clapped a great straw hat on his head, and pointed to it with a grin, as much as to say, I'll have the first laugh.

"Anybody might tell by my appearance," said he, "that we are going where cotton and sugar flourish. Miss Tuke, as medico of this ship, give me leave to prescribe a parasol, whilst the sun stands high. I can feel the heat of these decks through my boots."

"I am not afraid of sunstroke," she replied. "Look, Mr. Walton!" she suddenly cried, in a voice as clear as a bell, "look at that steamship yonder!" Mr. Norie ran for the opera-glass. "How beautifully distinct she is—a toy—a tiny ivory carving! Is she a great ship, Mr. Walton?"

I looked and answered, "About four thousands tons. Does that convey any idea of her size?"

"Not the faintest idea."

"Imagine a toy terrier alongside one of those mastiffs; so would the *Lady Maud* appear alongside yonder steamer."

She took the glass from Norie, and had a long, long look.
Had the surgeon not kept his eyes on her, I should, as she
could not know I stared ; but two men admiring their hardest
at once was unfair. I surrendered the job to Norie, and
directed my eyes to the ship. She was an Indian or American
boat, very long, brig-rigged, sharply defined upon the horizon ;
but the refraction of the light left a sharp tremulous void between her hull and the water, and gave her the appearance of
steaming through the air, with her bottom within a foot of the
blue, marble-smooth sea. She was the only vessel in sight
that way; and her solitary presence somehow made the ocean
look more lonely than had nothing but the water been visible.

We were heading about S.S.E., which brought the Isle of
Wight almost over our stern. Sir Mordaunt, seeing me looking at the compass, dropped his paper and joined me.

"She seems to know the road, Walton, don't you think?"
said he, looking with a well-pleased face at the water.
"Yonder must be St. Alban's Head, Purchase?"

"Ay, that's right, sir," answered Purchase. "This vessel's
a fine one to steer, sir ; easy in the hand as a child's perryam-
bulator."

It was impossible not to laugh at this pronunciation, and to
cover my mirth I said, "Ay, skipper, after your old Geordie,
eh? nine inches of freeboard, and a tiller that shoves you half-
way down the companion, and bows like a doubled-up Dutch-
man ! "

Purchase moved his jaws as if he was gnawing upon a junk
of tobacco, and by the way he looked at me, and the hard
cock he gave his head, I fancied he was meditating a rejoinder ;
but Sir Mordaunt diverted him by asking where he was steering the yacht to.

"Into the fairway track, sir. Running for the Chops as we
be, there's no call to keep the land aboard."

Such a course might have been proper for a big ship, but
with a blue sky overhead, and a pleasant breeze over the quarter,
a vessel like the *Lady Maud* did not want a twenty-mile offing.
Besides, it seemed a pity to sink the pretty coast, which we
could have kept in sight until abreast of Weymouth, picked up
again at the Start, and kept as far as the Lizard. However, it
might be that old Purchase was not sure of his lights and bearings in these parts, and if so he was wise to keep the open sea
about him, for he had only to steer west when he hit the fairway, and he was sure not to miss the North Atlantic.

"What regulations will you have, Sir Mordaunt?" I asked. "Of course the crew will be divided into watches."

"I leave everything to Purchase," said he.

"I shall muster the men in the first dog-watch," said Purchase, eying me sternly, as if suspecting my questions meant more than met his ear, "and divide them into watches, as *you* say, sir; me taking the starboard watch, and Mr. Ephraim Tripshore, as mate, heading the port watch. That's accordin' to Cocker, as I believe."

"Aren't you tired of steering, Purchase?" said Sir Mordaunt. "Why not let one of the men relieve you?"

"So one of 'em shall, sir, so one of 'em shall, when the correct time comes," answered Purchase. "Meanwhile, as I'm answerable for this vessel, please, gentlemen, to let me give her a clear horizon afore another man takes my place." And he clung to the wheel with a very resolute and Briton-strike-home kind of look, and frowned at the foretop-gallant sail as if his feelings were injured. Sir Mordaunt was visibly impressed. In his eyes, Purchase was a stout and manly tar, all of the olden time. For my part, now that I saw he could steer (which on the mere testimony of his extravagantly nautical appearance I should not have believed), I felt able to hope that he might also know how to take sights.

Though it was drawing on for four o'clock, the sun still bit fiercely, and I was glad to quit the neighborhood of the wheel for the pleasant shadow of the mainsail, where sat the ladies and Mr. Norie, with a low table in the midst of them covered with cool drinks. The deuce is in it, thought I, if this touch of the sea don't hearten up Lady Brookes for the cruise. The sparkling breeze kept the leaning spars as steady as a flag-post; so motionless was the surface of the sea that our bowsprit end did not rise nor fall an inch above or below the horizon to which it pointed; and yet all the while the vessel was slipping through the water at five or six knots an hour. And, oh, the sweetness of the warm wind buzzing among the canvas, like the hum of a drowsy congregation in church!

"The Isle of Wight grows cloud-like," said I, pointing astern. "But see, Miss Tuke, how St. Catherine's Point away yonder crowns the blue water! If this were December, one might swear that those white cliffs were snow-covered plains. Do you know, Sir Mordaunt, that such a day, and such a ship, and such a sea should make even a Chinaman poetical?"

"Providing he was not seasick," said Lady Brookes, smiling.

"What a pity some one doesn't invent a cure for seasickness!" exclaimed Miss Tuke.

"There is only one cure for it," I observed, "and I am happy to say that I am the discoverer of it."

Lady Brookes looked at me.

"Let us have it, Mr. Walton," said Norie. "If it's a real specific, I'll engage to make you one of the richest men in England."

"The beauty of it," said I, "lies in its simplicity. When you feel ill, think of something else, and your sufferings will cease."

"Pshaw!" said Norie.

"Oh, I am not likely to have the doctors with me," I continued, "because there's nothing learned in the prescription, and no drugs are wanted. But let me tell you a story, Lady Brookes. A friend of mine patented a marine invention, which he had to carry to sea to test and improve. He was a martyr to seasickness, and the absolute necessity of quitting the land for even a couple of hours' tossing on shipboard was a hideous condition of his patent. But every invention has something of Frankenstein's giant about it, and the man who makes a discovery must be prepared to have his brow wrung—the correct phrase, I believe, Miss Tuke—'When pain and anguish wring the brow,——"

"Yes, yes; 'a ministering angel, thou.' Fire away, Walton!" said Sir Mordaunt, filling a meerschaum pipe.

"Well, Lady Brookes, my friend went to sea with his discovery, and I accompanied him. The only vessel he could hire for the run was a screw-steamer, shaped like a log of wood, in my judgment the most awful roller ever launched. 'I shall never be able to stand it!' exclaimed the poor fellow, quivering in his shoes as we stood looking at her from the pier side. I comforted him by saying that the heavy ground-swell was the very thing he should desire, as he wanted all the motion he could get to properly test his patent. We embarked, and the vessel steamed out, and no sooner was she clear of the harbor than she went up and down like a rocking-horse. One moment you might have touched the water with your nose——"

"With your what?" interrupted Sir Mordaunt.

"I said, with your nose—providing you weren't a negro, I mean. I expected, of course, to see my friend writhing on his back. But he had fixed his instrument, and discovered that his calculations were wrong; the correction of the errors engrossed his mind. He could think of nothing but his invention and his blunders, and though he could hardly keep his legs, he never uttered so much as a groan. In short, *he forgot to be seasick*. Mr. Norie, what say you to that, sir? If it don't prove that seasickness may be stopped by compelling the mind to think of other things, I'm a Frenchman."

An argument followed, and everybody was against me.

"It's absurd," said Norie, "to suppose that nausea can be checked by mental excitement."

"Do you mean to tell me," I exclaimed, "that a cry of fire would not rout every seasick passenger, and cure him until the fright was over?"

No, he would not even allow that.

"Then if that wouldn't cure him," said I, "death itself wouldn't."

"You'll have to improve on your discovery, Walton, if Norie is to make you a millionaire," said Sir Mordaunt, laughing. "But as none of us mean to be seasick, we'll forgive your failure."

"Don't say that, Mordaunt," exclaimed his wife, rather pettishly. "I am quite prepared to keep my cabin until we get home again."

"No, no; we must overhaul some excitements to bring you on deck, and cure you long before we return," said I. "I'll warrant my prescription, only, of course, I must have the physic."

"But you said just now, Mr. Walton, that we do not want to meet with any adventures," observed Miss Tuke, slyly.

"Nor do we," exclaimed Sir Mordaunt, emphatically. "Let us keep the object of this cruise steadily in mind, and pray that it may be happily attained."

His earnestness made us all serious, and I was pleased to see his wife glance at him rather gratefully.

CHAPTER III.

In this manner the afternoon passed, the sun crept over to our starboard beam, but shortly after four o'clock the schooner's helm was shifted, and the vessel brought to a course west by magnetic compass; and then the sun was over our port bow, and the sea under its blinding light an ocean of flashing gold down to the very stem of the yacht.

Tripshore, the mate, was at the wheel now. He was a plain, pale, sandy-haired man, not nearly so marine-looking as old Purchase so far as clothes and complexion went, yet he had the appearance of a better seaman than the other, and I admired him for that, as he stood airily holding on to the spokes, with his head floating on his neck like a bubble, as first he squinted at the compass, and then aloft, and then to windward, and then withdrew one hand from the wheel in order to wipe his mouth.

We had run the coast very nearly out of sight. Here and there upon the horizon, bearing N. N. W., were blobs of film and the darker shadow of the Bill of Portland. But though there was little to be seen that way, the seaward prospect was tolerably lively, with a number of little coasters buzzing down Channel like ourselves, and close together, and a tall, old-fashioned brig that dropped astern as though she had an anchor in tow, and keeping pace with us, having edged up from the eastward, a long, low, beautifully modeled wooden ship, painted black, with a gilt figure-head, and gilt band along her sides, and white boats. She carried sky-sail masts, though the yards were not crossed, but her royals topped a beautiful sweep and surface of canvas, and the white cloths which she lifted against the rich blue sky had both the softness and brilliance of foam. She held her spars erect, for there was not weight enough in the wind to give her a list, and the dignity, elegance, and blandness of her appearance were absolutely *human*. It was impossible to watch her without thinking of some graceful, swanlike woman "walking in beauty." The trembling water gave back no image of her shining sails, but the shadow of her hull was dark in the sea under her, and defined the thin line of foam racing along her side like a cord of white wool unwinding at her stem and trailing far astern until it vanished amid the blue sparkles.

"A full-rigged ship will always be the noblest example of man's handiwork," said Sir Mordaunt, who had been watching her in silence. "She is a real creation—a living thing, full of instinct, owing her life to that same breath of heaven by which we exist. All else is more or less *mechanical*—of the earth, earthy—and illustrates its perishableness by the very qualities which keep it flourishing. The grinding of a steam-engine makes us feel how small a flaw will stop it, and we think of coal and gauges and rivets. A grand building is stationary ; it is wonderful, but it is dead. But a sailing ship ! Look at that beautiful vessel! Is she not sentient? She might have been born of the very element she rides—her hull of the deep-sea rock, and her sails of the storm-driven foam. What think you of that, Walton, for *real* poetry ?"

"Lovely, indeed ! A heaven-seeking pigeon, Sir Mordaunt, with a fáct under its wing. I often regret that so many fine things have been said about ships. There's no room left for modern imagination."

"So much the better," piped Ada Tuke, "for now we shall stand a chance of getting plain English and the truth."

"Don't be sarcastic, my dear," said Sir Mordaunt.

"Indeed, Ada is right," quoth her ladyship. "That vessel may appear a live thing to you, Mordaunt, but to me she only suggests the idea of close cabins and a craving for dry land."

I looked to see if she was in earnest ; for at that moment the ship that was not above half a mile to leeward of us was as beautiful as a dream, a symmetrical pearl-like cloud against the blue—with a flash and tremble of foam at her forefoot and along her glossy side that was thrown out with all the effect of a cameo or a bit of relievo work by the pale blue water running up beyond her and meeting the azure heaven by the breadth of a hand over her bulwarks. One would have thought that the owner of such lustrous if listless eyes as Lady Brookes's must have had some sensibility to be stirred by that lovely sea-piece. Perhaps had her husband not praised the spectacle she would not have found it so insipid. But it was certain she did not mean to be courted into liking the water or anything that swam on it (I won't say *in* it). The ocean was the doctor's prescription, and she took it as she would a dose of castor-oil.

"Lady Brookes likes inland scenery," said her husband. "Agnes, you remember your first impression of that little valley near Limoges? Very few people, Walton, can admire the beautiful in every expression of it. Now an object like that ship is a finer sight in my eyes than, for instance, the grandest flower show you could walk me through. I don't care for flowers. I never could get further than telling the difference between a rose and a violet." And he wound up with some commonplaces on dissimilarity of taste, with benignant reference to his wife throughout, wanting to please her, and apologize for her too.

It was time to drop the subject ; but Miss Tuke was hugely ad-

miring the beautiful ship, that was now so close to us that we
could see her people gazing at our yacht from the quarter-deck
and forecastle ; and she began to ask me questions about the
names of the sails, and if I could imagine where the vessel was
bound to, and so on. The ship was sailing faster than we, and
heading along a course that must carry her across our bows.
Tripshore at the wheel eyed her with a bothered look, and old
Purchase gazed at her sullenly over the forecastle bulwark, with
his chin resting on the back of his great hands. Had I
had command I should have luffed the yacht, so as to let
the ship forge well ahead, and then put my helm up ;
but whether because Tripshore would not shift the wheel
without orders, or because Purchase did not see what
might happen, the yacht was kept steady. Presently the ship
was no more than three cables' length on our lee bow, and her
great heights of canvas looked like a tower into which we were
heading as neatly as we could steer. Very recklessly, and almost spitefully as I thought, the helm of the ship was changed
and her braces being untouched, the weather halves of her royals
and foretop-gallant sail were aback. The maneuver threw her
almost athwart our hawse ; and I said to myself, '' Now for a
collision, and a week's delay at Dartmouth for repairs."

Purchase jumped up with a roar.

''Where are you coming?" he yelled, tossing his fist at a
group of men who were looking at us over the stern of the ship
with folded arms, and grinning at us like baboons. " Hard
up there ! Tripshore ! hard up, man ! "

The spokes revolved like the driving-wheel of a locomotive
in Tripshore's hands, but for some moments we were all in
confusion, our crew dancing about and shouting at the ship,
Lady Brookes calling to her husband, and Norie swelling the
shindy by bawling to me to tell him if there was anything he
could do. Had it not been for Lady Brookes's alarm, I should
have laughed outright, for Purchase, whilst running aft, kicked
a coil of rope and fell with his whole length handsomely, his
brass-bound cap hopping some fathoms away from him, exposing a pate as bald as a new-born baby's, and rather redder.

We cleared the ship, and when all was safe, our men let fly
a broadside of insults at her. All the answer they got was a
yell of derisive laughter. Sir Mordaunt was in a towering passion. He whipped out his note-book, and, posting himself in
a prominent place, went through some wild dumb-show with
the idea of terrifying the people aboard the ship by letting

them see he was taking down her name, which, by the way, was the *Victoria*, of Middlesboro'. Knowing what an excitable race sailors are, I planted myself in front of the ladies, so as to hide the vessel from them, and fend off, so to speak, any nautical terms her men might bestow on us, which, I flatter myself, was a wise precaution on my part, for I was afterward privately told by Sir Mordaunt that the pantomime of some of the seamen, when they saw him elaborately posture-making over his pocket-book, was of a character that utterly effaced the poetical impressions which had been excited in his mind by the beautiful appearance of the ship.

So far as Lady Brookes was concerned, the experience was an unfortunate one, for it made her fretful, and stopped her husband for the rest of the day from talking before her about the pleasures and beauties of the sea, and the agreeable prospect the cruise offered. I did my best to reassure her, but she would not hear me.

"The sea is *full* of danger, Mr. Walton ; as a sailor, you must know that," she exclaimed.

"Not half so full of danger as the land, Lady Brookes. Think of the carriages and cabs and carts which are day after day running over people and into one another. Take a street crossing in a crowded throughfare, with horses prancing all about one, and blowing their steam into one's very ears. I had rather be in a gale of wind. At sea you have no burglars, no pick-pockets, no intoxicated tramps, no excitements of that kind. All is plain sailing, with here and there a few waves."

"You will never be able to convince me against my will," said she, with a cold smile, that showed I was making her angry. And she repeated, for the fourth or fifth time, that nothing but her husband's anxiety about her health could have prevailed upon her to take the voyage.

"Well," thought I, as I left her, "I hope we sha'n't have too much of this. We have not even hove up the Start, and yet here has been as much grumbling as should serve for a trip round the world."

We dined at six. Up to within twenty minutes of that hour we had carried the same steady pleasant breeze that had blown us lightly out of Southampton Water, but it had suddenly veered to the south and east, and the water all that way was a dark blue under the merry sweeping air. I stood with Miss Tuke, watching the swift race of foam creaming and hissing past, and sparkling in the sunlight in green and yellow and pale pink bubbles, as though the reflections of some gigantic prism illuminated the snow-white swirl. Oh, the fresh sweetness of that wind shooting into the nostrils out of the luminous green hollows of the little seas over which the yacht sped, with scarce the lifting by an inch of her bows !

Its inspiration was unpoetical, however, for it made me as hungry as a wolf. The first dinner-bell rang. I handed Miss Tuke down the companion, and a few minutes after four bells had been struck upon the yacht's forecastle (we kept our bells going as regularly as a man-of-war) we had all gathered round the cabin table—all, that is, except Lady Brookes.

"She has no appetite, she says, and complains that her back aches," said Sir Mordaunt, ruefully. "That abominable ship upset her nerves. I wish she were not so timid."

"She can't do better than lie down and keep quiet," said Norie. "The sea air is strong, and she must learn to face it by degrees."

"No, no, it isn't the sea air; it was that infernal ship," answered Sir Mordaunt. "Why, even old Purchase was scared. Did you see him go head over heels, Walton ? "

"I did, and thought his object was to let us see what a fine head of hair he has."

"My dear sir, he's as bald as an egg," said Norie—an observation that settled the question of the youth's native land.

When I think of the conclusion of our voyage, the interior of the cabin as we sat at dinner on this the first day rises clear and bright as a painted picture before me. It was, as I say, our first dinner—so far as I was concerned, our first meal aboard the *Lady Maud*, and the impression I retain is due to that. One had only to look around to guess that Sir Mordaunt must have spent a small fortune in equipping this yacht as a home for his invalid wife. Her sleeping-berth told a story of prodigal outlay, and a glittering pendant to it was this dinner-table, sparkling with silver and crystal and flowers.

A plain man like myself, whose income is too narrow for show, though ample for happiness, who had passed many years (considering my age then) in a rough calling, and who had but very imperfect notions of the character and flavor of those high-flying luxuries which only very long purses indeed can bring down, is no doubt easily impressed. But I cannot be wrong in speaking of the luxuries and elegancies with which Sir Mordaunt had crowded the cabins of the *Lady Maud* as examples of superb taste and polished hospitality. I remember, as I looked around me, thinking, "Good Lord! imagine this schooner in a collision, and all these fine things going to the bottom!" Taking it all round, it was a high tribute of a husband's love to a wife. In reality Sir Mordaunt was as plain a man as I in his tastes. Had he been going this journey alone, he would not have had silver on his table and silk and velvet in his cabins. A cot and a blanket would have sufficed him for a night's rest—a simpler bed, even, than would have suited me—and he would have enjoyed his bit of corned brisket off a plate of cheap china, and swigged down his pint of claret with all imaginable relish out of a two-penny tumbler. Who could look at his kind face, and the concern in his eyes as he would give a half-glance—showing where his thoughts were—in the direction of Lady Brookes's cabin, and not heartily hope that the recovery of his wife's health would repay him for the loving trouble he had taken, the worry her peevish disposition and reluctance had caused him in arranging and proceeding on this voyage across the Atlantic?

" The breeze does not freshen with the setting of the sun," said I, noticing the gradual recovery of the swinging trays, and catching the softening hum of the wind gushing through the open skylight out of the mainsail with the tremors and mixed notes of a distant band of music. " Listen, Sir Mordaunt, to the plashing of flat falls of water to windward. I don't like to hear those sounds when I'm in a hurry at sea. What pleases me is to look over the bows and see a semicircle of foam arching out on either hand like the white arms of a swimming girl."

" When shall we come to the place where the water at night looks on fire? " asked Miss Tuke.

" You'll have to wait, my dear," answered Sir Mordaunt.

" Do you mean the phosphorus? " said Norie, with an expression on his face that threatened natural philosophy.

" Oh, don't call it phosphorus! " she replied, laughing. " Explanations of beautiful effects spoil them. I like the way sailors speak of it," said she, looking at me, " when they tell you they dropped a pail over the side into the water, and brought it up shining like gold in candlelight."

" Ay, ay ; that's how Jack talks," said I.

" No, no ; that's not poetical enough for Jack," exclaimed Sir Mordaunt. " What he would say is, ' Bill, d'ye know, when we chucked a bucket overboard, I'm blessed if it didn't come up like new Jamaica rum all afire.'"

"Scientific authorities curiously differ from one another on the cause of those phosphorescent effects," said Norie. "In the voyage in search of La Perouse they are ascribed to small gelatinous and transparent molecules. But others say it's the decayed spawn of fish. And some call it crabs."

"They might as well call it cauliflowers," said •Sir Mordaunt.

"You're bound for the right waters, if you want to see it in perfection, Miss Tuke," said I. "But let me tell you a phosphorescent sea is not always a desirable thing. I was once becalmed in the latitude of the Andaman Islands, and at sunset the whole of the sea right away round the horizon was blood-red. It scared us all to see it. Half an hour after the sun was góne the ocean kept this awful color, proving that the sun was not the cause of it ; and what made the scene more fearful, the sky in the *east* was a pale crimson, just as though the sun, like a clown in a pantomime, had jumped through one window merely to pop his nose out of another. As the flush faded out of the sea, as the night deepened in fact, the water grew bright with fire ; and presently we were afloat upon a surface of flame—how shall I describe it?—an ocean of red-hot glass. But oh, the barometer ! It had sunk an inch and a quarter in two hours ; and sure enough, before ten o'clock had been struck, our ship was on her beam ends, with the water up to the main hatch, nearly leveled by as furious a cyclone as ever struck a vessel."

"I am glad Lady Brookes doesn't hear you, Walton," said Sir Mordaunt. "After that yarn, every flash of phosphorus would distress her as a portent."

"But why," said I, "do you discourage Miss Tuke by telling her she'll have to wait some time before seeing those luminous effects ? I have beheld this very water through which we are now spinning brilliant with green lights."

"Ay, but you don't find these northern waters flash as the sea does in the tropics," responded Sir Mordaunt. "What my niece has in her mind is a kind of oceanic snapdragon—a mighty surface of wavy blue or green fire—a very devil's bowl, with sharks instead of plums swimming about in it."

"Only let me see such a sight ! " cried Miss Tuke, clasping her hands and dropping back her head into a fine heroic posture.

"Wouldn't you prefer an earthquake ? " asked Norie, gravely. "They're plentiful in Jamaica, and I dare say Sir Mordaunt wouldn't mind cruising about Portland Bay or the north of Morant Point until one happened. They say it's a most impressive sight to see a negro village sliding down a mountain's side."

I couldn't stand the fellow's sober face, but laughed out, leaning back in my chair and wiping my eyes until I was ashamed of myself.

"Why, Mr. Walton," said he, "perhaps you don't believe that an earthquake will dislodge a whole town, and send it rattling down a hill?"

"Oh dear yes! I was laughing at the image presented to my mind of a crowd of negroes chasing a hill that was running off with their houses," I replied, meeting Miss Tuke's eyes, and nearly bursting out again. "I know what negroes are, Mr. Norie, and the noises they make when in pain or alarmed. But we ought to be able to manage without earthquakes."

"Besides, Mr. Norie, an earthquake is a *landsman's* diversion," said Miss Tuke, contemptuously emphasizing the word I have underlined. "We, you know, are sailors, and have nothing to do with what goes on ashore."

I wish I could express the mingled sauciness and seriousness of her manner. Sir Mordaunt surveyed her with a fatherly eye of pride and affection. The angle of the deck brought the skylight overhead into the focus of the rays of the setting sun, and the warm red light was caught by the looking-glasses on the port side of the cabin and flung in a whole veil of radiance—soft as the illumination of a stained-glass window—upon that part of the cabin where the girl was sitting, and filled her hair with sparks, as though reflected in gold-dust, and gave a faint pink tinge to her beautifully clear skin, and threw up her rounded figure against the cabin wall that lay in shadow beyond her. I am unable to describe her dress, as I have no memory for such things, but I remember that she wore a thick plait on her head that might very well have passed for a gold crown, so lustrous was her hair, and that she had a cloudy gauze-like frill—however it may be called—round the collar of her dress, and no jewelry, except a thin watch-chain round her neck, not even a finger-ring.

Presently she left the table to go to her aunt. The steward put a box of cigars upon the table, real Havana tobacco, as I speedily discovered. It seemed almost a profanation to smoke in such a cabin, and I wondered how Lady Brookes would relish our easy manners if the fumes reached her berth. Sir

Mordaunt, filling a great meerschaum pipe, flung himself along the lee lockers, and made a pillow of his arms, and Norie sat pulling swiftly at his cigar, as though the sooner he made an end the better he should be pleased.

There was not the faintest motion in the vessel. She was, indeed, still leaning under the fresh draught of air, but the swinging trays hung over the table without oscillation. The cabin was resonant with the humming of the wind up aloft, and by listening I could hear the noise of the rending of the smooth water by the stem of the yacht, and the hissing of the bow wave breaking into foam abreast of the gangway.

"It should take a deal of this to tire a man," said I.

"You mean a man who likes it," replied Sir Mordaunt. "But, Lord bless me, Walton, there's a deal of cant in yachting. I know owners of yachts—fine vessels, too—who after lying a fortnight in one harbor will creep away on a smooth fine morning to another harbor a few leagues distant, and stop three weeks there. They call it yachting! They might do as well with a wherry. Take one of those yachtsmen's trips from the Isle of Wight. After spending a month at Cowes, the owner of the vessel—who you may be sure is a mighty nautical fellow in his brass buttons and naval cap—orders the anchor to be got up, and away they go for Weymouth. They stop at Weymouth a fortnight. Their next voyage shall be to Teignmouth. Here three weeks are consumed in sitting under an awning and fishing over the side. Torquay is not very far off, and so our friend goes to Torquay, and there he stops until it is time to lay the vessel up. I once asked a friend of mind who did this sort of thing regularly—who kept a large yacht, but hated the sea as cordially as my wife does—why he went to the expense of a small fortune a month in making water excursions which he abhorred, when he could visit all the principal sea-board places by rail for the cost of his men's wages for one week. 'Pooh! pooh!' said he, 'you're always sneering.' But I meant no sarcasm."

"Your niece would shame some of those fellows, Sir Mordaunt," said Norie. "I think she would like to be on the water all the year round."

"Her father was a sailor—that may account for her taste."

I asked if her father was living.

"No, he died—why, it must be now over twelve years since —off the west coast of Africa, where he was then commanding a small vessel of war. What a fine, handsome man he was !—

3

a real heart of oak ! Why, I see him, Walton, as I see you ;
his brown face and bonnie blue eyes, and hair like a lion's
mane tossed upon his forehead ! " He blew out a great cloud
of tobacco smoke, and lay behind it, silent, musing and pensive.

"And Mrs. Tuke ? " I asked.

" Dead too, Walton—dead too. She was my only sister, and
I felt her loss terribly. The news of her husband's death broke
her heart. I don't mean this metaphorically. She died half
an hour after the news was given her, and as the doctors
could not account for her death, her body was examined, and
her heart found ruptured. What think you of that, Norie ? "

"It admits of a physiological explanation," replied Norie,
putting down his cigar, half smoked out.

"Ay, of course," said Sir Mordaunt, choking off the science
that was threatened. "But what an illustration it is of
woman's love ! "

"I should say your niece inherits her parents' fine qualities,"
I exclaimed.

"She does. She is brave and good and warm-hearted, and
it is most fortunate that my wife thought of asking her to join
us. You see," looking at Norie, "it is unavoidable that Lady
Brookes should not always be able to preserve that gentleness
of temper which was one of her delightful qualities down to
the time when her health gave way. It was necessary that
she should have a companion—one of her own sex, I mean—a
friend and equal, to read to her and talk, and be with her.
Ada fits the post to a hair, and I'm glad she promises to
thoroughly enjoy the run. Shall we go and see what's doing
on deck ? "

We climbed the companion steps and emerged into a glorious
crimson evening. It was half-past seven by the clock under
the skylight : the sun was a vast magnificent, rayless
globe, throbbing, and still of a most dazzling glory, poised
over the flashing sea in the west ; and all away in the
south the water was crisp with the breaking heads of the
little seas. The *Lady Maud* was sailing very fast, as any
one might have told by following the narrow milk-white
wake to where it vanished in the far, dark blue distance astern.
The wind was extraordinarily rich to the taste, and blew as
warm as a woman's breath in the face. It had come around
another point into the southward during dinner, and we buzzed
along with our square yards well against the lee rigging, and

with plenty of mainsheet coiled down near the after grating. There were smacks and bigger vessels scattered about—the dark brown canvas of the former as red as blood in that light—standing down channel; and broad upon the weather bow was a yacht apparently steering for the Isle of Wight —an immensely lofty vessel, cutter-rigged with the squarest mainsail I ever saw (indeed, the gaff was very nearly as long as the boom), and a long, narrow, racing hull, so slender that it was wonderful to see such a mighty vc'ume of canvas supported by it. Her lee rail was very nearly level with the foam, and the water all around her and astern was white with her rushing, as though she were in the midst of breakers.

"There's one of those vessels which are pleasanter to watch than to be aboard of," said Sir Mordaunt, dryly.

Beautiful she certainly looked when we got a windward view of her, showing so much yellow metal that you might have sworn her hull was made of brass. But what pleasure people can find in holding on the weather rail of a deck that slopes up and down like the side of a wall, in carrying on until the lee bulwarks are under water, with a fine prospect of turning turtle if anything jams when the order is given to let go, I cannot imagine.

Just before eight o'clock Purchase called the crew aft, and divided them into watches. He read out their names, and the men stepped on one side or the other according to the watch they were put into. Sir Mordaunt stood near the skylight, smoking his pipe, and was evidently much impressed by Purchase's square nautical figure and deep sea voice, and the peremptory gestures of his hand as he sung out the names. The men looked a very respectable company as they stood in a crowd near the gangway. They were in uniform, of course, with the name of the yacht in gold letters upon their caps, and white drill or duck breeches and white shoes. Some of them had bushy whiskers, and showed their throats like men-of-war's men. When Purchase had gone through the names, he cleared his pipes, took a squint astern to see if Sir Mordaunt was listening, and spoke out as follows : " Now, my lads, here we are bound to the West Hindies, with a beautiful vessel under our feet, and an A 1 gent as our boss. The voyage, as you all know, is undertaken for the cure of her ledship's health, and may the Lord keep his eye upon this hooker for that reason ! " Here he gave another squint astern to see if Sir Mordaunt was still listening, and then walked a few paces to leeward and

spat over the rail into the water, after which he came back.
" Men, we all know one another, and that's a good job. We're
not aboard a coalman. I don't say it'll be all nothen to do but
to sit down and be blowed along, unless we runs short of holy-
stone, and lose pride in this here lovely whiteness and brightness," pointing to the decks and to a brass binnacle just before
the foremost skylight. "But it ain't colliering, mates. No
calking wanted here, boys, and the clews, ye see, fit the yard-
arms," looking aloft ; "and the gear don't want greasin', nor
the duff washin' to get the coal dust out of it. So, mates, as
we're bound to be comfortable, give three cheers, one for Sir
Mordaunt, t'other for her ledship, and one for the vessel. Take
your time from me."

The men were on the broad grin all the time the old fool
harangued them, but they cheered as they were told, and
heartily enough ; yet the whole thing to me was as loose and
unsailorly as a scene in a play—what with the spotless white
decks never to be met in that perfection in any other craft than
a yacht, and the flowing rig of the men, and old Purchase in
this brass-bound cap. All that was wanted, when the skipper
ended his speech, was a band of music to strike up, and a song
sung, the whole concluding with a marine ballet. I wondered
that Sir Mordaunt did not see how theatrical and unshipshape
was this bit of sailorizing in his skipper ; but instead of looking at it as I did, he was pleased and gratified by the cheering.

"A most characteristic speech, was it not ?" said he, as old
Purchase went forward in the tail of the men. "Just what a
hardy old salt would say. I wish Lady Brookes had been on
deck, and seen the men grouped in front of the old chap."

The evening was gathering fast, and the moon in the south
grew brilliant as the red flush in the west faded. I lounged
about the deck with Sir Mordaunt, and he then went below to
his wife. It was the best hour of the day, cool with dew and
the blowing of the wind ; the moon flashed up the sea in silver
under her, and in the east the stars were shining like riding-
lights down to the horizon. There were three or four men in
the bows of the yacht, and their voices came aft in a faint
gruff murmur ; but from that point to where I stood, near the
after-skylight, the deck was deserted, and beautiful the sight
was of that deck, as white as paper in the moonlight, with the
shadows of the shrouds ruled in thin but deeply black lines upon
it and upon the white hollows of the gaff foresail and mainsail,
which gleamed—to compare a big thing with a little thing—

like the inside of an oyster-shell, a pearly surface shot with faint shadow ; while swelling above these spacious concavities the topsail aft, and the staysail between, and the square canvas forward, topped by the little beautifully cut top-gallant-sail, looked as vague as puffs of steam under the stars.

Observing somebody to leeward gazing at the sea under the main boom, I peered at him, and presently made out that it was Tripshore, the mate.

" I doubt if this wind will hold very long," said I, crossing over to him.

"I don't think it will, sir. It's inclined to slacken away to nothing," he answered, stepping back a pace, and casting his eyes aloft.

" Where should we be about now, think you, Mr. Tripshore ? " said I.

" Well, as I reckon, we should be coming on to Portland High Light presently," he replied, pointing away out on the lee bow.

" Why on earth does the skipper take this wide offing ? " I asked. " I should have imagined that, as an old coalman, he would have been glad to keep the land in sight as long as ever he could. Is this your first trip with him ? "

"Ay, sir, I never set eyes on him before."

" What are *your* experiences as a sailor ? "

" Why, I've been yachting for the last three years ; but all my time before was spent in big ships."

" And what sort of a crew have you got together, Mr. Tripshore ? Pretty good men, eh ? "

" Well, it's like this, sir ; they're just about the average kind of yachts' crews—a mixture ; a few smart sailors, several middling ones, and several bad ones, I should say—sogers, sir ; but taking 'em all around, I reckon they'll do."

I stood talking to him for some time, for his manner of speech brought up old days in my mind. It was like being at sea again in the old hookers I sailed in to hear him. I was sure he was a better man than Purchase, and thought it would have been a good job had he got the command instead of the other.

Gradually, as we stood conversing, the vessel lost her list, and the sharp *shaling* of the water to leeward subsided, and now and again the main-boom swung in. To leeward of us, about half a mile ahead, and showing about three points over the starboard bow, was a small lugger-rigged smack that was holding her own against us in a manner that proved her a fast sailer for a craft of her kind.   I was examining her through a night-glass, and picturing her little cabin, and the men asleep on the shelves, and letting my fancy run loose on her, when a pretty voice at my ear said : "The wind is dying away, Mr. Walton.   What a pity !"

It was Miss Tuke, and alongside of her was one of the big mastiffs, with his back on a level with her hand.

"I am glad you have come on deck," said I ; " for you would be missing a lovely night by stopping below.   There will be no wind at all soon.   But what should that matter ?   We are not timed, and the longer we can keep Lady Brookes at sea, the stronger her health will grow.   Is she coming on deck ? "

"No ; she is in bed," she answered, "and Uncle Mordaunt is reading her to sleep.   What a good husband he is !   Did you ever try to read anybody to sleep ? "

"Never.   But I fancy I could do it, though ; and more quickly than most people."

"It's very heartless work," said she.   "When one reads aloud one likes to be admired for good delivery, or one wants the book to be admired.   But to read in order to make a listener sleepy is a real hardship.   It must be like steering the phantom ship I have read about, that is always trying to double the Cape —tiresome work, Mr. Walton, and nothing to be gained even if the Cape *should* be doubled."

"I should wonder at your simile if Sir Mordaunt hadn't told me you were a sailor's daughter," said I.

"Yes, my dear father was a sailor," she answered, in a low, sweet voice.   "If I had been a man, I am sure I should have been a sailor.   It is a hard life, no doubt, as you said ; but there is no nobler and more manly profession."   And after a pause, "What vessel is that out there ?"

"A smack.   Take this glass ; you will see her plainly." She looked, and then gave me the glass and went to the compass, and as she peered into it the haze of the lamp sparkled in her hair, and her face looked like a piece of exquisitely sculptured marble.

"Weren't you in the merchant service ? " she asked, coming back to me.

I told her yes.

"Isn't the Royal Navy better ? " said she.

"No doubt," I answered.

"I don't believe you think so, though," said she, laughing.

"The merchant service turns out finer seamen, because in the merchant service a man goes through a training he never gets in the navy," said I. "The life is harder, the experiences always of a practical kind, and there is no playing at sailor, as there is in the navy. But the navy man has the better social position ; all the sea songs which are made are about him ; he puts state money into his purse, wears a uniform, and his ship is always clean."

"Yes, and how beautiful his ships are, too ! " she cried.

"How many years ago are you speaking of, Miss Tuke ? "

"I suppose I must say when I was a little girl, for then it was that I saw a frigate called the *Impérieuse*. If I knew your sea terms I could describe her. I can see her now, resting like a swan upon the water, with a broad white belt painted along her, dotted with cannons, and majestic masts, and crowds of white frocked sailors upon her decks, and red-coated sentries at her side. If I were a man, what would I give to command such a ship ! "

"Oh, you are speaking of the age of wood ; we are now in the age of tanks. I remember the *Impérieuse ;* I saw her in China, in the Bay of Pechili, and alongside of her a sister ship, the *Chesapeake*, with Admiral Hope's flag flying. Ay, they were lovely fabrics indeed. We shall never see their like again for every picturesque quality that made the fifty-gun frigate the loveliest object in the world."

Here Norie forked his body through the companion ; he stood sniffing and looking around him, and presently spied us under the main-boom.

"Surely this can't be the sea ! " he exclaimed. "Where are the waves ? Why, it's like Windermere, or an Irish lake ! "

"You cannot have waves without wind," answered Miss Tuke, "and you see, Mr. Norie, there is no wind," and as she said this the foresail flapped heavily, and the main-boom swung in almost amidships, and forced us to quit that part of the deck.

"But there's no swell," pursued the doctor. "Do you notice, Miss Tuke, that the vessel doesn't heave in the smallest degree ? "

This was true enough. The water was indeed extraordinarily smooth, and had been so all day, but never so noticeable for that as now, owing to the burnishing of it by the moonlight, and the falling of the wind, and the reposeful shadow that girdled it. Even the light canvas was giving an occasional flap as the expiring draughts of air came and went, but these were the only sounds aboard the schooner. The fellows had come out of the bows, and but one man stood there now ; the rudder-head never stirred, and the wheel chains were as quiet as the backstays ; there was not an atom of motion in the hull to strain a timber or to cause the faintest jar. We stood for some time without speaking, and wondering at the silence, which the darkness in the north, and the flood of brilliant silver in the south, and the beautiful stars burning brightly upon the sea-line, and the ebony surface upon which our vessel hung, made mysterious enough to subdue the feelings, when suddenly we heard the sound of a concertina, and a male voice singing to the simple melody, stealing across the sea from the direction of the smack on our lee bow.

"Hush !" whispered Miss Tuke, lifting her hand.

We listened.

" 'Tom Bowline,' as I'm a man !" cried I. "Fancy a fisherman singing 'Tom Bowline !' How the rascal warbles ! "Faithful be—low he d—d—did his du—oo—ty !' Ah, what a lovely old song is that !"

"You can't hear the words, surely ?" exclaimed Norie, straining his ears.

"No ; but don't I *know* them, doctor ? 'And now he's gone aloft !' Methinks I behold the spirit of the old tar listening. Do you see him, Miss Tuke—with your mind's eye, I mean—finely silvered over by this moonlight, his pigtail upon his back, and a junk of tobacco standing high in his bronzed cheek ? Imagine if this sea—this very identical piece of water we are looking at—could give up its dead ! What a wonderfnl variety of costumes !—Romans who were tossed overboard from old Cæsar's galleys ; Vikings who had been blown through the Straits of Dover, and foundered in sight of fleering native Britons ; Armada Spaniards ; De Ruyter's Dutchmen ; Yankee privateersmen. Heavens, what an array of doublets, ruffs, peaked beards, steeple-crowned hats, horse-pistols, and swaggering figures, *à la* Paul Jones."

"Upon my honor, Mr. Walton, it's enough to make a man afraid to look over the side," said Norie.

"The music has stopped !" exclaimed Miss Tuke. "How soft and yet how clear the tune was !"

"No thanks to the man, who, I'll wager, has a hoarse pipe, nor to his concertina, an odious instrument even when well played," said I ; "but to this beautifully polished surface of water, which sweetens the sounds that glide along it, and to the distance that lends enchantment. Figure some noble tenor —Rubini, or Mario, or Giuglini—singing to a soft band of music away out yonder. If moonlight and music and feeling and water can make a smacksman's song a sweet sound, think —oh, think—of a great artist sending his rich flute-like notes rolling across that breathless surface! Why, Mr. Norie, every fish with ears to hear would float up out of the black depths to hearken, and cod and turbot and soles, ay, and the brown dab and the silver sprat and the green crab, might be had without the bother of shooting a trawl."

"Forward, there!" sung out Tripshore, who had been pacing the deck abreast of the gangway; "lay aft some hands, and get a drag upon the lee forebraces!"

The fellow on the look-out echoed the order, and in a few moments several dark figures came along, coils of rigging were flung down, and the yards were braced up. The noise brought Sir Mordaunt out of the cabin.

"Hillo, Walton!" he cried out. "Has the wind all gone? Why, just now we had a stiff breeze."

"All but gone, Sir Mordaunt."

"Is that you, Mr. Tripshore?"

"Yes, sir."

"What are you doing?"

"Trimming sail, sir. The draught's drawed ahead; but it'll be failing us altogether presently."

"We're booked for what the Spaniards call a furious calm," said I.

It was, however, the right sort of weather to make one's self comfortable in. Chairs were brought, the steward placed decanters and glasses upon the skylight, and there we sat in the moonshine, which was now so brilliant that I could have read a book by it.

I inquired after Lady Brookes. She was asleep. "And the best thing, too, for her," said Norie.

"And sleeping very soundly, Norie," said Sir Mordaunt, cheerfully. "Oh, depend upon it, the doctors are right. There's nothing like sea air."

I heartily agreed with him as I lay back in the very easy chair that had been placed for me, watching the smoke of my cigar, blue as steel in the moonlight, go up straight out of my mouth. But though there was no air to be felt on deck, the light canvas was faintly drawing aloft, and the occasional sob-

bing of water under our counter was a sure indication, upon
that perfectly smooth surface at all events, that the yacht had
steerage-way.

We were in the midst of a mild argument, the subject of
which had been started by Norie. Presently I noticed Tripshore, who was stumping the port side of the deck as regularly
as a sentinel in front of his box, suddenly stop, and peer at the
sea over the weather bow, sheltering his eyes with his hand
from the moonlight. After a bit he went aft, and spoke to the
fellow at the wheel, and then he returned, and stood sheltering his eyes and staring.

"I fancy Tripshore has sighted something worth looking at,
to judge by the attention he is giving it," said I, unwilling to
be the first to address the man.

Sir Mordaunt broke off in what he was saying, and called
out, "What do you see, Mr. Tripshore?"

"Why, sir, what looks to me uncommonly like a ship's boat
adrift," he answered, pointing in the direction into which he
had been staring.

We left our chairs and went to the side, where we stood peering and peering.

"I see it, uncle!" exclaimed Miss Tuke. "Look at the big
star there, like a lantern over the sea : the object is exactly
under it."

"In the very wake of its light," said I, and I went for the
night-glass.

"Isn't it a boat, sir?" asked Tripshore.

"Certainly," I answered, after a prolonged squint; "but I
don't see anybody in her."

The glass passed from hand to hand, and all were agreed
that it was a boat that had gone adrift, unnoticed, whilst towing
astern of a ship.

"Can't we edge down to her, somehow, Tripshore?" said
Sir Mordaunt. "I should like to have a close look at her."

"I'm afraid there's not much edging to be done, sir," responded Tripshore, grinning and casting his eyes round the
sea. The breathlessness of the calm that had fallen could be
seen in the water under the moon, where the magnificent flashing silver reflection was as motionless as a surface of illuminated looking-glass. And yet, wonderful to relate, on looking
over the side, I saw the schooner was still obeying the im-
pulse of some very phantom of a draught of air, overhead, for
there were bubbles crawling by, and ripples as fine as the

wires of a piano-forte breaking from her stem, and resembling silver threads upon the dark water as they came aft within the sphere of the moon's reflection.

"You might shove her up a little, do you know, Mr. Tripshore," said I. "She ought to bear it. Here we are, moving without wind, which proves that the *Lady Maud* is bound to go, no matter how you head her."

He immediately told the man who was steering to starboard the helm. That the vessel was moving was shown by her creeping round so as to bring the moon on the port bow.

"Why, Sir Mordaunt," I exclaimed, "you've got a wonderful ship here! Of course there is a current of air aloft, but would any man believe that a yacht of this tonnage will answer her helm on such a sea as this?"

> "'The helmsman steered, the ship moved on,
> Yet never a breeze up blew,'"

chanted Miss Tuke, melodiously, at my elbow.

"Don't go on with those rhymes, or you'll come to dead men, Ada," said the baronet.

"It beats cock fighting," exclaimed Tripshore, looking up at the canvas that hung without a stir. "I thought the draught was ahead just now, but favoring it must be, if it's anywheres about at all. Yet there's no use worriting the men by box-hauling them yards about, sir," said he, looking at me. "If our anchor was over, I should reckon some big fish had got hold of it, and was showing us the way down Channel."

"Quarter deck, there!" bawled the man on the lookout in the bows. "There's a boat away out yonder ahead of us!"

"What are ye hollerin' about?" growled Tripshore. "We've been watching of it this half-hour. Why didn't you report it before?"

"'Cos I didn't see it," answered the man.

"Yachtsmen are like new-born puppies when they get upon the sea—blind for several days," rumbled Tripshore in his gizzard, looking at me.

A quarter of an hour passed, by which time the boat was about a third of a mile distant. But the yacht had now come to a dead stand. I threw the end of my cigar overboard, and watched it, but it did not shift its position by a hair's-breadth. A wonderful calm, truly! Often afterward I recalled that picture—the sea like ebony in the east, but gloriously radiant

in the south ; nothing in sight but the little boat, and the smack
on the starboard beam, looking like a fold of gray mist upon
the dark water ; the sky black as ink on the skirts of the haze
which floated around the small, brilliant, yellow moon, and all
up aloft as silent as the grave.

"Heaven have mercy ! what's that ?" Pooh ! only the cold
snout of one of Sir Mordaunt's great dogs upon the palm of my
hand.

"Why, Walton, man, what a shout ! Do you know you
have made me drop my cigar ?" exclaimed Sir Mordaunt ; and
he stooped and groped about the deck.

"I beg to apologize," said I. "I was a million miles high
among the stars, and to be brought back to earth by that
rascal's nose was really too great a trial ;" and I shook my
fist at the splendid brute, who contemplated me with a languishing eye, and half a fathom of tongue hanging out of his jaws,
as if he were trying to bolt the ensign. Miss Tuke was shaking with laughter. I believe she had shoved the dog's head
against my hand.

"That boat bothers me," said Sir Mordaunt, looking at it
through the night-glass. "Now that we have neared her, she
seems more like a wherry than a ship's boat."

"I wonder Johnny Fisherman hasn't sighted her," said I.
"But be she what she will, it must take us all night to come
up with her if there's to be no more wind than what we have
now. So, Sir Mordaunt, if you like to order me away in one
of your boats, I shall be happy to overhaul the little derelict,
and give you a report upon her."

"A good idea, Walton ; but why should you have the
trouble of going ? Tripshore there——"

"No, no ; I'll go."

On this the necessary orders were given, the watch came
aft, and presently I was in the stern-sheets of one of our smaller
boats, rowed by a couple of men, and heading for the source
of our puzzlement.

"Do you see the phosphorus now, Miss Tuke ?" I shouted
as we shoved off, calling to her as he stood, with her uncle
and Norie, watching us from the yacht's side. Every dip of
the oars flashed the water up in fire, and whole clouds of the
green radiance revolved in the wake of the boat. I looked at
the yacht when some distance from her, and heartily wished
Miss Tuke had been with me, to see the beautiful moonlight
picture. The vessel was more like a phantom than a real

"I had to grasp his collar to save him."—Page 45.

thing ; her sails pale and visionary, the water under her as black as ebony, and reflecting like wan and fainting stars the points of tremulous brilliance kindled in her mirror-like sides by the exceedingly clear and powerful moonbeams.

It took us about ten minutes to reach the boat, but it was not until we were quite close that I could see that no ship had ever owned her. She was, indeed, a pleasure-boat, painted a light blue ; the head of her mast, that had been unstepped, projected over the bow, and the clew of her lug trailed in the water over her side. The men threw their oars in : we glided alongside and grasped the gunwale.

"Just as might ha' been sworn ! " said one of my fellows. " Here's a dead man in her."

I stood up and looked into the boat. The first object my eye rested upon was the figure of a man lying at full length upon his breast, with his face hidden in his arms. The mast was along the thwarts, but a portion of the sail was in the bottom of the boat, and the man lay upon the canvas. There were a couple of oars, with their blades projecting over the stern, and I immediately noticed a bundle of man's clothes— trousers, coat, waistcoat, shirt, hat, and boots, a complete rig out—in the stern sheets. I jumped into the boat, followed by one of the men.

" Is he dead, think you, sir ? "

" Help me to turn him over—gently."

As we raised him he moaned, then gave a deep grunt, and immediately afterward uttered a loud, prolonged shriek, and sprung to his feet with such frantic energy that the boat was all but capsized by him, and I had to grasp his collar to save him from falling overboard.

" Where am I ? " he shouted, staring about him in the wildest manner, and then peering into my face. "Oh, my good God ! " he groaned, "my brother's drowned, and I've been drifting about in this boat since seven o'clock this morning, if to-day's Thursday ; " and catching sight of the clothes in the stern of the boat, he burst into tears, and wept and sobbed most grievously.

"Here," said I to the yachtsman, "hitch the end of this painter to your aftermost thwart, and tow us to the schooner. Bear a hand, men, as I'm afraid this poor fellow is starving."

Saying which, I put my hand upon the young man's shoulder, and in a manner obliged him to sit down. So far as I could read his face by the moonlight, he looked about five or six and twenty years old. He was dressed in a light tweed suit, and a small telescope was slung at his back. He was as white as a corpse, and shivered and shuddered incessantly, even to the extent of his teeth chattering ; quite dazed, too, and staring an instant at me, and then at the boat ahead, and then up at the moon, and around the sea, with an air of stupefaction that was like madness, until his eyes fell upon the clothes in the stern sheets, whereupon he would moan as though suffering an agony of pain, and twist and turn about in such a fashion that I was obliged to keep my hand ready to collar him, lest he should writhe himself overboard. I asked him one or two questions ; but beyond learning that his boat had been blown out to sea from Weymouth, and that his brother, who had been his companion, was drowned, I could get no information from him. He was as muddy and confused as a man in liquor, and could only stare and groan and topple about in his misery.

As we approached the yacht, Sir Mordaunt called to know what I had found. I would not answer, for fear that Lady Brookes, whose cabin port-hole was sure to be open, should hear me and be alarmed. However, when we were close enough for the people aboard the schooner to see two figures in each boat, a dead hush fell upon them—no more questions were asked.

We got the boats alongside, "Catch hold of that rope," said I to the poor fellow ; but he was too weak to gain the deck unassisted. Sir Mordaunt's good heart stood in no need of explanations : he took one arm and Norie the other, and between them they carried him to a chair, and forthwith administered a bumper of cold brandy grog. The spirit acted like magic, and the poor creature drew himself erect, and looked earnestly and intelligently about him.

"Our friend," said I, " will be all the better for something to eat. He has been drifting about the Channel in his open boat all day."

Instantly Miss Tuke ran below, and returned with a plate of cold meat and bread, which she placed on the skylight before the young man. He seemed mightily embarrassed by the kindness shown him, and utterly miserable too ; for though he eat with avidity, he would pause every minute to sigh deeply, and once I saw the bright tears drop off his cheeks on to his plate.

We drew away whilst he eat, and stood looking at his boat and talking in whispers about him. The clothes in the stern had a dreadfully significant appearance, knowing, as we did, that they belonged to a drowned man. After a little I went back to the young fellow, and asked him if he would have some more meat. He said no ; and then grasping my hand, thanked me in the most moving manner for saving his life.

" You feel pretty well again, I hope ? " said Norie.

" Much better, I thank you, sir." And looking away over the sea, he exclaimed, with a gush of grief : " I have left my wife at Weymouth, and the long absence will have broken her heart. And oh, my poor brother ! my poor brother ! "

I saw Miss Tuke clasp her hands, and I own I was much affected.

" How came you in this wretched plight ? " said I.

" Oh, sir," he answered, " I can tell it you all in a few words. I am clerk in a London bank, and my brother was in the Weymouth post-office. I had got a fortnight's holiday, and brought my wife to Weymouth for a change of air. My brother owned the boat you found me in, and last night we arranged to have a sail before breakfast this morning. We started, and sailed a long distance out, and then my brother said before we returned he would bathe. He undressed and jumped into the sea, and was swimming very well, when all at once he cried out, his arms stood up out of the water and he disappeared. I tried to row the boat round to where he had sunk, but she was too heavy and the wind too strong, and, besides, he never rose again," said he, looking at us with his white face, and stretching out his quivering hands in a manner strange indeed to see.

" Here, take this, my man," said Sir Mordaunt, pouring out another nip of brandy.

The poor fellow swallowed the dose, and then continued :

" I know nothing of the management of boats, and I was made foolish by the dreadful suddenness of my brother's death. The Bill of Portland was in sight, and I put the oars out and rowed in that direction ; but besides being a bad rower, I found the oars too heavy, the wind was sideways and against me, and I felt ill and weak with sorrow and fear. I had soon to give up, but I thought of my wife, which made me resolve to set the sail and try to reach the shore by sailing. I hoisted it up, but I found, owing to my ignorance of steering and adjusting the sail so as to catch the wind properly, that I was leaving the land instead of approaching it. I looked about for help, but there was only one vessel in sight, a long way off ; yet I thought I might be able to overtake her, or at least get near enough to make them see that I was in distress. So I turned the rudder, and the wind being strong and behind me, the boat ran very fast along, but not fast enough to reach the vessel, which gradually faded out of sight. I saw more vessels, but all of them a long way off, and not knowing where I should be blown to, I took the mast down, hoping that by remaining stationary I should be noticed by some passing ship. But though the sail was down, I knew that I was being blown further and further from the land ; and what with that and the thought of my drowned brother, and my wife waiting for me, wonder I did not fall crazy," said he, looking strangely. Then, after a pause, he exclaimed, suddenly, "Pray, what time is it?"

I told him.

"How am I to get home?" he cried, starting up and flinging a look round the sea. "Is Weymouth far off?"

"Now don't worry yourself," said I ; "we'll put you in the way of getting home."

Sir Mordaunt looked at me as if he would ask how *that* was to be done.

"You see, my friend," I continued, "that we are in a dead calm ; and without wind, you know, a sailing vessel is help-less."

"Yes, sir, I know that," he answered, sadly, "But I'm thinking of the fear and grief my long absence will cause my wife."

Miss Tuke sidled up to me, and whispered faintly : "Oh, Mr. Walton, do advise Uncle Mordaunt how to land him. His distress is quite heart-rending."

"Mr. Tripshore," said I to the mate, who stood looking at us from the other side of the skylight, "have you made Portland High Light yet?"

"No, sir, and I don't reckon we shall make it. We've too much offing."

"How far distant is that light visible?"

"Why, in clear weather, about twenty mile, sir."

"Now you see how the case stands," said I, addressing the young man, who had been eagerly listening. "I should say that Weymouth is a good full thirty miles distant from this point, and so we can't possibly land you by a boat. But yonder," said I, pointing to the smack that lay becalmed about a mile and a half abreast of us, "is a vessel that will set you ashore near to Weymouth, I dare say. That's all that *can* be done, I think, Sir Mordaunt?"

"Ay, to be sure," answered the baronet, briskly, as though relieved of a perplexing consideration ; "and if they won't land you for charity, they'll do it for money, I have no doubt."

"Oh, I'll pay them, with pleasure, sir," replied the young fellow, plunging his hands into his pockets, just as a man would who is not quite sure of finding what he seeks.

Sir Mordaunt waved his hand with a benevolent gesture, and then crossed over to Tripshore and gave him some directions in a low voice.

The mate went to the side where the yacht's boat lay, and called to the two men who remained in her, "One of you cast that boat's painter adrift, and chuck the end up to me." Here he ducked as the rope came aboard, caught it, and took a turn with it. Then thrusting his head over the bulwark, he mumbled out some instructions. The little boat shoved off, and I saw her shoot out of the shadow our vessel threw upon the water and head for the smack, the thole-pins cracking as the oars were brandished, and a tiny wake behind her, like a string of glow-worms.

"Don't allow your mind to be uneasy," said Sir Mordaunt, coming back to the young fellow. "I'll see that you are put in the way of getting home, and meanwhile keep your heart up by reflecting that you'll soon be with your wife."

"You are very good—very good, indeed, sir," answered the other, in a trembling voice. "This has been an awful day for me."

And indeed there was no occasion for him to say as much, for he had the most broken-down look I ever saw in a man. His voice quivered, he kept on clasping and unclasping his hands, and stealing wild looks around the sea, and now and again he would smear his hand over his forehead, as though he struggled to collect his mind or to help himself to discover that he was not in a dream.

"Were you asleep when I found you ?" said I.

"I couldn't tell you, sir. When it grew dark my loneliness became horrible. The wind dropped, and the boat made no noise, and the silence was shocking. Several times," said he, sinking his voice, and looking at Ada Tuke as if constrained by her sweet face—marble-like in the moonlight, and beautiful with sympathy—to address her, " I imagined I saw my brother's body in the water near me. A dreadful fit of horror came upon me at last, and I threw myself into the bottom of the boat : but whether I fainted or fell asleep from exhaustion, I can't tell

4

you, for I remember nothing more until I looked up and saw you bending over me, sir," turning to me.

"Take some more brandy," said Norie, observing, as indeed we all did, how the poor fellow was shivering. "A whole gallon wouldn't affect you in your present condition." And he whispered to me : "What an imagination ! It will play the devil with his nerves when he gets home. I should be sorry to swear that he won't sicken and die of this day."

Miss Tuke now began to talk to him. How very gentle and sympathetic and cordial she was with the poor fellow ! She did him more good than the brandy. He told her how long he had been married, and where he lived in London, and that the baby was considered more like him than its mamma, though it had her eyes, and resembled her when it smiled, and so on and so on. Sir Mordaunt listened approvingly, Norie with a grin, and I with wonder. What was her receipt for making this poor dejected, shipwrecked cockney cheer himself up?

"She'd be worth her weight in gold at an election," Norie mumbled in my ear. "She'd get all the votes for her man."

"Do you see anything of the boat ? Mr. Tripshore ?" said I, presently, crossing to the mate, who hung over the starboard bulwarks.

"I think I hear her, sir," he answered, and straining my ears I caught the measured creaking of oars.

In a few minutes the boat grew distinct in the moonlight, and there looked to be a load of people in her. As she drew near, however, I saw that there were only four persons, our own men and two strangers ; but these last, sitting right aft, bowed the boat's stern down to within an inch of the water, whilst her bows were cocked up, so as to expose over a yard of her keel.

"Who have you there ?" hailed Tripshore.

"Two of the men out of yon smack," was the answer. "They're willing to land the gent for a sovereign, so we brought a couple of 'em along to row him aboard in his own boat."

The boat sheered alongside, and Sir Mordaunt told the fishermen to step up. They came rolling in over the gangway with the laborious, clumsy sprawling peculiar to smacksmen. They were both of them as warmly clad as old Purchase ; their legs, above their knees, were incased in enormous boots drawn over thick stockings : each man wore a stout blue knitted jersey, covering I know not how many thicknesses of flannel, and yellow sou'westers with hinder flaps which stuck out astern of their heads like the tail of a bird.   I never beheld more powerfully built men, nor finer specimens of the complete English smacksman, as they stood with their long, muscular arms hanging down their sides, though curved at the elbows, and terminating in huge half closed fists like rounds of beef; whilst their eyes glittered in the moonlight as they rolled them upon us under their heavily thatched brows, and their short strong beards forked out over the swathings round their necks like the back of a perch, and curiously corresponded with the projection of the flaps of the sou'westers at the back of their heads.

Sir Mordaunt explained how we had found the young man, and said that he wished him to be put ashore at Weymouth, if possible, and as soon as any wind came.

" Weymouth ? " said one of them, tilting his sou'wester over his nose, that he might scratch the back of his head.   "We ben't going to Weymouth.   We belong to Brixham, and 'ur goin' thur.   Won't Brixham do ? "

"Where is Brixham ? " asked the young fellow, faintly, and inclining his body toward the smacksman with an air of painful eagerness.

"Where's Brixham ? " echoed the fisherman.   " Why, it's close to Dartmouth, and about six mile as th' croo flies from Tarquee.   Eh, Tummas ! "

'' That's aboot it," answered Tummas.

" How can I get from Brixham to Weymouth ? " inquired the young man, in his tremulous way.

" By rail, I reckon. There's a railway, ben't there, Tummas ? " said the first smacksman.

And the other answered, " Zure there be, William, though I ne'er wur on it."

" Look here, men," said Sir Mordaunt, cutting all this short. "This poor young gentleman has been floating about in an open boat all day—since seven o'clock this morning.   His wife is at Weymouth, and he wants to get back to her as soon as ever he can. You have offered to carry him to Brixham for a sovereign, eh ? "

" We've offered to set him ashore for a zovereign, zur," answered the smacksman who had replied to the other questions.

" Well, I'll give you a couple of sovereigns to land him at Weymouth."

" Zay three, and we'll do it," exclaimed the fellow, quickly.

The greedy rascal made me lose my temper.

"Why, what are you?—Zulus!—that you want to be paid before you act like English seamen!" I cried. "Don't you know that there are hundreds of fellows along your coast who will risk their lives at any moment of the day or night to save a fellow creature from drowning, without thought of or chance of reward, whilst here are you bargaining and squeezing like a pair of old clothesmen before you'll give a hand to restore this poor gentleman to his friends? What *are* you, I say—Zulus?"

"Zooloos be d——d!" said the fisherman. "We belongs to Brixham, I towd ye. We've got to get a living like other foalks, and if we puts into Weymouth, we'll be losing near a day o' time."

"Take the offer, Willaim," grumbled his mate. "Take the offer. What's the use of making a disturbance?"

William hung in the wind and breathed short; and then said, "Very well; two zovereigns, then."

Sir Mordaunt gave him the money, upon which the young man went up to the baronet and said something, but what, I did not hear. Sir Mordaunt laughed and motioned with his hand, and said, "Pray, now, jump into the boat, and let the men row you to the smack."

"May God bless you, sir!" said the young fellow; then shook hands with us all round, giving Miss Tuke a respectful bow as he left her, and went over the side into the boat. The moonlight was full on him, and when he entered the boat he raised his leg in the act of crossing a thwart to get into the stern-sheets, but the sight of his brother's clothes seemed to petrify him. He cried out, "Oh, dear!" as though he had been shot, and shrunk away, and though the fishermen told him to go and sit aft, he shoved past them into the bow of the boat, where he threw himself down upon his knees and hid his face under the gunwale. The smacksmen looked at him, and then up at us, and their perplexity proved that our fellows had said nothing to them about the drowning of the young man's brother.

"Shove off!" I called, thinking it best to let the man explain as they went along.

The burly smacksmen each seized an oar, lifting it with one hand as a lady would a paper-cutter, and away they went, Tummas standing up and rowing, his face looking forward, fisherman fashion, and William stretching his back close to where the young man was squatting. We watched the boat until she was swallowed up in the mist of moonlight that over-hung the dark water like a white fog, and then, Sir Mordaunt, pulling out his watch, exclaimed, "Why, Ada, my dear, it's ten o'clock. Pray go and see if your aunt is awake, and if so, and she should want to know the cause of the commotion, tell her the story, but leave out the drowning part."

As he said this, four strokes were told upon the bell that hung just before the foremast. Miss Tuke at once bade us good-night, and went away."

Norie gaped loudly. "Sir Mordaunt, with your permission, I'll go to bed. The sea air has got into my eyes;" and he followed Miss Tuke.

I, however, was in no hurry to exchange the freshness and sweetness of the night air for the close cabin, and Sir Mordaunt being of my mind, we lighted fresh cigars and quietly paced the deck.

"Would any man think," said I, "that we are literally at sea?—for, considering how well into the Channel we are, we may fairly call these waters the ocean. Not a stir, not a tremor."

As I spoke, a beautiful bright shooting-star flashed over our mast-head, leaving a long trail of silver upon the sky, and ex-piring in a puff of glittering smoke.

"Hush!" exclaimed Sir Mordaunt, softly. "By listening you should hear the report."

The silence was so profound, and the run of the meteor so rocket like, that for an instant I was bitten by my friend's fancy, and actually caught myself straining my ear. I broke away with a laugh.

"Do you think those stars *do* make a noise when they ex-plode, Walton?"

"Impossible to say; but I like the idea. The notion of a burst of thunder following their extinction, and floating away in organ tunes through those silent spaces, is Miltonic."

"I wonder what becomes of the fountain of spangles which they throw up when they burst?"

But this was drifting into album stuff, so to get clear of it, I talked of the young man we had saved.

"What a change from the bustle of the City of London to the loneliness of an open boat *here!* The moment he said he was in a London bank, I though of the clattering of gold and silver coin in the copper shovels those fellows use, and the swarms of people round the counters, and the tumult of voices and scratching of pens and flapping of ledgers, and the rattle of cabs outside. And then I turned my eyes upon that silent surface. Do you know, Sir Mordaunt, the fellow must have either an extraordinarily strong or an extraordinarily weak mind, not to have been driven daft. He was not alone : his companion was his drowned brother, who was continually shaping himself upon the water."

"Shocking !" exclaimed Sir Mordaunt, shuddering. "Walton," said he, speaking in a subdued voice, " I hope to God there is no evil augury in this business ! I don't like it ; I wish we had not encountered that boat."

" Why, but for our meeting it, it is fifty to one that the poor wretch would have perished," said I.

"Ay, I am glad of it for his sake : but still, to tumble, as it were, upon a corpse on the very threshold of our journey ! "

" Call it a sign of luck," said I. "That's my interpretation of everything, and the only effectual way of getting rid of uncomfortable omens."

"What are considered as omens among sailors ? " he asked, with quite enough interest and other symptoms of an uneasy mind to make me suspect that, in his present mood, it would not take much to throw him off his voyage.

"Marine omens," said I, " are very numerous.   Jack doesn't like dead bodies.   He doesn't like drowned cats.   Composants worry him——"

" What are composants ? "

"Sort of graveyard blue-lights which come out of a gale of wind, and bring up at the yard-arms, or on the stays, or at the end of the flying-jibboom."

"Ah ! and what are the other omens ? "

"A good deal depends upon the amount of rum served out," I replied.   "In teetotal ships omens are not numerous."

He laughed, and said : " Hang the boat ! I wish that smack had found her first.   Well, Walton, we can't do more than pray that all will go well with us."

" Yonder's a slant of air coming along," broke in the prosaic tones of Tripshore, who crossed over to our side of the deck and pointed.

Brilliantly clear overhead, not a shred of cloud among the stars, and yet there was the breeze coming "out of nothing" right in the wake of the moonlight, which meant dead ahead for us, and making a picture worth watching ; for the wind, as it breezed over the magnificent space of silvered water, broke up

the brilliant reflection as it advanced, dimming, or rather frost-
ing, the white radiance where it was in contact with it, but leaving it ahead as burnished and placid as a sheet of polished metal.
It came slowly, and we could see the starlight shivered like
bits of looking-glass in the water within a cable's-length of us
before it was fanning our cheeks.

"Trim sail, the watch!" rattled out Tripshore. "Get a
drag upon those head sheets. Lay aft here, some of you men.
Wheel, there—steady as she goes. How's her head?"

"Southwest by west, half west, sir."

"The smack feels the draught, Sir Mordaunt," said I
"Round she heads for Weymouth—nor' nor'east, as Tripshore
would tell us."

The breeze briskened up merrily. It was doubly delightful
after the spell of calm, and appeared to blow Sir Mordaunt's
doubting fancies clean out of his mind. Under gaff topsails
and three jibs, and the main boom very nearly amidships, and
the weather leeches quivering in the moonshine, the schooner
looked right up into the warm westerly wind with erect spars,
and with the foam gleaming past her in a manner that made
one see she knew the trick of going to windward. In this way
we were swarming along when half-past ten was struck, on
which we threw the ends of our cigars overboard, and went
below and to bed.

CHAPTER IV.

A COMFORTABLE bed is a small thing to talk about, but a fine
thing to enjoy. Considering how large a part of life is spent
in bed, allowing only eight hours out of the twenty-four there,
if you choose, a man is wise to lie soft and warm. For my
part I have no opinion of those Wellingtonian notions of hard
palliasses and pillowless bolsters. If I can't be manly without
racking my bones all night, I would rather remain without any
sex to speak of. The science of upholstery hit upon the most
perfect bed for comfort, rest and refreshment when it designed
the spring mattress, and hair mattress on top of it. That was
my bed aboard the *Lady Maud ;* and as I bundled into the
snow-white sheets, and dipped my intellectual brow into a pillow of down—soft as the feel of water when a man floats on
his back—I felt that the cynics would have to exert themselves

into an uncommon effort of eloquence to persuade me that life isn't worth having.

I was sleeping soundly when the steward knocked at my door and sung out that it was eight o'clock. As my consciousness brightened, I took notice, first, that the bracket-lamp, screwed against a timber near my head, was oscillating like a pendulum ; next, that the sunshine flashed into and faded out of the little cabin in a very windy manner ; and lastly, that there was a great sound of creaking and groaning and splashing and foaming going on all around me.

"So ! an honest breeze of wind at last !" thought I, as I sprung out of my bunk, and began to topple about after my clothes ; and the springing, swashing, hopping motion of the craft putting an uncommon buoyancy into my mind, I tuned up my pipes :

" ' Another pull, my lads ! belay ! ' "

Here I hauled on my small clothes.

" ' Up with those yards, and let her go ! ' "

Here I fought my way out of my night-gear.

" ' Ours is the ship to run away
When stormy winds abeam do blow.' "

Now, thought I, for a dip ; for I had noticed a capital bath, with a shower-box rigged up over it, in a bit of a room just before the skipper's cabin ; and I opened the door to peep out, as I did not want to plump against Miss Ada or her ladyship with my hair unparted.

No sooner was the door open than an extraordinary noise greeted my ear. What *can* that be ? thought I. But a moment's hearkening solved the mystery. It was, indeed, nothing more nor less than poor Norie *roaring* with nausea in the cabin facing mine. First he would moan like a dog at the moon, gradually increasing the intensity of the sound, and hoisting it up a whole octave, until it ended in an explosion—a complete blow-up—after which he would fall to the moaning again, regularly followed as I have described. But however heartily I may have sympathized with him, I could do him no good ; so, the coast being clear, I bolted forward, clawing along the side of the table in the cabin like a parrot along a perch—for the motion of the little vessel was lively enough to dance me off my legs —and reaching the bath-room, soused myself, and went aft again, inconceivably refreshed. Silence now reigned in Norie's cabin. As I arrived abreast of it, the steward came out.

"Is Sir Mordaunt up yet?" I asked.

"Yes, sir, this hour gone. He's on deck, sir."

"Mr. Norie seems very bad."

"Terrible sick, to be sure. Almost alarming at times, sir," he answered.

"How long has this breeze been blowing, steward?"

"Why, it's been fresh since four o'clock, so Mr. Purchase told me, sir."

"How is her ladyship?"

"I've not heard that she's much inconvenienced by the motion. But her maid's down, sir, quite helpless, poor thing," and he pointed to the cabin next Lady Brookes's.

"And Miss Tuke?" I asked, determined to get all the news at once.

"Miss Tuke is on deck with Sir Mordaunt, sir."

Hearing this, I made haste to dress myself; but before I went on deck I opened Norie's door and looked at him. His cabin was the counterpart of mine in respect of fittings and furniture, excepting that the bunk was right under the scuttle or port-hole. Our friend was to leeward, and as the schooner was lying well over, the port-hole was submerged, and all that could be seen through it was the bright green water sluicing past the thick plate-glass like a mill race, and gurgling and thundering as it went. Some light, however, came down through the bull's-eye in the deck overhead.

Norie lay in his bunk, with a counterpane over his legs, though his toes were visible at one end of it. He was the completest picture of a seasick man that the most experienced imagination could body forth—head on one side, mouth open, eyes filled with water and rolling vacantly, hair over his forehead, the whole tinted with the hurrying, quivering green of the sea through the port-hole.

"Sorry to find you in this plight, Mr. Norie," said I. "Can I do anything for you?"

"Don't talk to me, Mr. Walton; I can't speak," he groaned. "Curse the sea! I thought I could stand it."

"You'll be able to stand it presently—have no fear. Once well rid of your 'longshore swash, you'll take a delight in the rolling deep.

He motioned with his hand, and looked so abject, that I had no heart to offer him further consolation.

" Tell the steward to keep near me," he gurgled as I went away.

On putting my head through the companion, I found Sir Mordaunt and his niece standing close beside it. I wished them good-morning, but at the top of my voice, for what with the washing of the seas, and the booming of the breeze aloft, there was the devil's own noise about. Sprawling aft to look at the compass, I found the schooner lying her course, with the wind a couple of points free. Of all foamy, sparkling, windy mornings, this was one of the grandest I can remember. The wind a summer gale, sweeping and singing over seething heights of running surges ; the water among the foam as green as emerald, and as radiant and clear ; above our mast heads a sky of violet —a most delicately tender blue—with masses of cloud resembling the vast enlarging puffs of powder smoke from the mouths of some gigantic cannons, sailing with the majesty of squadrons of line-of-battle ships across it ; and a windward horizon studded with the snow-white shoulders of similar masses of vapor soaring from behind the sea. The life of the magnificent scene of rolling waters was made wild and almost tempestuous by the whirling shadows of these noble clouds, for where they touched the deep the water was an olive hue and the foam a dead white ; whilst in the sun, against the very outlines of these shadows, the sea was a sparkling light green, with white smoke scattering along it, like bursts of steam, from the heads of the surges as they broke in flashes of blinding light. Over this tossing surface the schooner was splashing and jumping, under a double-reefed mainsail and two jibs. Every minute, as she bobbed her cutter-shaped nose into the hollows, the spray flew over her forecastle in a glittering cloud, and her forward cloths were dark with the saturation of it to half the height of the stays. The watch were in oil-skins, and shone like oil, but all the wet was forward. From a fathom abaft the foremast to the taffrail the sand-white decks were as dry as an old bone ; though at times, when the creaming seas heeled the powerful little vessel over to leeward, the keel of the quarter-boat looked almost within a foot of the water, and the foam alongside spat and bubbled and hissed some inches above the covering-board.

" This repays us for last night's delay, Walton," exclaimed Sir Mordaunt, with his face all aglow, and his hair blowing about his ears, and his beard under his arm.

" I am glad to hear from the steward that Lady Brookes isn't troubled by this dance," said I.

" Not in the least. My niece says it is owing to the bed. It is a fine bed, I admit ; but though it prevents my wife from feeling the pitching and rolling, it doesn't qualify the effect of going up and down : this sort of movement, I mean," said he, as the schooner was thrown up by a sea, and then sunk into the hollow left by it as it ran away roaring and hissing to lee-ward. " Depend upon it, she is going to prove a real sailor, and I'm thankful to Heaven for the mercy."

" And how is it you are not prostrated, Miss Tuke ? " I asked, looking at her with great admiration ; for the strong wind had kindled a bright flush in each cheek, that made her eyes as brilliant as the water where the sun touched it, and her white teeth and red lips and happy enthusiastic expression might have served as hints for a picture of the Goddess of Health. She shook her head, and laughed merrily, balancing herself with the ease of an old sailor to the motion of the vessel, and beating me hollow in that respect ; for she kept her hands by her side, whilst I took care to keep a grip of the top of the companion.

" Poor Norie is very bad, Sir Mordaunt," said I. " It wouldn't do now for one of us to fall ill. Our friend couldn't prescribe."

" I'm very sorry for him," replied Sir Mordaunt, "but I wish he didn't think it necessary to make such a noise. He told me he was a good sailor. The doctor I wanted, who was a naval surgeon for some years, wouldn't come : his practice was too good to jeopardize by leaving it for a summer. However, I have known Mr. Norie for some time, and Lady Brookes is quite safe in his hands. I suppose he'll get over his seasickness in a day or two. But he needn't hurry ; none of us will want him professionally, I hope."

Presently old Purchase stumped along the lee side of the deck, and touched his hat to me as he passed.

" Good-morning, captain," said I. " The schooner knows the scent, now she has the wind—eh, captain ? "

" You're right, sir," he answered, with a grin that crumpled up his face like a block of mahogany that has been shriveled by heat. " I never see any wessel hold her own better. Look over the starn, sir, and ye'll notice she don't make a hair's thickness o' leeway."

Dress as he would, he was always a terribly nautical man to look at. He had a black sou'wester on, the inner rim of which came as low as his eyebrows, and oil-skin leggings, and a rusty pilot-cloth coat pretty nearly as long as a parson's.

" Whereabouts are we now ? " I asked.

" I give us till ten o'clock to-night to be abreast o' the Start, onless the wind comes free, in which case we ought to be well on the Scillies," he answered.

" At that rate, Sir Mordaunt," said I, " we should be clear of the Channel in twelve hours."

" Yes, and no very great run either, Walton.   This head sea bothers the boat.   Mark, now, as she jumps at that wave ! " The light green surge struck her full on the bow, and burst in a storm of snow over the forecastle.   " Do you notice how it stops her ?   Purchase, dont spare your canvas.   Let her have all that she will carry."

" She's got as much as she wants, sir," answered the skipper. " I'm a man as never drives a willing wessel, sir.   My arguey-ment is, no craft is built to sail on her side, and the more you bury her, the more you give her to drag along.   This here double-reefed mainsail keeps the yacht wholesome.   And isn't it pressure enough, gentlemen ?   Look at the weather stan'ing rigging ! "

I was glad to agree with him, but gladder still to hear the steward in the cabin ringing us down to breakfast.

" Only three of us this time," said I, as we seated ourselves. " When shall we have the pleasure of Lady Brookes's com-pany ? "

" Before Norie's, I dare say," answered Sir Mordaunt, with a laugh.   " But let us leave well alone, Walton.   My wife swings without suffering in that excellent hanging bed of hers, and I want her to graduate for the sea in it.   Ada, my love, you will have to look after your aunt whilst Carey is on her back.   Lucky you stand this tumblefication so handsomely."

A tumblefication it was, and the harder to get used to because we had woke up into it, if I may so say, after having gone to bed in smooth water.   On deck, the racing and jumping and foaming of the yacht were a delight, and the strong wind a noble cordial, but in the cabin the motion was exceedingly un-comfortable.   It was not like the stately heaving up and sweep-ing down of a large ship, a steady oscillation that enables a man to count twenty betwixt the plunge of the bow and the rising of the stern, and that gives him time to nicely regulate the conduct of his legs, but a wobbling, squelching, jerking movement that tossed you back whilst you were endeavoring to prevent yourself from being pitched on to your nose, and that set every visible object sloping in half a dozen different directions in a breath. Used to the motion of big vessels, I own it bothered me greatly at first.

The breakfast, by reason of this same dance was by no means a comfortable meal. Most of our time was engrossed in preventing the contents of our plates from sliding on to our laps, and in watching a chance to snatch our cups from the swinging trays that tossed over our heads. The steward's was the worst lookout. To watch him coming along from the direction of the kitchen with a plate of muffins in one hand and a dish of ham in the other, stopping abruptly every now and again, and taking a hurried squint first at one plate and then at the other—like a nervous young gentleman playing a tune upon the piano, and first cocking his eye at the bass keys, and then twisting it on to the treble—ought to have moved my pity. I managed to keep my face, in spite of the laughing devil in Miss Tuke's eyes ; but when at last he fell down with a rack full of toast, and I saw him sprawling after the pieces, that scattered like a pack of cards, and presently get up and rub his nose and look at his fingers, as though his nose was burned, and he expected to see the skin come away, I fairly exploded, but with a result that was utterly unexpected ; for, lying back in my chair to have my guffaw out, at the moment the vessel lurched somewhat heavily to leeward, over I went on my back, and bringing up against the cushioned locker, lay, like to suffocate with laughter. I regained the table, with my face, as I could feel, as red as a powder-flag. Sir Mordaunt, grinning broadly, hoped I was not hurt, and Miss Ada, looking at me with the flush of suppressed laughter in her cheeks, said, "A very proper rebuke, Mr. Walton, for ridiculing your fellow-creatures in misfortune."

We scraped through the meal, and then dispersed on merciful errands—Sir Mordaunt to see his wife, Miss Tuke to comfort the prostrate Carey, and I to condole with Norie. I found him no better. He turned his blood-shot eyes on me with a haggard look of remonstrance, as though he suspected I came to quiz him.

"Is there anything you would like?" said I. "Try a glass of cold brandy ; it may settle your stomach."

" I've got no stomach to settle," he answered. "It's all gone away overboard."

"He meant this as a figure of speech, but any one would

have taken it literally on seeing his face. He could scarcely articulate, and could not do better than lie motionless ; so I came away, and filling a pipe, crawled on deck, and stowed myself under the lee of the skylight.

A head-sea in the English Channel, until the water broadens into an ocean abreast of the Lizard, is the most unpleasant in the world. There is no room for the waves to get big, in the sense that ocean waves are big, and the passage of a small vessel over them is all chop, chop, and sputter and stagger. Once clear of this spiteful tumble, the deck takes an agreeable buoyancy from the long regular heavings of the deep sea surges. I was much struck by the appearance of a brig on our lee beam, and could appreciate, by watching her, the action of the sharp, short, slopping sea through which our schooner was biting and squeezing and jumping. She was ratching, like ourselves, under lower topsails and foresail, and she toppled about like a buoy. So short were the waves, that before she could settle her stern into a hollow, a succeeding sea had buried her bow, when, breaking into dazzling foam to a level with her figure-head, it would shoot up in a cloud of mist, like the smoke of a waterfall, as high as our foretop, and blow away on her quarter as though a cloud of vapor had burst out of her fore hatch. As she veered astern—for we passed her rapidly—the character of her rolling could be better perceived ; and the jerky dislocating tumble, the sprawl of the masts, as if they must lay their lengths along the sea, the sharp recovery, the submersion of the stern down to the taffrail, and the great yawning heave of the bows, showing the yellow metal down to her forefoot, and the water pouring out of her hawse-holes and head-boards like the foam from a driven horse's mouth, made her for all the world resemble a man hammered by a crowd of ruffians, and kept from falling by the blows rained upon him from all sides.

The strong wind held all day, and the yacht was really miserable, with her frothing scuppers and streaming forecastle. The men liked the head sea as little as any of us, and the only creatures who appeared to enjoy it were the dogs, who were incessantly springing about the decks, and barking at an extra heavy lurch, and shaking their coats free of the constant showers of spray which they were forever plunging into the bows to receive.

But at four o'clock the wind hauled away into the south, and though it blew with undiminished strength, yet the shift seemed to have deprived it of half its force. A reef was shaken out of the mainsail, and the reefed foresail set, and under this increased canvas the yacht drove like a thing possessed. The foam flew away from under her counter, and the tail of the wake looked to be dancing among the seas of the horizon; there was no longer the old severe pitching, even the rolling was moderated by the steady beam pressure, and no more water flew forward, unless it were now and again a bucketful of spray that flashed over the weather bulwark with the sparkle of a mass of brand-new silver coins, scattering as they went.

This was the right kind of sailing; a warm strong summer gale abeam, the sea a leaping surface of green and white, a fine sky overhead, with the swollen vaporous masses of the morning replaced by a surface of feather-shaped clouds, very high and scarcely moving, and the yacht buzzing along like a steamer, with a belt of foam to windward, which the wind that swept out under the foot of the mainsail blew up in flakes, as though the inside of a feather-bed had gone adrift.

That night at a quarter before nine I was chatting with Sir Mordaunt in the cabin when Tripshore put his head into the skylight, and told us that the Lizard lights were in sight. We bundled on deck, and looking away on the starboard bow, there, like a fire-fly hovering over the deep, was the last of the English shore-beacons we should see. The sunset had gone out of the sky, and the moon was on the other side of the vessel, and where the Lizard light was, the sea was a great throbbing shadow.

"Those lights, if I remember rightly," said I to Sir Mordaunt, "are visible about twenty miles distant, so we know how far we are from the old home."

"They are, I think, the first lights a sailor sights when homeward bound from the south," he answered, "unless he happens to be blown near the Scillies. How many eyes must have watched for those sparks! What hopes and fears they must have kindled! Well, good-by, old country!

> ' Much as we have loved you,
> We'll dry the tears that we have shed before.
> Why should we weep to sail in search of—'

health, eh, Walton? But many days must pass before we see those cliffs again, or behold that little spark yonder. And meanwhile may God have us all in His keeping!"

We stood looking at the light—for the two beacons appeared

one at that distance—and at the foaming sea around us (upon whose southern horizon the moon was shedding its soft white fires), and hearkening to the piping of the wind up aloft, and the strong permanent hissing of the water at the bows of the yacht, whilst the far-off light got gradually smaller and smaller as we edged away toward the limit of the sphere within which it is visible, until it was no more than a needle's point of brightness, and only apparent when the eye was directed a short distance from it. At last it vanished, and there was no light at all that way except the stars twinkling blandly upon the water-line.

"Gone, Sir Mordaunt. This is really bidding our native land good-night." And I piped up :

> " ' Yon sun that sets upon the sea,
> We follow in his flight ;
> Farewell awhile to him and thee—
> My native land, good-night.' "

"Two more lines, Walton," cried Sir Mordaunt.

> " ' Let winds be shrill, let waves roll high,
> I fear nor wave nor wind.'

And there we stop. "Yonder's our home," he exclaimed, pointing over the bows of the schooner into the west. " A solemn mystery to head for. What mighty mariners have vanished in its immensity ! Look at the gloomy desolate wild now, and think of Columbus breasting it in a vessel that might serve one of our ships for a long-boat, steering by no other illumination than the light that never was on sea or land. But come, let us go down and toast the *Lady Maud* in a glass of soda and brandy. The old girl has whipped us bravely down the English Channel, and she deserves all the encouragement we can give her by our good wishes."

Had we been bound to the West Indies with a freight that required dispatch, we should have been put into fine spirits by the noble wind that blew us out of the English Channel, for it lasted all that Friday night and the following Saturday, and by way of favoring us to the utmost, veered to the eastward, so as to enable us to make the necessary southing ; and for all these hours the yacht pelted under exactly the same canvas she had on her when we sighted the Lizard light, and we grew as used to the sweeping roar of the passing foam, and the humming of taut shrouds, and snow-white cloths tearing at the bolt-ropes, as passengers in steamships to the throbbing of the engines.

We were rather surprised when sitting down to dinner on Saturday to observe the door that shut off the sleeping berths open, and Norie emerge. He was yellow and haggard, and stood for some moments holding on to the door stanchions, evidently too nervous to let go ; but presently, making a dash, he struck out for the table, reached it without mishap, and swung himself into a chair.

"An unexpected pleasure," exclaimed Sir Mordaunt, looking at him with surprise. "We all thought you were in bed."

"So I was," he answered ; "but I felt hungry, Sir Mordaunt, and as I considered the symptom a good one, I was determined to encourage it."

And hungry he unquestionably was. I never saw any man make a larger dinner. But from that moment he complained no more of seasickness.

Lady Brookes, however, still kept her cabin, nor had I set eyes on her since Thursday. But next morning, after breakfast, whilst Sir Mordaunt and I were smoking our pipes on the grating abaft the wheel, her ladyship suddenly uprose through the companion, assisted in the rear by her maid Carey, who in turn was helped along by Miss Tuke. We both ran up to her.

"Why, Agnes, this is brave ! this is encouraging ! " cried Sir Mordaunt, to whom it was very evident his wife had not unfolded her intention. "Walton, kindly shove that chair along. Carey, go and fetch a cushion for her ladyship's back. Ada, my love, throw the shawl over your aunt's knees ; " and for some moments all was bustle : it was like the arrival of a member of royalty at a ball.

The invalid had chosen the right kind of morning for her first appearance. The strong wind had failed in the morning watch, so old Purchase had told us ; there had been a calm for an hour ; then a breeze had sprung up in the northwest, and that was the wind now blowing ; every stitch of canvas had been piled upon the schooner, and she was softly and quietly sweeping over the deep blue fathomless sea, like an albatross blown along by its outstretched tremorless wings, gliding up and running down the long ocean swell, the long intervals between whose bright and foamless acclivities were too wide to make the regular motion inconvenient or even noticeable. The men were in their Sunday rig, lounging about the deck forward,

5

some of them smoking, some reading, some looking over the side at the luminous curve of water which the passage of the yacht arched over from either bow, and their smart clean dress prettily heightened the effect of the exquisitely white decks and the beautiful heights of gleaming sail which soared into a light blue sky, frosted in the east with minute spray like clouds, whilst in the west it was an untarnished summer azure. It was surely a delightful picture to come upon after a three days' imprisonment in the cabin, and Lady Brookes's face brightened as she looked around her. Moreover, she was gratified by the pleasure her presence on deck gave her husband ; and this, and the commotion her arrival among us created, put her into excellent spirits. Even the mastiffs seemed to suspect that there was to be no more seasickness aboard the *Lady Maud*, and breathed hard, and exposed their tongues, and shoved about among us, as though in search of some means to un- burden their minds of those feelings for the expression of which they could find no other vehicles than their tails.

Whilst we stood talking, some men came aft to spread the awning ; and whilst this was doing, Purchase drew a red ensign over the quarter-deck capstan.

" For divine service, my dear," said Sir Mordaunt, answering the question in his wife's face.

This was as it should be ; and presently the whole ship's company came aft, and gathered around the capstan. It was a pretty sight. First, the men in a crowd upon the white deck, all very clean and smart in their tidy dress, standing bare- headed and for the most part in reverential posture ; then the bright color of the ensign, with Sir Mordaunt's fine, tall, long- bearded figure inclined over a great church service ; and to the right of him Ada Tuke's pretty face and amber hair, crowned by a little hat and a long dark feather, thrown up by and finely contrasting the knot of rough sailors' countenances behind her ; and in another place, Carey, the maid, between the elbows of two seamen ; and just behind her the cook, with his one eye turning about in his sour face, and Purchase varying his devo- tional aspect by an occasional professional squint up aloft.

All the incidents of a man's progress to a great misfortune take a strange, pathetic significance after the trouble has hap- pened, and he looks back and thinks of what went before. He then finds how full of meaning some things were which at the time went past as the veriest commonplaces. This was our first Sunday at sea, and our gathering together to worship God knits all those people to me, so to speak, in a manner that makes that picture moving to recur to, though at the time I never could have believed the memory of it would affect me as it does. I have but to put down my pen and close my eyes, and I see all those men, and Sir Mordaunt in the midst of them, and his wife (the only one among us seated), with her gaze fixed upon the prayer-book in her lap ; and more than that, I see the great ocean stretching into the sky all around us, and have before me the very aspect of the heavens in the south, and the leagues of flashing sunlight in the water. In thinking of it I feel like a child looking at a picture in a soap-bubble. The whole scene moves, and is full of exquisite color. It is close to me ; I am wondering at the brilliance and the life of it !

And now it is gone ! And so shadow-like becomes the yacht and her little company of men and women, nay, and those very waves

> " That o'er th' interminable ocean wreathe
> Their crispèd smiles,"

so unreal as a part of the vanished experience, that I seem to be as one who has acted with phantoms and taken part in a performance whose fabric was a dream.

CHAPTER V.

FRIDAY, June so-and-so ; eight days out ; longitude about 15° W., latitude about 39° N., which is near enough, as I have no other log-book than my memory to go by.

I awoke early, and finding the cabin close and the sky shining like blue silver through the port-hole, I bundled on my clothes and went on deck. It was a little after six ; the sea was smooth and flecked with foam ; what wind there was was abeam, and the yacht was heading southwest under a crowd of canvas. The watch on deck were washing down, and the sunshine flashed in the glass-clear water which they sent gushing from the buckets, whilst they swabbed and scrubbed, with their trousers turned above their stout white calves, and made the schooner as busy as a hive with their movements.

Purchase was in charge, and seeing him standing near the binnacle, " taking in " the yacht, with his hands behind him and his legs apart, I went up to him and said good-morning.

"Another fine day, captain. The weather has favored us wonderfully so far."

"It has that, Mr. Walton, sir," he answered, giving me a rather wandering look, and with an expression of suppressed mirth that might well be described as a smile rolled up in his face, though no words could convey the hilarity among the wrinkles and the mixed suggestions of his brown and purple countenance. "Oncommonly fine weather we've had, and no mistake; and I don't know that I'm a man as can ever get too much of it," he added, with an effort to recover his gravity, and lifting his eyes—which resembled faintly illuminated cairngorms twinkling in the deep caverns under his brows—to the heavens.

I stood to leeward of him, and a puff of wind breezing my way made my first suspicion certainty. The aroma of rum, or some equally strong spirit, was a most decided flavor in the air. "Hang me if I believe that complexion of his *is* weather," thought I, twisting a glance at his red nose and fiery cheekbones; "and Lady Brookes may have keener eyes than her husband." However I had never smelled drink upon him before, and so I was not all disposed to take notice of his present condition, that was in no sense pronounced, and that might be very well due to a dram taken on an empty stomach.

"Yes," he continued, bringing his eyes from the sky, and with the humorous expression breaking out among the mahogany wrinkles again, "fine weather is always sootable to my feelings. If I had my way, breezes after this here pattern should be the prevailing winds, and the sea would never be rougher than what you see it now. But mind!" said he, with the insistence of a man who is resolved that you shall know he understands his own meaning, "I'm not going to say that all sailors are like me in this here fancy for smooth water and six-knot breezes. Some likes pickles strong and some likes 'em mild. I likes 'em mild, and the same here with cheese. Some sailor men don't object to gales o' wind, providing they blow the right way; and some prefer the draughts of air such as they tell me ye get down in the latitood of Captain Cook's islands, where ye a'most forget the names of the running gear for the want of using it. Now, Thomas!" he suddenly bawled, "mind where you chuck that water. Shut the skylight, one of you. Steady as she goes, William," turning to the man at the wheel. "How's her head, William?"

The fellow gave the course; but I noticed that he bit his

under lip and looked astern, holding the little wheel with one
hand.   The truth is, the joke lay not so much in the dash of
drink that made the old fellow's face laughable to look at and
his deep salt voice diverting to hear, but in the collier-like
mannerism it forced out of him.   His dress only travestied
him.   What he wanted was a musty old beaver, and a long
coat, and a red shawl round his throat, and a framework of
grimy decks, and a surface of patched cloths stretched upon
yards made for other vessels.   Yet I am bound to say he knew
navigation—enough, at least, to enable him to point his sextant
and prick some kind of course.   The first day he came on deck
"to shoot the sun," I thought he only exhibited the instrument
to bamboozle Sir Mordaunt, and that he had no other notion of
finding his way to the West Indies than by dead-reckoning,
which latter I suspected from the care he took to keep the log
going.   But I was undeceived when he sung out, "Strike eight
bells," though I had like to burst with laughter when I saw him
bobbing after the sun, staggering about the deck, with the
sextant to his eye, as though some one had given him a blow,
and he was trying to reduce the swelling by a cold application.
    "Isn't that a ship yonder?" I said, pointing over the bow,
having suddenly caught sight of a speck of gleaming white
against the sky where the vague horizon met it.
    He bobbed and sheltered his eyes, and after cleansing them
several times by means of wedging his knuckles into the
hollows in which they lay buried, exclaimed, "Ay, it's a sail,"
and so saying, went for the glass.   He was a long while
bothering over the focus, and when at last he adjusted the
tubes to his vision, he was unable to hit the object, repeatedly
dropping the glass and looking for the sail, with one eye
closed.
    "Give me the glass, captain," I exclaimed, impatiently, for
I was beginning to think the man more muddled than I had at
first suspected, and noticed with annoyance the amused glances
which the fellows who were cleaning the decks cast at him ;
for it did not at all please me that a man holding the responsible position that Purchase filled should jeopardize the disci-
pline of the vessel by making himself ridiculous in the eyes of
the crew.   I took the glass, but was afraid to look the old fool
in the face, for fear of laughing ; I therefore quitted that side
of the deck.   There was not much to see.   The vessel ahead
was on a line with our bowsprit end, and only her highest
canvas was visible.   The sunshine, however, poured full on

the stranger, and made what was shown of her very clear and sharp against the sky, whereby I perceived that she was a square-rigged vessel, but whether bark, or ship, or brig I could not tell.

I went below for a cold bath; and when I came on deck again, at eight o'clock, Purchase's watch was up, and he had gone to his cabin. Nobody belonging aft excepting myself had turned out, and as all the crew were getting their breakfast, the only persons on deck were Tripshore and the man who steered. The mate touched his hat to me, and not knowing I had been on deck before, pointed out the vessel ahead, that, greatly to my surprise when I perceived that she was going our way, we had risen considerably whilst I was below.

"Yonder should be either a very slow boat, Mr. Tripshore," said I, "or else the *Lady Maud* is sneaking along much faster than she appears to be going."

"There's no weight in the wind, sir, pretty as it is," answered Tripshore; "and that chap ahead, I dare say, now, is loaded down to his chain-plate bolts; whilst, if you'll look around you, you'll see there's nothing to stop the *Lady Maud*—the sea like silk, the draught steady enough to keep everything pulling, and a square-sail on her light and big enough to blow her along in a calm."

This was true. I ogled the stranger again, and judged from the height of her topsails, which were just visible, that she was a large Indian or Australian ship. I put the glass down, and asked Tripshore if the skipper was below.

"Yes, sir; he went below when I relieved him at eight bells."

"He must have knocked about a great deal in the sun in his youth," said I, gravely, watching Tripshore's face. "It's not to be supposed that his nose caught the color it wears in the North Sea."

He laughed, but made no answer.

"Sir Mordaunt," I continued, "says his complexion is owing to weather. What do you think, Mr. Tripshore?"

"It's not my place to take notice of things which don't concern me, sir," he answered, but so significantly as to make me see he followed my drift.

"Why, perhaps not, if the things *don't* concern you. But if you happen to be a passenger aboard a vessel, her captain's character and skill and habits ought to interest you, I should say, Mr. Tripshore, seeing that your life is in his hands, and

that it entirely depends upon him whether you shall be drowned
or not."

"That's right enough, sir," said he. "The captain of a
vessel ought to be a man of first-rate character, and I don't
know that the people who are along with him haven't a right
to watch his character, and notice when it's shipshape and
when it isn't."

This was all the justification I needed for having spoken to
him about Purchase. For though I had made up my mind to
say nothing about having noticed the old man the worse for
liquor, I was bothered, if I had not been surprised, by the
discovery, and hoped, by speaking to Tripshore, that he would
hint to Purchase I had spoken as if I suspected an intemperate
habit in him, for that might frighten him, and hold him away
from the bottle. Perhaps as a man who knew something about
the sea I found a significance in the incident that would have
escaped a landsman. The perils of the deep are numerous and
dreadful enough, but there are none worse than a drunken
captain. It was enough to think of our sleeping below, and
the schooner in charge of a man thick with rum, and blinking
in the eyes of a squall, to make me anxious and determined to
watch him. But, as I before said, I would take no further
notice of what I had observed beyond talking to Tripshore, so
that he might advise Purchase to be on his guard; that is, if
they were friendly, which it was out of my power to inform
myself upon, as they were rarely on deck together for any
length of time, and what passed below was hidden from me.

Norie arrived from the cabin shortly before breakfast, but I
did not meet the others before the meal was on the table.
Who had given orders for the provisioning of the *Lady Maud*
I never knew. I doubt if it were Sir Mordaunt, for the foresight
could only have been shown by an old and experienced sea-
caterer. Considering that our live stock consisted only of
poultry, I have often wondered how the cook managed to
stock the table so sumptuously, though at the time I took what
came without speculation. Our breakfasts in particular were
always remarkable for plenty and variety. On a fine day like
this, when the sunshine lay upon the open skylight, and the
drawn curtains softened the light, and fresh currents of air
breezed down through the windsail with force enough at times
to keep the leaves of the plants and flowers trembling, no
prettier scene could be imagined than the *Lady Maud's* cabin.
Nothing but the motion of the vessel could have persuaded you

that you were not in some low-ceiled, richly furnished apartment ashore—that is, after finding a fictitious *raison d'être* for
the solid mainmast that pierced the two decks, and attributing
the radiant stand of arms against the bulkhead to some capri-
cious decorative fancy.

"There is a small excitement ahead of us," said I, as we
seated ourselves at table ; a large full-rigged ship, that we are
overhauling in fine style. If this light wind holds, we shall be
well up to her by noon."

"I hope, Mordaunt, you will give orders to Purchase not to
go near her," said Lady Brookes.

"No, no ; we'll keep to windward of her—eh, Walton ? "
exclaimed Sir Mordaunt.

"Will that be a safe place, Mr. Walton?" her ladyship
wanted to know.

"As safe as if she were out of sight," I answered. "But,
Lady Brookes, you mustn't pretend to be nervous now. You
have beaten the worst part of the sea, and after such an exploit
you should have the nerve to face even a fire."

"Well said!" cried Sir Mordaunt. "And let me tell you
that this same sea is behaving to you as a generous enemy
should. Norie, do you know of any drug that could work the
change I see in my wife's face? Believe me, for brilliant eyes
the ocean breeze is better than belladonna; and for beautiful
complexions, what is sarsaparilla compared with salt oxygen ? "

It was evident that Lady Brookes did not the less relish her
husband's references to herself because she looked as though
she were deaf.

"What do you think of salt oxygen, Miss Tuke, for a new
medical term ? " exclaimed Norie, with the admiration in his
face that was a standing part of it whenever he turned it upon
Miss Tuke.

"If it's unintelligible, it should suit the doctors," she answered.

"Are you keeping an account of this voyage, Walton ? " sung
out Sir Mordaunt. "Logging it, as you nauticos say ? "

"Why, no ; nothing has happened to make a beginning
with. No use putting down latitude and longitude and state
of the weather *only*. Let a whale run into us, or let Purchase
fall overboard and vanish in the hold of a shark, and I'll fire
away."

"At that rate, I hope you'll find no occasion to write at all,
I'm sure," quoth her ladyship.

"If ever I should attempt to tell the story of this cruise," said I, "the yarn will consist merely of loggings. There'd be no *story*. I'd tell the truth, and that's all ; enlarge, but not imaginatively, upon the 'observations,' which you know make a part of every log-book."

"The best sea-books are of that pattern," said Sir Mordaunt. "What are *Tom Cringle* and *The M dge*, and Dana's fine book, and Herman Melville's, but logs—amplified jottings? Your profession has never produced a finer writer than Michael Scott, Walton. There is more beautiful poetry in one page of Michael Scott's sea descriptions than in all the 'Islands' and 'Corsairs' and 'Shipwrecks' put together. But then you must *know* the sea, to enjoy him, whereas you can relish Cooper and Marryat without ever having been further than Gravesend ; and that, I suppose, is the reason why they are more popular than the other, though they have not a tithe of his genius."

"Why don't *you* keep a record of this voyage, Miss Tuke ?" said Norie, rather languishingly. "Our friend Walton, I dare say, would furnish you with the sea terms, and I should very much enjoy reading your descriptions of us all."

"Would you ?" said she, with a cold smile in her eyes that made the apparently naïve question a mighty malicious thing to my ear, though Norie took it as Peter Bell took the primrose.

Lady Brookes laughed. Miss Ada was so much brighter and cleverer than the man who addressed her, that no woman could have watched the two faces without being pleased.

"Ah, I would indeed," said Norie. "Sir Mordaunt, pray beg your niece to keep a journal of our travels, and I'll tell you what I'll do. If we have time for a run ashore when we get to Jamaica, I'll botanize and philosophize, and make out a learned chapter about the night-hawk, and the tern, and the pelican, and the hawk-billed turtle, and the lignum-vitæ, and the brasilletto, and the wild cinnamon——"

"Ay, and the green cabbage, and the pearly onion, and the land-crab, and the floury yam," said Sir Mordaunt, laughing. "If my niece is to write a book, she must get her interest out of the sea. If we touch anywhere it will be to fill our tanks, not to philosophize, nor to yellow-feverize either, Norie. Besides, man, how long do you suppose we mean to be away ? This is not a voyage round the world."

" And the time flies," said I. " Eight days out already ! and it seems but yesterday that we were bowling down the English

Channel.   Wh'en and where, I wonder, does your skipper mean to strike the northeast Trades ? "

" Where do they begin ?" asked Miss Tuke.

" About seven or eight hundred miles further south than where we now are," I answered.

" Do you think your skipper knows anything about those winds ? " asked Norie, jokingly.

But Sir Mordaunt resented this in his mild-mannered way, not only because he had great confidence in his captain, but because he did not like any doubt to be cast upon the fellow's capacity in the presence of Lady Brookes.   So at least I read it.

" You ought to know, Norie—but you *do* know, for I remember telling you—that Purchase has been to sea ever since he was a boy, and has sailed as man or as master in all sorts of vessels, in all sorts of seas, and in all sorts of weather.   *You*, Walton, should be able to assure our friend that so old a sailor as Purchase must know the winds as well as he knows his two hands."

" Say what you please, Mordaunt, about him," exclaimed Lady Mordaunt, unexpectedly, " I am still of opinion that he drinks."

" Nonsense, Agnes !   Why should you believe such a thing ? Have you ever seen him drunk ?"

" Well, if he doesn't drink now, the time is not long past when he *did* drink : of that I am sure," said she, emphatically. " Mr. Walton—nay, I'll ask *you*, Mr. Norie—did you ever see such little, watery——"

" Groggy ? " suggested Norie.

" I say such little, watery, *filmy* eyes, in the face of a man who has been sober all his life ? "

" Never," answered Norie, anxious after his correction to make amends by agreeing warmly.

" You *must* clear your mind, Agnes, of this melancholy prejudice against an excellent old seaman," said Sir Mordaunt, after bestowing a look of reproach on Norie.   " Walton will tell you that the weather produces effects upon the face which might easily pass for symptoms of drink."

" Ay," thought I, " but the weather doesn't make a man's breath smell of rum; " but I held my peace.   The subject was dropped by Lady Brookes rising, and presently we were all on deck.

I looked in the direction of the ship, and observed that her courses were now visible, and, as I might tell by an attentive examination of her through the telescope, a fragment of her hull. She resembled a small moon poised upon the blue horizontal line, shining as blandly as if the canvas had been self-luminous. The light breeze still held, and the schooner was slipping through the water very nimbly. Indeed, shortly after we arrived on deck the log was hove, and the speed made out to be five knots, which I thought remarkable, considering the lightness of the air. The lofty rig, however, of the *Lady Maud* greatly helped her in light breezes. She carried no spinnaker, but instead a square sail that was made of very fine canvas. light as duck, and that was set from the deck ; and I have seen it full and round, and the schooner breaking the brass-like waters into ripples and churning up a wake under the pulling of it, when the other canvas has hung up and down without a stir. We had that sail set now, and every other cloth besides, including a foretop-mast studding-sail that overhung the water and shone in it like a shallow bottom of silver-sand ; and every sail being as white as milk, and the sunshine white too, the appearance of the stately, gleaming heights, silently doing their work, was exceedingly beautiful.

We gathered together under the awning, for the sun was very fierce, but after a while Miss Tuke went below, and began to play and sing. She had no " touch," as it is called, but her voice was pretty, and as she always chose words set to real tunes, I was fond of listening to her. And so the morning crept by until old Purchase came on deck, just before noon, to hunt after the sun, having apparently slept off the effects of the dram he had swallowed in the morning watch.

By this time we had overhauled the ship to within a couple of miles, and there she lay, steady as a cloud, about two points on our lee bow. I had not been giving her much attention for some time, owing to a very lively novel I had taken from a pile of volumes upon the sky-light ; but being disturbed by old Purchase's sprawling search for the sun, I looked up and noticed how near the ship was, and so, putting down the book, I took the glass and examined her.

She was a long, frigate-built, merchantman, with painted ports. Her square yards and short royal mast-heads made her look very handsome aloft. She had a long poop and top gallant forecastle, and big cabin windows, which caught the sunshine and flashed streams of light in the still blue water under her. Her sails were beautifully cut, her large channels gave the standing rigging a wide spread ; and, deep as she was, yet I

could just catch the greenish gleam of her copper a trifle below
the sparkling blue surface over which she was faintly moving.
I noticed with some wonder that she had a number of flags
hanging along her awning, in such a way as to hide all that
part of the deck save the taffrail. This gave her an uncommonly gay appearance. The flags were of all colors, and the
contrast of them with the white awning and the black and white
sides of the ship was very striking.

On a sudden I caught sight of her name, painted in large
characters on her stern.

"Sir Mordaunt!" I exclaimed, looking around, "I recognize
an old friend yonder. Ten years ago I was second mate of
that ship. She's the *Dido ;* and bound, I have no doubt, to
Sydney, New South Wales."

"Very curious, indeed!" he exclaimed, coming over to me
and taking the glass. "It only proves what a little world this
is—even at sea." He ogled the ship. "But what is the meaning of those flags? It isn't the Queen's birthday, is it? Are
they having a ball aboard of her?"

"There's a jollification of some kind going on," said I.
"Can you make out any of her people?"

"I see some figures at the taffrail."

"Let us signalize her," said I.

"To be sure!" he exclaimed. "Here, Purchase," he called,
"signal that vessel, will you?"

The old fellow had "made eight bells" some time before.
He put down his sextant, rolled aft, and hoisted the ensign.
Miss Tuke now joined us, and we stood watching. Presently
a spot of red glimmered at the ship's stern, it soared, and the
red ensign languidly fluttered at the peak.

"Hush!" cried Miss Tuke ; "don't you hear the sound of
music?"

I listened a moment.

"Plainly enough," said I. "What on earth are they about?"

The strains of a band of instruments were distinctly audible,
though what wind there was blew athwart us and toward the
ship.

"Can't you ask them by flags what they are doing?" said
Miss Tuke.

"Quite easily ; but we shall be within hail presently, and
that will save us the bother of spelling over the signal-book,"
I answered. "How strange to light upon the old hooker all
these leagues down here!"

And I fell a-musing, thinking of the months I had passed in her, the watches I had kept on her poop, the old crew whose faces and names I could distinctly recall, and the incidents of the voyage. I own my heart warmed up at the sight of that ship. I was proud to be able to point to her, and say that over and over again I had had charge of her in the long watches, for she looked, as I have said, a beautiful object upon the blue of the deep sea. Indeed, there was no handsomer vessel of her kind afloat. But it was not only her appearance that kindled me ; the present seemed a mere dream when I looked at her, and nothing real but the life I had passed aboard of her. Any sailor will understand my feelings. Jack's love of a ship in which he has sailed and been well treated is a genuine sentiment. I knew every plank, every rope, I might say every nail, in that fabric.

Looking around, I caught Miss Tuke's eyes full upon me.

" I dare say you would rather be in her than here," says she.

" My dear child," exclaimed Sir Mordaunt, " you should hear Walton talk of his blankets having been stolen——"

" Not in *her*," I interrupted. " No, I was very comfortable in that boat. But don't you believe, Miss Tuke, that I wouldn't rather be where I am. I think of her as a man might of an old sweetheart. The sight of her makes him pensive ; but does that mean that he is sorry they didn't stick to each other ? "

"One always returns to one's first love," said she, laughing.

"So this meeting proves," said I. "Sir Mordaunt, you must lay me alongside—not to board her, but to talk. Perhaps I know her skipper ; and, besides, we can hear the music, and if Lady Brookes won't object, we might turn to and shake a foot to it, to keep the people yonder company. But I should like to know the meaning of that jollification. Cheerfulness is rather uncommon in a ship a few days out from home."

" Perhaps they have a great man on board," surmised the baronet ; "and this may be his birthday."

" Maybe a governor. A governor becomes a great man the moment he quits London," said I.

" I wish this yacht were a steamer," said Lady Brookes, pettishly—having been looking for some moments through the skylights at the sails, which were faintly stirred by the swell—with an expression of lassitude in her face.

" Why, Agnes, I would have hired a steamer, my love, had not the whole summer been before us," answered Sir Mordaunt.

" But you would not have been so comfortable.   The smell of
the engine-room is always about.   On such a day as this it
would be exceedingly unpleasant ; and the throbbing and
champing of the engines is very harassing in a small vessel."

"'That is so, indeed," said I, backing my friend as usual in
these encounters.   "Steam is all very well for dispatch, but
when you are not in a hurry you must choose a sailing vessel.
You enjoy expectations in a sailing ship which steam defrauds
you of.   How will the wind blow?   Will this calm last?
When a breeze springs up, will it be foul or fair?   In a steamer
you don't think of these things.   You plod on like a pack-man.
The fine old traditions, the seamanship, the beating to windward, the reefing down, the lying to, the running or scudding,
are all blown away by steam.   Jack has chucked his tarpaulin
overboard, blacked his face, and gone with a shovel into the
bunkers.   He is no longer sailor, but stoker, and all our maritime notions have been melted down into the propeller."

"I don't think you would like the *Lady Maud*, aunt, if she
were a steamer," said Miss Ada.   "There would be no snow-
white sails," lifting up her beautiful eyes, "and we should be
constantly peeping into the looking-glass, to see if there were
smuts on our noses."

" Better smuts than stagnation," murmured her ladyship.
"We may be stuck without motion upon this sea for the next
month."

Evidently the heat made her peevish, and besides, as an invalid, certain obligations of temper were imposed upon her
which she was bound to fulfill.   I changed the subject by
talking of the ship ; and when lunch was over we all returned
on deck, Lady Brookes excepted, who complained of languor
and went to her cabin, though I was inclined to attribute her
withdrawal to spleen.

———

CHAPTER VI.

WE had passed an hour over luncheon, and on arriving on
deck I was surprised to notice how we had neared the ship in
that time, though the calm was now profound, the water running like a surface of oil into the sultry horizon, where the sea-
line trembled in the haze of heat, and was here and there
indistinguishable from the swimming sky.   Whether vessels

becalmed together at sea do actually attract each other, as sailors believe, I cannot positively say ; but their tendency to close is unquestionable, and is often a source of inconvenience and even of danger when there is a swell on.

The ship had swung with her stern dead on to us, but owing to the shadow cast by the tent-like envelopment of flags and awning over her poop, it was impossible to see along her decks ; but there was a small crowd of people looking at us over her taffrail, and we could see their faces, though too far off to distinguish their lineaments.

" We might hail her, Sir Mordaunt," I suggested, " and find out where she's bound to, and what the jollification is about."

" Call to her, will you, Walton ? You know what to say."

" Purchase had better sing out first," said I. " He's skipper, and I mustn't usurp his functions."

On this he turned to Purchase and requested him to speak the ship. The old chap clambered on to the bulwark, and passing his arm round a backstay, bawled in his deep, gruff, wheezy note, " Ship ahoy ! "

After a short pause a figure jumped on to the taffrail. " Hillo ! "

" What ship is that ? " rattled out Purchase.

" The *Dido*."

" Where are you from, and where are you bound to ? "

" From London, bound to Sydney, New South Wales."

" Didn't I say so ? " said I.

" What's the name of your yacht ? " came from the ship.

" The *Lady Maud*, from the Hisle o' Wight, bound to the West Hindies ! " vociferated old Purchase, pulling off his brass-bound cap, and mopping his bald pate with a red handkerchief which he extracted from the bottom of his head-gear. At this point the band of music, that was apparently stationed on the forecastle, struck up " Auld Lang Syne," and Purchase dropped with the unwieldiness of a bear off the bulwarks. It was now my turn. I sprung on to the rail and waved my hand, in token that I had something to say. The man who had answered Purchase looked toward his forecastle and made a gesture, and after a bit the music stopped.

" Ship ahoy ! " I shouted.

" Hillo ! "

" Will you be good enough to give me the name of your commander ? "

" Captain Robert Spenser."

"He was chief officer when I was in her," said I to Sir Mordaunt. "See now if he recollects me." I again addressed the ship. "Will you ask him if he remembers Mr. Edmund Walton, who was second officer under him in Captain Turnbull's time?"

This conversation had brought a crowd of people to the stern of the vessel. They were as thick as flies, and I noted a number of heads forking over the side of the ship, trying to catch a sight of us, while some men got into the main and fore rigging to look.

"Perfectly well," came back the reply, as clear as a bell, over the polished surface between the two vessels. "Are you Mr. Walton?"

"I am."

"I'm Captain Spenser."

I pulled off my hat and flourished it, a salutation he returned with a hearty gesture.

"Ask him to visit us, Walton," exclaimed Sir Mordaunt, much interested in, and even excited by, this colloquy. "These are the mild adventures I enjoy."

I hailed my old shipmate again, and asked him to come aboard, an invitation he promptly accepted; and in a few minutes a couple of midshipmen jumped into the white gig that was slung over the stern of the *Dido*, and she was lowered smartly into the water and hauled round to the gangway. After a short delay, during which, I presumed Spenser had dived below to furbish himself up for his visit, he got into the boat, in which four more midshipmen had seated themselves, making a crew of six, and shoved off; and had the *Dido* been a man-of-war, no better effect could have been produced than that white boat ripping up the sea under the flash of the long gleaming oars, and the ship behind gently immersing her deep sides in the shining swell, and bringing them out, and a couple of feet of her copper as well, sometimes, all glittering and streaming with wet; whilst the center folds of her symmetrical canvas, that looked like marble against the blue, flapped smartly into the masts, and sent across the water the musical clanking of chains and the chafing of blocks and the quick rattle of reef-points.

The boat came alongside, and I received my old friends at the gangway, We shook hands cordially, and I introduced him to Sir Mordaunt and Miss Tuke.

It was many years since I had seen him, but I should have known him at once. He was, when I was at sea with him, and still remained, one of the best-looking men I had ever seen, fair, sunburnt, slightly above the middle height, his profession stamped upon every movement, yet without the least nautical assumption or "shoppishness," of a most amiable disposition, at this time barely forty years of age, and as excellent a seaman as was at that time afloat.

"Why, Walton," cried he, "this, to be sure, is an extraordinary meeting. Have you command here?" looking about him with great admiration. "I thought you had cut the sea— driven out of it by a legacy?"

I briefly explained how I happened to be in the yacht, and the object of the cruise.

"You are acting wisely, Sir Mordaunt," said he. "I am sure the run will greatly benefit Lady Brookes. I have a man there," pointing to his ship, "a first-class passenger, who has entirely lost his voice, and can only speak in a whisper. I am going to carry him round the world, and I'll wager before we are north of the line again he'll be able to bawl as lustily as yonder old gentleman," indicating Purchase.

Wine and tobacco were brought, and we seated ourselves for a chat. He told me that he had commanded the *Dido* for the last four years, that she was still in the trade she was engaged in when I was her second mate, and had become a favorite ship with the colonials who visited England.

"You appear to have a great number of people on board," said Sir Mordaunt.

"One hundred and sixty-nine passengers, all told," he answered. "There are above a hundred emigrants."

"But what is the meaning of those flags along your awning, and the music, Spenser?" said I. "Are your passengers celebrating their escape from the mother country?"

"No. It's a romance—as interesting, Miss Tuke," said he, addressing her, "as any exciting chapter in a novel. I'll tell you the story in a few words. Among the cuddy passengers are a Mr. and Miss Wheeler. Mr. Wheeler is an old gentleman, and Miss Wheeler (as I will still call her) is a young and pretty girl. Of course it is no business of mine to make inquiries about my passengers, but no sooner were we fairly under way, and I had leisure to look about me, than I found my curiosity tickled by this couple. That they were father and daughter I did not doubt, but I could not understand the girl's miserable dejection. She was incessantly fretting, so much so that I was positive more was behind this misery than leaving home.

6

Well, to make the story short, four evenings ago I was talking to some passengers near the wheel, when I heard a great noise of quarrelling upon the quarter-deck. I went forward to see what the matter was, and saw old Mr. Wheeler flourishing his arms like a wind-mill, and abusing a young man who was looking at him very quietly. A crowd of persons stood around, listening evidently with great astonishment to the old man's violent language, and wondering at the youngster's meek reception of it. I went down on the quarter-deck, took Mr. Wheeler by the arm and led him into the cuddy, and asked him what the matter was. He was fearfully excited, and hardly able to speak. However, after a while I managed to calm him down, and then he told me his story. He was a widower, very fond of his daughter, and anxious, of course, about her future. The girl, behind his back, had fallen in love with a young fellow, and betrothed herself. Mr. Wheeler found this out, and tried to prevent them from meeting. That, of course, was a hard job for a man engaged every day in business in the City," said he, laughing, "and I suppose his efforts failed. Afraid that his daughter would elope, he resolved to carry her to the other side of the world—to Sydney, where he has a sister. He made arrangements for a year's absence, and took ship in the *Dido*. But love is not to be outwitted by old age. I suppose Miss Wheeler told her sweetheart what her father meant to do ; for, will you credit it ? the rogue paid his money for the 'tween-decks ; came aboard in the dark, and lay hid among the emigrants until the ship was clear of the Channel. So here they were all together again, and the old man worse off than had he stopped ashore. Mr. Wheeler, happening to be standing at the break of the poop, noticed young Stephenson—that's his name—upon the quarter-deck, saw through the whole thing, rushed down, and fell upon him with his tongue. And what, think you, is the upshot of this marine romance ? " continued Spenser, laughing heartily. " You will, of course, hold me responsible, Miss Tuke, when I tell you that, my heart being melted by the poor girl's grief and the young fellow's loyalty, and learning from old Wheeler that Stephenson was a gentleman by birth, that his antecedents were honest, and that there was nothing against him but his poverty—no great crime in a lover when his sweetheart's father earns three thousand a year, which, I believe, is old Wheeler's value—I went to work to reconcile the enraged parent to what I told him was a stroke of destiny ; and getting some of the passen-

gers to help me, reasoned, urged, entreated, and so effectually
got him into a corner that, after sulking for a day, he called
us to his cabin, and said that, since matters had come to that
pass, he would risk no further disgrace, and had therefore resolved that his daughter should be married at once.   And
married they were—this very morning ; and the weather being
fine, we dressed the ship and we are going to have a feast
and a dance this evening."

"So, Miss Tuke," said I, "here is a real adventure for you
at last."

"I would like to have seen them married," said she.

"It was a very pretty sight, I assure you," exclaimed Spenser.
"We have a parson aboard, and everything was perfectly ship-
shape.   We turned the cuddy into a church, and all hands put
on their Sunday clothes ; and as we have a good many ladies
among the first-class passengers, there was no want of color.
Speeches were made at lunch, which we called breakfast in
honor of the occasion, and the flourishing of pocket-handker-
chiefs was quite touching.   The bride and bridegroom made
a really good-looking pair.   But you must dine with us,
Sir Mordaunt.   Miss Tuke, you will come, I hope?   We've got
a band of music aboard—three or four fiddles, and a harp and
a trombone and a cornet, most of which are among the steerage
passengers, though the cornet belongs to the cuddy ; and as
we shall light the decks, and all hands will dance—the saloon
passengers aft, the others on the main-deck, and Jack on
his forecastle—the sight will be worth seeing, and help to relieve the tedium of a sea-voyage.   We dine at half-past five."

Sir Mordaunt hung in the wind a minute or so over this
invitation to dinner.   I was afraid he was going to refuse,
which I should have regretted, as Spenser was full of heartiness,
and might have misconstrued a refusal.   Miss Tuke looked
anxiously enough at her uncle to make him see she wanted
him to accept.   Suddenly he said : "You are very good, captain, and we shall be happy to join you.   But what about the
weather?"

"Have no fear," said Spenser.   "Leave the weather to me."

"You can safely do that," said I.   "The weather and Spenser
are old cronies, and thoroughly understand each other."

"I hope Lady Brookes will accompany you," said Spenser.

"I shall certainly endeavor to persuade her," answered Sir
Mordaunt.

Captain Spenser remained on board the yacht for about a

quarter of an hour, during which time Sir Mordaunt showed him over the vessel, whilst Miss Tuke and I and Norie talked with the midshipmen, whom I had called up out of the boat to look at the yacht and drink a glass of wine. In those days of large and handsome sailing ships the merchant service was reckoned scarcely inferior to the navy ; and having regard to the difference between the numbers, there were as many gentlemen afloat in one service as in the other. When I was in the *Dido* she carried twelve midshipmen, most of them lads from Eton and Harrow, and with one exception only, the sons of gentlemen. She had now but eight midshipmen, six of whom had pulled their skipper aboard of us, and very gentlemanly young fellows these six were, with a dash of schoolboy shyness that was not unbecoming, and a frank, straightforward way of answering questions. They were rigged out in white trousers, cloth jackets, and brass-bound caps, with a gold badge over the peak ; no waistcoats, but, instead, large silk handkerchiefs loosely tied round the open collars of their shirts. Of course none of them knew me, for I had given up the sea when they were little boys at school ; but they soon saw that their ship had been an old home of mine by the questions I asked.

After a while Sir Mordaunt came up from below with Captain Spenser, who, after swallowing another bumper of claret and lighting a cigar, got into his boat, telling us, in his hearty fashion, not be later than five, and not to trouble about the weather, for that he would warrant the calm for some hours yet ; and as the oars dropped into the sea, that was like a sheet of quicksilver, he raised his hat, and away dashed the boat, soiling the beautiful, breathless, burnished, and yet slowly heaving surface like moisture upon a looking-glass.

Shortly after he was gone Lady Brookes came on deck. She stood a moment or two in the companion, looking at the ship —not as if to admire the delicate and ivory-like fabric that swung upon the water, which her reflection filled with color, so as to remind me of the silver plate of a daguerreotype, with various hues shooting across it at every heave of the swell, but —as if considering that she was too close, and a source of danger.

"How near we are to that ship, Mordaunt !" she exclaimed. "You can distinctly hear the people laughing and calling."

"Don't be afraid, my love," he answered. "The least breath of air will waft the yacht clear of her. We have just had a visit from her captain, a most gentlemanly, sailorly man, an old friend of Walton's, and he has asked us to join them in a merry-making they are holding over a most romantic incident." And he told her the story of old Wheeler and his daughter, and wound up by saying that Captain Spenser was anxious she should dine with him, and see the dancing.

" But how are we to reach the ship ? " said she, looking doubtingly and yet as if she had a mind to go too.

"Why, in that boat," answered her husband, pointing to a whaling-built semi-lifeboat hanging at the davits.

" Oh," said she, drawing back in her chair, "if that's the only way of reaching the ship, " I'll stop where I am."

I should have liked to ask her if she could suggest any other way.

"There will be no danger, aunt," pleaded Miss Tuke. "You will be very much amused. Captain Spenser is an exceedingly agreeable man ; and think of the romance, aunt ! It would make me miserable for the wind to get up and carry us away, without seeing the bride and her husband."

"And old Wheeler," said Norie.

But it was no good. If there were any other mode of getting on board the ship she wouldn't mind going ; but nothing, she said, could induce her to trust herself in a little boat. And the glitter in her eyes, and the twist in the corners of her mouth, made us all see that it was time to leave off persuading her.

I was afraid Miss Tuke would have been disappointed after all ; for shortly after four o'clock the water in the southwest darkened under a small wind that came along over the breathing swell very slowly, but still, as I thought, with a promise of holding in it. They saw it on the ship as soon as we did, and before it reached us Spenser hailed the yacht, to say that if there was any weight in the coming slant he should not expect us to stop, though he was quite willing to lay his mainyards aback for a couple of hours, if we would heave the schooner to and go aboard. However, the puff turned out to be a mere cat's-paw, that expended itself in a few minutes, leaving the water glass-smooth again, and fading away from us in the east like the shadow of a cloud running over the sea ; but it was of some use too, for it enabled us to forge ahead of the ship, and give her a wider berth, though it left us within speaking distance, and near enough to let us see her people, and have the whole image of the vessel before us in bright and beautiful completeness. When the time came for us to go, Sir Mordaunt did not much like leaving his wife alone ; observing

which, Norie very humanely offered to stop and keep her ladyship company, for which I was not sorry, and, the boat being
manned, we got into her and headed for the ship. As we approached, the band on the forecastle struck up, "See, the con-
quering hero comes!" which made me laugh heartily.

"Do you notice the women looking at us over the bulwarks?"
said I to Miss Tuke.

"I must ask Captain Spenser to let me go over the ship,"
said she. "I should like to see where the emigrants sleep and
live."

"I'll take you below," I answered.

"I hope the saloon passengers won't think us intrusive,"
said Sir Mordaunt. "I was for declining your friend's invitation at first, and proposing to visit him for an hour after dinner;
but I wasn't sure that my wife wouldn't come, and I thought
it would be a pleasant break for her, and a real experience to
remember and talk over."

"A ship's captain may entertain whom he pleases, and I
think you'll find the passengers will consider themselves honored
by your company," I answered.

The whole length of the ship's bulwarks was lined with heads
watching us as we approached, and I fancy that we were all
three somewhat embarrassed to find ourselves the cynosure
of so great a number of eyes, and being rowed to the martial
music of the band. They had thrown a gangway ladder over
the side, with white man-ropes to hold by and a grating at
the bottom to step out upon. We swept alongside in man-of-
war style, hooked on, and I jumped out, giving Miss Tuke a
hand, and followed her and Sir Mordaunt on deck. Spenser
and his chief officer received us at the gangway; but though
memory and my old traditions were never stronger in me than
at that moment, I confess, after the quietness of the schooner's
deck, the crowds of emigrants, seamen, and other people who
congregated near the gangway to see us arrive, coupled with
the buzzing of the band, the cackling and lowing and bleating
of live stock in the long-boat, pens, and hen-coops, the crying
of babies, and the appearance of the decks, dark and even grimy
looking, after the yacht's, the great coils of running rigging,
the massive bulwarks, the huge water-casks, and all the rest
of the big ship's heavy equipment, were positively bewildering.

We were conducted on to the poop, where a number of well-
dressed ladies and gentlemen were walking or sitting. Owing
to the flags and the awning, this part of the vessel was in

'Spencer and his chief officer received us at the gangway.'—Page 86.

shadow, and very grateful and pleasant the gloom was.   Standing at the foremost end of the poop, and gazing aft, was like looking through a canvas tunnel.   The deck here was white enough, and all the brass-work finely polished, the shadow variously tinted by the blues and reds and yellows of the flags, and at the extreme end was the large wheel, with the steersman holding it, his figure in the sunshine, and making a striking object against the rich blue of the sky over the taffrail.

The very first persons we were introduced to were Mr. Wheeler and his daughter and son-in-law.   The bridegroom was not particularly good-looking, but his manners were gentlemanly, and he had very kind, honest eyes, and a pleasant laugh.   So much I remember of him.   But his wife's face I have before me now—a most beautiful face indeed : no artist ever painted or described anything more harmonious and uncommon. Rich auburn hair, violet eyes, a lovely figure, a smile that broke like a light upon her countenance, and a soft damask rose-like flush on her cheeks.   I wondered, when I looked at her, where the deuce my friend Spenser's eyes or heart could have been, that he had mentioned her charms to us so lightly and dispassionately.   Her indescribable beauty made her husband a much less heroical character in my opinion than I had been disposed to consider him.   To follow such a piece of witchery as this to Australia, even as a steerage passenger, was a sample of fidelity or fascination infinitely beneath the worth of the prize.   Had he swum down the Channel after the vessel, or turned privateersman and captured the ship, and borne away his true love to a tropical island, in ballad-story fashion, I would have credited him with some appreciation of his duty as the lover of such a girl.   But merely to book himself as a third-class passenger in the ship in which his sweetheart was outward bound, to risk nothing worse than a spell of 'tweendecks life, with the chance of gaining not only a lovely girl, but an heiress—pooh ! the thing was too commonplace.   He was no longer romantic—merely a lucky dog.

I fancy Spenser was rather proud to introduce Sir Mordaunt to the passengers, and they seemed very happy to meet the owner of the handsome schooner-yacht they had been admiring all day.   However, we had scarcely time to do more than bow, when the first dinner-bell rang, and everybody bustled below to dress.   A very agreeable, well-dressed Australian lady took charge of Miss Ada, and carried her to her cabin, and Sir Mordaunt and I followed Spenser into his den, where we put down our hats and trimmed our hair, while our host bustled about, full of excitement and gratification ; lamenting Lady Brookes's absence, and offering to send a boat for her ; envying Sir Mordaunt's ownership of the *Lady Maud ;* cracking jokes over the recent nuptials ; squinting at his log-book, and giving me the result of his "sights" at noon ; calling up merry recollections in me by swift reference to the old skipper we had sailed under— all in a breath, as I may say.

The second bell rang, and we sallied forth into the cuddy. The scene was a lively one. A long table ran down the center of the great cabin, with a short one across it atop, making the shape of a T ; and these tables being dressed for dinner, covered with plate and china and glass and flowers, made the cuddy look as if a Lord Mayor were going to give a feast in it ; whilst punctual to the summons, out of the row of cabins which flanked the table on either hand issued the passengers, talking and laughing, silk dresses rustling, fans playing ; and presently we were all at the table, Sir Mordaunt and Miss Tuke beside the skipper at the head, I plump opposite the bride and bridegroom, and next to old Wheeler, and all the way up and down, and cross-wise at the top table, an agreeable alternation of male and female figures.

A strange scene to tumble upon in mid-ocean ! I looked at Sir Mordaunt and his niece, and saw they were taking it all in, and heartily enjoying the novel experience.

Passenger vessels of the *Dido* class are fast becoming things of the past, and I am disposed to dwell upon this interior, and the whole picture of the vessel because in a few years hence it will be hard to meet anybody who remembers that kind of ship, or who will be able to realize that the average time oc-cupied in making the voyage from London to Sydney was be-tween three and four months. The *Dido* was ten days out (so her chief mate told me), but her passengers had recovered from their sea-sickness, and had got to know each other, as I might easily have guessed by looking around me. Most of them were Australians, returning from a visit to England, well-bred, quiet people, extremely genial in their manners, without an atom of brag or swagger in them, and nothing whatever about them to distinguish them as colonials.

Every passenger seemed to look upon us as his own particular guests, and Sir Mordaunt and I were being constantly called upon to drink wine with one or another—this genial fashion surviving in the ships of the *Dido* class long after it was extinct ashore—and we were all three of us fairly embarrassed by the attention paid us. Still, it was very nice, though it increased my regret at Lady Brookes's absence, because her presence would have added a great zest to her husband's gratification. Miss Tuke enjoyed herself thoroughly. She won everybody's heart within reach of her eyes and voice, and the whole spirit of the scene—delightfully novel and entertaining to her—was reflected in her sweet and radiant face.

I was careful to take wine with the bride and bridegroom, to the former of whom I made the most gracious bow I was master of, as a feeble expression of the admiration she had kindled in me ; and when this performance was over I turned to old Mr. Wheeler, and conveyed all sorts of good wishes for the young couple into his ears.

"I suppose you know, sir, how it all came about?" said he. He was a rather pompous-looking old chap, with a face like John Bright's, a great satin stock round his neck, and stiff shirt-collar, which obliged him to move his body as far as his waist—or where his waist ought to have been, for he was as round as an apple under his waistcoat—when he turned his head.

I answered that I had heard the interesting and romantic story from my friend Captain Spenser.

"I certainly hope they *will* be happy," said he. "In the meanwhile, I don't like the idea of taking a voyage to Australia for no other purpose than to get home again. I left London at a great inconvenience to myself and others, and I see no prospect of returning under the time I expected to be absent."

"You could transfer yourself and baggage to the first home-ward-bound ship you meet," said I.

"If we come across one I shall do so, sir. As yet we have encountered nothing but your yacht, and she is not going the way I want to take," he answered. "But it may all be for the best," said he, with an effort. "I am reconciled. I shall settle them in Australia, if we get there, where Mr. Stephenson may be able to add to his wife's income. And—and I hope they *will* be happy."

He gulped down the contents of the wine-glass, and looked severely at the swinging tray opposite him. I caught his daughter eyeing him nervously, but her husband whispered something to her, whereat she smiled and turned her face to-ward him, with a look so brimful of love and happiness that I was ass enough—seeing that I was not the recipient of that glorious expression—to feel a good deal moved by it. Out of the fullness of the heart the mouth speaketh.   Old Mr. Wheeler seemed to have been more candid with me than he intended, for he hung back after this, as though he feared that any topic we should get upon would lead him back to this business of his daughter.

It was close upon seven o'clock when we left the table, and knowing there was not much to be seen of the sea from the poop, in consequence of the flags, I left the cuddy by the quarter-deck entrance, and stood there a few minutes, looking at the yacht and the water.   The evening was quite breathless, and the ocean a polished surface of pale violet under the deep pure azure of the heavens, upon which not a fragment of cloud was visible.   The yacht lay full in the setting sun, about three-quarters of a mile on our port bow.   She had swung broadside on, and lay heaving her fine symmetrical length upon the swell, that shook the folds of her canvas so as to make those milk-white spaces flash and fade in alternations of shadow and rounded brightness.   Dozens of emigrants sprawled upon the bulwarks and on the forecastle, looking at her ; but many others were eating their suppers on deck, squatting in whole families round their hook-pots of tea and tin dishes of biscuit, and the savings of their midday meal of salt pork or junk, and making the decks of the fine ship picturesquely squalid.   Indeed, the scene in the hands of a good artist would have made a canvas likely to detain you in front of it a long while.

Whilst I stood gazing I heard my name softly called, and looking up, I saw Miss Tuke leaning over the brass rail that protected the forepart of the poop.   Alongside of her stood the first mate, a man named Woodman.   I joined them ; and as I ascended the poop ladder I caught sight of Sir Mordaunt in the midst of a crowd of passengers, talking and laughing, and evidently in high spirits.

" Mr. Walton," said Miss Tuke, "remember your promise to take me downstairs to see where the emigrants sleep and live. Mr. Woodman is kind enough to say he will accompany us."

" By all means let us go," said I.   " But first let me ask you what you think of this scene.   Is it not a sight worth coming to see ? "

" It is, indeed.   I should have been very sorry to miss it. How foolish my aunt was not to join us ! Everybody is so kind and agreeable.   I am sure," said she, looking behind her, " had Uncle Mordaunt been the Prince of Wales, the reception he has had couldn't have been more hearty and gratifying."

As she said this, Spenser bustled out of the crowd that was gathered around the baronet and came running our way.

"I say, Mr. Woodman," he sung out, "are the boat's crew about? I mean the yachtsmen. Just tell them to jump into the boat, will you? Oh, Miss Tuke, I beg your pardon! And, Walton, how have you been getting on, old friend? I've prevailed on Sir Mordaunt to let me row over to his ship, and try my eloquence upon his wife. She ought really to be with us —and the doctor, too. I'll bring 'em both—I'll bring 'em both!" And in a high state of excitement, with his fine eyes aglow and his handsome face flushed, he toppled over on to the quarter-deck, and in a few moments was rowing for the yacht.

"Lady Brookes won't come," said Miss Tuke, laughing and shaking her head. "He'll soon tire of trying to persuade her."

Here Mr. Woodman joined us, and without more ado we left the poop. One way into the 'tween decks was by the booby-hatch, as it is called—or·*was* called, for marine things have changed names since my day. This was a square hole just under the break of the poop, with an almost perpendicular ladder down it. There was a quantity of raffle on the main-hatch, though one of the gratings was off for the admission of air; but there was no ladder, and so we could not get into the 'tween-decks that way. Miss Tuke looked down into what must have resembled the bottom of a well to her, and hesitated; but just then a woman, holding a baby in one arm, forked out of the gloom, gained the deck, and went forward.

"If *she* can come up, I ought to be able to get down," said Miss Tuke.

"Let me go first," said I, "so that, if you should fall, I shall be at hand to shore you up."

"And if you will give me your hand," said Mr. Woodman, "I will support you from this end."

She put her foot over—it was a very small one—and with our help reached the lower deck safely. The mate was for shoving forward into the gloom at once, knowing the ropes; but Miss Tuke and I preferred to stand and gaze for a minute or two, until our eyes got their right focus. Then, bit by bit, the old familiar scene (to me) grew defined among the shadows. The first object that courted the eye was the immensely thick mainmast, that looked as big as the funnel of an ironclad, between the decks. Beyond was the main hatchway, the gratings of which let down a little light, but not enough to penetrate far, nor to perplex the illumination of a lamp that hung near the mainmast, and that swayed to and fro as the ship leaned with the swell. There was a long row of berths on the port side, into one of which I poked my head, meaning that Miss Tuke should look, but instantly shut the door, on perceiving a woman and two children lying in the upper bunk, and a man sound asleep under a big top-coat in the lower one. Woodman was more fortunate, and lighted on an empty berth that was a very good sample of the rest. Here were three bunks filled with rude bedding, miserable straw mattresses, coarse brown blankets, and petticoats and breeches in bundles for pillows ; a couple of crazy old boxes on the deck, which I suspected, by the look of the hinges, had been dashed about by the motion of the ship, and forced to vomit their wretched contents more than once ; and here and there a tin dish, an old cap, a boot.

" How would you like three or four months of this sort of thing ? " said I to Miss Tuke.

" I could not imagine anything more unendurable," she answered.

Woodman laughed.

" You see it at its best now," says he. " To thoroughly appreciate it, you should be here in dirty weather, when the hatches are battened down, and all the emigrants below ; when there is no light beyond what that lamp gives, when the ship is straining heavily, and sea-chests and women and children go fetching away with every roll, and when some of the men are singing, and some of the women quarrelling, and all the youngsters are squalling. Eh, Mr. Walton, I think you have an emigrant ship's 'tween-decks in perfection at such a time ? "

Though most of the owners of the cabins were on deck, some score or more were below. In one place four men, dressed as English artisans, seated round a chest and playing at cards, silently and with a certain austere earnestness ; in another place a woman, seated on a bundle of some kind or other, against a large box that served her for a table, around which were gathered five children, to whom she was handing pieces of biscuit, whilst a baby lay against her bosom that was barely concealed by a small red shawl over her shoulders. Here a man lay flat on the deck, his head pillowed on his arms, and his eyes fixed on the huge beam directly over him ; there a couple of infants quarrelled over an old rag that had been twisted up into the

likeness of a doll, with a rope-yarn tied around it to distinguish
the head from the stern.   None of these people took any notice
of us.

Miss Tuke looked about her without speaking.   It was all
new to her, and painful to see.   The poor woman feeding her
children, with the baby at her breast, the whole of them miserably clothed, and their meal no more than black tea and biscuit, formed a really moving sight ; because in addition to
what the eye saw, the imagination added the pain of quitting
her native country, perhaps for good, the misery and suffering
of a long voyage, with a strange land at the end, without, it
might be, a friend to give her a welcome.   But God tempers
the wind to the shorn lamb.   Certainly these people did not
feel their condition with the acuteness that a woman like Miss
Tuke, who could only think of their lot in contrast with her
own, would imagine.

There was not much more to see, except the midshipmen's
berth, into which I put my head, but found the long, narrow
cabin, with its double row of bunks and slip of table, traveling
on stancheons, empty, for the young fellows would of course
be on deck, waiting to cut a caper, and to show off their buttons
and white pants.   So we made for the booby-hatch, and helped
Miss Tuke into the pure air, much after the manner in which
we had assisted her below.

As we emerged I saw a crowd of people at the open gangway, and, to my surprise, who should come over the side but
Lady Brookes, gallantly handed up by Spenser !

"Hang 'em ! those good-looking fellows can do anything
they please," said I to Miss Tuke ; and we went forward to
welcome her ladyship, and congratulate her on her courage.
She threw alarmed glances around as she stepped on board, as
if she was frightened by the number and appearance of the
emigrants who crowded the main-deck to see her arrive.   Captain Spenser's gallantry, however, knew no limits, and deserved
silk stockings and a laced coat ; for, holding his hat in one
hand and her ladyship's fingers in the other, he conducted her
on to the poop, where I wondered he did not get in front of her
and walk backward.   Presently she was in the thick of the
passengers, alongside her husband.

" Now Sir Mordaunt's happiness will be complete," said I.

" There's Mr. Norie ! " exclaimed Miss Tuke ; and, catching
sight of her, he ran up to us.

Of course he had arrived with Lady Brookes, but I did not

see him come over the side. He was all bustle and satisfaction and chatter.

" The captain was irresistible ! " he exclaimed. " Such a coaxer I never listened to. Miss Tuke, you should have seen Lady Brookes melt away under his entreaties ! Heaven defend us ! had there been any wind, and that handsome fellow had proposed to run away with the yacht, dash me if I don't think——"

" He'd have carried you with him, eh ? " I interrupted, noticing that Miss Tuke looked away, as if she thought the medico was out-talking his judgment ; for, undoubtedly, the difference between Sir Mordaunt's age and Lady Brookes's did somehow make wild talk of this kind more of a mistake than it seemed to be. " Look at those decks, Norie, and congratulate yourself upon having yonder beautiful, milk-white, quiet sea-home to return to when we have had enough of this ; " and I pointed to the yacht, that the swing of the ship brought on to our port beam, and whose nose was at us, bringing her two masts into one, which swayed their snow-like canvas from side to side like the languid beating of an albatross's wing, while beyond her the large summer stars were shining with the green and blue brilliance of diamonds, though astern of us the flush of sunset still illuminated the heavens, and flung a most rich and lovely twilight upon the face of the breathless deep.

Conversation, however, was no longer possible, for the band of musicians, who had been fiddling and blowing on and off all day long, got together close to where we were standing, and struck up a piece of dance music. It seems that all the fellows were professionals but one, so the music was fairly good, and quite excellent to dance to. Whilst these fellows were tuning up, several of the crew of the *Dido* were running about the decks in a high state of excitement, rigging up lanterns of various kinds and sizes around the poop and along the main-deck. The illumination was not brilliant, but it was very effective, and nothing in its way could have been more striking than the appearance of the people shifting their colors as they passed out of the light into the shadow, with here a red lantern flinging its ruby flood upon a space of deck where the luster lay like a great blood stain, and there a coil of rope, a water-cask, a fathom of chain-cable brightly irradiated by a white light, through which the people came and went like a procession of ghosts, the gloom lying dense on either side resembling a flood of black water between silver and purple banks ; whilst on high were the vague, pallid sails, and over them a heaven crowded with stars.

The band, having finished its overture, struck up a quadrille. In a great hurry Norie asked Miss Tuke to give him the dance, and she consented. I preferred to look on, and so I got into a corner and watched the proceedings.

The poop was full of gliding figures. I saw Sir Mordaunt dancing with the bride, and very handsomely he twirled her about, turning out his toes in ye ancient fashion, twisting the calves of his legs round, flourishing his arms, and behaving most graciously; and I also beheld my friend Spenser, who was the baronet's *vis-à-vis*, rolling about in a fine nautical style, with a very bouncing fat and fair partner, whose waist he took every opportunity that presented itself to clasp and spin round with, as though the only way to dance a quadrille was to waltz through it, and as though he reckoned that dancing was an idle entertainment if it did not involve a fair proportion of hugging.

On the main deck and forecastle the emigrants and seamen were hopping about in great glee. Their exercise had no reference whatever to the music, only in so far as the fiddling and strumming gave them an excuse to kick up their heels; for their performances were strictly original, and as numerous as the men, women, and children who took part in them, and this made the whole scene exceedingly amusing. I own I laughed heartily at some of the antics I witnessed, particularly at the sailors, some of whom kicked off their shoes, that their legs might feel lighter.

And yet, full of broad humor as the whole scene was—and even the behavior of the select folk aft was not free from this quality, for some of their postures and movements were quite absurd—it was impossible to lift one's eyes from the decks to the spacious, gleaming leagues of silent ocean, bounded by the glittering sky, and black as ink under it, though brightly reflecting the luster of the larger stars in thin flakes of silver that seemed to be melting and slowly sinking in a thick trickle of white, burnished, molten metal, without finding one's merriment checked. The thought of the minute speck this ship made upon that boundless surface, and the littleness of the people whose whole world it was for a time, and the paltriness of the pastime, pathetic in its paltriness, that made them merry, became too violent for mirth when that soundless, breathing, ebony space of ocean was looked at.

But thoughts like these would not do. I broke away from them, and picking a road through the dancers, reached the place where Lady Brookes was sitting, and after a few compliments upon her pluck in leaving the yacht, asked her if she would give me the next dance. No, she was quite unequal to dancing, she replied ; but she was very amiable, and seemed impressed and amused by the scene, and flattered by the civilities shown her.

Presently the quadrille came to an end, and Sir Mordaunt and Miss Tuke and Captain Spenser and some others joined Lady Brookes. But the band would not give us much rest. In a few moments they burst out into a waltz, which I danced with Miss Tuke, and was heartily enjoying, when suddenly, as we whirled past Sir Mordaunt, he called to me. We stopped, and went back to him.

"Look, Walton," said he, pointing right over the stern ; "isn't that a breeze of wind coming?"

I immediately saw the troubled starlight, and the sharper horizon way down upon the north-east.

" Yes," I answered, "there comes some wind, certainly ; but it may prove only a cat's-paw."

" We ought to get on board the yacht, Mordaunt," exclaimed his wife, suddenly, and even sharply.

" Well, complete your dance, Walton. I can't interrupt Captain Spenser," he said, laughing, as the skipper, grasping a lively partner, flew past us as though he were in tow of a comet.

We finished the waltz ; but by the time the music had ceased the wind was all about us, and the chief mate bawling orders over the poop rail.

" Keep those yards aback ! Don't forge ahead of the yacht ! " panted Spenser, breathless after his capering.

Sir Mordaunt went up to him with his hand extended.

" My dear sir, you are not going yet ? You'll disappoint us all if you don't stop and join us at the table below ! This is only a summer draught—it'll be all gone in a moment."

But Sir Mordaunt would go. It was no cat's-paw that was blowing, but a steady, gentle breeze, that might freshen fast for all we could tell ; and Spenser, probably guessing this himself, and certainly seeing by Lady Brookes's manner that entreaties would only tease her, ordered the yacht's crew into the boat, and at the same time hailed the schooner, to let them know we were coming. Then followed so much hand-shaking that my arm ached again with it. Every soul aboard crowded the sides to see us get away, and as we shoved off they gave us a hurricane cheer, which we answered with hearty good-will. In a few minutes we gained the yacht. Lady Brookes and Miss Tuke were carefully handed over the side, the boat hoisted, the sails trimmed, and the schooner, slightly leaning to the soft wind, was sliding as noiselessly as a sleigh over the long-drawn, invisible undulations. Neither our departure nor the coming of the breeze, however, stopped the fun aboard the *Dido*. The music struck up again whilst our boat was hoisting, and at the same time they swung their yards, and got way upon the vessel. The moon would be late in rising, but the starlight was strong, and the ship was tolerably distinct, and stood up upon the black water like a rock covered with snow. They had removed the flags around the poop, so as to come, no doubt, more readily at the braces, and left the lanterns exposed, which at that distance looked like a number of lights ashore ; so that, with the music, you might have imagined it was a small town out there, and the people winding up a holiday.

We all stood looking at her ; but I believe Miss Tuke and I found her most significant, for we had seen her 'tween-decks, and, as it were, looked into her inner life. She was making a more southerly course than we, which imperceptibly widened the distance between us, and diminished her visionary and swelling proportions. The increasing interval was curiously defined by the sound of the music, that grew bit by bit more thread-like and minute, until there buzzed such a tiny humming, amid which, nevertheless, the tune and time of it could be accurately followed, as you would have supposed only a band of Lilliput musicians could send up.

"She will soon be out of sight," said Lady Brookes, who stood all this while holding her husband's arm and watching the ship.

"Wonderful to think of that vessel—that mere fragment like a chip of mother-o'-pearl—being full of human beings, and that she typifies the whole great world by the cargo of hopes and passions and sorrows and ambitions which she carries over this black ocean !" exclaimed Sir Mordaunt.

"You want to look at a ship from a distance, to comprehend what a very small thing man is," observed Norie.

"Small in point of size," said I, "but a wonderful little chap for all that. I am never less ashamed of my species than when I see a ship, and think of the pluck and genius and science it means."

7

" I can hear the music yet," exclaimed Miss Tuke.　"They must be still dancing."

" Well, I thoroughly enjoyed myself," said Sir Mordaunt. " A queer adventure to stumble upon, Walton, and I shall remember the tea and the dance and the lighted decks while I live.　Spenser's a fine fellow, a gentleman, a handsome man, and, no doubt, a complete sailor.　If this calm had lasted, we should have returned his hospitality.　But there they go!" stretching forth his hand : "symbolizing life—the child and the bride, the old man and the young, rich and poor, all melting away in the gloom!　Who's poetical among us ?　Here's a subject for a sonnet."

" It's been done over and over again," said I.

"And it's too late for poetry," quoth Norie ; and pulling out his watch, he put it to his nose, and called out, "Only half past nine, though ! I thought it was after ten."

Three bells were struck, whereupon Lady Brookes bade us good-night and went below, leaning on Miss Tuke's arm.　By ten o'clock the ship was invisible upon our weather quarter, and the *Lady Maud* was spinning before a rattling breeze, spitefully worrying the water under her, and flashing the white foam away from her side, as though like a sentient thing she had been fretting over her enforced idleness and meant now to take her revenge.

CHAPTER VII.

Our meeting with the *Dido* was certainly a pleasant break, and for a day or two afterward we talked of nothing else.　As the time went by without anything happening worth noticing, I could not but flatter myself that our cruise would prove as uneventful as the most timid passenger could desire.　I speak mainly in reference to Lady Brookes.　If she enjoyed the cruise, it was certain to do her good.　On the other hand, as Norie said to me, all the virtue of the sea-breezes would stand for nothing against a capsizal of her nerves or any depression of spirits.

Nothing could have been more delightful than our run into the Horse Latitudes.　Gales and dead calms, terrible thunder storms and breezes, fair one hour and foul the next, are the characteristics of these parallels, which (so historians say) got the name of " Horse " because, during the union between England and America, numbers of horses were exported from the mother country, and it was reckoned that more of the animals died in these baffling, thunderous and treacherous latitudes than in all the rest of the passage.   It was our luck to carry a strong breeze of wind, about two points abaft the beam for over five hundred miles, and noble sailing it was : I don't say for speed, for the vessel's best qualities were not exactly hit by the wind, but for the freshness and liveliness and lastingness of it. We drove along under a top-gallant-sail and foretopmast studding-sail, which means that every cloth, with the exception of the square-sail, was on the yacht ; and small as she was it took two men to steer her, and then they had as much as they could do.

Many a time I would go right forward into the bows, and hang over the rail for half an hour at a time, watching the beautiful appearance of the bow-wave curling out like a curve of molten green glass, and preserving this lovely arch for a distance of some fathoms, where it flashed into a mass of snow and white smoke, and was washed by the rush of the brilliant surges against the yacht's side, to recoil in a more dazzling smother of foam. The vessel's beam kept the decks comfortable, and her list, except when hove to in a gale of wind, would never be so acute as to rob her spars of the majesty of subdued inclination ; and when my eye wandered from the pouring green and silver of the surges under her bows to the canvas on high, it was always with a thrill of delight and admiration, for the swollen spaces shone like white metal in the central cloths, and, with the deep blue sky beyond them, were almost blinding to look at ; and it kept the heart dancing to mark the whole effect of these gleaming towers leaning over the swiftly flying belt of foam to leeward, the sloping decks glittering like dry white sand, with here and there the sparkle of glass or brass as a yaw or a come-to dodged the lustrous object into the sun-beams, whilst for leagues round the water was throbbing and leaping under the sharp bright gale.

It was on one of these days that, whilst looking over the bows, I spied something in the water that made me beckon to Miss Tuke. Norie was talking to her, but she left him without ceremony, though he immediately followed her.

" Look ! " said I, pointing to the water about twenty feet to windward, where a shape that resembled bright emerald was cutting along close under the surface, and keeping way with the yacht without any perceptible action of the fins or tail.

"There's another ! " shouted Norie.

"And another!" echoed Miss Tuke. "What are they, Mr. Walton?"

"Dolphins," said I. As I spoke, the fish I had first seen, a fine fellow, measuring, I should think, very nearly five feet, leaped clean out of the sea. He was as green, I say, as emerald whilst in the water; but the moment he shot out of it his body became a bright yellow, all but the fins, which were of the color of olive, and he looked like a solid body of burnished gold flung up out of the foam. He was long enough in the air to enable us to observe his build, and I took notice of his long jaws and flattish head and bright eyes. His playfulness set the others jumping, but they had not this fellow's beautiful bright yellow. One was like sulphur, another almost white, like clouded silver, without any sparkle; yet their wonderful gracefulness, the miraculous shifting of their hues from brilliant green in the water to metallic yellows and whites when out of it, made them a fine sight to watch; and so delighted was Miss Tuke that she called Sir Mordaunt and her aunt to come and look, and we all stood gazing until the fish, for some reason, shot away from us, and though our own speed was at least nine knots an hour, yet these dolphins vanished right ahead of us like arrows discharged from our forecastle. The eye lost them in a breath. Had they been dissolved in the green water by some instantaneous chemical process, their vanishment could not have been more amazingly sudden.

This noble wind carried us without a flaw well into the middle of the Horse Latitudes, and then left us. We reckoned ourselves too fortunate to have got it at all to grumble at its cessation; but still the calms and the heavy swell and the bothersome light airs were not the easier to bear because of the slant of luck that had carried us down to them.

It was on a Thursday morning that the breeze failed us. It was so oppressively hot in the cabin that Sir Mordaunt told the steward to get a couple of tables on deck, and set them out for lunch. On deck, at all events, some currents of air were to be felt from the flapping of the huge mainsail as the vessel rose and sunk on the swell, and the awning was an effectual shelter from the sun, though so great was the heat that the pitch between the white planks was as soft as beeswax. The lunch was like picnicking; dishes and bottles and glasses on the deck, where they were not very likely to capsize; one of us with a plate on his knees, and Norie balancing himself on the skylight.

I remember it was on this occasion that I took particular notice how well Lady Brookes was looking. Her complexion was some shades fairer, or at least clearer, than it was when we left England. There was real life in the luster of her eyes, whereas, before, I had been struck with their want of spirit, that was hard to reconcile with their sparkling. I complimented her warmly on her improved looks, wishing perhaps rather to please her husband than her, for I cannot say she was a woman I much liked, though she had some good qualities, and her want of amiability was, I dare say, owing to her health, or at least to her habit of thinking of herself as a sufferer.

"I certainly do feel very much better, Mr. Walton," she replied.

"The voyage will re-establish you," said Norie. "But then you are fond of surprising us, Lady Brookes. Who could have imagined you would prove so excellent a sailor at the start? and now here you are drawing in health and spirits from a temperature in which I simmer like a boiling lobster;" and he pulled off his hat, and swabbed his pale face, that shone as though a flask of oil had been emptied over him.

"You were afraid that the heat would prove too much for my wife, Walton," said Sir Mordaunt, whom her ladyship's admission had greatly pleased. "But you see I am right. I could not have chosen a better cruising ground."

"How much further south have we got to go?" asked Miss Tuke.

"Why, I don't know what course Captain Purchase means to steer," I answered. "Jamaica lies on the parallel of eighteen degrees north. Where time is no object, one can find a good many entrances into the Caribbean Sea. Do you know what the skipper means to do, Sir Mordaunt?"

"I believe he intends to head for the Mona Passage, and feel his way along the Haytian coast," he answered. "I leave everything to him, for he traded among these islands, you know."

He happened to be on deck, dressed (as usual) as if it was the month of October, and this sea the German Ocean, and I should have liked to ask him what his plans were. But whether Tripshore had repeated my conversation to him, or whether he resented my opinion of him, which I dare say my manner had conveyed, though not purposely, of late he had avoided me, giving me very short answers to my remarks, until it had come to my taking no notice of him at all. This posture of his made me unwilling to strengthen his ill-will by putting any questions which he might interpret into a doubt of his judgment ; moreover, Sir Mordaunt was so well disposed toward him that I should have acted an unfriendly part in emphasizing my doubts of his capacity as a seaman and navigator.

Lunch being over, I went to the side of the vessel to light a cigar, and catch the draught from the fanning of the mainsail. The swell was rather heavy, and there was not enough wind to steady the schooner, and her canvas swung and rattled with every roll, filling the air overhead with loud reports, like the explosion of small arms. Yet there was enough weight in the wind to keep us moving ; and every now and again, as the stem of the yacht chopped down, a great mass of foam would be hove away, that covered the water for many fathoms around us with a hissing and seething surface, the effect of which was very striking, owing to our extremely languid passage through it. It was the color of the water, however, that made these churnings impressive. I never remember seeing the ocean, out of soundings, and above all in tropical latitudes, with so strange an appearance. It was a greasy dark olive green, as thick and slimy-looking as paint, with a singular sheen upon it, such as a cobweb catches from the sunlight, as though coated with oil ; and under this sluggish and sickly surface the swell ran in lazy folds, and the eye could trace these slow and portentous heavings to the very nethermost water-line, where the dark green hills rose and sunk in undulations of a wintry sharpness of outline against the sky, that was a pale blue down there.

The sun, that stood very nearly over our mastheads, was but lazily reflected in this sea : the flashing was sullen, with a reddish tinge ; but this was, indeed, the color of the sun.

"All this would be very tropical," said I to Sir Mordaunt, who had joined me, and said something about the appearance of the weather, " but for the look of the sea. Under such a sky as this it should be a beautiful blue."

"What do you make it, Walton ? Are we going to have a storm ?"

"Have you looked at the glass recently ?"

" Just before lunch," he replied. "It is steady."

"It doesn't seem reasonable to talk of a storm when there's not a cloud to be seen," which, in fact, was the case at that time. " But——"

I was proceeding, when all on a sudden my eye caught sight of an object that, though it kept my mouth wide open, stopped my talking as if by a stroke of magic, and I gazed and gazed, with my cigar half lifted to my mouth, and doubting my own sanity for the moment.

"Why, what do you see, Walton? What *are* you staring at in that manner?" exclaimed Sir Mordaunt, greatly surprised.

"Look!" I cried. "Follow my finger—*there!* Do you see it?"

He peered, and then catching sight of the object, made a step backward in his excess of astonishment.

It was the picture of a dismasted ship, inverted, high above the water-line, and hanging in the air. I rubbed my eyes and looked again. The vision was absolutely perfect. It seemed to be at least half a mile high, and was the representation of a ship, or a bark, submerged to her bulwarks, with three stumps of masts standing, the center one of which was considerably taller than the others, with apparently some fragments of canvas set upon it. But what struck me as the most amazing part of the spectacle was that, though the vessel had all the appearance of being buried as deep as her waterways in the sea, there was no similitude of a sea under, or rather above her. It was like a water-color drawing upon the sky."

"A most beautiful mirage!" exclaimed Sir Mordaunt. "Agnes! Ada! Come here quickly. Come and see a wonderful sight!"

Whilst the ladies hurried up to him, I ran for the glass.

"What is it. Mordaunt?" I heard Lady Brookes say, in a tone of alarm.

"It looks like a ship falling from the sky!" exclaimed Miss Tuke.

By this time the men on deck had caught sight of the phenomenon, and stood staring at it with all their might, and expressing their astonishment in a regular buzz of voices. I never could have believed that refraction would fling an object that was no doubt sunk some distance below the horizon to so great a height, and whilst enormously magnifying it (for the whole spectral fabric, with its three masts, was clearly to be viewed by the naked eye), leave it so exquisitely sharp too. It was this magnification that enabled us to see the mirage, for though the low freeboard of the schooner did not give us a wide horizon, yet the distance of the water-line was sufficiently great to dwindle a ship upon it into a mere speck.

The glass I leveled was a powerful one, and the vessel stood up before me as though she were not two miles off. I examined her carefully, and perceived the mirage to be the reflection of a bark upside down, apparently water-logged, and a complete wreck. She was rolling with a very regular motion, and I cannot describe the impression produced by this movement in a *picture*, with no water to be seen, as though she were sunk to her scuppers in the bright transparent *air*, and with the blue and somewhat hazy sky all around her. On the stump of her foremast she had her fore-yard standing, that swayed to and fro with her rolling, and she had a main-trysail set, though the lower portion of it seemed to be in rags.

"Look, Sir Mordaunt," said I. "You can see her very plainly with this ; " and I handed him the glass.

"Ladies, will ye please cast your eyes aloft?" suddenly rattled out old Purchase. "There's another sight overhead."

"A sun-dog!" I exclaimed. "The air's like a looking-glass."

And, sure enough, over against the sun was another sun—the very ghost of a sun—a wan, sickly, yet perfectly distinct and luminous orb.

"What the deuce does *that* mean ? " said Sir Mordaunt, staring up at it, as were all hands. " *Two* suns ! What part of the world is this, now ? "

"Oh, twin suns are common enough," said I, keeping back in the hearing of Lady Brookes—who was apparently agitated by this conjunction of phenomena—the information that these sun dogs are by ancient mariners regarded as the forerunners of bad weather. "But yonder is a real puzzler. Surely a more beautiful mirage never was seen."

"There must be a wreck under that reflection," said Norie.

"You may be cocksure of that," said I.

"And there may be living people on board," said Miss Tuke, almost in a whisper, as though awed by the object.

Her words appeared to put a thought into Sir Mordaunt's head. He gazed at me earnestly, and said :

"It may be a signal, set up by heaven itself, to bring us to the help of some poor sailors there. We ought to run down and have a close look at the vessel. How far distant will she be, Walton ? "

"Not very low behind the sea," I replied, "to judge by that reflection. The masts, you observe, are perpendicular with the horizon. Were the vessel far down, those masts would be in-clined."

"Let us steer in that direction," said Sir Mordaunt, with

great seriousness, and looking at the beautiful painting upon the heavens as though it were some holy vision. And then he gave the order to Purchase.

The mirage bore as nearly as possible W. S. W. The shift of helm brought the light easterly wind on our quarter, but made the schooner look right into the eye of the swell, and her courtesying was fast and even furious, and occasionally she would bury her bow as high as the hawse-pipes in the surface of foam which her chopping motion dashed up out of the sickly green water, and sent seething for some fathoms ahead and on either side of her.

But all this while we stood looking with something of a breathless manner at the beautiful and wonderful illusion of that wreck afloat in the transparent air, projecting our heads over the rail to have it in sight, for it was now over our bowsprit end. It remained in view for about twenty minutes ; it then began to fade gradually, like a rainbow, but its decay might be better likened to the extinction of a bright image in a looking-glass upon which you softly breathe. It soon entirely disappeared, yet the phenomenon of the double sun remained visible for some time after. When that was gone, we saw the reason of these disappearances in the stealthy thickening of the atmosphere, until the azure grew so dusty as scarcely to look blue. The wind hung in the east, but it fined down perceptibly, and I counted upon a strong westerly wind following in due course, from the swell that was running up to us from that direction. Although we were protected from the sun's heat by the mist upon the sky, beyond which the luminary was a well-defined throbbing ball of flashing reddish-yellow shorn of his blinding rays, the heat was terribly oppressive, and if it had not been for the currents of air which the pitching of the schooner sent circling along the decks, it would have been scarcely endurable. It was as bad as the atmosphere of a closed glass-house on a summer afternoon.

Although I had often heard talk of mirages at sea, and had indeed been shipmate with an old seaman who had witnessed much such another sight as we had beheld—for I remember the account he gave me of a full-rigged ship having been visible for nearly three-quarters of an hour upon the sky at a great height above the water—yet the only thing of the kind that I had ever encountered was that of the southeast coast of the Mauritius, that was hove up by refraction and rendered distinct to us when we were leagues from the point whence, under ordinary circumstances, it should have been apparent ; and I recollect the consternation of the captain at the apparition, his conclusion being that he was seriously out in his calculations. Such a picture as that which had just melted made a great impression on me, and indeed we were all equally affected, and could think and talk of nothing else. Sir Mordaunt, I am persuaded, found something supernatural in it ; that is, in the circumstance of a vessel having her miserable condition denoted by a heaven-created signal, visible for I know not how great a distance.

"I dare say it was a mirage of that kind that first suggested the Phantom Ship," said Miss Tuke.

"Very likely ; and certainly, so far as the object we saw was concerned, it *was* a phantom ship," I replied.

"And the two suns!" exclaimed Lady Brookes. "Really one would suppose we had sailed into an enchanted land."

"Assuredly they that go down to the sea in ships see the works of the Lord and His wonders," said Sir Mordaunt, very solemnly. "Even now I behold something like a phenomenon, only this time it lies in a contrast. Mark the horrid green of the sea, and the chilling appearance of it under yonder smoky blue. One would suppose that such a sky as that is only to be seen over a town full of factories. And how the *Lady Maud* labors! I never saw the sea burst away from her so sullenly before, and yet we can barely be moving two miles an hour."

"It just occurs to me," said I, "that the bark may be visible from your top-gallant-yard there. It should be worth while trying to make her out before the atmosphere thickens, which will happen presently."

Saying this, I called to the steward through the skylight, and asked him to hand me up the telescope case, into which I put the glass, and slung it over my shoulders.

"What are you going to do, Walton?" asked Sir Mordaunt.

"Going aloft to look for the wreck," I answered.

"What! to the top of the mast?" ejaculated Lady Brookes.

"To the very tiptop," I answered, laughing heartily, and away I went. I had forgotten, however, that only the lower rigging was rattled down, and that half the climbing would have to be accomplished by "shinning." But I would not back out of it, and so I sprang into the shrouds and trotted aloft, blackening my hands very tidily with the tar that lay like soft black glue upon the hemp, and was presently perched upon the top-gallant-yard, watched by some men on the forecastle, and by old Purchase from the main deck, who scowled at me under the great red hand with which he protected his eyes, as though he wondered what my game was now, and if this were another move in the direction of taking the command away from him.

At this elevation I was a great height above the sea, as the *Lady Maud* was very loftily sparred for a vessel of her tonnage ; and steadying the glass against the side of the mast I carefully swept the water ahead to a distance of four points on either bow, but nothing was to be seen. I had more trouble to make this inspection, however, than I had reckoned upon, for the motion up here was uncommonly severe, and although the square canvas was furled, yet the quick swinging in of the jibs, and the jump of the foresail as the little vessel pitched, wrenched and jerked the masts very unpleasantly, and with the heavy swing of the rolling, obliged me to keep a fast hold with one hand. But, as I say, there was nothing to be seen, and stowing the glass away in its case, I sung out my report to Sir Mordaunt, who with the ladies and Norie had come along to the foremost end of the awning to watch me. But before descending I lingered a few minutes to observe the singular appearance of the sea, whose unwholesome green, sluggishly swelling and falling, was infinitely more impressive to watch from this height than from the deck, in consequence of the magnitude of the expanse my elevated position enabled me to survey ; whilst below me—the only object in sight upon this great world of waters—was the hull of the yacht, looking no more than a beautiful toy vessel, but with her proportions defined as I had never before had a chance of seeing them, and constantly dashing out a quantity of foam from under her bows, the form of which was exquisitely marked by the curve of the rails upon the churned up-snow of the water under the bowsprit.

On gaining the deck my first business was to get rid of the tar on my hands. This I effected by sending the steward to the galley for a little slush. Soap and warm water did the rest. Before I returned I peeped at the barometer, but noticed nothing beyond a little increase in the concavity of the mercury.

"It is very odd," said Sir Mordaunt, "that you can see nothing of the wreck."

"She will be further off than we think," said I, "and yet not much further off either ; and if a man were stationed aloft I should expect to hear his hail at any moment. But what is your object in running down to her ? Do you suppose there may be men aboard ? "

"Yes," he answered; "that is, if she's not an illusion. I wish you had seen her, though, for we don't want a goose-chase." He added, sinking his voice: "What think you of the weather? For my part, I don't like the look of it at all."

It certainly had a portentous appearance, but I told him that the worst of it might prove to lie in its aspect, as the depression of the mercury was very trifling. The afternoon drifted away slowly, but though on three several occasions a man went aloft to look for the wreck, she remained invisible. Lady Brookes turned to her husband when for the third time the report came that there was nothing in sight, and said, in her nervous, irritable way, "Mordaunt, if there is no vessel, what could that reflection have been?"

"There *must* be a vessel somewhere in that direction, my love," he answered. "We are moving very slowly, and" (turning to me) "I suppose, Walton, as she had lost the upper portion of her masts, and has only a little fragment of sail showing, we are not likely to see her until she is pretty close to us."

"Ay; and then again," said I, "the atmosphere is as thick now as it was transparent before." And I turned my eyes into the west, that is, over the starboard bow of the schooner, where I noticed a gathering darkness that could not be called clouds, for there were no vaporous outlines to be seen, but rather a shading of the sky, that was dark on the water-line, and that lightened softly and gradually until it merged into the dusty blue that prevailed overhead and down to the sea over our stern and quarters.

About half an hour before we went to dinner the light air completely died out. This made the swell of the sea all the more unpleasant, and the *Lady Maud* wallowed in it heavily; but she raised no foam now; though sometimes she would dip her gunwales so deep that the water burst through the scupper-holes in flying jets of spray, as though a force-pump were at work behind them.

Tripshore was now on deck, and when the wind failed us he gave orders to strip the yacht of all but her foresail and forestay-sail, or standing jib. Sir Mordaunt and the ladies were below when this was done. I went to the mate, who was always very civil to me and well disposed, and spoke to him about the mirage. He had heard about it from the men, and his opinion was that if the air was clear the wreck would now be in sight. I asked him if he thought we were going to have dirty weather.

He looked around him and answered that the sky was puzzling, and he couldn't understand the color of the water. Sighting that sundog, he said, wasn't over hopeful, yet there was no uneasiness in the glass, which was strange if that sky meant anything. He added : ''It's more like thunder than wind, I reckon ; yet I don't know but what we may get a stiff breeze from the westward betwixt this and midnight.''

''You're ready for it when it comes,'' said I, glancing at the naked mainmast.

'' No use letting the vessel knock her canvas to bits when it can't sarve her, sir. Besides, there's no good in keeping such tall spars as them buckling and jumping. They'd be none the worse for housing.''

I stood a few moments looking at one of the big mastiffs, that had jumped on to the taffrail, and was barking now and again in a deep angry note at the water as it swelled up almost flush with the rail when the vessel sank her stern. There was something very fine and picturesque in the brute's posture as he balanced himself to the lifting and falling, whilst with cocked ears and gleaming eyes, and shining fangs just distinguishable under the black leathern-like flesh of his jaws, he snapped with a deep-throated note. I called to him, being afraid that he would slide overboard during one of the heavier dips, upon which the fine animal sprang on the deck, and greeting me as he rushed past with a friendly dig of his cold moist nose against my hand, tumbled over his companion, and the two fell to skylarking about the decks.

Norie wanted to be scientific at dinner, and explain the cause of mirages and twin suns. I suspected that he had peeped into some book upon those subjects whilst dressing, for he talked like a man whose ideas were new. But for Miss Tuke I believe we should have listened to him ; but as fast as he began she drew him away artfully, and having interrupted him, spoke to her aunt, or asked me or Sir Mordaunt a question. So he gave up after a bit, but he took her gracelessness with something more than amiability, and fixed such an admiring gaze upon her that I noticed Sir Mordaunt and his wife exchange glances over it.

It gradually grew dark as we sat talking and eating. They had furled the awning, which enabled us to see through the skylight, and I remarked the lurid tinge in the atmosphere, but without commenting upon it, as I guessed by Sir Mordaunt's reserve that he wished me to hold back all forebodings in his

wife's presence.   He and I, however, were, I think, alone in observing the increasing shadow.   The others put it down to the
evening ; but it was not time for the sun to go to bed yet, and
the darkness that almost immediately follows the descent of the
luminary in the tropics was of a very different complexion from
the brooding, oppressive, reddish haze that had apparently
covered the whole sky, and that was casting down a hot, faint,
obscure light of its own.

" How fearfully the vessel is rolling ! " exclaimed Lady
Brookes.   " The motion and the heat make me feel giddy."
She put her hand to her forehead, and Miss Tuke passed a
smelling-bottle to her.

" Let me advise you to lie down," said Norie.

" My cabin is so hot," she answered, peevishly.

"Not hotter than it is here, ·nor even on deck ; and you will
not feel the motion in your bed, Agnes," said her husband.

She hesitated, and looked up at the skylight, and then
seemed to acquiesce.   I jumped up to offer my arm, for my
self-balancing properties were better than her husband's ; but
I was scarcely on my feet when a glare of lightning flashed
upon the skylight, and illuminated us all as though a rocket had
been sent up, and at the same moment an unusually heavy
swell striking the vessel, rolled her so sharply over that a
number of plates, glasses, spoons, and such things toppled off
the table, and fell with a great crash upon the deck.   Lady
Brookes squealed out, and for some minutes all was confusion,
for the vessel, having rolled one way, must come back again,
and bury the other side of her, whereupon more things fetched
away from the table, and the din of breaking china and glass,
and the jingling and clattering of the fragments on the deck,
were bewildering enough.

" There is not the least occasion to be alarmed, Agnes,"
exclaimed Sir Mordaunt, holding by the table, having been
absolutely unable to rise from his chair during that wild and
unexpected roll of the vessel.   " Walton, you know that in
these tropical climates lightning is as common as sunshine, and
not a jot more harmful."

" Perfectly true," I shouted.   " In the Malacca Straits I have
been able to read a book right through my watch on deck by
the incessant play of the lightning."

Here Miss Tuke went to her aunt, and began to coax her to
lie down.   Sir Mordaunt added his voice, and Norie backed
him, and at last she yielded and disappeared with her husband

and niece, whilst Norie withdrew to his own cabin, and the steward groveled about on the floor, picking up the broken china and glass. I finished my wine, preparatory to going on deck. Presently Sir Mordaunt returned, looking very much annoyed.

"Now, Walton, what think you is the next joke?" said he. "Her ladyship's maid has tumbled into her own bed, and lies with the sheet over her head, quivering like a jelly in an earthquake. She's afraid of the lightning, and you may hear her declaring in a stifled cry that she wouldn't show her nose to save her life."

"Lady Brookes can do without her, I daresay," I answered, laughing. "But in a time of real danger all these quiverings and hidings wouldn't sweeten misfortune, Sir Mordaunt—eh?"

"Don't for Heaven's sake talk of danger, real or imaginary!" he said, sending a glance through the skylight. "Steward, when you have collected that mess, light the lamps, will you? And get my water-proof coat ready to hand to me when I call for it."

We lighted our cigars and went on deck. There should have been at least another hour of daylight left; but it was already as dark as evening, though I did not take particular notice of this until I reached the deck, as my eyes had got used insensibly to the gradual infolding of the gloom whilst we sat at dinner. Looking up, I saw that the sky overhead and in the west was covered by a curtain of dense vapor, which, owing, I suppose, to the light of the westering sun, was of a deep, forbidding, bronze-like hue over our masts, though it brightened into an ugly and sallow orange toward the east, where the vapor was not so dense; but in the west the sky was like a pall of motionless smoke, thick, bluish, most portentous and sinister. The sun was behind it, and totally hidden. Under this frightful heaven for frightful it truly was—lay the sickly heaving sea, almost black in the western shadow, but drawing out into its ghastly sallow green as it stretched away under the lighter sky of the east.

"It is long since I saw such a sight as this," said I to Sir Mordaunt. "It will be black as ink presently."

Another sharp flash of lightning shot out of the smoky thickness in the west, and I marked the spark whirl zigzag across that part of the sky—a perfect fork of wire-like flame—and vanish in the sea. We listened, but no thunder followed.

"I don't like that silence," exclaimed Sir Mordaunt, uneasily.

"If that flash was so far off that the thunder it made is inaudible, what will the lightning be when it's overhead?"

"I'd as soon be in a vessel as anywhere else in a thunderstorm," said I. "How rarely you hear of a ship being struck! The masts and spars offer so many points that the lightning is scattered by them."

Purchase and Tripshore were both on deck, and most of the men, this being the second dog-watch, though it was probably the heat and the appearance of the weather that held them in a crowd forward, puffing at sooty tobacco-pipes, and constantly looking up and around. The gloom increased every moment as the sun sank deeper and deeper into the darkness in the west on its way behind the sea, and very soon the lurid orange tint went out of the sky, the water-line—nay, the deep itself—grew indistinguishable, the outlines of the little vessel faded, and there was nothing to relieve the eye but the binnacle lamp that filled the air with a soft haze, and the illuminated skylights, and the bull's-eyes in the decks over the berths, which twinkled like glow-worms from the lamplight under them.

The yacht labored heavily upon the swell, and the small canvas that was exposed on her flapped heavily. The creaking and groaning were startling, for the silence upon the sea was profound, and there was no other sound but what came from the vessel, whose plunging and wallowing filled the air with the loud gurgling and sobbing of water—most unpleasant noises to hear in that darkness. There was no more lightning; but the heat! it made me feel as if I were stricken with a raging fever. I went to look at the compass, to see where the yacht's head had swung to, and perceiving a figure standing a little distance behind the fellow at the wheel, I took it to be Tripshore.

"What do you think this is going to be? Not a tempest, I hope," said I.

"If a tempest's thunder an' lightning, then it's a tempest that's coming," answered a deep wheezy voice, that gave me to know I had addressed old Purchase.

I could see nothing of him but his outline; but no sooner did he open his mouth than the same spirituous smell I had before detected in him filled the air.

"A tempest generally comprises wind," said I, willing to test his condition by a little discourse. "But so old and experienced a sailor as you should be able to predict the weather as faithfully as a barometer."

"It 'ud be a poor job if I couldn't tell the weather better than a b'rometer," he answered, shuffling his feet about, and talking with a certain thickness of voice, which the fumes he distributed around him found a complete reason for. "What I says is, b'rometers be damned. I never was shipmates with one afore I took charge here, and if any man can say he's seen me looking at it for the purpose o' guessing the weather, I'll give him leave to make me swaller the mercury in it. Isn't that right, Tom Hunter?"

This was addressed to the man at the wheel, who, seeing the indecorousness of the skipper's language in my presence, and guessing his condition, and being evidently surprised by this sudden appeal, answered with a short uneasy laugh. That laugh, however, appeared to serve as a hint to the old man; for, without ceremony, he shuffled away to the other side of the deck, or, at least, to some place where he was clean out of sight. I went forward a few steps.

"Is that you, Mr. Tripshore?"

"Yes, sir."

"Do you know that Mr. Purchase is the worse for drink again?"

He made no answer.

"It's an abominable state of things," said I, "that in the eye of such a night as this the skipper of a vessel full of human beings, who look to his skill and judgment for guidance and safety, cannot keep himself sober. I shall certainly speak to Sir Mordaunt about him, though not now, as I want this storm to pass away first. I noticed that you have the whole foresail set. If there should be a cyclone in that blackness —and you should be prepared for the worst—you will be show-ing a whole ocean of cloths too much for the first outfly. Why not close-reef it whilst there is no wind?"

"I named that to Mr. Purchase, sir," answered Tripshore, "but he said no."

"He's too drunk to know what he says," I exclaimed, warmly. "Go and reason with him. If he refuses, give the order yourself. I'll take care you are supported." Here Sir Mordaunt, who was standing somewhere forward of the star-board main-rigging called to me :

"What's the matter, Walton? I hear your voice buzzing like a bumble-bee's. Anything wrong?"

"I was merely exchanging a few words with Mr. Trip-shore," I replied.

8

"I've been watching a strange object in the water. Look now ! do you see it ? "   As he said this the side of the deck we occupied swung into a hollow, and the water stood up close : and about a fathom away I saw the outline of a large fish revealed by a glancing of phosphorous that dimly shone around it, so as to make it seem like a luminous shape as it stealthily sailed, apparently within six inches of the surface, toward the bows of the yacht.   Is it a shark, Walton ? "

"Yes, that should be a shark," I replied.

We watched it until the light it made was no longer visible.

"It's a great pity that those brutes cannot be put to a use, like the whale or the seal.   There'd be some chance of their becoming extinct then in a few generations," said Sir Mordaunt, lighting another cigar ; and raising his eyes, he rapped out : "I say, Walton, just look overhead ! It is the very quintessence of night kept from falling by our mast-heads. What fearful, unspeakable, unsearchable blackness ! What's become of the lightning, think you ? "

"We shall have it presently," I answered, wondering if Tripshore was doing as I had requested.

Sir Mordaunt approached the skylight, and called to the steward in a soft voice to hand him up his water-proofs.   I requested the man to get mine too ; and while I stood waiting, old Purchase went forward, shuffling along the deck like a fisherman, and I heard his thick gruff notes ordering the watch to lower the foresail and close reef it.   This eased my mind. As I bent down to take my oil-skin from the steward, Norie came out of his berth.

"How's the weather, Walton ?" he called, looking up.

"Black," I answered.

"Is it going to rain ? " said he.

"I reckon it is," said I.

"Then here goes for volume the second," said he, and he very wisely bundled back to his cabin.

If the storm was not right overhead, it was assuredly not very far off.   I never remember a more uncomfortable time. The breathless silence, the voluminous heaving of the black water, the impenetrable blackness, were sufficiently subduing ; but the worst sensation was the feeling of expectation that the ponderous, brooding shadow excited—the wonder what was going to happen—whether it would open and let down an ocean of flame, or whether there was a gale behind it, or whether it would pass away as breathlessly as it had come up.

But our doubts were soon resolved. We had scarcely shipped our water-proof coats when some rain fell. Each drop was as big as an egg, and though the fall did not last longer than a man could count twenty, yet so great was the weight of the drops that the deck boomed to the fall. Then came a pause, with nothing breaking the silence but the gushing sounds of water sluicing out of the scupper-holes into the sea. I was in the act of addressing Sir Mordaunt, when a flash of lightning of the very color of sunlight struck through the blackness; nay, had the sun himself looked out in his full glory, he could not have spread a more piercing, wide-spread splendor. It was like looking at the yacht and the sea in the light of full noontide. How the eye could master so many objects in that breathless gush of yellow flame I cannot tell, but I could not have seen more had five minutes been allowed me. The masts, the line of bulwarks, the group of men standing motionless near the foremast in a crouching posture, some of them with their hands to their eyes, the whole sea black as ink, leaning its sharp ebon circle against the sulphur-colored radiant heaven—all these things I saw in that one second, and then the darkness was insufferable, thick as dense folds of midnight vapor, not a stir nor moan of air in it, of an opacity that made me pant, as though the black envelopment suffocated me. The flash fell from right overhead, and it seemed that the crash must follow before the blaze went out. This expectation made the two or three seconds of silence that followed appear as long as a minute; but then came the most ear-splitting roar that had ever deafened me. A crash indeed, not a succession of peals, but one stupendous, unechoing explosion, that, smiting the oily surface of the water, boomed away in a dreadful roar, sinking and sinking its cadence until it became a soft melodious echo in the distance. But scarce had it faded when another sun-bright flash filled the sky. This liberated the rain, and it came down in a sheet, and the deck was so covered with immense hailstones that it was like treading on shingle. And now, as if two squadrons of aerial line-of-battle ships were engaging one another immediately over us, the air was filled with whizzing darts and lances of flames, dazzling crimson and yellow sparks, wild zigzag streams of fire, very showers of it, which filled the water with their tumultuous reflections, until it seemed that a thunder-storm was raging over as well as under us. And the thunder was as ceaseless. I could not have counted two between the explosions. The fierce, frenzied rattling, the ponderous booming, the sudden sharp explosion, mingled together and combined to produce one dreadful uproar. But all this while there was not a breath of air. The rain fell down in perfectly perpendicular streams, as could be seen by the lightning, that kept the heavy sheet of water sparkling like the surface of a tall cascade in the sunshine.

In the very thick of the hullabaloo I heard a woman's voice shrieking.

"Hark!" I shouted to Sir Mordaunt, as we stood together close against the starboard quarter-boat; and we ran, splashing and floundering, over to the companion. The yelling and squealing below might well have made any one believe that murder was doing down there; and the incessant crashing of the thunder, and the fierce lightning that kept the whole sky flaming, gave these female shrieks a character very fit indeed to thicken the senses and make goose-flesh of one's skin.

Sir Mordaunt bundled below at a rate that was like to break his nose for him, while the water poured out of the brim of his hat and streamed away from his oil-skins as though he had just been fished up out of the sea alongside. I followed him, in a wild state of mind, fearing that some one in the cabin had been struck by the lightning. But I soon saw what was the matter. Miss Tuke and Norie were kneeling upon Lady Brookes, who lay flat on her back on the floor, kicking up her heels, flourishing her hands, and screaming and laughing at the top of her voice. She was in hysterics; but if Norie hadn't bawled this out to us, I should have believed her clean out of her mind—raving mad, in fact. It was certainly a most painful scene. Her ladyship, as I have said, was a fine, well-made woman, and the fit made her as strong as a man. The united strength of Norie and Miss Tuke could hardly prevent her from rising; and before Sir Mordaunt and I could get near enough to lend a hand, she fetched Norie such a cuff over the head that if he had not been holding on to her it must have sent his heels into the air. All the while, too, she kept shrieking and sobbing and talking nonsense, whilst the frame of the yacht trembled to the thunder shocks, and the cabin was filled with a succession of blinding flashes, sometimes yellow, sometimes blue, which came so swiftly one after another that it was like blinking the eyes against a strong and lasting blaze. I heard Norie tell Sir Mordaunt that he was obliged to hold her ladyship down to prevent her rushing on deck, and that he had been calling for assistance to get her to her cabin, as she was too much for him with only Miss Tuke to help. Sir Mordaunt immediately pulled off his dripping oil-skins ; and, dropping on his knees, seized his wife's hand and entreated her to be calm, himself so agitated that his broken words were scarcely intelligible. Presently she grew quieter, and then Norie made her swallow some brandy ; and with the doctor supporting her on one side and her husband on the other, she went staggering and sighing to her cabin, keeping her eyes tightly closed that she might not see the lightning.

"What a fearful storm, Mr. Walton !" exclaimed Miss Tuke, holding her hand over her eyes too, for some of the flashes as they darted through the skylight were blindingly brilliant. "How long do you think it will last ? "

"It will be passing very soon. It's just a tropical outbreak. Had you lived in the West Indies you would be laughing at all this whizzing and booming," said I, but not very honestly : for I took it to be as dangerous a storm as could have burst upon us, and there is no West Indian living who would not have been awed and alarmed by it.

"I never saw such lightning before," said she, "nor heard such terrific thunder. There ! see that !" she cried, raising her voice to a shriek, as one of the sharpest flashes which had yet fallen seemed to set the whole cabin on fire, and was instantaneously followed by an explosion that sounded as though a magazine full of powder had blown up. There was no use trying to put heart into her in the face of such an uproar as that. I advised her to join Lady Brookes, and bustle about, and take as little notice as possible of the lightning ; and then went on deck again, first peeping at the glass, and observing no change in it.

The truth is, I could not persuade myself, from the indication of the mercury, that a tempest of wind—short-lived, indeed—would not follow this thunder storm ; and this being my expectation, and knowing that Purchase was in no fit state to command the schooner, should a sudden extremity confront us, determined me to keep a lookout for myself, for it was evident that Tripshore would not act independently in Purchase's watch ; and, moreover, it would be Purchase's watch on deck until midnight.

The storm played furiously, and continued to do so for upward of a quarter of an hour after I returned on deck, during all which time the rain fell in torrents and flashed up the sea

into a surface of phosphorescent foam by its weight ; but not
a breath of air slanted those lines of water, which sparkled in
the lightning in greens and blues and yellows, so as to make
the whole scene one of awful beauty, truly, indeed, as though
heaven were raining fire—an illusion that was perfected by the
flames in the sea, which might have made you suppose the
ocean itself was burning.

Both Tripshore and Purchase remained on deck, and the
men forward crouched, with scarcely a move among them,
under the bulwarks. I constantly looked aloft to observe if
the lightning had damaged us there, but nothing was touched.
I could not be mistaken in that. Some of the flashes were so
vivid that I could follow the masts to the trucks, and see the
little vane at the head of the mainmast ; and yet it was certain
that the electric fluid had run over the yards and spars as
water might, for at times I had perceived sparks of intense
brilliancy whizzing along the topsail sheets, which were chain,
and along the jackstays, and flying off into the air, just as you
may note the white fires flash away from the wires of an
electric battery.

But in a quarter of an hour, as I have said, it became
evident that the worst of the storm had passed, and that the
body of it was veering to the eastward ; and presently looking
into the west, I spied what might very well have passed for a
ship's light, a small yellow star, and then another, and yet
another, until, and while the storm was solemnly moaning in
one direction, and the heavens all that way were tremulous
with the glare of lightning, the sky in the opposite direction
was quite clear, and the stars shining. But the storm had left
the calm as dead as it had found it, more breathless in one
sense, if I may so say, by the weight and fury of the rain having flattened the swell and diminished the rolling of the vessel,
that before had wafted draughts of air along the deck.

I took off my oil-skin, and hung it over a belaying-pin to let
it drain ; and whilst I was doing that Sir Mordaunt came on
deck, followed by Norie. He approached me close, to make
sure of me, for it was still very dark, and exclaimed :

"Oh, Walton, thank God the storm is over ! I really believed at times that the yacht would have been split in two,
and sunk like a bullet. Did you ever see more frightful lightning ? "

"Never ; and we want no more. How is Lady Brookes ? "

"Pretty nearly right again, but low, of course."

"If only a little wind would come," said Norie, puffing as though he were suffocated, "her ladyship would be herself. What she wants—what we all want—is air. An atmosphere chock full of electricity, not to speak of flashings of fire and crashings of thunder, such as might make a man believe the day of doom had come at last, plays the deuce with weak nerves."

"How wonderful is this calm, after that hellish uproar!" exclaimed Sir Mordaunt, removing his hat, and looking upward.

The stillness was indeed wonderful, for the muttering of the departing storm was too far off to vex the ear; indeed, it seemed to define and heighten the silence, like distant music in the dead of a peaceful summer night ashore. The play of the lightning flashed faintly as far as the zenith, but left the glowing stars in the west undimmed, and nothing was to be heard but the plashing of large drops of moisture draining from the yards and rigging, and the soft tinkling of water trickling into the sea from the scupper holes.

"It is seldom that so wild and heavy a storm passes so breathlessly," said I. "But if I am not very much mistaken, we shall have a breeze of wind from the westward presently. Yonder sky is clearing fast."

"In that case it will be foul for us to reach the wreck," said Sir Mordaunt.

"Certainly it will; but I had clean forgotten the wreck," I answered.

"What should be done?" he asked. "I am sure that mirage was meant as a call to us, and I should feel exceedingly uneasy if we missed the vessel."

"Why," said I, rather struck with this remark, for I had always considered my friend as of a literal and prosaic cast of mind, "if the wind should come westerly, all that can be done is to put the schooner under easy canvas, and ratch her leisurely in the direction where we suppose the wreck to be. A bright lookout for the vessel should be kept."

"I'll go and speak to Purchase," said he. "I am determined to have a look at the wreck, if she is to be seen, and the wind will let us approach her," and he walked over to the skipper.

"Sir Mordaunt seems quite bitten by that mirage," said Norie. "I hope, if we are going to look for it, it won't keep us bothering about here long. It's simply roasting work without a breeze. Both day and night are equally insupportable, especially the night. When are we going to get those northeast trades you once spoke about?   Have they given up blowing, think you?"

"I used to know where they are supposed to begin, but I won't swear to the latitude now," I answered, listening all the while with one ear to the humming and grumbling of the conversation going on between Sir Mordaunt and Purchase near the wheel.

Meanwhile the watch below had quitted the deck at the sight of the stars, and gone to their hammocks, and here and there a man was slapping about him with a swab.   Just before Sir Mordaunt rejoined me, I caught sight of a breeze of wind darkening the star-lit water in the west, and in a moment or two Purchase rolled forward, calling upon the watch to make sail in his deep sea roar, to which rum, or whatever his liquor might be, had given a shrewder huskiness.   Sir Mordaunt took my arm, to draw me away from Norie, and asked me if I had spoken to Purchase during the evening.   I answered that I had.

"Did you notice anything peculiar about him?" said he.

"I thought he was rather drunk," I answered.   "Is that what you mean?"

"I won't say that—I won't go so far as that," said he, in a subdued, anxious voice.   "But I am afraid the man has been fool enough to swallow more than his head can carry."

"And not the first time either," said I.   "Not very long ago I found him muddy and merry in his watch on deck, and when I smelled his breath to-night, I resolved to speak to you seriously about him, though I should have waited for the morning."

"I must talk to him," he exclaimed.   "I must call him into the cabin to-morrow and rate him.   Mind you, Walton, the man's not *drunk*.   I don't even say he's muddled.   He's just a little thick.   I am sorry you have noticed this in him before.   Still, it won't do to be *too* critical.   Here you have a fine bluff old seaman who has run us to this point safely and well, and before we condemn him let us make sure he is not one of those men whom a very small drop of spirits intoxicates."

"No, no," I interrupted; "his nose doesn't blush for nothing. A red nose is the drunkard's conscience; and if Purchase can't swig down half a pint of raw rum without winking, I'll forfeit fifty pounds."

But Sir Mordaunt would not hear this.   He said (of course very kindly) that I was prejudiced—which I did not deny;

that it would be unfair to take an extreme view of the old man's indiscretion ; that if drinking was a habitual vice with him, the matter then would be a very serious one, but that he had only been detected twice slightly the worse for liquor since we had left England. "Slightly, I say," he added, "because it does not prevent him from attending to his duties, as you may judge for yourself"—pausing to give me an opportunity of hearing the skipper singing out to the men. "I have not spoken to him, so let us give him a chance. It is a hundred to one if he repeats this folly."

A hundred to one if he doesn't, thought I ; but I would not pursue the subject, mainly because I did not want to figure as an intruder nor to be thought unreasonably prejudiced, and also because I could not help seeing it was my friend's dread of alarming his wife that made him reluctant to witness anything seriously significant in Purchase's "indiscretion." However, I might now take it that he would watch his captain critically, and spare me the burden of a secret which I should hardly have liked to part with, though I should feel I wronged my companions by witholding it.

But already the breeze had reached us, and the water was rough with it, and the yacht under her mainsail and standing jib was scraping along, looking well up to the bearings which Sir Mordaunt was anxious to make. And here I am bound to say that Purchase understood his master's directions, and had acted properly in keeping the schooner under easy canvas and ratching leisurely. Sir Mordaunt took care to call my attention to this, and was evidently pleased because I had nothing to say. The breeze freshened slowly but steadily. Every vestige of the storm had long since vanished, and the stars were now dipping to squadrons of clouds sailing up from the west in swift procession, and in appearance so much resembling the trade clouds that, had they been coming up from the north and east, I should have believed that we were leaning before the first of the regular winds. The breeze gathered weight fast, and presently the water was all white to windward of the yacht, and the booming of parted seas at the bow as regular as the grinding of a crank. After the oppressive heat of the calm, the sweeping air was as invigorating and delicious as an iced cordial. It speedily dried the decks, and I could see the dark patches of moisture upon the mainsail growing bit by bit more pallid, until the great sail stood like a moonlit cloud up and down against the heaven of the horizon.

CHAPTER VIII.

By half-past ten I was very sleepy.   Miss Tuke had come on deck, and kept Sir Mordaunt and me company in a few turns; but Norie, who made one of us, managed to hook her arm under his, pretending that the deck was not safe walking, as though *he* (whose gait was a convulsive stagger compared with her beautiful, elastic, buoyant tread) could prop her up. But she was disposed to be complaisant, and presently he sneaked her over to the lee side of the deck.   If this did not delight me, I was solaced by remembering that she had often snubbed him briskly enough, and I construed her kindness into a little compliment to his amiable reception of her mild derision.

But, as I say, at half-past ten I felt very sleepy.   There was nothing in sight, the wind was piping grandly, and the yacht having been put about for a short board, so as not to miss the wreck by going to leeward of her, had settled down on the port tack, and was jerking along, her weather leeches shivering, and her sharp nose biting an opening through the short, black, foam-topped surges.   It seemed a pity to be cruising about after a kind of phantom ship when we could have laid our course at nine knots an hour, and made perhaps a fair run out of these humbugging latitudes.   But there was too much humanity, though based, methought, on a somewhat airy foundation, in my friend's resolution to allow me to utter a word against it.

I was awakened by a sharp rapping on my door, and on opening my eyes was surprised to find the daylight broad upon the porthole—it did not seem to me that I had been asleep above an hour.   I asked who that was, whereupon the steward put his head in and told me that the wreck was close by, and Sir Mordaunt would be glad if I'd come on deck.   I immediately rose and dressed myself.   It was easy to judge, without going on deck, that there was a considerable sea running, and a very strong wind blowing, for the yacht was plunging sharply, and every now and again I could hear the sharp rattle of spray upon deck, while the washing of the sea against the side of the schooner was exceedingly heavy and noisy.   In less than five minutes I was out of my cabin.

Sir Mordaunt stood close against the companion, gazing to leeward, and when he saw me he pointed with great excitement to the sea, crying, "There she is, Walton! I told you the signal was not put into the sky for nothing. How are we to rescue them?"

I looked and saw a large water-logged vessel—apparently a bark—upon our lee beam. She was a complete wreck, and recalling the features of the mirage we had beheld on the preceding day, I perceived that this was the vessel that had painted the reflection in the air. Her foremast was gone just under the top, though the foreyard still swung upon it, supported, it seemed to me, by the truss. Her maintopmast was standing, but her mizzenmast had been broken short off at the deck, and stood up like a huge bunch of sharp, jagged, white splinters about two feet high. Portions of her deck forward were blown out. Only a sailor can figure to his mind the image of confusion and wreckage aloft, masses of black rigging hanging over either bulwark, the maintop-gallant mast swinging over the topsail-yard, upon which the furled sail lay in rough heaps of canvas, with the gaskets hastily and clumsily passed, as though by men who had worked in an extremity.

But this was not the spectacle that fixed my eyes. The hull of the vessel was sunk to about six inches below her washboard, so that nothing but her bulwarks prevented the water from standing to that height upon her decks; but about three feet abaft the starboard fore-rigging the bulwarks were smashed level with the decks, making a fissure about two yards wide, through which, as the hull slowly rolled, with the most sickening, languid movement that can be imagined, the water flashed out in a roaring coil of foam, as though a sluice gate had been opened. She had apparently had a deck load of timber, for though most of it was gone, a number of planks still littered the decks, lying one athwart the other in hideous confusion, with fragments of the galley and fore-deck-house, which had been split to pieces, lying amongst them, together with such a raffle of gear, broken spars, pieces of canvas, and the like, that no description could give you the barest idea of the dreadful picture of shipwreck that immersed hull presented.

There was another deck-house aft, close to the wheel (or where the wheel had stood), which the furious seas had left uninjured; and upon the top of this structure were three men and a woman, lashed to a thin iron rail that ran around the top of the house.   On examining them through a binocular glass, I perceived that two of the men were scarcely clothed, having no more than their shirts and drawers on, whilst the woman had a sailor's jacket buttoned over her shoulders ; but her black hair was loose, and blew out in a cloud from her head—a small matter for me to take notice of, and yet one that gave a most melancholy wildness to that miserable group of human beings.   Meanwhile, and very frequently, the seas, dashing themselves against the weather bulwarks of the wreck, shot up in long sparkling masses of green water, that blew in scattering clouds over the deck, and again and again the men and the woman were hidden from our gaze by bursts of spray which momentarily veiled the whole of the after-part of the bark.

It was indeed blowing a very stiff breeze of wind, and the pitching of the yacht to the strong Atlantic sea that was running was made fast and almost furious by her being hove to under a treble-reefed gaff-foresail, with her nose right into the wind, to prevent her forging ahead of the wreck.

I do not say that the sight of those men of themselves would not have made a most thrilling and irresistible appeal to us for succor ; but how that appeal was heightened, so that it raised a passion of anxiety in us—at least I can speak for myself and Sir Mordaunt—by the presence of the poor woman, I will leave it to your own heart to conceive.   All our crew stood forward looking at the wreck, and constantly directing their glances at us, as if to guess our intentions, and Purchase and Tripshore were together near the wheel.

"Walton," said Sir Mordaunt, who seemed to be stirred to the very soul by the sight of those people on the bark, "you'll not wish me to apologize for rousing you up at this hour.   I want you to advise me.   Purchase is dead against our lowering a boat in this sea, and says we should stand by the vessel until the weather moderates.   But this wind may last for another week, or it may freshen into a gale and blow us away. Meanwhile how long have those people been in that situation ? For all we know, they may be starving, Walton.   You see they have no boat, and cannot come to us.   We are bound to succor them, and at once."

I took a hurried look around the sea, and said, " Yes, at once."

"At all events, the attempt must be made," he continued, in a manner so agitated that his words rolled over one another as they tumbled out of his mouth. " I'll cheerfully share the danger. I'll go in the boat."

" No, no," said I ; " if you'll put the job into my hands, I'll answer for the right kind of attempt to save them being made."

" You are a good fellow," he cried. " For God's sake go to work."

His charging me with this matter convinced me that he had found old Purchase more obstinate than he liked to admit. But it was impossible to look at the wreck and wonder at his emotion. The people made no signs to us, unless a sign was meant by the woman, who sometimes raised her hand. They hung together like corpses ; but no doubt their reason for keeping still was that if they unlashed themselves they stood a great chance of being swept overboard. Although we were hove well to windward, and abeam of the wreck, the send of the sea was settling us faster to leeward than she was traveling, and every heave carried us nearer. This, however, was no great matter, for the yacht was perfectly under command, and a shift of the helm would speedily forge us ahead of the wreck. As it was, we were now near enough to make our voices heard, so, jumping on to the rail, I hailed the vessel. One of the men, he that was most fully dressed, replied by lifting his arm.

" Are you English ? " I shouted.

He motioned affirmatively. This was fortunate, for had they been foreigners I must have found great difficulty in making my meaning intelligible. At my first call, the men clapped their hands like shells to their ears, to catch my words, and the passion of eagerness expressed by this posture made them the most moving figures in the world.

" We mean to send a boat," I hallooed ; " but as we can't risk sheering alongside, we'll drop under your stern, and as we pass, you must jump. Do you follow me ? "

The man again raised his hand.

" See that you get the woman over first."

This injunction was likewise heard and understood. I sprang on the deck, and ran up to the mate.

" Mr. Tripshore," said I, " yonder is the biggest boat," pointing as I spoke, " and fortunately she hangs to leeward. Will you please sing out for volunteers ? I'll take charge, and if you'll accompany me, I shall be glad."

" I'll go, sir," said he, promptly ; and immediately went along the deck and called for volunteers. All the men came

tumbling aft, that is, all the sailors among them. My utter
disregard of old Purchase had put him into a great passion ;
and he was additionally mortified by the quickness of the men
to come into an errand which he had advised Sir Mordaunt
against.

"It's nothen short o' murder ! " he rattled out, straddling up
to Sir Mordaunt, and struggling to control his rage. " If Mr.
Walton's a sailor, he'll know that this is no fit sea for a yacht's
boat to be lowered into."

"Keep back ! " shouted Sir Mordaunt, impetuously. " Mr.
Walton knows what he is about. Don't interfere with him."

What more passed I cannot say, being busy from that moment with choosing my men for the boat. She was a six-oared
boat ; but I could not fully man her, for, though I saw it would
be hard work pulling to windward, which we should have to
do to regain the stern of the vessel, yet those people on the
wreck must make the boat dangerously deep in such a sea if
six men manned her. I therefore chose three of the best hands,
and told Tripshore to take stroke.

"When we go clear," I called to Sir Mordaunt, "let Purchase
make a board to windward, and then wear and heave the yacht
to, to leeward of the wreck." And so saying, I jumped into
the stern sheets, shipped the rudder, the men seized their oars,
and we were lowered.

The boat hung by patent clips, that is, by hooks which flew
open and released her the moment she touched the water and
eased the falls of her weight. But for this we might not have
got away without a ducking, or something worse. As it was,
five men hanging upon the davits in a heavy boat made a
dangerous weight for those iron fixtures to sustain, and I own
I held my breath as we were lowered. But there was no other
way of launching ourselves. The yacht rolled so heavily that
at moments her lee rail was flush with the water, and by bringing the boat to the gangway we should not only have risked
staving her, but some of us must have broken our legs or necks
in getting into her. Yachtsmen, however, are nearly always
good boatmen. We were lowered handsomely, though carefully, the boat touched the water, the hooks flew open, and
the fall-blocks rushed past our noses as the yacht rolled from
us, and hung like a cliff over our heads. In an instant we
were swept up and away from the side of the schooner, which
swung heavily toward us, sinking low until we looked down
upon her white decks, which lay like the side of a hill.

" Give way !" I bawled ; the oars flashed, and there we were heading dead for the stern of the wreck.

Our boat was like a whaleman's, sharp at both ends, and with a good spring. She was a kind of life-boat, too, fitted with wooden, tubular, air-tight casings. She topped the seas like a cork, and yet at the first start the height and volume of the waves made me forget the wreck. I could think of nothing but our situation. At one moment we were in a hollow, in a dead calm, with the foam of the summit of the mountain of water behind us blowing like a flight of white-breasted sea-birds high over our heads ; the next, we were on the top of the huge surge, the boat end on, the bowman right over my head, and a chasm behind us that was like looking down a precipice.

However, with a strong effort of will, I drew my mind away from all this, and fixed my attention on the wreck, where I beheld the poor creatures engaged in unlashing themselves, whilst one of them, grasping the woman, was crawling along, and shoving her as he went to the extremity of the deck-house, where a short ladder would enable them to reach the taffrail. Happily the wreck lay so very low in the water that it would be nothing of a jump from her into the boat. I sung out to the man who pulled the bow oar to make ready to catch the woman, and at the same time I told the other fellows to lay upon their oars, as the boat had way enough, and stand by to back water when we got under the stern of the wreck, so that we should not shoot past too rapidly.

Yet never was nicer steering wanted than now ; for if I directed the boat too near the stern, there was the chance of a sea lifting us under her counter, and smashing us into staves ; whilst, on the other hand, if I gave the bark too wide a berth, the woman would never be able to reach us by jumping. I pulled myself together, and watched the send of the boat on the seas steadfastly. The woman stood on the taffrail, waiting for us, grasped by the man, who crouched down behind her, with his hands locked in her dress. Every now and again a column of water ran up the bark's quarter, and smothered them, and I could see the woman at such moments beating the air with her hands, and then rubbing down her face, whilst her long black hair, that hung for a bit in its saturated state down her back, would lift, and then blow out straight upon the strong wind.

Calculating the distance as accurately as I could, I headed the boat so as to hit the water about five feet from the taffrail.

The wind and the waves rushed us along.   When about twenty feet distant I shouted to the men to bury their oars and stop our way somewhat.   This was done, and then we were under the vessel's stern.

" Jump ! " I shouted.

The woman, dashing back her hair, made a spring, with her arms outstretched.   The bowman caught her, and the boat trembled as her body fell into his arms.   In a moment we had swept past the vessel, but the woman was safe in the bottom of the boat.

It was now necessary to row to windward in order to drop down again past the vessel's stern.   It was tedious and perilous work, but there was no other way of rescuing the men.   We should have been stove alongside the groaning and squelching hull, or chucked right on to her.   But when we rounded to get to windward again, there was just one moment when I believed we should say good-night to the world.   The boat was flung up by a savage sea that was shaped like a cone, and tossed into the air on the prong of this evil surge, as though Neptune had speared us with his trident, and was forking us aloft ; and the fellows who tugged at the oars, missing the water, swept the blades through the air, and fell head over heels off the thwarts.   Yet this very accident was probably the saving of us ; for the weight of the men being in the bottom of the boat kept her keel in the water, though as that sea ran roaring away under her, a vertical line would have cut through her two gun-wales.

After rowing a certain distance, I put the boat's head round again for the wreck, and as we drifted close alongside the stern, we maintained our position there by means of backing water long enough to enable two of the three men to drop among us.   Another struggle to windward, and another row-ing past the wreck, enabled us to get the third man ; and with our miserable freight lying in a silent heap in the bottom of the boat, we made for the schooner, that had gone away to leeward, and lay hove to, waiting for us.

But only half our errand was accomplished, and the worst part remained.   We had saved the unhappy people, but how were we to put them and ourselves aboard the yacht ?   Every time we were spun up on top of a sea I saw her plunging and rolling under her reefed foresail, dipping her bows so deep that two-thirds of her rudder came out of water, and heeling over to leeward until it seemed that another foot of inclination

"When about twenty feet distant I shouted to the men."—Page 128.

would lay bare her keel; and then down we would plump into
hollow, where there was not a breath of air, and nothing to be
seen but the water toppling in mountains above us, and the
sky, which we looked up at as though from the bottom of a
well.   The tumbling of the schooner on the one hand, and our
own sickening sinkings and risings on the other hand, were
pretty broad hints of the difficult and dangerous job that lay
before us.   There was only one plan to adopt, and when we
were close to the schooner it entered my head.   Sir Mordaunt
and the ladies and Purchase, indeed everybody aboard the
yacht, were intently watching us, and in order that they should
hear me, I steered as close to the stern of the schooner as I
dared venture, and shouted at the top of my voice for them to
reeve a whip at the foreyard-arm, and sway us aboard, as that
would be our only chance of reaching the deck; and I also
bawled to them to heave us a line, which I protest none of
them seemed to think of doing.   Old Purchase appeared quite
dazed, and stared at us like a fool, and we should have been
swept away to leeward by the wind and sea like smoke, if the
fellow who held the wheel had not let go of it and swung a
coil of rope at us, the end of which was cleverly caught by the
bowman; and presently we were riding at about ten feet distance from the vessel, our weather oars being kept overboard
to hold the boat clear of the side.

In a few minutes a whip was rove at the foreyard-arm, with
a guy, leading over the bulwark rail, to steady it.   "A bowline on the bite," as it is called, was made at the end of it, and
the man on the yard overhauled the whip until the bowline
came to our hands.   The woman was raised, and the bowline
slipped over her, and watching our chance, I shouted to the
people aboard the schooner to sway away.   The poor creature
shrieked as she was swept out of the boat into the air; and
never shall I forget her appearance as she swung aloft a few
moments, with her gown rattling upon the wind like a flag,
and her hair streaming out, and her arms tossing wildly.   I
recollected Miss Tuke saying that she hoped we would meet
with adventures, and I wondered what she would think of *this*
as an incident.   It was like seeing a person hanged.

I believe the woman had been unconscious to the moment
of the men lifting her up to pass the bowline over her shoulders,
and no wonder the poor soul kept screaming, if, as I suppose,
she only recovered her sensibility to find herself hanging over
the foaming water at a height of sixteen or eighteen feet.

9

But the guy was manned, and she was carefully drawn on board ; and very quickly the bowline was again overhauled into the boat, and one of the shipwrecked men fitted into it, and sent aloft.

The relation of this business is easy enough, but the acting in it was a tremendous experience. First, we had the utmost difficulty to keep the boat from swinging away from or sheering against the yacht's side. We had all to crouch low in her, and do our work as we squatted in her bottom, for fear of over-setting her. As the seas passed under her she would lean over, and keep us breathless ; and one moment she would be hover-ing on the summit of a sea that gave us a clear view of the foaming waters beyond the yacht's decks, and the next the yacht had vanished, and nothing was visible but the wall of green water that sparkled and hissed and roared between her and us. On the other hand, the rolling of the yacht's masts tautened and slackened the bowline so wildly that it was a real agony to wait for and mark the moment when to sway away. I myself narrowly missed an ugly ducking, not to mention a broken limb : for, all the shipwrecked men having been got aboard, Tripshore insisted on my going next, whereupon the bowline was caught with plenty of slack. and tossed over my shoulders. I gave the order myself to hoist up, and whether from flurry or worry chose the wrong moment, *i.e.*, when the boat was at the bottom of a sea instead of being on the top of it, the result of which was I found myself traveling into the air with the boat and the sea in full chase of me, and coming much faster than I was going. Fortunately a swing of the yacht cleared me of the boat, which, had she struck my legs, must have broken them ; the boiling water rose to within half a dozen inches of my feet, and then subsided, leaving me swinging over a huge roaring hollow. However, before I could completely realize my position, they had swayed me over the bulwarks, and with a hearty thrill of delight I once more felt the solid deck under my feet.

Sir Mordaunt wrung my hand and was good enough to com-pliment me warmly on the manner in which the rescue had been effected. He told me that his wife and niece were below with the woman, and begged me to go and change my clothes, which were indeed wet through. But this I answered I could not do until I had seen the men aboard, and the boat at the davits. In a manner, I felt responsible for their safety, more especially as Tripshore remained in the boat to hook her on, leaving nobody in command but Purchase, whose inactivity during our return from the wreck had by no means improved my opinion of him as a seaman.

When all the men but Tripshore were dragged over the side, the boat was dropped astern, and carefully hauled under the davits. All hands came aft and tailed on to the falls, but before the boat was alongside I flung the end of a bowline into her, and shouted to Tripshore to put it under his arms, so that, should he fall overboard, we could fish him up without trouble. This undoubtedly eased the man's mind, and made him work more coolly. And certainly never did he stand in greater need of his nerves, for nothing but a steady eye and nimble hand could have saved the boat, that, as the yacht leaned down, rose to a level with her rail, and then sunk below under the bends, until I had to fork my head over the side to see her.

" Hoist away ! " and the boat came up hand over hand.

" Thank God for that ! " said I, as the falls were belayed, and Tripshore, throwing off the bowline, jumped on to the deck. " Now, Sir Mordaunt, I'll go and shift my clothes ; " and down I bundled, exulting, as any man would, over our successful exploit.

There was nobody in the cabin, but I heard voices in Carey's berth as I passed to my own, and supposed that the ladies had carried the poor woman there, and were giving her a dry outfit. I made short work over my own toggery, and in five minutes was on deck again, by which time the reefed mainsail had been hoisted, and the yacht was breaking the seas as she started afresh on her cruise. The wreck was broad on the weather quarter, and I stood in the companion looking at her. There is no inanimate object that appeals so pathetically to the feelings as a deserted wreck tossing upon the high seas. Shorn of her beauty, her masts broken, her rigging trailing in confused heaps, surrounded by the great ocean that makes her desolation supreme, she resembles a dying creature : she seems to know her fate, and to be faintly struggling to save herself from vanishing in the fathomless grave that slowly sucks her down. The sunshine flying between the clouds flashed in the snowstorms of spray which were hurled over the almost submerged hull ; the foreyard swayed wildly, like a beckoning arm entreating us to stay ; and here and there along her side black fragments of bulwark stanchions or such things stood out when the coils of green water had poured from her decks and left them exposed ; and they so resembled motionless human beings, standing drowned and supported by their death-gripe, that it was impossible to behold the illusion without a thrill.

Old Purchase stood near the wheel, looking very dogged and sullen, but Sir Mordaunt was not on deck. Catching sight of the steward, I called to know where the baronet was. He replied that Sir Mordaunt was in the forecastle, seeing to the shipwrecked men. I went to the forecastle hatch, and sung out to know if I might step down.

"Come along, Walton, come along," shouted Sir Mordaunt; so I stuck my toes into the up-and-down ladder, and dropped into the forecastle.

This was my first visit to this part of the vessel, and I was surprised by the roominess of the interior, considering the tonnage of the yacht. There was a double row of bunks on either hand, a good-sized square table that traveled on stanchions, so that it could be hoisted up out of the way when not wanted, with lockers around. The deck was white, everything very clean, and the place in excellent order. But you felt the motion here as it was to be felt in no other part. It was like standing at one end of a seesaw plank, and the jump was often sharp enough to make one reel. The roll of the bow wave, and the sound of the solid surges smiting the resonant fabric, and recoiling in a smothered hissing and seething, might have passed for a thunder-storm heard in a cellar.

The three men whom we had rescued sat at the table, eating with slow motions, and yet with a kind of avidity that was made distressing to witness by their languor, which was that of men in the last stage of exhaustion. Such of the yacht's crew as were below stood at a respectful distance looking on, while Sir Mordaunt leaned with one hand upon the table, talking to the poor fellows and encouraging them. They all three threw down their knives when they saw me, and rose very shakily from their seats, and whilst they extended their hands for me to shake, thanked me in broken tones, and one of them with the tears gushing out of his eyes, for having saved their lives. I was quite unprepared for this, and for a moment was unmanned by their pitiful faces and the corpse-like drooping of their figures, and by the low melancholy pitch of their voices, which quivered with emotion.

In the hurry and anxiety of the rescue, I had taken no notice of their appearance; as they jumped into the boat, they had been let to lie in the bottom, where of course, from my place aft, I had not been able to see them. I now ran my eyes over them, and never was the cruel usage that the sea gives to men whom it has mastered more lamentably illustrated than by these figures. It is true they had got on some dry clothes, lent them by the yachtsmen, but their faces were most miserable to see. The fire of famine and mental suffering sparkled in their deep-sunk eyes; their lips were white, and were scarcely defined upon their flesh; their cheeks were hollow, and there were excoriations, which looked like burns or scaldings, upon different parts of their faces; whilst their nerveless, shaking hands resembled fat or wax, swelled up and made to look like lepers' hands by the salt and the ceaseless washing.

I sat down opposite them, and Sir Mordaunt said :

"Their vessel was the *Wanderer*, bound from Pensacola to Liverpool. They had been four days in their awful plight, Walton, when we rescued them."

"Do you mean four days without victuals or drink?" I asked.

"Yes, sir, so help me God!" answered one of them, in a hollow, broken voice. "We got caught in a gale o' wind that almost knocked us to pieces, and in that same gale we started a butt, I reckon, for the water came in fast and drowned the vessel."

"What has become of the rest of the crew?" I asked.

"Why," answered another man—he that had cried when he took my hand—"the gale left us only one boat, and we got that overboard, and all hands crawled into her. But afore we could get her clear, a sea chucked us against the ship's side and stove us. Three of us got on deck, and I caught the woman by the hair—she's the captain's wife, sir—and dragged her up. All the rest went down. We heard them screamin', but we could do nothing, and it was soon over."

"Did you sight nothing in those four days?" I inquired.

"Ay; a big steamer passed us—she must have seen us—but she never stopped," replied the other man—one answering after the other, in turns, as though they felt the need of relieving one another.

"You were right, you see, Sir Mordaunt," said I, in a low voice : "that mirage was surely a Heaven-directed signal."

And I own when I looked at those men, and reflected that but for that mirage we should never have sighted the wreck, I perceived so clearly the will of God in the adventure, that I sat a while silent and awed by the wonder and mercifulness of it, and by the closeness it brought me to an act of the Creator that made the Divine operation, if I may so say, a visible thing.

We staid about ten minutes talking to the men, in the course of which I gathered that the crew had originally consisted of fourteen souls, and that these men who were saved were able seamen : that their ship was only two years old, and her cargo worth a deal of money ; but that nothing could have resisted the gale that struck them, which from their description, I took to be a cyclone, of which the skipper must have headed his ship into the thickest and most dangerous part, in ignorance perhaps, of the nature of those rotary storms. I advised the poor creatures turn in and sleep as long as they could, and Sir Mordaunt and I came away.

He held my arm as we walked slowly aft. He was much affected, and could hardly speak for some moments.

"Oh, Walter," he exclaimed, presently, "how little people ashore know of what goes on at sea! How impossible it is to understand the horrors of shipwreck without experiencing it, or beholding it in its dreadful reality as we have!" And he extended his hand as he said this toward the water-logged bark that was now a long way astern, and scarcely to be seen amid the spray that dashed over her and veiled the ruins of her spars. "When I went into the forecastle, one of my crew whispered to me that at the sight of the food two of the ship-wrecked men burst out crying. It will not bear thinking of. I have never been brought face to face with human misery like this before."

"Nay, don't let us bother over it," said I. "The men will do, and the ladies will no doubt pull the poor woman through. That's a capital boat of yours. No ordinary quarter-boat could have lived in this sea." And I looked at the running and splashing and hissing surges, which sometimes swelled up white with the foam of our driving stem to within a foot of the bulwark rail, and leaped and sparkled far as the eye could reach, banding the deep with a rugged circle ; while over the frothing waters the cloud shadows sped in rushing crowds, making the wild, free, streaming leagues of water piebald with violet patches and the sunlight's white splendor.

I put my head into the skylight to see if breakfast was ready, and perceived the dishes on the table, and the steward in the act of reaching for his bell. Indeed, the job of saving the shipwrecked men had occupied more time in performing than it takes in reading about it. It made me wonder to think how long we had been in the boat, and among the seas, for though it had not seemed a long while to me, it was hard upon an hour and a half from the time of our quitting the yacht to the moment of hoisting the boat to the davits.

Lady Brookes and Miss Tuke and Norie entered the cabin as we went down the companion steps, and I was rather taken aback by Miss Tuke coming up to me, with her hand outstretched, and telling me that I had acted "as a real sailor would," and the like. I thanked her for her good words, and there stopped, secretly relishing these compliments too much from *her* to deprecate them, and yet not wanting the action to take one particle more of significance than it deserved.

"Here at last is a real adventure for you," said I. "Already the *Lady Maud* has saved five lives—counting the cockney we found adrift in the Channel as one. But the poor woman—how is she?"

"Oh, Mordaunt," exclaimed Lady Brookes, answering the question by addressing her husband, "she is such a poor, delicate creature. Her husband was the captain, and he was drowned with the others when the boat upset. She was starving and ravenous, and yet she could not swallow, and she might have died with the food before her, for the want of being able to swallow, if Mr. Norie had not made her drink water with every mouthful."

"To bring the muscles into play," said Norie.

"Well ; but what has become of her? is she in bed?" asked Sir Mordaunt.

"Yes, in Carey's bed," answered her ladyship.

Good Sir Mordaunt heaved a sigh. "Think of the poor creature exposed for four days and nights to the seas breaking over that sunken hull! How can flesh and blood bear such suffering? And her mental anguish ! "

"*There* you hit the worst part of shipwreck," said I. "It is not the hunger and thirst only, it is the thoughts of your own lonely, miserable doom, the friends far away, who may never know what has become of you, the memory of the people who have been drowned in your sight——"

Here Sir Mordaunt interrupted.

"Pray, Walton, hand me one of those eggs," and he winked ferociously.

"Oh, Mordaunt!" cried Lady Brookes, hysterically, "I wish we were safe at home ! "

"Are you not as safe here?" he replied. "Come, come, my love, don't let the shipwreck trouble you."

"It's no more than passing a tombstone in a journey," said I. "That wreck means just as much as a grave that your eye lights on as you drive along in a carriage."

"Just as much and just as little," exclaimed Norie. "It points a moral, of course. But who's afraid?"

"You have not seen the woman, Mr. Walton," said her lady-ship, in a trembling voice, and very pale. "Mordaunt, her eyes were like live coals, and you should have seen her as Ada and Mr. Norie supported her through the cabin, with her long black hair as wet as sea-weed plastered over her hollow face!" She hid her eyes in her hand and shuddered violently, whilst Sir Mordaunt looked at me with a melancholy shake of the head, as though he would say, "I was afraid of this from the beginning."

We went on with our breakfast in silence, none of us in particularly high spirits, and we certainly did not stand in need of any emotional outbreak in Lady Brookes to depress us. For my own part, I was beginning to feel the effects of the excitement and anxiety of the time spent in the boat, many years having passed since I had been engaged in so rough and hazardous an adventure, and my training ashore had not been of a kind to enable me to support such an experience very sturdily; so, when breakfast was over, I went to my cabin, and threw myself on the bed, meaning merely to rest myself, instead of which I fell asleep.

For three hours I slept, and when I awoke I felt buoyant with the refreshment of that sleep. It was still blowing very fresh, and the sea was high, and the yacht plunging over the surges, and frothing the water for a league away astern of her, and driving through it nobly under a treble-reefed mainsail and standing jib, the gaff-foresail having been taken in whilst I was below. The sun was high, and all the clouds gone. Indeed, the sight of that strong sea, and the sound of the wild wind storming through the rigging, and all overhead a liquid, beautiful, tropical azure, untarnished by the smallest puff of vapor, made me pause when I had gained the top of the companion steps, and look up with wonder. It was more like being off the west coast of South America, where heavy gales rage under blue skies, than in the North Atlantic.

But what a scene of brilliance was the sea! The beams of the high sun made a mirror of the whole surface of it. The flash and quiver of foam alternated with the poising coils of glittering water, and every wave that broke flung up a great shower of spray that fled ahead of it on the wings of the wind like a torn veil of silver thread, so that the whole expanse of the leaping, boiling, sweeping, and seething deep was covered with this flying mist of salt, which sparkled like jewels in the glorious sunshine, and flung a rainbow-like radiance over the face of the ocean. The clearance of the sky might have been accounted for by the wind having shifted a couple of points to the northward. This shift was good for our comfort by diminishing the angle of the deck ; but though the schooner showed but few cloths, the pressure made her tremble as she ran, and it was like watching the bottom of a water-fall, where the cascade meets the rushing stream, to see the water shoot up at her bows, and fly clear of her decks in an avalanche of snow, and strike the hissing seas twenty fathoms to leeward of her.

I found Norie reading to Miss Tuke, she sitting and listening, with her hands folded and her eyes half closed. I thought him lucky to be able to read well enough to engage her attention. Sir Mordaunt stood alone, looking at the sea.

"I'm glad indeed, Walton," said he, "that I made no objection to your going off to the wreck. The poor creatures must have perished had we carried out Purchase's idea, and waited for the wind to go down. But you acted bravely, Walton, very bravely, and I am proud that my men should have backed you so well. They shall not go unrewarded."

"Praise them as much as you please," said I. "They deserve encouragement. But let us have no more about my part of the undertaking. Why, is not that one of the shipwrecked fellows yonder?"

And there, sure enough, just to leeward of the foremast, was the first of the men who had jumped from the wreck. He was squatting on his hams, and smoked a short pipe, the bowl of which was inverted, and around him stood a group of the *Lady Maud's* men, listening to his yarn with rapt attention, their figures swaying to the motion of the vessel. He was like Coleridge's ancient mariner, with his glittering eye and pale forefinger, which he scored the air with as he talked.

"I've been watching him," said Sir Mordaunt, "and wondering what we are to do with the poor creatures. We must keep them, I suppose, until we arrive at Kingston, and God knows they are heartily welcome."

"Unless we fall in with a homeward-bound ship," said I.

"To be sure; and then we can transfer them.   I had never thought of that."

Just then the man caught sight of me.   He instantly stood up, and pulled off his hat.   I beckoned to him.   He rammed his finger into the pipe bowl he was smoking, and thrusting the pipe into his breeches pocket, came aft.   I wish I could describe his manner; the working of his pinched and hollow features; the twitching of his hands, as though he would embrace me; and the speaking and moving expression of gratitude that softened and humanized his eyes, though, but for that look, the fires which famine and anguish of mind had kindled in them, and which still burned there, would have made them shocking to see.

"I am glad you are hearty enough to be about," said I. "But it would be better for you to keep your bunk, I think. After what you have gone through, you want rest quite as much as food."

"I can't rest, sir; I can't be still," he answered.   "It's fearful to be quiet, and shut my eyes, for then it's all happening over again.   No; I'd rather be on deck, sir—leastways if you don't wish otherwise.   God bless you, sir!"

"How are your mates?"

"Sleeping like dead men, sir.   But talking and keeping my mind going does me more good than sleeping, said he, quickly, as if afraid that his reference to his mates would make us send him below.

I now told him that it was our intention to put him and the others aboard the first homeward-bound ship we should meet that would take them, and that if we failed to meet with such a vessel, we should land them at some West Indian port, most probably Kingston.

"But we'll take care to land you where you will find a ship to carry you home," said Sir Mordaunt.

The poor fellow was very grateful, and thanked us humbly for our kindness.   Miss Tuke left Norie alone with his book, and joined us as we talked to the man, and spoke to him in a way that reminded me of that night in the Channel, when she stood soothing and cheering the fellow we had found in the boat.   There was no affectation in her sympathy and liking for sailors.   She saw further into their life than most girls would, and found something to move her in the thoughts of the great mysterious ocean into which Jack sails, and the lonesomeness and suffering of the fate that often befalls him.   Here,

now, was a figure that would have affected a more insensible
heart than hers. Suffering such as this sailor and his mates
had endured gives a kind of sanctity or mystery to a man, and
the compassion he excited was mixed with an awe that was
not to be hindered by his rough speech and broken-down bearing.

I was somewhat surprised that Sir Mordaunt made no further
reference to the part old Purchase had taken in the business of
the rescue. I thought he would have coupled his unsailorly
half-heartedness on that occasion with his grogginess on the
preceding evening, and found the two strong enough to support a prejudice. I did not even know whether he had spoken
to the man about his trick of overdoing his drams, nor would I
inquire. A conversation might have taken place between them
when I was asleep, and Purchase would, of course, know
what excuses and what promises to make, and what to say for
having opposed the sending of a boat to the wreck. As Sir
Mordaunt said nothing about him, I considered it would be an
intrusion if I volunteered any further opinion on him in his
capacity as skipper. But this self-imposed reticence of mine
only served to increase my distrust and harden my contempt
of the old man as a seaman.

It was not until the evening of the day of the rescue that I
saw the woman whom we had saved. It was after dinner. I
had been smoking a pipe on deck, enjoying the headlong wind
that showed no sign of abating, and that was driving us foaming and dancing athwart the parallels toward the trade-wind,
and promising us a fast and noble run to the West Indies. I
stepped below to refill my pipe, and on entering the cabin,
saw the woman sitting in an arm-chair, talking to Lady
Brookes and Miss Tuke.

She looked at me vacantly, not remembering my face ; but
when Lady Brookes (who had recovered her spirits, and given
up lamenting—for a spell—that she was not ashore) said,
"This is Mr. Walton, the gentleman who steered the boat,"
she jumped up, and grasping my right hand in both hers,
kissed it again and again, and when she let it go it was wet
with her tears.

Although she was very wan, with the aspect of emaciation
that characterized the three seamen, she was certainly not so
formidable as the picture that Lady Brookes drew of her at
breakfast had led me to suppose. Her hair was brushed and
braided—it was black as ebony, and very abundant—and the

bight of the braided loops fell low on her back. She had ex-changed her torn and soaked gown for a dress belonging to Miss Tuke; and I perceived that she possessed a figure that suffered nothing even from contrast with Lady Brookes's fine shape. She was of the middle height, and I thought that when health had colored her lips and cheeks afresh, and filled out her face, she would turn out to be a handsome woman. Her age apparently did not exceed four or five and twenty years, and she did not look older than that now, in spite of what she had gone through. I also noticed what I was hardly likely to perceive when I had heard her voice amid the thunder of the wind and the cannonading of the surges storming the disman-tled wreck—I mean that she was Irish. Her accent was very rich, but educated, so that there was nothing in it that I could illustrate by spelling. There was plaintiveness and winning and drawing music in her tones, as she poured forth her thanks to me, with the bright tears flowing down her hollow face. But it would be idle to write down her words; for, greatly as they moved me, yet the pathos of her gratitude was rather in her eyes, in the motion of her hands, in the soft vibration and vary-ing harmonies of her voice.

"Will you call my husband, Mr. Walton?" said Lady Brookes. "He does not know that Mrs. Stretton"—for that was the woman's name, it seemed—"has left her cabin."

Forthwith I summoned my friend, who got up from under the weather bulwark, where he was smoking, and throwing his cigar overboard, followed me into the cabin. There was a bland, consoling courtesy in the manner in which he took the woman's hand and spoke to her that was incomparable in its way. He put fifty inquiries to her about her strength and health, and the like, and wound up by letting fall her hand, and raising his own, and thanking God with lifted eyes that his yacht had been the means of saving the lives of the sufferers.

He then spoke to her of his proposal of transferring her and the men to a homeward bound ship; or, failing that, of land-ing them at Kingston, Jamaica.

"Are you going to Kingston?" she asked, eagerly.

He answered that he had not intended at first to put into any port; but that the yacht would probably have to touch somewhere for fresh water, and that he would choose Kings-ton, for the sake of the magnificent scenery of Jamaica.

"I have a brother-in-law who is a shipping agent in Kings-ton," said she, still speaking anxiously, but in a subdued voice ; and she was proceeding, but stopped, with a look of embarrassment.

" In that case," said Sir Mordaunt, immediately, seeing, as we all did, indeed, the reason of her hesitation, "we will gladly decide to carry you to Kingston."

" You are very, very good, sir. I should not have had the boldness to ask so great a favor. Indeed, such kindness, following my trial, is more than I can bear," and the poor thing again burst into tears, and cried and sobbed most piteously.

Sir Mordaunt was just the man to be affected by a woman's tears ; and while she cried he kept his face hung, and his features worked as if he would cry too. Miss Tuke, by way of diverting all this sorrow, led the poor young widow to tell her story to Sir Mordaunt. I thought at first that this was like putting her on the rack, but speedily saw that it did her good to talk of her troubles.

She had only been married a few months, she said ; indeed, she married her husband in the very week the bark sailed from Liverpool. We all sat listening with a kind of fascination whilst she told the story of the gale and the wreck and the capsizing of the boat, by which all the people but four perished. The muffled roar of the sea outside ; the sharp shrieking of the wind in the rigging, which latter sound echoed in clear notes down the skylight and companion ; the wild lifting and plunging of the schooner ; the creak and grind of timbers and bulkheads ; the quick dislocating jumping of the swinging trays, and the rattle of the fire-arms in the rack ; and the significant patter of spray, like a heavy fall of hail upon the deck—gave such a color to her narrative as kept us all hearkening with rapt attention to her round and fluent accent, made passionately plaintive by the horrors of her memory. I think I sce the picture now ; Lady Brookes, watching the speaker with her black eyes all ashine, and her hands tightly folded, and her lips compressed, and her brows gathered ; Miss Tuke, full of sympathy and wonder and fear ; Sir Mordaunt, supporting himself by the table, balancing his tall figure to the heavy lurches, smoothing down his beard, sometimes looking at the woman, and sometimes around him at us, with an expression of consternation ; I, full of hearty pity for the poor bereaved soul, who sat telling her story with dramatic power, but utterly unconscious of the effect she produced—clasping or extending her hands, one moment sinking her voice until we had to lean forward to hear her, then wildly exclaiming, then stopping to cry.

She made me shudder when she came to the starving part of her story.   In the evening light her face was as white as death, and her fiery black eyes were something to shine in the skull of the very spirit of Famine.   That day of the thunder-storm was the third of their sufferings, and the calm was a long agony to the parched and helpless and hopeless wretches.   The froth stood upon the lips of the men, and one of them put his teeth to his arm, but his heart failed him ; and as she told us this, carried away by the previous memory, and anxious that we should fully grasp the anguish we had released them from, she acted the things—raised her arm to her lips, with her burning eyes fixed on Lady Brookes's face as she did it ; whereupon, with a sudden choking cry, her ladyship started to her feet, and fell into a dead swoon in the arms of her husband.

Poor Mrs. Stretton was panic-stricken by the effect of her story.   "Oh, it is my fault—it is my fault !   How rash I am— how wicked !" she cried, and sprang to Lady Brookes's side, and kissed her hand, and committed a hundred extravagances of grief, whilst I tumbled upon deck to fetch Norie, whom we had left there watching the sea, and quite unconscious of the thrilling drama that was enacting below.

"I say, Sir Mordaunt," exclaimed the doctor—as he bent over the unconscious woman, who lay upon the floor, with her head on Miss Tuke's lap, whilst her husband swabbed her face with toilet vinegar or something of that kind, and Mrs. Stretton (whose ability to move at all, after what she had gone through, was amazing to me) groveled on her knees with a smelling bottle, which she held to Lady Brookes's nose—"this won't do.   If her ladyship is to be sent into fainting fits in this fashion, I'll not answer for her life."

Sir Mordaunt made no answer, but he looked terribly grieved and upset.   After the regulation quantity of slopping and slap- ping, Lady Brookes came to, and was carried off to her berth in state, Miss Tuke heading the procession, Sir Mordaunt and Norie holding each an arm of her ladyship, and cutting fantas- tic figures as they toppled to and fro upon the heaving and bounding deck, and Carey the maid and the unhappy captain's wife bringing up the rear.

Glad to be quit of the business, I went on deck, where I found Tripshore, with whom I had a long yarn over the inci- dent of the morning ; and when I had done with him, I had the deck to myself for half an hour, though from time to time I would find myself taking a furtive squint down the skylight to see if Miss Tuke were coming my way, for I was growing sentimental enough about that girl not only to enjoy her company, not only to relish the occasional snub she bestowed on Norie, and any half-suppressed impatience of him that she exhibited when he drew alongside of her, but even to indulge in fond and foolish dreams of the future.

If this confession, however, makes it appear that I was in love, then more is conveyed than is true. I was not in love with Ada Tuke. I was only warming up toward her. I enjoyed thinking of her and I dwelt upon the possibility of my falling in love with her as an agreeable dream that might one day be realized. Any young fellow who has been boxed up for some weeks with a pretty girl in a vessel will understand what I mean. A man rarely falls seriously in love with a girl at sea. He plays round and round the emotion, warms himself by it, and enjoys its light; but he seldom or never burns his wings. He waits till he gets ashore to do that. The steady earth helps him to concentrate himself. At sea the tumblification keeps him diffused.

For that half-hour, however, I managed to do very well alone. The sea was a noble companion, and the voice of the strong clear gale overhead full of eloquent meaning. The night had fallen, but it was most brilliant with stars. They lay as thick as dust, and the planets looked like little moons, so round and full of light were they, so bland and large and serene and steady. Now and again a meteor that filled the sky all round it with light, like the showering of a port-fire, would sail athwart those stars, and puff and vanish in a smoke of spangles. The sea was a magnificent sight, all ashine with fire. The summit of every surge was luminous and in the hollows the greenish streaks flashed and faded in cloudy radiance like brimstone. I could see the phosphorus sparkling upon the forecastle as the yacht dipped and shipped a smother of water over her weather bow; and sometimes, when the surges ran up her without breaking, and fled along with the strong wind over the vessel's nose without touching her, the air all that way seemed on fire with the bright rush. Indeed, it was blowing hard. If the *Dido* had this wind, she would be under double-reefed topsails. The brave little schooner stormed grandly through the pelting surges, swelling out the foam by half her own length ahead of her every time she dropped a courtesy, and sending the black and shining water hissing and roaring away to windward of her, and sweeping it astern into a wake that might have served for a thousand-ton ship.

I stood for nearly a quarter of an hour watching that wake rushing away from me, full of whirling, and eddying fires, into the leaping leagues of darkness, and listening to the clank and jerking of the wheel-chains, and the booming of the wind in the hollow of the drum-like mainsail, and the crashing of waters to right and left as they soared and coiled over, and broke into wildernesses of snow under their own weight.

CHAPTER IX.

But this fine wind did not last through the night. When I came on deck at eight o'clock next morning the wind was away in the southeast, a gentle breeze, and the swell of the sea fast going down. There was a small bark on the lee horizon, standing to the north, too far off to be of any use to us for transshipping the wrecked men. She remained in sight until after breakfast, and seeing her put it into Sir Mordaunt's head to call the three men aft, and talk to them.

They presently arrived and I was struck to see how the rest and the food had pulled them together. Sir Mordaunt at once told them that he had consented to carry Mrs. Stretton to Kingston, where she had friends; that if they liked the notion of going as far as Kingston, he would convey them there, but they must decide. He would either take them to Jamaica or transfer them to the first homeward-bound. ship we could signal. What was their choice?

After looking at one another, and talking a while among themselves, they replied that they would rather be put aboard some homeward-bound ship; they were strangers to Jamaica; had no idea of what chances there were of getting a ship that way; whereas at Liverpool there was a tidy bit of money for them to take up as wages, and scores of vessels in want of hands.

"But we hope you'll make use of us whilst we're with you, sir," added the fellow who had acted as spokesman. "We're willing to turn to and do any mortal thing we're put to. It worries my mates as much as it do me, sir, to know how to show ourselves grateful ; for merely thanking of you, and calling blessings on you and your party, sir, don't carry the meaning in our hearts half as fur as we want it to go."

"There's no occasion for you to work," answered Sir Mordaunt. "We have plenty of men. As for gratitude, you have already thanked us enough. Your business is to take rest, and recover your strength and spirits."

And so that matter ended, and the poor fellow went forward.

In obedience to Norie's injunctions, it was agreed among all us people aft not again to refer to the wreck before Lady Brookes, nor indeed to speak upon any topic in her presence that was at all likely to capsize her nerves. Norie told me in confidence that the action of her heart was weak, and that a fainting fit might end in death. "I don't want to go into the matter with her husband," said he, "for fear of distressing him ; but we owe it to them both to keep her mind cheerful. And I have told Mrs. Stretton to avoid all reference to her trials as she would poison, though, poor creature ! it's rather too much to expect her to look easy, with her husband drowned a few days ago, and with the memory of ninety-six hours of famine and salt-water scouring to fill up her mind."

"Is this cruise doing Lady Brookes any good, think you ? " I asked.

"Certainly it is," he answered. "But hysterics and swooning have put her back."

"But it was the lightning that sent her into hysterics," said I. "We can't prevent thunder-storms from gathering."

"Why, that's true enough," said he. "But a thunder-storm isn't always happening ; whereas, if I had not put you on your guard, the wreck would find you all in talk for the next fortnight, and every meal would be embellished by allusions to drowned bodies, storm-swept decks, starving men languishing to swallow their own bones, and other light and pleasing topics of that kind."

Nothing particular happened that day. Indeed, it was one of the quietest days we had passed. Lady Brookes kept her cabin, and her husband was nearly the whole time with her. I saw very little of Miss Tuke, very little of the doctor, nothing at all of Mrs. Stretton. After the thunder-storm, and the strong wind, and the excitement of the wreck, the calm weather fell like a pause upon us all ; and when we met at meals, I noticed an unusual gravity of manner in Sir Mordaunt and his wife and Miss Tuke, so much so that the meals that day were the dullest we had set down to : even Norie seemed to have lost his tongue.

At dinner I asked what arrangements had been made for Mrs.

10

Stretton's accommodation, and was told that she would share Carey's berth, and take her meals with her.

"She said she would rather not join us here," said the baronet, "although I pressed her to give us her company.   This shows a very modest, retiring character.   Yet what pleases her should please us."

However, some time after, Norie told me that he had taken the young widow aside, and begged her to keep as much as possible for the present out of Lady Brookes's sight—to wait until the recollection of the shipwreck should have faded out of her ladyship's mind.   He said that Miss Tuke had told him of the dramatic power with which Mrs. Stretton had related her story, and said he : " You see, Walton, that though she might promise not to talk so graphically again before Lady Brookes, she might forget her vows should the conversation drift toward her sufferings and widowed and destitute condition—for I suppose you know that her husband's death leaves her penniless ! —and it is my duty as medical adviser to protect Lady Brookes against all risks of further ' capsizals,' as you call them."

To all this I made no answer ; but I could not help thinking he bade fair to make a fool of his patient by humoring her gim-crack nerves in this way.

The morning of the fifth day, dating from the rescue of the shipwrecked people, broke in a dead calm.   I came on deck about an hour and a half after the sun had risen, and found the sea like a lake, though heaving softly with a light swell that ran languidly along the path of the sun.   Glancing aft, I saw a female figure standing at the bulwarks, leaning her face on her elbows, and looking into the water.   I believed for the moment that it was Miss Tuke ; but hearing me, she looked round, and then I perceived that it was Mrs. Stretton.

In all those days I had only seen her once, and then I had caught but a glimpse of her down the skylight as she passed through the cabin.   Consequently I was very greatly aston-ished by the change that had been wrought in her appearance. She was no longer the wild, white, haggard woman we had rescued.   Pale indeed she was, but her cheeks had plumped out, her lips were red, the hollows under her eyes had filled up and lost their livid tint.   Her fine black eyes flashed back the sunshine, and were beautifully clear and soft as a gazelle's, with a rich expression of melancholy.   She wore one of Miss Tuke's dresses.   I could not describe it for the life of me ; but though a dressmaker would have given her more room about the bosom, her scissors could not have cut the dress more finely into the waist, and furnished a more free and sweeping in-curving down the back.

Indeed, I was so much surprised by the change, and by this apparition of a picturesquely handsome woman rising up, so to speak, out of the ashes of the deplorable figure we had rescued—shrieking as it was swayed into the air over the boiling water, with its black tresses floating like a burst of smoke from her head upon the gale—that I fairly hung in the wind as she came up to me with both hands extended, and could scarcely answer her cordial greeting, melodized by the Irish accent I have spoken of ; nor am I certain that I didn't blush.

" Why, Mrs. Stretton," said I, "if I had met you ashore in a crowd, I believe I should not have known you."

" Oh, yes, I am recovering my health : I wish I could say my spirits," she answered.

" I hope you are pretty comfortable below ?" said I.

" I meet with nothing but kindness," she replied, looking as if she could cry. " I thank God for finding such friends. I believe my sorrows would have broken my heart had I been thrown among rough people. For, oh, Mr. Walton, I loved my husband ! I miss him so much—so much ! "

I said nothing, for in the face of a sorrow of this kind it is best to be quiet. To give her time to rally, I went to the compass, though there was no use looking at it, for there was not a breath of air, and the swell had swung the schooner with her head to the north ; and then I went to the taffrail, where I had not stood a moment when my eye was attracted by a shark lying close under our counter, motionless as a log of wood, near enough to the surface to allow about an inch of his dorsal fin to fork out through the oil-like blue of the water, and to enable me to see his eyes, which methought he raised with a most languishing expression, as though he said, " If you *would* but oblige me, and tumble overboard, my dear sir ! "

This was a sight, I thought, that should divert the widow's grief. So I called to her : " Mrs. Stretton, pray come and look here. Here's something that should be feminine, for I reckon it twigs my sex, by the way it ogles me."

She came along quietly, and looked over ; but she had barely glanced at it when the creature slowly sank, but without any perceptible motion of the fins or tail, drawing down and fading until it was indistinguishable in the clear, azure, fathomless deep.

" Doesn't that prove what the brute's gender is ? You perceive she vanishes at the sight of a woman," said I, wanting to see a smile upon my companion's face.

But my joke missed fire. Her thoughts were evidently fathoms below me—with the corpse of her husband, I dare say—and I saw a tear drop with the flash of a diamond from her eyes into the sea. Just at that moment one of the mastiffs came up to us, and rubbed her hand with its cold moist snout. She cried out, and recoiled a yard, with as much stately horror as ever I saw in a tragedy actress. Her cheeks were as white as the deck, and her eyes on fire; but instead of laughing when she saw the dog, she put her hands to her face, and her bosom rose and fell vehemently.

"Get away, you brute!" said I, motioning the fine animal forward. "Mrs. Stretton, you are not the only person he has scared by his trick of shaking hands with his nose. That black snout of his once brought me from the stars with a run, and made me whoop like an Indian."

As I said this, a pretty voice behind me exclaimed, "What's the matter, Mr. Walton?"

It was Miss Tuke. I wished her good-morning, and explained that Mrs. Stretton had been frightened by the mastiff.

"He frightened me, indeed," said the poor woman, apologetically; and then asking Miss Tuke what time it was, she said something about Carey waiting for her, and went below.

"You choose an early hour for flirting, Mr. Walton," said Miss Tuke, gravely.

I asked her what she said. She repeated her remark.

"But don't you know," said I, "that I am no longer a sailor; that is, a man who will flirt with anybody? When I am in a flirting mood, I don't choose widows."

"Don't you think her a good-looking widow?" she asked.

"Yes, I do; I think her a handsome woman."

"And considering that you saved her life—" said she, pausing.

I was not displeased. "We were looking at a shark," I answered.

"But she had her hands to her face, and seemed very much agitated when I came on deck."

"Your kind heart is at fault for once," said I. "We had seen a shark. Let me find out if the creature is there still." I peered over the taffrail. "No, he keeps out of sight, afraid that nobody will fall overboard if he shows himself. Well, Miss Tuke, when I saw the shark I called to Mrs. Stretton and she came and looked. The shark faded into the depths, but the widow's imagination followed it, and went beyond it, as I may guess from a tear that fell from her eyes. Her thoughts were with her husband—the drowned body of her husband ; and I have no doubt that her mind's eye was upon the beloved face when the nose of the dog touched her hand. The sensation of that cold nose upon her hand, when her mind was full of her drowned love——"

" Oh, Mr. Walton, you have said enough. I am ashamed of myself. But you know I was joking."

" I hope you were," I answered, rather pointedly.

She blushed a bit, and said, ''Don't you think Mrs. Stretton pretty ?"

"Didn't I say yes just now to that same question ? " I exclaimed, laughing out at her.

" If you had known how handsome she was, would you have been more anxious to save her ? "

I thought it best to answer with a nod, at which she laughed heartily, and said,

" Now I wonder what can have become of the shark ? "

I took another squint over the stern, but there was nothing to be seen of the fish.

"That's where the shark *was*," said I, pointing. "Give him time, and like hope in the human breast, he will rise, being of a hungry nature."

At this juncture arrived Sir Mordaunt. "Another dead calm," said he, sniffling and sniffling, and addressing Tripshore, who had the watch till eight o'clock. Then trotting up to Miss Tuke and me, he wished us good-morning. "D'ye know," said he, " I doubt if we shall get a chance to send our shipwrecked men home. The Atlantic appears to have become a Dead Sea as regards ships. Why do we sight no steamers ? "

"We should be in the track of some of them," I replied. " But we shall stand a better chance of meeting vessels soon, if your skipper's navigation is correct, for the Trades can't be far off."

" My dear Walton," exclaimed Sir Mordaunt, "whenever you have occasion to mention Purchase, you invariably speak as though you had not not an atom of belief in the man's capacity."

" I have never concealed from you that my opinion of him is not a high one," I answered.

" Is it because he commands a yacht ? "

" No, no. Tripshore is a yachtsman, for the matter of that," said I ; " but I think very well of Tripshore as a seaman."

" Why don't you find out what time it is by the sun, as Purchase does, Mr. Walton ? " said Miss Tuke ; " and then you'll be able to tell us if the man understands navigation."

" I don't want Walton to do anything of the kind," exclaimed Sir Mordaunt. " For myself, I have full confidence in Purchase, and I should be very sorry for him to suppose he had given me reason to distrust him as a navigator, which would certainly be his impression, Walton, if he saw you taking observations. Then again, Ada, if your aunt should see Walton with a sextant in his hand, she would imagine that Purchase did not know his business ; and as she is already prejudiced against the old man, you know well how such a notion as that would worry her. And suppose Purchase, believing us all to have no confidence in him, should throw up his post in a fit of disgust ? There would be a dilemma ! "

" Not if Tripshore would take his place," said I.

" But Tripshore is not a navigator, Walton. He is only an able seaman. He has never passed an examination. I doubt if he could handle a quadrant."

" Well, so far as I am concerned," said I, " pray don't suppose that I want to check Purchase's working. The suggestion was Miss Tuke's, not mine. It's over ten years since I took an observation, and I am not at all anxious to begin again."

Suddenly Miss Tuke, who was looking over the stern, called out, " Mr. Walton, here is your shark."

. And there, sure enough, was the ugly brute, close under the surface of the water, this time exhibiting the barb of his tail as well as nearly the whole of his top fin.

" A shark is one of the conventional interests of the deep," said I, as we all three stood looking. whilst the fellow at the wheel stepped aft by an arm's-length from the spokes to look too. " No voyage is complete without a shark."

" We ought to kill him," said Sir Mordaunt ; " but we don't want him on deck. Our ship's not big enough for that fellow to dance upon."

" And they makes a great mess, sir," said the man at the wheel. " Ye've got to chop 'em into little bits, to kill 'em ; and they're full o' blood."

" Oh, we're bound to kill him ! " I exclaimed. " It's a duty we owe to our fellow-creatures. Is there such a thing as a shark hook on board ? "

"There are two or three in the forecastle, sir," answered the man.

"Suppose we hook him, Sir Mordaunt, and belay the line with his head out of water, and a bowline round him as a preventer guy? He'll then make a good target, and there are guns enough below."

"Let us wait until after breakfast," he answered. "The shark is evidently in no hurry to be off, and by that time my wife will be able to tell us whether the discharge of fire-arms will annoy her or not."

Soon after this we went to breakfast; but whilst we were waiting for Lady Brookes, Carey came to say that her mistress did not feel well enough to join us.

"Did I apologize to you, Mr. Walton, for having doubted that there was a shark under the stern?" said Miss Tuke presently, and when breakfast was fairly under way.

"Neither for that nor for darker suspicions," I answered.

Seeing her uncle looking, she told him how she had gone on deck and found me and Mrs. Stretton alone; and how the poor widow had her hands to her face, and appeared greatly agitated; and how I had said that my companion had been frightened by a shark ("No, no; by one of the mastiffs," I interrupted); "but that," she went on, without changing her face, "when we looked, there was no shark to be seen."

Norie was laughing heartily in his sleeve. Apparently he took it that it was my turn now. It was certainly not hard to see that he relished this new idea of Miss Tuke.

"But the shark has re-appeared, Sir Mordaunt," said I, "to prove my story true."

"Do you mean to say, Walton," exclaimed Norie, with a sly roll of his eyes toward Miss Tuke, "that Mrs. Stretton—a sailor's wife, bear that in mind—was agitated even into burying her face in her hands by the sight of a shark?"

I answered by once more explaining that the poor woman had hung over the side in a brown-study, thinking of her husband, no doubt, whose body floated in the deep, as they all knew, and not very many miles away, and that the cold nose of the dog touching her hand had given her a great fright. "And that's just the story," said I, with an emphatic nod at the doctor. The foolish creature smiled, and shook his head. He would not let me off, at least before Miss Tuke.

"It's hardly a subject for a joke," said Sir Mordaunt. "To me it is a wonderful thing that the poor woman bears up as she does.   To be starved, and knocked about and drenched **day** and night by roaring seas for some days, is bad en**ough**; but when you add the death of a husband to such an experience, it must be crushing."

"We have done our best to comfort and cheer her, uncle," said Miss Tuke.

"Yes, my dear, I know that.   You have been very kind and good to her," he replied.

"It is a pity that she will not join our party here," said I, rather spitefully, and looking at Norie.   "She is a very well-spoken woman, and it's a treat to hear her voice.   But privacy is the privilege of even good-looking mourners, and we are no doubt right to respect and uphold it !"

"She is too graphic," said Norie ; "and we have a very cherished patient to remember."

"Yes, we must think of that, Walton," exclaimed Sir Mordaunt.   "Norie showed great discretion in advising Mrs. Stretton to keep herself retired for a while.   Should grief master her in the course of a conversation, she might make my wife faint again, and the object of our cruise ought not to be defeated if we can help it."

Here I thought of the shark, and seeing the shadow of old Purchase upon the skylight, I asked the baronet to hail him and ascertain if the fish was still astern.   This was done, and the answer (delivered in a voice that seemed to come out of the middle of a feather-bed) said that the shark remained in sight.

Before we left the table Sir Mordaunt went to his wife, to tell her, I suppose, that we meant to shoot a shark, and that she was not to be frightened by the report of fire-arms.   Apparently she did not object, for the steward was told to follow us on deck with some of the guns out of the rack.   We bundled up the companion steps, and I immediately ran aft, and looking over, saw the shark sure enough.   A light draught of air had come up whilst we sat at breakfast, and the schooner was breathlessly creeping along over the transparent sheet of azure that looked like liquid blue glass.   The shark, however, maintained a distance from us that he never shifted by the breath of a hair, though I could not detect any movement in his body.   He was fully twelve feet long, and with his huge shovel-nose, and hump-like fin, and tremorless iron-skinned and most powerfully built body, looked as treacherous, malignant, and deadly a brute as any man would delight to slaughter.

"See how he follows us, Walton !" shouted Sir Mordaunt.

"How the dickens does he keep himself moving ? Mind, Ada ! For God's sake, don't lean over the taffrail like that ! Where's the fishing-gear ? Let's kill him or put him to flight—get rid of him somehow. It's abominable to have him hanging dead in our wake, as though he smelled death in the air."

In a few minutes a big shark-hook was brought, the chain hitched to about a dozen fathoms of stout line, and the hook baited with a lump of salt beef.

"Stand by, some of you, with a running bowline when he's gorged the hook," said I, addressing several of the crew who had come aft to give us a hand ; and so saying, I threw the great baited hook overboard. '

Our taffrail was not very high above the water, and whenever the swell lifted the yacht's bows we were dipped into very unpleasantly close quarters with the shark, who ogled us all in turn, as though his palate could detect no difference between such a delicacy as a hairy seaman with a face like leather and the soft and delicate Miss Tuke. It gave one a strange sensation in the midriff to meet that evil cannibal eye, and to reflect with what horrible celerity and fiendish absence of all compunctious visitings the owner of it would accommodate the biggest man among us with a free passage in his enormous hold.

The moment, however, the bait splashed in the water, the brute dropped astern two or three fathoms, as if affronted by so poor a mouthful when we had it in our power to oblige him with dainties so very much more nourishing and filling. Yet to a hungry shark even a lump of salt meat is better than nothing ; though I could not help fancying that the beast divined our little game, or already had earned some experience of baited hooks, to judge from the manner in which he approached and smelled at the beef, and then recoiled from it, before making up his mind to bolt it.

I gave the hook another fathom of line, and this veering the bait nearer to the shark, overcame his last lingering scruple. With a sweep of the tail that filled the water with bubbles and eddies astern of him, he rushed at the bait, turned over, and his pale blue belly flashed under the glass-clear surface. The next instant he had bolted the beef and was making off with it. But I had already taken a turn with the line over a belaying-pin, and the rope instantly tautened upon the monster, and swept his huge shovel nose round after us.

"Tail on here, men !" I shouted. "Haul him along, and make ready with the bowline."

The scene then became uncommonly fine—five of us sweating and hauling upon the line at one end, and the shark furiously resisting us at the other. This was by no means my first shark, but none that I can remember ever showed the activity of this fellow. He gave us as much sport as a small whale would with a harpoon in its back. At one moment he would be on the surface, with his square nose hove out of the water, lashing up the foam as though a whirlwind were playing around him ; then he would dive with such tremendous force that the whole five of us were swayed aft as though a locomotive had got hold of the line.

We were all laughing and bawling and blowing and hauling, and raising a mighty hullabaloo over this business, when I saw one of the mastiffs spring on to the taffrail and look at the shark. His eyes were on fire, his black jaws were quivering with excitement.

"Mind the dog ! he'll be after the shark !" I shouted. But before the words were well out of my mouth, the noble animal gathering himself together, launched into the air ; and scarcely had the plash of his body reached our ears, when the other mastiff, rushing past us like a flash of light, cleared the taffrail at a bound, and there were both dogs in the water, making for the shark.

Sir Mordaunt greatly prized these dogs, which were indeed noble and valuable animals, and instantly sang out :

"Get the boat over ! Never mind the shark ! Save the dogs, men !"

"Put your helm down, man !" I shouted to the fellow at the wheel. "Stop the schooner's way ! Don't you see we are going faster than those dogs can swim !"

Old Purchase, who had held aloof while we were playing the shark, now came sprawling over to the starboard quarter-boat, vociferating at the top of his voice, and greatly increasing the confusion. Meanwhile, and before the men had let go the line, I had thrown it over a belaying-pin, and was holding on to it, balancing myself so to speak, against the weight of the shark, when, as I was eagerly looking at the dogs, which were now astern of the shark, that had been towed past them by the motion of the yacht, the line gave to my weight, and I fell flat on my back, the line heaping itself on my face and breast by the force of the involuntary jerk I gave it.

"The shark's off ! The hook has carried away !" I roared. "Look out now, or the fish will have the dogs !"

"The shovel nose of the shark overlapped the tawny hide."—
Page 155.

In hot haste I scrambled on to my feet, and rushed to the taffrail. The schooner having come round to the wind, had brought the dogs abeam, and they were swimming around and around, about fifty yards distant from us, apparently in search of the shark, that had disappeared. Sir Mordaunt stood whistling to them with all his might, but whether because their blood was up, and they wanted to fight the strange beast they had seen us struggling with, or because they enjoyed their bath too much to be in a hurry to come out, they showed no disposition to obey their master's summons.

All this while the men were bothering over the boat. Something was foul, and Purchase's noisy bawling and showing off did not help the fellows. There were enough seamen for that job, and I did not offer to help, but stood looking and looking, wondering where the shark was, and if he had made off for good, and if there were others about. Just as the boat splashed into the water, I caught sight of a black fin sticking out of the varnished blue, about a pistol-shot from the dogs. One of them had seen it, and was making for it. I involuntarily tossed my hands up, shouting :

" See, Sir Mordaunt, there's the shark ! If your men are not quick, he'll have that dog."

The baronet rushed to the side where the boat lay, and literally yelled to the men to make haste, stamping on the deck, and pointing, with a perfect frenzy of impotent anxiety.

But it was too late. In the eagerness of the noble animal to come at its foe, it was swimming so vigorously that its head was high out of water, and now and again it uttered a short savage bark. But on a sudden the fin disappeared, and I could distinctly see the great fish sink by the length of a man's body below the surface. With a quick swing of the long tail the monster darted forward, its belly glistened as it came uppermost, and the dog, baffled by the sudden vanishing of the black fin, had turned its head toward us, when its body darted up out of the water as though it made a spring, the shovel nose of the shark overlapped the tawny hide, one terrific squeak came from the poor beast, with a most agonizing note ringing through it, and then fish and dog disappeared, leaving a great stain of blood-colored foam upon the water.

Miss Tuke shrieked out, and Sir Mordaunt stood as white as death. By this time the boat had got away, and a few strokes of the oars brought it abreast of the other dog, which was immediately collared and dragged over the side ; and when pres-

ently the animal was handed up on deck it was trembling as
never did I see a dog tremble before.   It did not offer to shake
its wet coat, but crouched, all streaming, under the after-grating.
   This incident depressed us greatly.   We stood looking in
silence at the crimson patch upon the water that staid in one
compact stain like oil, whilst the men hoisted the boat, and the
vessel's head was put round to her course.
   "We'll say nothing about this to my wife," said Sir Mordaunt, addressing us all generally.
   "Certainly not," answered Norie.
   "If she asks where the dog is, of course we must tell her
it fell overboard," continued Sir Mordaunt.   "But not a word
about the shark. "
   "Not a word," said I.   "Do you see anything of the shark,
Miss Tuke?   I would give something to avenge the poor animal. "
   We all peered, but sharkee had found as huge a meal as he
could manage in the big dog, and had made sail.   I hauled in
the end of the line, and found that one of the links of the chain
had parted, yet it had looked a very strong chain, and stout
enough to have swung three such fish aboard all at once.
   "Anyhow, he has got the hook in his inside, Sir Mordaunt,"
said I ; "and I am much mistaken if that's not a pill that will
presently stop any more cabbaging on his part."
   This, however, was no consolation to the baronet, who was
greatly distressed and vexed by the loss of the dog.   He called
to the steward to carry the guns below, and getting under the
awning, lighted a cigar, and smoked with a very moody face.
   "Adventures are crowding rather more thickly than we want,
Miss Tuke, don't you think?" I asked.   "We shall not be able
to say that our cruise lacked incident."
   "I wish I hadn't seen the dog killed," she exclaimed, with
the horror of the thing in the expression of her eyes.   "I shall
never forget it, nor the poor creature's scream."
   "Do you want any more adventures?"
   "Not I.   Another such a one would set me crying to be
home."
   "After such a tragedy as that water-logged bark was the
theater of," said I, "the death of the dog makes but a poor
business.   If you are going to find a long memory in what has
just occurred, what sort of memory, think you, will yonder
men"—and I pointed to the three seamen who were in the
bows of the schooner—"and the poor woman below preserve?"

"Don't put my imagination on the rack, Mr. Walton," she answered. "You will make me hate the sea as much as I thought I loved it."

"Oh, pray don't do that thing, because if you make yourself hate the sea, you know you may follow it up by hating sailors."

"There is no fear of that," she answered, archly, and smiling in my face.

This admission was made exceedingly agreeable to me by the manner in which it was said. Looking round, and seeing Norie on the skylight sucking at a cigar, and watching us, I could not forbear smiling; but she was as grave again as a nun at her prayers, gazing at the sea, and evidently in no mood for a light chat. So I placed a chair for her near her uncle, and fetched her some books; and then fixing an easy-chair in a spot where the light air that was keeping the main-sail quiet breezed down softly under the awning, I lighted a pipe, stretched my legs, and gave myself up to a spell of indolence and honeydew tobacco. My position enabled me to command the deck, and Miss Tuke in particular I had very plainly in my sight. I thought she looked prettier this morning than I had seen her before; but then, to be sure, it was always my impression every time I saw her. No girl's face that I can remember meeting so regularly improved on acquaintance as Miss Tuke's. Then, again, all her postures and movements were bewitchingly lady-like. I glanced from her to her uncle, and then I had a short spell of thinking about him.

It was not perhaps very easy to feel sorry for my warm-hearted, hospitable friend, when I looked round upon his beautiful vessel, and thought of the wealth that enabled him to possess and mantain such a luxury, and when I likewise remembered that his health was equal to the enjoyment of all the pleasures his fortune could command. And yet I could not think of his wife, and believe that he was a happy man. He certainly did not look so now. I had never seen him more dejected, which made me think he was mixing up some foolish fears and fancies with the destruction of his dog.

On the other side of the skylight sat Norie, lazily surveying Miss Tuke, whose back was turned toward him, and occasionally glancing at me with his black, monk-like eyes, which looked as dusky as an Indian's in the shadow of his wide straw hat. From him my eyes went to old Purchase, who had been stumping this side of the deck until I located myself upon it, when he immediately changed sides to get away from me. The old fool hated me, and was jealous of me, and I don't say I hadn't given him cause. Sweltering as was the day, he was dressed in thick pilot-cloth, and it was difficult to look at his sour and wrinkled face, and the dim eyes he cast sometimes upon the sea and sometimes upon the sails, without laughing.

The men had spread a short awning over the forecastle and were seated under it, busy on various small jobs : but where the decks were unshadowed the air was quivering with the heat that struck up from the planks, between which the pitch was bubbling : and the foremast and standing-rigging trembled and waved in the haze, and seemed to be winding round and round like revolving screws. There was enough wind to keep the sea flashing, and most beautiful was the effect of the diamond-like scintillation upon the soft deep blue of the water. The sky was cloudless, but the rich azure of the zenith lightened as it drew toward the horizon, until it was nearly as pale as silver where it met the deep ; and in the fiery hot air the ocean boundary waved as though a mountainous swell were rolling around.

Suddenly the fellow who was steering called to Purchase. I turned, and saw him pointing over the starboard bow of the schooner ; and getting up to look, I immediately perceived the smoke of a steamer, but very faint, and like the bluish thread of a spider, leaning into the northern sky.

I went over to Sir Mordaunt, and startled him out of a deep reverie by exclaiming that yonder was a steamer apparently coming our way. He jumped up, and was full of life in a moment.

"If that be so, Walton," said he, "we may be able to send the rescued men home."

This was my thought too. I fetched the glass and looked at the smoke, that presented a curious effect, owing to the refraction on the horizon, that threw the point whence the smoke issued above the water. There was nothing as yet to be seen of the vessel, but by the inclination of the smoke, and its steadiness, I could not doubt that the steamer was heading our way. I continued watching for her about ten minutes, at the expiration of which time I could make out, with the help of the telescope, that was a very powerful one, the projection of a mast and square yards above the horizon ; and soon after the whole hull drew up, though to the naked eye she was a mere speck upon the very verge of the mighty surface of blue sea, upon which the sunshine gleamed and faded with the sinking and rising of the light swell, like the fluctuating luster in a moving sheet of shot silk.

It was now seen that she was heading dead for us, and Sir Mordaunt sent his niece below to tell Lady Brookes that a steamer was coming our way.

"How shall we convey our wishes to her?" said he to me.

"Purchase should know," said I.

"Purchase!" he called.   "I want that steamer stopped, that we may ask her captain's permission to send the three men to her—that, is if she is going home.   How shall we stop her!"

"How shall we stop her, sir?" wheezed the old fellow, giving me a piratical glance, as if he guessed there was some trick of mine in that question.   "Why, it's a case of distress: so half-mast the ensign, jack down."

It was plain from this that the man knew nothing about ships' signals, for he should have flown colors signifying "I wish to communicate."   But as a coalman, he probably had handled no other bunting in his life than his old ensign.

I ventured to suggest that the half-masted ensign with the jack down was a very extreme signal to display, and would make them believe our vessel in imminent danger.

"If you know better than me, Mr. Walton, perhaps you'll tell Sir Mordaunt what *your* idea of signaling is," exclaimed the old man, stormily.

"Pray please yourself," I replied, preserving my gravity with an effort.

He began to address Sir Mordaunt, who cut him short by saying, "Hoist what you choose, Purchase; hoist what you choose, man : only see that you stop the steamer."

"I take my orders from *you*, sir," replied Purchase, with angry emphasis; and forthwith bundled aft, and with great ostentation of gesture bent on the ensign and hoisted it, union down and half-mast high, making us appear in a terrible plight indeed. I nearly suffocated with laughter whilst watching his face as he gazed up at the mast-head and shook a turn out of flag halyards.   If Sir Mordaunt had been capable of anger, I believe he would have been sharp upon me then : but his gentle disposition would never let him go beyond a remonstrance.

"My dear Walton, pray don't quiz the old man," said he. "He may have forgotten the art of signaling by flags."

"But couldn't he look into the signal-book to see what he should do?" I replied.   "Suppose *me* ignorant, my ignorance goes for nothing. But *his* ignorance is ominous, even in so small a matter as bunting. "

"Don't be afraid of him," said he, smiling. "I'll warrant you that he carries us home safe enough. "

"Let us say nothing about that, Sir Mordaunt, for here's your wife. "

He hastened to meet her and get her a chair, and in a trice was busy about her, pointing out the ship, adjusting a cushion to her back, and so on.

Miss Tuke came to me, and said in a whisper: "Do you remember, when the shark seized the poor dog, that I screamed? Well, my aunt heard that scream, and asked what it meant. I told her that one of the dogs jumped overboard for a swim, and that it had frightened me. I wish her health did not make these fibs necessary. But having told her this, I repeat it to you, that the fiction may be maintained."

"I am afraid among you all that you are spoiling your aunt," said I.

"It's Uncle Mordaunt's wish," says she, quickly.

"Well, then, *he's* spoiling her. If I had a nervous wife, I'd humor her nerves, I believe, but my humoring should be an education, too. A poor shipwrecked widow, like the woman below, should not scare her, and she should be able to see a shark eat a dog with just as much sensibility as you showed, and no more."

"That puzzles me rather, but it doesn't matter," said she. "At all events, I am sure you mean to compliment me. But you will remember that I am not an invalid, and I see that you still think of the poor widow."

I laughed outright, whereupon up marches Norie.

"What's all the fun about, Walton ? "

"Don't be suspicious ; we weren't talking about you," said I.

"Aren't you haunted by that poor brute of a dog ? " cried he. "You were the cause of his death. You *would* fish for that shark, and by hooking him you excited the poor animal, and made him jump overboard."

"Hush, pray ! " exclaimed Miss Tuke, with a glance at her aunt.

He made a hideous grimace. " Heaven preserve me ! I had clean forgot. Why, what a monstrous ship is that yonder ! What is she ? A man-of-war ? "

She was approaching us very fast. Her hull was green and red, with a profusion of gilt that looked like gold-lace upon her

bow. She was brig-rigged, with raking masts, and a square
yellow funnel leaning aft, and apparently not far short of three
thousand tons burden. She looked to be aiming straight for
us, and the heavy sheer of her iron bows made her resemble a
small island coming along. Two sparkling columns of water
spouted up at an angle from each side of her stem, and their
summits rose to close under the hawse-pipes, but as they
arched over they broke into foam, and girdled the dark red bottom of the speeding hull with a band of snow, the ends of
which met under her counter, and streamed away in a glittering milk-white line across the blue sea until the eye lost sight
of the delicate trail in the far distance.

When she was about a mile off, her people hoisted English
colors, and slowed the engines, as you could have seen by the
drooping of the two shining bow waves, like the gradual turning down of a fountain. I have no doubt the sight of our flag
made them reckon upon coming across something tragical ; and
through the glass I could make out swarms of heads along the
line of bulwarks watching us.

"Stand by to hail her, Purchase," exclaimed Sir Mordaunt ; and
we all gathered together in a cluster abaft the main-rigging to
see her, whilst our men bustled about, letting go and tricing up,
and dowsing canvas, that we might not swim out of earshot.

Now that we knew by her flag she was English, and took it,
of course, that she was going home, we looked at her with an
interest which, if you have crossed the ocean and been for days
without speaking a vessel, you will sympathize with. She
made the picture of home rise before us vividly—the English
Channel, with its beautiful shores ; the yachts whitening the
offing round the Isle of Wight ; the crowded Downs, with low-
lying Deal sparkling beyond the glittering shingle ; the noble,
busy Thames, and the garden-like lands beyond its banks. A
group of men were upon her high skeleton bridge, and one
stood at the extreme end of it, waiting to hail us when near
enough. Presently the turn of her wheel by a couple of spokes
canted her head, and she drew out slowly (her engines being
stopped), and we watched with admiration as she floated abreast
of us the gradual unfolding of her immense length, and the beauty
of the whole picture of her red bottom coloring the blue water
under her, and her green sides full of flashing windows and
her massive stem standing up and overlooking the sea like a
sheer cliff, whilst a trickle of gray smoke floated languidly
toward the sky out of her short leaning funnel, and her rigging

11

veined the heavens like a spider's web. Her poop was of middling length, protected by a very low bulwark surmounted by brass stanchions and white life-lines, so that we could clearly perceive the crowd of saloon passengers, seated or standing, and watching us from under the awning. There were a great many women, dressed in all manner of gay colors, and Miss Tuke hit the character of the picture neatly when she said to me that those people looked like a garden party out on a cruise. Binocular glasses and telescopes bristled at us from all parts of the vessel. I could well imagine the wonderment excited by the inverted and half-masted ensign aboard a yacht with a crowd of smartly dressed seaman in her bows, well-dressed people aft, and the whole apparently coming up to a high standard of safety, luxury, and equipment.

"Schooner ahoy !" came ringing from the steamer.

"Hillo !" bawled Purchase.

"Why have you that distress signal flying ?"

"We've three shipwrecked men aboard that we took off a water-logged bark," vociferated Purchase ; "and if you're bound for Hengland, will'ee let us send 'em aboard you ? "

There was a curious movement among the people on the poop at this, and the man who had hailed us stumped along the bridge to where the knot of men were. I could not help thinking that the information they had got was a disappointment to many of them. A good deal of excitement had been promised by our flag, and Purchase's statement was no better than an anti-climax. Presently the man returned to the end of the bridge, and sang out, "We'll send a boat ; " and after a short delay a boat swept round under the stern of the huge vessel, in charge of one of the mates—an individual in a long coat with gilt buttons, and a square-peaked cap. A short ladder was thrown over the side, the boat hooked on, and the mate stepped aboard. He raised his cap very politely, and glanced round him with much curiosity, and then took a squint at the ensign, as if he could not reconcile that flag with the small business that had caused its display.

"I am glad that nothing is the matter with you," said he, addressing Sir Mordaunt, at once guessing him to be the owner.

"We hardly knew what to expect when we saw that signal. "

"You are bound to England, I presume, " said Sir Mordaunt.

"We are sir,—to Glasgow, from New Orleans."

"That's a bit out of the men's track," said I to the baronet.

"Why, no," he replied ; "not if I give them the means to

get across to Liverpool. Would your captain take the poor fellows?" said he addressing the mate.

"Certainly," was the reply. "I shall have to trouble you for the particulars of the rescue. Which are the men?"

They were called, and came aft. Dressed in the clothes lent them by the yacht's crew, and having quite recovered their health, they looked very tidy, likely seamen.

"This gentleman," said Sir Mordaunt to them, "tells me that the captain of yonder steamship is willing to give you a passage to Glasgow. I know that the port you want to get to is Liverpool; but as you are anxious to get home, here is a chance you should not miss; and if I give this gentleman sufficient funds to pay for your journey from Glasgow to Liverpool, your being landed at Glasgow won't make any difference to you."

"We can only say, Thank you, and God bless you, sir!" answered one of them.

"You still have the clothes you wore when you were rescued?" continued Sir Mordaunt.

"Yes, sir."

"Well, you will keep those you have on, and the two suits will serve you as a kit. I'll make it right with the owners of those clothes."

The poor fellows tried to thank him again, but the words stuck in their throats.

"Bear a hand now, and get your bundles into the boat," said the mate; and they skurried forward, whilst the mate went into the cabin with Sir Mordaunt to take wine, and look at the entry in the log-book relating to the wreck.

In a very short time the three men were ready, and I saw them, as they said good-by to the *Lady Maud's* men, fling down their bundles and grasp each other's hands. Indeed, I never saw gratitude more movingly expressed than in the postures and motions of these poor sailors. They came to the gangway where I was standing, and one of them said, "We should like to say good-by to Mrs. Stretton, sir."

"To be sure," I answered, and went to the skylight, where I called to the steward to ask Mrs. Stretton to step on deck. She came immediately after Sir Mordaunt and the mate had arrived, and the three men, pulling off their caps, went up to her and held out their hands, one after another. I did not hear them speak; I believe nothing was said; it was merely a rough, pathetic seaman's grasp of the hand on their part. The memory of their long anguish, their drowned shipmates, all those horrors of famine and thirst, with Death the skeleton sitting among them on that water-swept deck, would well account for their parting in silence.   I had my eye on the widow's face as she shook hands with the first man.   It was firm, and she looked at him steadily ; but she broke down suddenly when she took the second man's hand, and dropped her face, unable to look at him ; and when the third man took her hand she was crying piteously.   Miss Tuke put her arm through hers, and led her away to the after end of the deck ; and I was glad to see her go, for it was painful that such grief as hers should be watched by so many eyes, though God knows there was no want of sympathy for her.

The men then bade us farewell.   Sir Mordaunt gave them his hand, and one of them held it as though he could not make up his mind to release it.   '' Good-by, mum !   God bless you, mum ! '' said they to Lady Brookes.

"Now my lads, jump into the boat," exclaimed the mate. '' But first let me tell you that this gentleman," indicating the baronet, '' has given me ten pounds for my captain to hold for you ;'' and then, as if he feared this would excite another demonstration of gratitude and cause more delay, he sung out : '' In with you, boys !   Chuck your bundles down."

The men dropped over the side, the mate, bowing to us all, followed, and as the boat shoved off, the three men stood up and cheered us.   In a very little while they disappeared under the stern of the great steamship, and shortly after the monster began to forge ahead.

It was a brave sight to see that huge and powerful fabric— that had lain motionless upon the swell which kept the yacht's masts swaying like a band-master's *baton*—divide the water under the hidden propulsion of her screw.   The trembling light under her quivered in her glossy sides, and the glass of her scuttles flashed and faded as her head came round to the north and east.   A great body of black smoke burst suddenly out of her low fat funnel, and the first belch of it shot up like a balloon ; but the breeze was too light to incline the dark and gleaming pillar until it had reached a certain height, when it yielded to a pressure of the current up there, and leaned over into a most graceful curl, which, as it blew further and further towards the horizon, looked like a gigantic bridge arching the blue water, whose surface mirrored the league of sooty coil in a straight dark brown line, that might very well have passed in the distance for a shoal of mud.

But though she made a fine show, yet she was sadly wanting in all those points of beauty which a sailing vessel offers. The pyramid of shining canvas, the stately leaning of the tapering masts, the swelling curves of the jibs, the lovely graduation of shadow and light upon the rounded cloths, and the sharp clear lining of the delicate rigging upon them, were all lacking. Strength, even in its most majestic form, was expressed by that mighty red and green hull heaping the sparkling blue water at her side, and a torrent of snow pouring away from under her elliptical stern, that was radiant with gilt configurations ; but there was no gracefulness. The eye had to seek the *Lady Maud* for that. And a beautiful sight she was, I make no doubt, for the passengers aboard that great receding steamer to watch. For as soon as the boat had gone clear of us, sail had been made, and such air as there was being abeam, every stitch of square canvas, and the studding-sails to boot, were piled upon the little vessel, until she must have looked like a big white cloud upon the sea. Soon the tinkling and churning of water alongside told us that the *Lady Maud* was contributing something to the rapidly increasing interval that now separated the two vessels. In three-quarters of an hour the great ocean steamship was no bigger than a nutshell upon the horizon, and when we went to lunch, nothing was to be seen of her but a smudge of smoke hovering over the spot where she had vanished.

CHAPTER X.

UNTIL the morning of the —— of July, that day making it over five weeks since we had sailed from Southampton, nothing happened that is worth recording. But on that morning the *Lady Maud*, being then under a mainsail, foresail and two jibs, the wind to the northward of east, and fresh, a squall blew up, and, half an hour after, a heavy gale of wind had stripped us of every fragment of canvas, saving the close-reefed foresail ; but the wind increasing in fury, this had to be furled, and we lay breasting the monstrous seas under bare poles, our topmasts struck, and the yards on deck.

Taking it altogether, the gale was as fierce a one of its kind as ever I can remember ; never indeed, approaching the force of a cyclone, though at midnight it came very near to being a hurricane. For hours and hours the ocean was like wool, and the sky like ink.   The heavy seas which rolled up carried the yacht bodily away to the westward, and I reckoned that the average drift of the vessel was not less than one and three-quarter nautical miles an hour for hard upon seventy-two hours of storm.

The gale blew for three days, and they were the worst three days that ever I had passed. The *Lady Maud*, though a powerful boat, and large for her class, was but a small craft to fight such sea as then ran ; nor did she make the weather we might have hoped from her beam and sheer. There were times when her plunges left nothing of her visible but her after, deck down to a few feet before the mainmast ; she looked to be smothered in a boiling caldron ; and one of those seas tore up the whole length of starboard hen-coops, and shot the fragments over-board like a flight of arrows, and robbed us of two dozens of fine poultry.

Our condition below was truly pitiable. It was the worst part of the storm. The gale was like a sirocco for the temperature of it, and the cabin, with the skylight closed and the companion shut to prevent the water from washing down, was hot enough to bake a joint in. But add to this intolerable atmosphere the frightful pitching, the sensation of being shot into the air with terrific force and velocity, and then falling with such headlong, sickeningly swift descent as to make you hold your breath with the belief that the hull would split open as it crashed into the deafening hollow, whilst the whole fabric rang with the howling and roaring of the tormented seas outside, and the ringing of the furious blast along the dark sky ; and every now and again there would be a deadly pause in the yacht's motion after one of her wild plunges, as if the sea she had shipped over her bows, and that had washed aft in a tempest of foam, had proved too much for her, and she was going down. Add this, I say !

No skill, no experience, was of any avail at a time like this.

The yacht lay to under bare poles, and the helm lashed, and whoever happened to be on deck to watch her stood right aft, for the seas which swept the forecastle made that part of the vessel as perilous as a raft, and no man could have staid there without being lashed ; nay, even then, he would have stood the chance of being drowned by the perpetual flying of water over him.

But our miserable condition below was lamentably aggravated by Lady Brookes's agony of apprehension. I believe, had the gale lasted another day, she would have died outright of fright. No food that I heard of passed her lips. She lay upon her swinging bed, moaning and screaming, until the power of making those noises failed her. At one period, indeed, her mind grew deranged, for I afterward learned that she had charged her husband with bringing her on this voyage merely to kill her, and stormed and raved at him until he ran in a state of distraction from her cabin.

His distress was truly deplorable. Between the horror of the gale on the one hand, and the alarming state of his wife on the other, he lost all nerve. I remember on one of those evenings being alone in the cabin, listening to the terrifying and thrilling bursting of the seas against the groaning, struggling, staggering hull, and very gravely doubting whether any of us would ever see the sun rise again, when Sir Mordaunt came through the door that led to the sleeping-berths, and passing his arm round an iron stanchion, stood looking at me without speaking a word, and his face as white as death. There was an expression of horror in his eyes which made them singularly brilliant and affecting to see, and I then took notice that he appeared to have aged by at least ten years since the morning.

"Come, come," I exclaimed, encouragingly, "let us keep up our hearts, if only for the sake of the women. You know Jack's old saying, 'While she creaks she holds.'"

"That may be," he replied, in a wild manner ; " but oh, Walton, it's killing my wife ! it's killing her ! it's killing her !" he repeated.

As I had not seen her, she having kept her cabin from the first hour of the gale, I could not offer an opinion ; but had she been anybody else but his wife, I believe I should have told him that a woman who could make such a hullabaloo as she had raised was not a person to die off in a hurry.

"Oh, Walton," he continued, "it's a dreadful blow to have my cherished hopes defeated in this way. I brought her against her will, and yet God knows I acted as I thought for the best. Even should this miserable gale leave us alive, it will have upset all the good she has derived from the cruise."

"I should strongly recommend you," said I, "to abandon all thoughts of returning home in the *Lady Maud*. Your wisest course will be to land your wife at Kingston, and accompany her to England in one of the mail-steamers. It is quite clear that Lady Brookes's nerves will not suffer her to receive any benefit from the sea."

"And can you be surprised?" he cried. "Feel this, now!" and, as he spoke, the yacht seemed to jump clean out of the water, reeling in her somersault until the edge of the swinging trays touched the upper deck, and I, from the port side of the cabin, looked down at Sir Mordaunt as though my head was out of window, and I was surveying a man on the pavement below. And then came one of those falls which always filled me with dread. The crash of the hull striking the water was as heart-shaking as the explosion of a great piece of ordnance, and the thunder of the near surges roared like the echo of the report. The deadly pause followed ; you could have heard the foam upon the deck seething and hissing to the very doors of the companion, and presently, when the brave little vessel lifted again, my face was wet with sweat. Ay, call me what name you please, my fine fellow ; but had you sat in that stifling cabin, and felt that prodigious heave and fall, and waited through that frightful pause to see if she would lift again, you must have a stronger head and heart than I, not to have perspired at every pore as I did.

It was impossible to go on talking. Even the few sentences we had exchanged had to be shouted, so wild and mixed were the sounds in the cabin. Norie lay sick and stupefied in his bunk ; he had been there since the preceding day. Miss Tuke and Mrs Stretton were with Lady Brookes. The widow, I had heard from Sir Mordaunt, had been unremitting in her attentions to her ladyship, and Miss Tuke had borne herself` with great courage. Indeed those two women were the real heroines of that gale; we men made but poor figures by comparison.

But to cut this part of my log short, the gale left us at noon on a day that made three days of furious storm. The wind fined down with astonishing rapidity. It seemed, indeed, to drop completely and at once. I went on deck to look about me, and stood transfixed and absolutely awed by the appearance of the swell. The height and power of the liquid mountains pass all power of description in words. The monstrous acclivities took their color from the sky, and wore the appearance of molten lead. They poured their gigantic folds along without a break of foam to relieve the livid, heaving, unnatural aspect ; and such was the rolling of the yacht, that with every dip of her gunwales she seemed to lay her masts along the water, and it was as much as a man's life was worth for him to let go his hold.

Figure such a sea, without a breath of air to ruffle the gigantic oil-smooth coils! The small rise in the glass did not encourage me to believe that we were going to have it all our own way yet. Clinging to the companion, I gazed around me to see what damage the gale had done us. Forward I could trace no mischief beyond the loss of the hen-coops; but, on looking at the davits, I saw that the fine quarter-boat with which we had rescued the survivors of the bark's crew had been smashed to pieces—she was no more than a mere skeleton, the stem and stern posts hanging by the tackles. But the long-boat amidships on chocks was safe, though it was strange that she should have escaped the seas which had washed over the bows.

The first to come on deck was Sir Mordaunt. He stood looking around him with the utmost astonishment.

"I can hardly credit my senses!" he exclaimed. "Why, just now it was blowing fit to tear the masts out! Is this only a lull, Walton? It may burst upon us from another quarter in a minute."

"I hope not," said I, " and I hardly think so. Once in my experience—it was in my first voyage—a gale left us as this has done, blew itself clean out, and fell dead. But I remember, that it left a better sky than that," I continued, casting my eye on the sooty stooping pall, and noticing the gradual thickening up of the horizon all round.

"How frightfully the yacht rolls!" he cried. "I hope we may not swing our masts overboard. To be reduced to a sheer hulk would about complete the misery of the last three days."

"No fear of that," I answered, "with those topmasts housed and those preventer backstays set up. Is that your doing, Mr. Tripshore?" I called, pointing to those additional supports to the masts, and addressing the mate, who stood holding on to one of the belaying-pins which girdled the foot of the mainmast.

"Yes, sir," he replied; "and they're all wanted. If there was any chance of this here tumbling lasting, I don't know but what I'd recommend Mr. Purchase to swifter in the rigging. But now the wind's gone, the swell will go too."

"Are we booked for any more bad weather, think you?" asked Sir Mordaunt.

"Well, it's hard to say, sir," said the mate, throwing a look around. "It's drawing on thick; but if any wind comes, it won't come hard whilst that fog hangs."

"Where's Purchase?"

"Below, sir, working out his dead-reckoning."

"We ought to know what he makes it," said I. "We've been blown by a long slant to the westward, and if the last observation he took—four days since, mind—was correct, his course should be to the eastward until he can get sights."

"I'll speak to him," said the baronet. "Tripshore, tell Purchase to come to me the moment he has worked out his reckoning, and request him to bring his chart."

The mate went below.

"Sir Mordaunt," said I, "will you tell me how Lady Brookes does? Is she better to-day?"

"She is not worse, Walton; but you will find her thin, and sadly changed. I have made up my mind to do as you suggested. I'll go home with her in one of the mail-steamers, and Purchase can sail the yacht to England. We will settle the matter later on. Only let this dreadful swell go down. I can hardly collect my thoughts."

He said this at an instant when an unusually heavy mountain of water heeled the yacht over until she lay almost on her beam ends; the spray shot in a fury of smoke through the submerged scupper-holes, and the toppling sea rose above the level of the bulwark rail. Had we let go at that moment, we should have whisked overboard as neatly as a man holding on to the gutter of a roof would drop into the road by relaxing his grasp. The wildness of the tumble appeared to daze the baronet, whose ashen-gray face showed such ravages from the worry, anxiety, and alarm that had possessed him during the storm as I never should have believed the human countenance capable of receiving the imprint of in so short a period.

As I stood looking at him, Mrs. Stretton came up the companion. I helped her up, and gave her a rope's end to hold by. She was very pale, and seemed worn out; her eyes had lost their brilliancy, and she reminded me of the appearance she had presented on the day of her rescue.

" You are wise to come on deck," exclaimed Sir Mordaunt. "I am afraid you have suffered much from your confinement below, and your devoted attention to my wife. Believe me deeply sensible of the sympathy and kindness you have shown her."

" I owe you my life," she replied, simply. " I shall never be able to repay you—nor you, Mr. Walton." And then looking at the sea, she cried, " The wind is gone, and yet in the cabin it feels sometimes as if the yacht were rolling over."

" We have seen the worst of it," said I; " though I should

prefer the sunshine to that mist which is gathering around us. Is Miss Tuke coming up ?"

"No ; as Lady Brookes is asleep, Miss Tuke has gone to lie down," she answered. "What a brave lady she is ! In the worst of the gale she never showed the least fear. Oh, I should tell you, Sir Mordaunt, that before Lady Brookes fell asleep we got her to eat a plate of cold chicken and drink some brandy and water."

"I am glad to hear that ; the food will put some strength into her," exclaimed the poor gentleman, with a little show of cheerfulness in his manner, that to me somehow made his aspect and tones exceedingly pathetic.

"Her ladyship is no longer afraid of you, then," said I, softly, in the widow's ear.

"No ; but Mr. Norie was very wise to keep me banished whilst there was a chance of my frightening her," she replied, whispering. "You can not imagine what a dreadful condition her nerves are in. Her behavior during the gale was like that of a mad-woman. What would have been my sufferings had I been as timid as she when I was with the poor men on the wreck ?" She shuddered, and sighed convulsively, and added : "I am so weary of the sea ! it is so cold, so cruel, so merciless ! Would to God it had spared my poor love to me ! The loss of all that we owned in the world would have been a little matter then."

Here Tripshore came on deck.

"Will Purchase be long ? " called out Sir Mordaunt.

"I don't think so, sir," answered the mate, giving me a queer look, the meaning of which I could not guess.

All this while we lay floundering and wallowing under our lower masts, with not a fragment of canvas showing. Sail was of no use to us until some wind came. An hour's idle beating and flogging upon those shooting, staggering, and swinging spars would have done our canvas more harm than three months of fair wear. The schooner lay broadside to the swell, that now and again depressed her so sharply that the green water poured over the bulwark rail on to the deck, and went washing as high as a man's knees over to the other side with the send of the vessel ; and the jerking and straining of the masts were so violent that it would not have greatly surprised me had the chain-plates drawn, and the lofty sticks gone away overboard.

About twenty minutes after Sir Mordaunt had sent for him,

Purchase emerged, and came clawing and lurching along to where we stood. He had a chart under his arm, and a sheet of paper in one hand. His face was unusually red, his cap was drawn low down over his forehead, and fake upon fake of blue spotted neckcloth coiled round his neck gave him such a strangled look as was disagreeable to see.

" Purchase," said Sir Mordaunt, " I am anxious to know what you make our position. We must have been driven a good many leagues to the westward, and the weather looks very ugly—very ugly yet, Purchase. No sign of the sun, and no promise of a star to-night;" and he stared upward and then around him with a dismal shake of the head.

The old man made no answer to this, but leaning against the skylight so as to balance himself, he opened the chart.

" Here, Mr. Tripshore," he exclaimed, in somewhat thick accents, " come and put your hand upon this chart where it curls up."

This was done, and Sir Mordaunt drew near the skipper, holding tightly by the skylight. I stood on the other side, but the chart was intelligible to me though inverted. Likewise I had a good view of Purchase, who the moment I looked at him close, I could see had been drinking. Sir Mordaunt found this out very soon, no doubt by the smell of the man's breath (for he stood next him). He drew up suddenly and stared at him, and then glanced at me, but said nothing.

" Here's the place where I makes the yacht to be," said Purchase, pressing his square thumb upon the chart. " Ye can read the latitood and longitood," he added, speaking in a greasy, neutral, low-comedian sort of voice, and surveying me with his small wandering eyes.

" What do you make it ? " demanded Sir Mordaunt, with a sternness I had never seen in him before, nor should have believed him capable of.

The old fellow raised the sheet of paper to his face, and after bothering over the figures, answered, " Latitood, twenty-five degrees ten minutes ; longitood, seventy-three degrees five minutes."

" What drift have you allowed for the three days ? " I inquired.

He made no reply.

" Don't you hear Mr. Walton's question ? " cried Sir Mordaunt.

" I've got nothen to do with Mr. Walton, sir," he answered. " You're my master."

The baronet repeated my question.

"About thirty mile," he answered, keeping his thumb stuck upon the chart in the queerest posture, as though he wanted to spin his hand.

"You may add another sixty miles to that, Sir Mordaunt, and then be within the mark," said I.

The old skipper looked at me with wandering eyes and a most evil expression in his face. I waited for him to insult me, when I should have told him he was drunk, and talked to him as I should have known how from my old sea training; but he held his peace, perhaps because he saw my intention.

"Here I see is the Crooked Island Passage," said Sir Mordaunt, after pausing to give Purchase time to answer my objection.

"Bearing south-by-west, half west," said Purchase. "'Tain't my idee to try for that passage, sir. I shall haul away to the east'ard under heasy canvas till the weather clears."

"That's just what you suggested, Walton," said Sir Mordaunt, with a gleam of satisfaction on his face.

Purchase looked at me, and was about to speak, but the yacht dipping heavily, he gave with it, lost his balance, and went rolling like a barrel down against the bulwarks. This was an accident that might easily have befallen him even had he been perfectly sober; but as we all perceived he was partially intoxicated, his tumble was like an emphasis upon his condition, and Sir Mordaunt looked away with an air of great disgust and irritation from the square scrambling figure, as the old noodle got up and lurched toward the skylight, with a purple face shining with perspiration.

Mrs. Stretton whispered: "He is intoxicated, Mr. Walton. He is not in a fit state to talk to Sir Mordaunt, and explain his navigation."

"This is not the first time," I replied, in a low voice. "But Sir Mordaunt will see him with my eyes now, I hope. He is less qualified, in my opinion, to command this vessel than the cook."

"That will do," said the baronet to Purchase. "You can take the chart below again."

"That's what I makes it, sir," replied the man, again reading the sheet of paper, and trying to steady his voice and comport himself as though he would have us see his fall was no evidence of unsteady legs. "Latitood, twenty-five ten; longitood, seventy-three five." And so saying, he rolled up the chart very slowly, and deliberately took a prolonged view of the sea, and watching his chance, sheered over to the starboard bulwarks, and clawed himself abreast of the hatchway, down which he disappeared.

Sir Mordaunt stood near me in moody silence, until Mrs. Stretton, who grew fatigued by her posture, asked me to hand her to the companion. I assisted her to descend the steps, and then returned.

"I am afraid you are right in your views of Purchase," said Sir Mordaunt. "He is again in liquor, and I fear the abominable habit is confirmed. Three times we have detected him, and who knows how often he may have been intoxicated in the night-time, when we were asleep? I am greatly deceived and disappointed. I could not have believed he would misbehave again after the conversation I had with him. But I shall say nothing to him. Let him carry the yacht to Kingston, which I have no doubt he'll be able to manage, and I will hand the vessel over to some agents to send to England. We have all had enough of this cruise. For myself, I can honestly say the last week has cured me of my taste for ocean sailing. Henceforth—if I am spared for any more yachting—I shall never go a mile beyond English waters."

"Well, as you say, the man has navigated us so far, and he may be able to accomplish the rest; and perhaps you are wise in resolving to say nothing to him," said I. "But he is out in his dead-reckoning—of that I am positive; though, as he means to stand to the eastward, his miscalculations ought not to greatly matter."

"When should we make Jamaica, think you?"

"This day week, with anything of a breeze," I answered. "I am assuming, of course, that Purchase's latitude is correct. His longitude I am sure is wrong."

"After his conduct to-day I shall stand no more on ceremony," said he. "I'll not consult the fellow's feelings. If you will take an observation—of course, if a chance occurs," casting a forlorn look at the sky—"you'll greatly oblige me."

"I can take a star in his watch below. He needn't know that I am topping him."

"Why didn't you suggest that before?" asked he, reproachfully.

"Pray remember how sensitive you have been about the man. You staved off all criticism."

"Because I had confidence. And mind, Walton, I am only

shaken now because he has broken his promise, and I find him drunk again. But you will do as you suggest? It will ease both our minds to know that his reckoning tallies with ours. And though he should have underestimated our drift to the west, that will not make his observations incorrect."

"Certainly not," said I. "But look there—and there! We shall get no stars to night. The horizon's not a mile off ; and did mortal man ever see the water of so hideously ugly a color before ? "

The thick mist that had been slowly gathering round, coming up from every point of the compass, like the four walls and ceiling which met and crushed the miserable prisoner in the story, had made the visible sea a mere narrow circle of water, which every moment was growing smaller and smaller. The swell, however, was fast falling, though it was still ponderous enough in all conscience ; and, owing to the diminished compass of the deep, had a more formidable appearance than it wore even when at its worst, owing to the majestic waving of the near horizon. The decks were full of currents of air, caused by the wallowing of the schooner, but there was no wind on the sea. The folds of the swell were as polished as glass. Yet the creeping girdle of mist, and the violent panting of the ocean, and malignant, sallow, bluish tint of the water as though it was putrefied, and the lowering lead of the sullen, motionless sky over our staggering masts, filled the mind with a spirit of foreboding miserable to feel and impossible to express.

When the luncheon hour arrived I followed Sir Mordaunt into the cabin, where we found Miss Tuke and Mrs. Stretton. Before taking his seat, Sir Mordaunt went to his wife's berth, and then returned, accompanied by Norie, who, although greatly nauseated by the detestable rolling, was making a manful fight with it. He had been in attendance on Lady Brookes for the greater part of the morning. This was the first time I had seen him for many hours, and we shook hands like people meeting after a long absence.

I found that Mrs. Stretton was to lunch with us, which I attributed to Miss Tuke's invitation. But now that she was constantly with Lady Brookes, there was no reason why she should not make one of our party, and drop her furtive life in Carey's cabin, and her secret meals with that lady's-maid. I was heartily pleased to see her among us. I had all along felt that Norie's banishment of her, merely because Lady Brookes might take fright at any reference to the horrors of the time spent upon the water-logged bark, was cruel usage to give to the poor shipwrecked woman, whose sex and loneliness, and the dreadful sufferings she had endured, gave her a powerful claim upon our tenderness.

"Do you think we shall have any more stormy weather, Mr. Walton ?" asked Miss Tuke.

I answered that it would be very unusual if we met with another gale, as this was not hurricane month. "The air," said I, "is very thick, but a little wind may scatter that, and expose the blue sky again, which I for one shall be glad to see."

"The motion of the yacht is much less violent than it was," said Sir Mordaunt.

"The swell goes down fast, thank Heaven."

"Walton," cried Norie, "you do not catch me coming to sea again. An old sailor once said to me. 'Master, a square foot of dry land is better than an acre of shipboard.' And often did that observation rise in my mind whilst I was praying in the gale, and wondering how long a stout young fellow like me would take to drown."

"If your fright was so great, I wonder your hair preserved its color," said Miss Tuke.

"My fright was very great ; I don't deny it. Several times I thought we had upset," he answered.

"That's an honest admission for our friend to make in the face of such courage as you and Mrs. Stretton showed," said I to Miss Tuke.

"The bravery was Mrs. Stretton's," she answered. "Had she not encouraged me, I should have been as frightened as Mr. Norie."

"The fog must be upon us," said the baronet. "How uncommonly dark the cabin has become ! "

"Hark ! What are they doing on deck ? " cried Norie, whose nerves were in a condition to be easily alarmed.

"Making sail," I answered, hearing the tramp of feet and the sounds of coils of running gear flung down. "There is a breeze coming, or arrived."

In a few moments the vessel heeled over to starboard, sure evidence that canvas was on her and that wind was blowing. The inclination greatly steadied her, and there was a sensation of buoyancy in her movements as she swung over the swell.

"Can you read that tell-tale over your head, Sir Mordaunt ? " I called out.

He stood up and looked at the compass with a pair of glasses that dangled on his waist-coat. The gloom was so deep that he had some difficulty to decipher the points. After a little he said :

"We are heading southeast by east."

I reflected, and said :

"That is not our course. Tripshore should be advised not to make any southing. We have a whole nest of islands under our lee."

He interrupted me.

"Let us go on deck, Walton, and see what they are about."

I threw down my knife and fork, and ran for my hat. Had it not been for the tepid temperature, emerging through the companion into the open air would have been like shooting into a London November day. The mist was as thick as smoke, grayish rather than white, owing to the sun being buried ; and had you flung a biscuit over the yacht's side it would have disappeared before it touched the water, so short was the span of visible sea from the yacht to the concealing folds of vapor. The mist was like a driving rain, and the decks were dark with the saturation of it. The breeze was sweeping the vapor in masses along with it, and whitening the near water with streaks and glancings of foam. The yacht was close-hauled. They had set the double-reefed mainsail and standing and outer jibs, and this canvas was as flat as pancakes under the tautly-bowsed sheets. Indeed, our main boom was very nearly amidships. The send of the head swell stopped the schooner's way, and she was jammed too close to the wind to take much propulsion from the canvas that was stretched like drumskins fore and aft her. I was bitterly vexed to find the wind sticking in the east. Tripshore came up to us the moment we appeared.

"Do you think you are wise in making any southing?" I asked him.

"Why, sir," he answered, "if Mr. Purchase's reckoning is right, we have plenty of sea room with our head at this."

"But Mr. Walton is persuaded that we are further to the westward than Purchase allows," said Sir Mordaunt.

"Give the matter a moment's consideration, Tripshore," said I. "Will you agree with Purchase that our drift during the gale was only thirty miles ?"

"I'm agreeable to double that, sir," he answered. "But even then there's nothing in the way, heading as we go."

"Fetch the chart," exclaimed Sir Mordaunt. "There's only one road to be taken—and that's the right one."

12

The man quitted the deck, and I walked aft, to see what leeway we were making. The wake was short, broad, and oily, and veered away on our weather quarter. With my hand upon the compass card, I made it about two points. This was as much leeway as one would look for in a ship under close-reefed topsails. It did not surprise me, however. I knew, under certain conditions, that few schooners could hold their own on a wind better then the *Lady Maud*, but the luff choked her. She was under small canvas, and, looking as she was almost right in the wind's eye, it was wonderful that she made any headway at all.

To save this leeway, I thought it would be advisable to ease off the sheets a trifle ; but the responsibility of making any suggestion in the midst of weather as thick as mud, and in the face of my complete doubts of Purchase's accuracy as to the position he affirmed us to be in, weighed down my anxiety, and determined me to hold my peace for the present. The weather, I said to myself, may clear before nightfall, and then I shall be able to find out where we are.

After a brief absence, Tripshore returned with the chart. We laid it upon the skylight and bent over it.

"You see, sir," said the mate to me, "if Mr. Purchase be out even by three times the drift he allows for, this here course of south-east-by-east heads us well into the open, away from that there raffle," indicating the Bahama group to the south of Providence Channel.

"But suppose our longitude should be to the west of 74°?" said I. "Go and look over the stern and mark the leeway, and then take notice of this island," pointing to the island of San Salvador.

"Ay, Walton," exclaimed Sir Mordaunt; "but why do you want to give us so much west longitude. Allowing that Purchase is out as far as you say, you don't believe that he is further out still?"

"I don't know," said I. "I have no faith in his calculations. Who can swear that his latitude is right?"

Sir Mordaunt peered at the chart, and then said—

"What do you propose, Walton?"

"Since you ask me plump," I answered, "I should like to see the yacht on the starboard tack."

"That 'ud be running away from where you want to go to, sir, wouldn't it?" said Tripshore, smiling, and speaking as if he thought me needlessly nervous.

"We certainly don't want to do that," cried Sir, Mordaunt, quickly. "We must get to Kingston as soon as ever we can."

I made no answer to this. Though Tripshore meant no offence whatever by smiling, he had annoyed me, nevertheless, by doing so.

"Go and call Purchase up," said Sir Mordaunt to the mate, "and tell him to bring the log-book, that we may go into the matter thoroughly. The fellow is not too drunk, I suppose, to explain his workings," he added aside to me.

I noticed that the mate hesitated.

"Cut along now, Tripshore!" exclaimed the baronet, impatiently. "This is an anxious time, and I must have Purchase on deck."

The man went away. At this juncture Miss Tuke and Norie showed their heads above the companion.

"Don't come on deck, Ada, don't come on deck!" instantly called out Sir Mordaunt. "This mist will wet you through. Norie, oblige me by handing my niece below; and keep the ladies amused there, will you?"

"With pleasure," answered the doctor. "But I say, Sir Mordaunt, if it's too damp for us, it's too damp for you and that fragile creature Walton. The air is full of rheumatism."

"Yes, yes; we'll be following you shortly. Away with you, Ada." And as they disappeared he said, "I don't want them to suspect any grounds for anxiety. My wife knows that the gale is gone, and is much easier in her mind. Ada's eyes are like a carpenter's drill. And faith, Walton, she does not need to be so sharp either, for your face looks as full of trouble as an egg is full of meat."

"I *am* bothered," I answered. "It's a devilish bad job, Sir Mordaunt, to be with a skipper you can't trust, and whose calculations you are sure are wrong, in weather of this kind, and with those leagues of Bahama Islands dead to leeward of us. And do you know, the wind freshens. It's breezed up since we have been on deck."

"Why doesn't Purchase come?" he exclaimed impatiently.

Just then the mate came along. He looked greatly worried, but without any hesitation he marched up to Sir Mordaunt and said, "I'm sorry to say I can't rouse Mr. Purchase up, sir."

Sir Mordaunt looked at him with astonishment, and then muttered, "It's *too* bad! it's *too* bad!"

"Has he been drinking since he went below, Tripshore?" I asked.

"He has, sir. His cabin is full of the smell of liquor. It's not pleasant for me to peach on a shipmate, but if ye'll go below, gentlemen, you'll see it all with your own eyes. He bargained for a four hours' spell, and has nipt fit to last him that time."

Sir Mordaunt took two or three impetuous strides.

"What's to be done?" he said, confronting me.

"What's to be done?" I ejaculated, almost contemptuously, I fear. "Why, break the drunken rascal out of hand, and take care to set the Board of Trade at him when you get ashore ; so that, by depriving the incompetent 'longshoreman of his certificate, you may put it out of his power to imperil human life."

My poor friend eyed me anxiously, and then turned to the mate.

"Very well," said he. "Mr. Tripshore, you will take charge of this schooner."

The man touched his cap and was about to speak.

"For God's sake let us have no refusal," cried Sir Mordaunt, quickly. "Mr. Walton will navigate the vessel."

"The run is only to Jamaica, Mr. Tripshore," said I. "Another week of sailing at the outside, I hope. If you like, I will keep watch and watch with you. Sir Mordaunt knows I have had confidence in you as a seaman from the beginning. You owe me something for my good opinion, so oblige me by giving the baronet the answer he wants."

The man still hung in the wind ; but after thinking a little, he said, "All right, sir. I'll take charge. You may depend on my doing my best."

"At four o'clock the watch below will be turned up, Sir Mordaunt," said I, "and the crew had then better lay aft, that they may be told of the new arrangement."

"Certainly. Do whatever you think proper," he answered, looking harassed to death by this new bother.

I went below to consult the glass, but it offered no promise of improvement in the weather. Norie and Miss Tuke sat in the cabin, and the former wanted to know why Sir Mordaunt and I kept in the drizzle. I made some answer and went up the steps, envious enough of the doctor's quiet enjoyment of Miss Ada's company to make me willing to call him aside and alarm him with a representation of our situation, and so stop his pleasure.

I went over to the chart again, and studied it attentively for some time, whilst Sir Mordaunt stood talking with Tripshore. The real trouble to me was, not being able to depend upon the observations Purchase had taken on the day before the gale. It is necessary that I should dwell upon this, that the sequel may be clear to you. Could I have been sure that his sights on that day were accurate, I should have been able to work out our position by the dead reckoning of those stormy days, so as to come near enough to the truth. But how was I to trust such data as an illiterate seaman like Purchase could furnish me with from his sextant? A trifling error by being repeated would bring him fearfully wide of the mark in a corner of the Atlantic that is studded with dangerous reefs and low-lying islands. I own I now sincerely deplored my want of resolution in not insisting upon checking the man's calculations by observations of my own. I had acted mistakenly in suffering Sir Mordaunt to put me off discharging what was a duty owing to every person in that yacht by his weak and unwise tenderness for Purchase's "feelings." And I was also greatly to blame in not having ascertained the latitude and longitude from the steamer into which the rescued men had been conveyed, so that we might have compared her reckoning with Purchase's.

But ten years' absence from sea had very greatly disqualified me professionally, as any man may suppose; and the weight of my present responsibility was not a little increased by this sense of my deficiency.

My disposition now was to put the schooner on the starboard tack. With her head at northeast, the whole clear North Atlantic (as I then believed) would be under our bows. Yet Sir Mordaunt's unwillingness to go north when our way lay south influenced me in spite of myself, and I could not forget Tripshore's quiet smile that was like ridiculing my anxiety.

I rolled up the chart, and going over to the mate, advised him to take a heave of the lead.

"Very good, sir," he answered, and went forward to give the necessary instructions.

After a little the deep-sea lead was got up, and the line stretched along. The vessel's way was stopped by her head being shoved into the wind and the lead dropped overboard. The "Watch O watch!" rang mournfully on the breeze as the fakes fell from the men's hands, until it came to Tripshore, who was stationed right aft. Seventy-four fathoms went overboard without giving us any soundings—hard upon four hundred and fifty feet, and no bottom.

"That looks as if the ocean was still under us, sir," said the mate cheerfully, as the line was snatched in a block, and the watch tailed on to haul it in.

Sir Mordaunt stood looking on, much impressed by these proceedings. He plucked up when he saw Tripshore grin and heard his remark, and said to me, "There is evidently plenty of water here, Walton."

"So there ought to be," I answered. "Meanwhile, Tripshore, I should recommend you to keep that lead line coiled down ready for an occasional heave. When you can't see you must feel."

All this time the mist remained abominably thick. It was indeed a very fine rain, and it blew along our decks in a kind of smoke. The swell was greatly abated, but the heads of the seas as they arched out of the vapor broke quickly, and with a certain fierceness, and poured in foam against our weather bow. The schooner, in consequence of being sailed so close, crushed through the water heavily and sluggishly, throwing off the spray to leeward in broad seething masses. With her housed topmasts and streaming decks she looked more to be struggling round the Horn than ratching in July upon the Western Atlantic. And, indeed, nothing but a low temperature was wanted to make me believe myself off the Horn, with the long Pacific swell under me, and the air as thick as a featherbed, and a sharp breeze rattling down out of the mist; just as I remembered it when our latitude was 63° south, though then the decks were covered with ice, and the salt water froze as fast as it was chucked aboard.

At four o'clock the watch below was called. Tripshore came to me and asked respectfully if I meant to stand Purchase's watch. I answered that I had offered to do so, and was quite willing to keep my word.

"I've been turning it over in my mind, sir," said the mate, "and I doubt if the men 'ud feel quite easy. You know what sailors are, sir. The crew have been taught to think of me and Mr. Purchase as their bosses, and of you as passenger."

"Who'll take turn and turn about with you, then?"

"There's Bill Burton, sir. Bill's our oldest hand, and a good man. The men 'ud mind Bill Burton."

Sir Mordaunt, who stood near, said, "As you are to navigate the yacht, Walton, it is only right that others should do the practical part. Tripshore takes Purchase's place, and so let Burton take Tripshore's, if, as you say,"—to the mate—"he is the best man for that duty."

"I'll warrant Bill Burton as a steady man, sir," said Tripshore. "He's as good a lookout as any sailor that I was ever shipmates with, and he's something more than a yachtsman."

"Let us consider that settled," exclaimed Sir Mordaunt. "And now the men should be told of the change. Send them aft, Tripshore, or the watch below will be going to bed." And as the mate went forward the baronet added, "Will you talk to them, Walton?"

"They'd like it better from. you," said I. "You pay them You are their master."

"Very well," said he, and he fell to stroking down his beard whilst he thought over what he should say to them.

In a few minutes they were all assembled. They were most of them in oilskins, which glistened with the wet, and they stood looking eagerly— this being a novel summons indeed, and they had no idea of what it meant. Sir Mordaunt coughed and fussed, and then rapped out :—

"I've sent for you to say that Mr. Purchase is no longer captain of my yacht. At this moment he is drunk in his cabin and incapable of coming on deck. Such conduct is scandalous in a responsible man. I don't believe he knows where we are within sixty or seventy miles, and yet there he is in his cabin, drunk and useless, and the weather so thick that you cannot see a boat's length from the side." ("It isn't the first time, sir," sung out one of the men.) "I know that. It's the third time. On the second occasion I gave him a good talking to, and he promised on his word as a man that he would not offend again. He's no longer captain. Our lives are too precious to be in the hands of a drunkard, though I always believed him to be a good seaman." (Some of the men laughed, but Sir Mordaunt took no notice.) "Mr. Tripshore will have command until we reach Kingston. Meanwhile, he will want somebody to help him to keep watch, and so I select William Burton. Step forward, Burton."

The man addressed made a stride, and looked around much astonished.

"You and Tripshore will head the watches," said Sir Mordaunt, "and I'll trust to your being a smart seaman to keep a bright lookout and help us all to bring the Lady Maud safely to an anchorage."

"I'm willing to obey any orders, sir," said the man, who was a short, thick-set, intelligent-looking fellow, with earrings, and a quantity of ringlets over his forehead and down the back of his neck, "but I hope this here setting me to head my watch means no difference 'twixt me and my mates. I'm only a plain sailor man, and don't want to be better nor my equils."

"They'll obey your orders, of course," answered Sir Mordaunt.

"That'll be all right, Billy ; don't bother about that, mate," said a voice.

Just then old Purchase made his appearance. He stood a short distance before the mainmast, holding on to the little companion that led to the part of the vessel where his cabin was. The absorptive power of his "bibulous clay," as Southey calls the drunkard's body, had drained the liquor away from his head ; but it was easy to see that he was by no means yet recovered, and it looked as if the sight of Sir Mordaunt made him unwilling to trust his legs. He blinked at us in wonder at seeing all hands together in a crowd on the quarter-deck, but was too muddled to perceive or guess the cause of the assembly. The crew were not conscious of his presence, but we who looked forward saw him at once.

Tripshore sidled up to me and whispered, "He lay like a dead man, when I tried to rouse him up. But he can smell anything going on, and he knows how to pull himself together, Purchase do."

It was probably the seeing Tripshore edge up to me and mumble in my ear that made old Purchase roar out violently, "How was it no one called me at eight bells?" and knitting his brows and looking very fierce, the better to disguise the lingering effects of the drink in him, he let go his hold of the companion and came lurching along toward us.

At the sound of his voice all the men looked around. He stopped after making a few strides, and planting himself on his legs by setting them wide apart, in which posture he presented the most absurd figure that ever I saw in my life, he roared out again to Tripshore to explain why he hadn't called him at eight bells, that is, at four o'clock.

"I'll answer you," exclaimed Sir Mordaunt, very sternly, dropping his head on one side and raising his arm. "More than half an hour ago the mate went to your cabin to tell you I required your presence on deck, but he found you so drunk that he couldn't arouse you."

" You call yourself a sailor "—Page 185.

"Me!" said the old fellow, putting on such a face that in an instant half the crew were broadly grinning. "Me—Purchase—drunk?" He tapped his breast and fell back a step. "No, no," says he, smiling foolishly, and looking around him; "this here's some skylarkin' of Ephraim Tripshore's. Tell Sir Mordaunt it's a bit o' tomfoolin', Ephraim. Lor' bless ye, mate! I never was drunk in my life."

"You're drunk now," cried Sir Mordaunt, warmly, seeing nothing diverting in this exhibition. Indeed, all the time he was incessantly glancing behind him at the skylights and companion, as if he feared that some echo of what was passing would reach his wife's ears. "You are superseded, sir. I shall discharge you at Kingston, and perhaps prosecute you for this conduct. You gave me your word that you would drink no more. You have broken your promise. You are a drunken fellow, and utterly unfit for the responsible position you have filled.. Go back to your cabin, sir. I have given the command to Mr. Tripshore, and William Burton will assist him. We shall manage very well without you, and a deal better than with you. So go below, Mr. Purchase, and don't let me see your face again, sir; and if I hear of you swallowing another drop of spirits before you are out of my vessel, I'll have you locked up in your cabin."

All this was delivered with an energy that surprised me in my friend. No doubt it was the nervous irritability induced in him by the worries, anxieties, and dangers of the past few days, and our present uneasy condition, that enabled him to rap out so smartly. The men were astonished at this vehemence in their mild-mannered master, but old Purchase was absolutely confounded. After the baronet had ceased, he stood staring at him with his mouth open, then slowly rolled his eyes around on the faces of the men, as though he would persuade himself by an inspection of their whiskered faces, ashine with the muggy, lukewarm, driving drizzle, that he was not in a drunken dream. Presently his gaze rested upon my face.

"Ha, Mr. Walton!" he bawled, extending his great clinched fist toward me. "It's _you_ I've got to thank for this, I suppose. It's you that's poisoned Sir Mordaunt's mind against me!"

I looked at him coldly. He was proceeding.

"Will you go away?" cried Sir Mordaunt.

The old fellow, retreating a step, shook his clinched fist at me.

"_You_ call yourself a sailor?" he shouted, in the thickest and

deepest notes I had ever heard rumble from him.   He drew a
deep breath, and added, ''You're a marine !   You're a sea
cook !   A sailor?   Why "—he drew another deep breath—"as
sure as ye stan' there——"

I was never a man to be menaced.   I stepped hurriedly
toward him, but at the first movement I made he rounded on
his legs and started for the companion ; and, drunk as he was,
he managed to scull himself along fast enough to swing himself down the companion steps before I could reach that hatch,
and vanished amid a half-suppressed shout of laughter from
the crew.

Sir Mordaunt had nothing more to say to the men, so they
went forward, and Bill Burton, as they called him, was left to
stump the deck of the schooner for a couple of hours.   I could
not help laughing at the gravity and look of importance the
man put on.   He had a nose like the bill of a hawk, and the
wet collected on his face and streamed away from the point of
his nose in large drops.   He stepped the deck as regularly as
a pendulum, his walk extending from the taffrail to abreast of
the mainmast, and every time he came to a stop, before slue-
ing round he would dry his eyes on the knuckles of his claws,
take a hard, steady squint at the fog on either side and ahead,
cast a prolonged look aloft, and so start afresh, swinging along
in a gait that was an indescribable roll, his arms swaying
athwart his body, and the fingers of his hands curled, as though
they still grasped a rope.

Sir Mordaunt now went below to change his clothes, which
hung upon him like wet paper.   I crossed over to Bill Burton
as he came along, and said it was a pity that Purchase should
not have held his drinking habit in check until he was ashore,
or until the weather improved.

'' Well, I don't mind telling 'ee, sir, I never took him for
much," he answered.   '' We all knew he was given to "—here
the man imitated the action of drinking—"for most of us in
our tricks at the wheel in the night, when you gents was turned
in, have seen him cruising about in a way that proved his
ballast was i' the wrong end of him.   But it wasn't for us to
take notice."

'' I should have supposed the speech he made to you, when
the watches were called for the first time, enough to ruin him
in the confidence of the crew," said I.

''Ay," he answered.   ''That were a rum speech.   I doubt
if he had his head when he talked that slush."

"What drift should you think we made in the gale, Burton? You'll allow for the send of the heavy sea, and recollect that our freeboard was tall enough to scud under every time we were hove up."

He reflected, and said, "Two mile an hour, might be."

"What do you think?"

"Well, I should say that, sir."

"That would bring it hard upon a hundred miles," said I.

"It wouldn't be much less," he answered. "I've been going to leeward two mile an hour under bare poles in a heavier craft than this vessel."

"Purchase allows only thirty miles for drift in the gale," said I.

He went to the rail to spit, as a mark of contempt. "My 'pinion is," said he, coming back, "he never saw a real gale o' wind afore this woyage."

"That's my notion, too," said I. "He's not only out in his dead reckoning, but I thoroughly question whether he was correct in his sights when he last took them. Therefore this thick weather and the wind dead in our eye is something to keep us uneasy. Even if Purchase's reckoning *is* right, the Bahamas are not far off. What instructions has Tripshore given you?"

"To keep her as close as she'll go, and take a heave of the lead every half hour."

"That's it. And let me add, if the vessel should break off by even a quarter of a point, put her about."

"Ay, ay, sir."

I went to look at the compass, and found it steady at south-east-by-south. The wind had not increased in weight, but it blew very fresh, and under the double-reefed mainsail the yacht's lee rail lay low upon the smother of foam which the bursting and chopping action of the little schooner threw up around her hull. The mist was as thick as smoke, and the water hardly to be seen outside the line of froth under the vessel.

"Is this thickness going to last?" I said to Burton.

"There's no tellin', sir. If you mustn't trust a squall ye can't see through, what's to be thought of stuff like this here?"

This sort of comfort might have suited Job, but it was of no use to me. I had been on deck all the afternoon, was wet through, as uncomfortable in body as in mind, and thought it about time to follow Sir Mordaunt's example, and dry myself.

"Keep a sharp lookout," said I, "and don't forget to 'bout ship if she breaks off," and, so saying, I gave my body a hearty swing, to shake off the wet and save the cabin carpet, and went below.

Norie was stretched along one of the lockers, reading. I pushed past, being too wet to bother with his questions, and going to my berth, dried and reclothed myself, taking care to lay out my water-proofs in readiness for my next visit on deck. I lingered over this and other little jobs, and when I returned to the cabin the lamps were lighted, and the steward was laying the cloth for dinner. Miss Tuke and her uncle and Mrs. Stretton and Norie were seated in a group near the piano.

My first glance was at the tell-tale compass ; the course remained unchanged. Sir Mordaunt, seeing me do this, called out—

"Every hour of this should be carrying us well to the eastward, Walton."

"With two points leeway," I exclaimed, with a shrug.

"Is there no means of preventing that leeway?" he asked.

"Setting more canvas would do it," I answered ; "but the vessel has as much as she wants. The other way is by easing the helm—but you know I don't advise that. Indeed, I have taken the liberty to order Burton to put the yacht on the other tack, should the wind veer to the south'ard by even a quarter of a point."

All this talk was Hebrew to Norie and the women, who sat looking on and listening.

" No doubt you are right," said the baronet.

"You know," said I, "that I should like to see the yacht on the starboard tack, heading well to the north-and-east."

"Away from our destination ! Let her break off, Walton, before you put Jamaica over her stern," exclaimed Sir Mordaunt, with a dull smile, and gravely shaking his head.

A short silence fell upon us. I broke it by inquiring after Lady Brookes ; and then Miss Tuke asked what her uncle and I had been doing on deck all the afternoon, "getting wet through, Mr. Walton, and risking all sorts of illnesses, as Mr. Norie will tell you."

"We've been watching the weather," I answered.

"Not much weather to be seen, Walton, said Norie. "This looks to me like November detached from the other months, and out for a cruise on its own account in the Atlantic. I shall behold the sun with interest when it shines forth again.

It has not been in sight since the—let me see——" He
counted on his fingers.   "D'ye call this *summer* cruising?"

"How long shall you stop at Kingston, Sir Mordaunt?"
asked Mrs. Stretton.

"I cannot say, madam; but not long, I believe," he
answered, with a look at me, to let me know that his intention
of abandoning the cruise on his arrival there was not yet pro-
claimed.   "We left England without meaning to touch at any
port, unless our fresh water ran short.   But the ocean," said
he, in a very sober voice, "makes a man's programme an idle
thing."

The poor woman sighed at this; and God knows, she had
reason.

Dinner was now served, and we took our seats.

"It is a great pity," said I, "that Lady Brookes keeps herself
imprisoned in her cabin.   Company and conversation should
do her more good than Carey and solitude."

"She is best where she is," said Norie; "certainly, until we
get fine weather.   Robust fellows like our friend, Sir Mordaunt,
have no sympathy with delicate nervous organizations.   A
hungry man wonders at another's want of appetite.   A man
whose heart beats strongly wonders at people feeling cold.
You should study medicine, Walton, if you want to sympathize
widely."

"Mr. Norie means that you should make people suffer first,
in order to feel for them," said Miss Tuke.

But talk of this kind was very flat, stale, and unprofitable to
me, and I dare say to Sir Mordaunt too, in our present humor.
I was repeatedly glancing at the tell-tale, hoping to find the
schooner breaking off, that we might have an excuse to get
upon the other tack.   Although it was only six o'clock, it was
as dark as a pocket outside with the fog, and the skylight
windows stood like squares of ebony overhead.   The heat was
no longer an inconvenience, owing to the draughts of chilled
air that breezed down through the windsail.   Likewise, the
swell was greatly moderated, and, though the piping wind
raised a bit of a sea, there was nothing discomforting in the
movements of the yacht.   In truth, we had been well seasoned
by the gale.   After the mountainous surges of the three days,
the tumble that a brisk wind stirred up was not a thing to
notice.

Sir Mordaunt was as reserved as I; the others chatted freely.
Mrs. Stretton, who had lived a few months in Jamaica, talked

about the scenery there and the negroes, and their strange
superstitions ; and I particularly remember her description of a
mountain, seen from the sea at sunrise—how the mountain on
top seemed a solid mass of red fire forking out of the snow-
white wreaths of clouds and vapor which girdled the lower
parts.   She spoke with animation, and her rich accents lent a
singular charm to her language.   She interested the baronet, in
spite of himself ; and it was the attention he gave to her speech,
while she was describing the Jamaica scenes she knew, that
warmed her up into fluency and spirit ; for she was *triste*
enough when we first sat down to dinner, and whenever she
was silent and listening to the others, the sad look came into
her face.   Somehow, I had never felt more sorry for her than I
did on this day and at that table.

The comfort and luxury of the rich sparkling interior was
made sharply sensible to the appreciation by the dismal, dark,
damp, oppressive weather without, and my heightened percep-
tion of it from this cause set me contrasting the situation of the
poor woman with hearty sympathy.   I thought of Lady
Brookes ; the love and solicitude bestowed on her ; her freedom
from anxiety ; her husband's ample estate, that made her life as
delightful as existence can be made for a woman by money in
the hands of a husband who lives mainly for her and her
pleasure ; and then I thought of this poor widow, newly
snatched from a horrible peril, her husband drowned in her
sight, and herself a beggar, as she had as good as hinted.

But sufficient for the day, thought I, is the evil thereof.   Let
us first get out of this weather, and find out in what part of this
corner of the Atlantic the yacht is, before we vex our souls with
other considerations.

CHAPTER XII.

Sir Mordaunt was the first to quit the table.   He apologized
for leaving us, and went to his wife's cabin, saying, as he
rose—

"If you are going on deck, Walton, I'll join you there
presently."

On this I quitted my seat, too anxious to linger ; and going
to my cabin, put on my water-proof coat and returned.   Miss
Tuke stood at the foot of the companion steps, looking up at
the darkness.   She said to me, with a glance around at Mrs.

Stretton and Norie, who remained at table, though the widow had followed me with her eyes as I passed along—"Mr. Walton," she said, in a low voice, "what makes you and Uncle Mordaunt so dull?"

"If your uncle is dull," said I, "and I don't know that he is, his wife's condition will answer your question about him. As for me, I am as cheerful as a man can be in a fog."

"No, no; you are dull too, Mr. Walton. Pray what is it? You can trust a sailor's daughter," said she, coaxingly. "Nothing you can say will frighten me."

"I give you my word of honor there is nothing whatever the matter. There is a dense sea-fog around us; and as Purchase's calculations, and, may be, the man himself, are not to be depended on, I am merely going to lend a hand on deck for a short while, to keep a lookout."

I saw she did not believe me, though I spoke the truth. She eyed me gravely and earnestly, and I was willing she should look as long as ever she pleased, for I, too, could look at her closely, with good excuse for so doing. Suddenly a little smile kindled in her pretty eyes, as she said softly—

"Well, Mr. Walton, join us here again as soon as you can. We are dull without you," and she went back again to the dinner table.

To my sight, fresh from the sparkling cabin, the air seemed pitch dark. I stood at the companion for some moments, waiting for my eyes to get used to this profound blackness. I then saw the rays of the binnacle lamp striking into the thick mist like luminous gold wire. Anon I could faintly distinguish the outline of the bulwarks over against me on the other side, and a fragment of the mainmast where the haze from the skylight fell upon it. But that was all. For the rest, as the French say, I might have had my eyes shut.

This being the second dog-watch, I knew Tripshore would be on deck, so I called his name.

"Here, sir," he answered, and came to my side.

"Have you kept the lead going?" I asked.

"Yes, sir," he replied, "but we get no bottom."

"And we want none, Tripshore. Have you seen anything of Purchase?"

"No, sir. His cabin door's to, and I allow he's turned in and asleep."

"The wind keeps steady," said I; "but so fresh as it is, I wonder it doesn't blow away this mist. The weather is thicker

than it was.   It's like smoke.   I never remember the like of it,"
said I, facing to windward a moment, and then gladly turning
my back on the blinding, penetrating drizzle.

" The men have grown anxious since Sir Mordaunt talked to
'em," said Tripshore, after a pause.   "They're not used to
weather o' this kind, and they've took it in their heads that Mr.
Purchase is all out in his reckonings.   His being in drink at a
time like this is a bad job, sir."

"We can manage without him," said I.

"Why, yes, sir.   It 'ud be a poor lookout if we couldn't."

" If the men," I continued, " were all of them salt-water men
like you, they'd find nothing to disturb them in the loss of such
a skipper as Purchase.   I feel as safe again with that drunken
fellow under the deck for good."

"Oh, it isn't *him* the men mind," he exclaimed.   "They
reckon nobody aboard knows where we are, and they don't
like that."

And small blame to them, thought I, but I said nothing.

"However, when the weather clears they'll brighten up with
it, I dare say," he added.

"You will remember, Tripshore," said I, "that you had
confidence enough in Purchase's reckoning to fancy that I was
over uneasy when I told Sir Mordaunt that I should like to see
the yacht on the starboard tack."

"You may be right, sir, though," said he, quickly.

"In my own mind," said I, "I am convinced that we are
further to the westward than we know of.   I may be wrong.
It is because I can't be sure, that I don't insist upon heading
away to the norrard."

" If you'll give the word, I'll put the yacht round at once,"
said he.

"Not without Sir Mordaunt's leave.   He wants to fetch
Kingston as soon as he can, and dislikes the idea of turning tail
upon it.   When he comes on deck——"

But before I could finish my sentence he arrived.   That is to
say, he came up the steps, but stopped before he reached the
top of them, and stood there like a man struck blind.

" My God !" he ejaculated, " what a night !"

I sung out cheerily, "Come along, Sir Mordaunt.   It'll not
be so black when your sight has lost the glare of the cabin."

"Oh, are you there, Walton ?" he cried, and came on deck,
but remained standing, as I had, in front of the companion.

"What a night !" he repeated.   "It is not yet eight o'clock.

Who is that near you ? "

" Tripshore, sir," replied the mate.

" What sail is the vessel carrying ? "

" Just what you left on her, sir—double-reefed mainsail, and outer and standing jibs. She's snug enough, and wants what she has if she's to ratch with the wind fore and aft her."

" Ay, and ratch she must," said I. " Tripshore is willing enough now, Sir Mordaunt, to see her on the starboard tack."

" But what's the good of going north, Walton," he answered, " when we are heading well to the east, and when we know from the chart that it is all open sea that way as far as the coast of Africa ? "

"Unless we have diminished our leeway," said I.

" There's no change in that, sir," interrupted Tripshore.

" Our true course now is southeast-by-south. Practically, then, we are steering a course parallel with the trend of the Bahama range. Nay, we are worse off even than that, for the trend of those islands is southeast. If we were certain of our whereabouts then we might find it safe enough to lie as we go. But in this weather, and without an atom of faith in Purchase's calculations, I'm for edging away to the norrard and eastward."

" Mr. Walton's right, sir," said Tripshore.

" Why, if you both think the yacht should be put about, let it be done," said Sir Mordaunt. " I'll not put my wishes against your judgment."

The necessary orders were immediately given by Tripshore, whose eagerness was not a little flattering to me after the reception he had given my opinion some hours before. The helm was put up to give the schooner plenty of way, and the brave little vessel, eased of her griping luff, began to *snore* through the water, whitening it all around until the phosphorus and the foam of it threw out light enough to enable us clearly to see the whole figure of the hull, though within the rails all was as ebony, save where the skylight and the binnacle filled a space of the midnight blackness with a golden haze and shining lines.

The men had to get the yacht round by feeling. They knew where the running gear led, and groped about until they came to the places. When all was ready the helm was put down, and the flying schooner shot into the wind, her mainsail rattling like a roll of thunder, and the great main boom tearing at its hempen bonds like an elephant straining at a lasso. In a few minutes the head-sheets were bowsed taut, and I went to the

13

compass and looked at it with a feeling of relief which I even then thought, and do still think unaccountable, considering that there was nothing but my distrust of Purchase to make me suppose our former course a perilous one.

Sir Mordaunt did not remain long on deck. I told him he could do no good by staying, and that he merely risked health by exposing himself to the malignant damp of this lukewarm, penetrating mist, and that I should not be long in following him.

And I was as good as my word. For after hanging about the deck for half an hour, the sight of the rich, comfortable, bright cabin, as I saw it through the skylight, tempted me beyond resistance. I waited until another heave of the lead assured me that there was nothing to be felt at eighty fathoms, and then I went below.

I believe our going below and sitting in the cabin reassured Miss Tuke. Besides, I was cheerful enough now that I had had my way, and Sir Mordaunt was likewise heartier and brighter in manner, as though his mind took its posture from my behavior. They say that coming events cast their shadows before ; but I can answer for our little company aft that not for a fortnight past had we been in a calmer and pleasanter mood. Besides, there was good news from Lady Brookes's cabin. Her spirits had recovered something of their tone, the smoother passage of the vessel had briskened her up, and Sir Mordaunt said that if the weather was fine to-morrow he hoped to have her on deck.

We were all careful to keep our conversation away from topics likely to recall what we did not wish to remember—the death of the mastiff, the water-logged bark, the terrible gale we had been struggling with. We talked chiefly of England, how strange it was to be without newspapers, and not to know what had happened in the time we had been away.

"Yes," says Norie, "think of the mass of news that will have accumulated by the time we return. Most of it we shall never hear."

"All my dresses will have become old-fashioned," said Miss Tuke. "How do the ladies dress in the West Indies, Mrs. Stretton ?"

"In the newest styles," she answered. "But I believe they look for their fashions to New Orleans and the American cities."

"Who import them from Paris," said Sir Mordaunt. "So, Ada, you'll not find yourself behind."

"But you'll give us no time for judging, Uncle Mordaunt," exclaimed Miss Tuke.

"Well, well, never mind about that now," said he. And then looking up at the compass, he turned to me and said, "Is this part of the Atlantic much frequented by vessels, Walton?"

"Not just hereabouts, I fancy. We're too far north for the West Indian steamers, and hardly in the track, I should say, for vessels bound to the Gulf."

"Pray let us talk of dress," exclaimed Norie. 'We've been so fearfully nautical lately, that it's quite a relief to think of shops and shore matters. Mrs. Stretton, you were saying——" And here we jabbered about West India dress fashions, and so plied the poor woman with questions that presently we were all talking about dress.

In this way passed the evening, until Miss Tuke, looking at her watch, said it was ten o'clock, and that she would go to her aunt and then to bed. Mrs. Stretton and she then wished us good-night, and withdrew. Shortly afterward Norie, who never showed any disposition to linger over the grog when Miss Tuke was gone, delivered himself of a loud yawn, shook hands, and went to his cabin. Sir Mordaunt lighted a cigar, I a pipe, and we sat for a while smoking in silence, listening to the stifled hissing of the water washing along the sides of the yacht, and to the straining of the bulkheads as the vessel rose and sank.

Presently, and without speaking, the baronet went to the foot of the companion steps and looked up.

"The night remains terribly dark," said he, coming back. "I had hoped to see a star. Surely such a fog as this must be very unusual here at this time of the year."

"You must be surprised at nothing that happens in the way of weather at sea," I replied. "I remember the master of a brig telling me that he once made a voyage from London to Barbadoes without meeting the North-East Trades."

"This dreadful thickness makes one think of collisions, Walton."

"I suspected that was in your mind," said I, "when you asked me that question about this part of the Atlantic being frequented by ships."

"But what do you think?" he inquired nervously.

"I should not allow any fear of that kind to trouble me," I replied. "The odds are a thousand to one against a collision in a great sea like this."

"You always put a hearty face on those ideas," he said, relaxing. "No doubt you are right; but this last week has tried me severely. Purchase, too, has worried me greatly; and such is my mood at this moment, that I would gladly give five hundred pounds to be safe in harbor—at Kingston or anywhere else."

"I hoped you had recovered your spirits," said I, grieved by this breaking down in him. "You have been very cheerful for the last hour or two."

He filled a tumbler with brandy and water, and swallowed a copious draught, and then sat silent, uneasily combing down his beard with his fingers, and holding his extinguished cigar, which he looked at without relighting.

"Shall you go on deck again?"

I answered, "Yes, to have a last look round."

He glanced at the skylight, as if he had a mind to go too; but, guessing his intention, I advised him to keep below, to go to bed indeed. "The chances are," said I, "that when you wake the sky will be blue, and the yacht buzzing merrily along under a bright sun to Jamaica."

"Ay," said he, "but do Tripshore and Burton know the course?"

"The schooner is in my hands," said I. "Only let the sun shine, and I'll engage that Tripshore and Burton run the vessel correctly. While this fog and this wind hold, we have nothing to do but to keep as we go."

He looked at me with a musing expression, and then, holding forth his hand, he said, "Very well, Walton; I'll obey your orders and go to bed. I commit our safety to you and Tripshore."

We shook hands cordially, and he went along the cabin, pausing, when under the skylight, to look out, and then closing the door softly after him.

I put on my waterproof coat and went on deck. It wanted twenty minutes to eleven. I thought the fog had thinned somewhat, and I crossed the deck to look to windward. Yet though the mist was undoubtedly less dense, gazing over the side was like staring at a black wall. The driving fog of fine rain made my eyes tingle, for the wind was strong, though so warm that it felt like the gushing of air from the engine-room of a steamer. Nothing of the water was visible but the boiling foam churned up by the yacht's bows thickly interlaced with long fibers of phosphorescent light. Sometimes, when a wave broke a short distance from the vessel, the flash of its foaming crest shone out through the mist, but nothing else of it was distinguishable.

Burton was in charge. I called to him, and told him that he must keep the schooner heading as she went. " Let her lie as close as she'll ratch," said I, "and shake it out of her. I would rather she crawled than ran, until the horizon clears. Those will be your instructions to Tripshore."

" Right, sir."

" How many men have you on the lookout? "

" Two, sir."

" Do your lights burn brightly? "

" I was forward just now, and they're as bright as the mist'll let 'em be."

"Tell Tripshore to see to that, will you? and to keep a sharp lookout. I'd give a deal of money, Burton, to know within ten miles where we are. This fog is a bad job after our long westerly drift. Have you any notion of the currents hereabouts? "

" No, sir," he answered. " But we should be right as we go. I was looking at the chart along with Mr. Tripshore, and it shows northern but open water to the east'ards."

" I shall be up and down all night," said I. " I may take some rest upon one of the cabin lockers, ready for a call. It may clear up suddenly, and you or Tripshore must have me up at the first sight of a star. Add that to your instructions, lest I forget to tell him."

We stood talking thus, and flitting about the deck, stopping now and again for five minutes at a time to look ahead into the pitch-black void, straining our eyes against the needle-like rain, in the hope of catching sight of a flaw, to let us know that the mist was breaking, until eight bells—midnight—were struck. The men forward thumped the fore-hatch, and bawled to the watch below to rouse out. Tripshore came aft. We heard him calling, otherwise we should not have known he was on deck.

" Here ! " answered Burton.

The mate, groping his way in the direction of the man's voice, walked up against me.

" Is this Burton ? " says he, feeling me, as a blind man would.

" No," I answered ; "he's to the left of me."

He begged my pardon, and said, "That scow-bank of a steward's turned down the cabin lights. Had he let 'em a be, the sheen of the skylight would have helped a man to see. It's

like being smothered up in a blanket, Bill.   I plumped agin the
mainmast as I came along, and allow I've lifted a bump the size
of a hen's egg over my right eye."

Burton repeated my instructions, and, after hanging about us
a few minutes, wished us good-night and went below.

I was weary enough myself.   A man usually is when he
would rather not feel sleepy.   The ten years I had spent away
from the sea had robbed me of the old seasoning.   The wet
and the wind bothered and tried me.   Nevertheless I remained
on deck another hour, occasionally conversing with Tripshore,
but for the main part hanging over the rail, first to windward, then
to leeward, vainly striving to see a fathom beyond my nose, and
watching—for the want of something to rest the sight upon and
relieve it from the oppression of the heavy darkness—the pallid
quivering of the rushing foam alongside, until the play of it, and
the shooting and throbbing of the whirling fires in it, made my
eyes reel.

Even if I had not been predisposed to lowness of spirits, this
spell of loneliness, and the foul black weather, and the groaning
and moaning of the invisible deep, with now and again the
shriek of a block-sheave high aloft, and the hollow flap of the
hidden canvas, and the numerous disturbing and startling
sounds which were jerked out of the rigging and spars in the
blackness overhead by the sharp yerking and jumping of the
schooner, were quite enough to depress me.

But at last my eyelids felt as if they were made of lead.
Once, while looking over the lee rail, I found myself dropping
asleep, and awoke with a kind of horror at the closeness of the
hissing foam.   I could resist the inclination to sleep no longer,
and, calling to Tripshore, told him I was going to lie down in
the cabin, and that he would find me on one of the lockers on
the port side coming abreast of the companion steps.

I then went below, removed my waterproof coat, and, putting
a soft pillow on the locker, laid myself along, completely
dressed, and ready to jump up at a moment's notice.   The
cabin lamps had been turned down, and yielded a very feeble
light.   I could have sworn I should drop asleep the moment my
head touched the pillow ; yet for at least twenty minutes did I
lie, looking at the feeble lamps swinging to the motion of the
vessel, and listening to the sounds in the cabin, and struggling
to work out a kind of reckoning to myself, so that I might
figure the yacht's position.

In the midst of this idle problemizing I fell into a deep slumber.

CHAPTER XIII.

I was awakened by a violent concussion. So heavy was the sleep from which I had been aroused, that I remained for a considerable space in a state of stupefaction. On my senses becoming active, I found myself sprawling on my back upon the cabin floor. I now supposed that I had been rolled off the locker by a heave of the vessel, and that the sensation of a strong concussion having taken place was due to my fall. I scrambled on to my feet, but scarcely was I upright when a terrible grinding and rending shock pitched me sideways on to the locker on which I had been lying. Men's voices were shouting overhead. I also heard the tramping of feet, the violent beating of canvas—above all, the roaring and rushing of water.

I sprang to the companion steps, and as I gained them there was another tearing shock—I know not how to describe it. To say that it was like the vessel going to pieces, will convey no image to your mind. Rather figure your sitting in a house, and one side of it sinking suddenly a foot or two, and every joist and strong fastening cracking and shrieking, and the roof and the whole structure trembling and groaning, as if the building must crash in. I stopped, struck to the very heart by the unbearable and soul-sickening sensation. At that moment I was grasped from behind. I turned, and saw Sir Mordaunt, dressed only in his shirt and trousers.

"What has happened?" he cried.

"We have either been run into or we are ashore—the latter, I think," I answered. "For God's sake get the women dressed, and bring them into the cabin;" and, releasing myself from his clutch, I sprang on to the deck. As my head came level with the companion the vessel heeled over—over—over yet! I crouched down, breathless and waiting, convinced that the yacht was going. I heard the men shrieking in the blackness as they fetched away with the angle of the decks, and fell helplessly into the lee scuppers.

When on her beam ends the schooner remained stationary. I knew by the bursting of the seas against her side, and by the fierce sounds of sweeping water over my head, that she had beaten round with her broadside to the sea, and so lay.   At the top of my voice I shouted out the name of Tripshore, but it was like speaking when a gun explodes.   The main sheet must have parted, for the sail I supposed lay fore and aft to the wind, and the slatting of it was like the crashing of thunder.   The sea to leeward was as white as milk, and the noise of its boiling was alone enough to deafen a man.   Added to this, every sea that struck the weather side of the vessel boomed with a deep and hollow note, and was followed by a wild splashing and tearing of water upon the deck.   Had I not kept the shelter of the companion when the vessel stopped at her sickening heel, I must have gone overboard, for a sea came pouring over the bulwarks that washed like an ocean of fire—so vivid was the phosphorus in it—as high as my waist, and tumbled down the steps in a cataract that was like to flood the cabin.   I had sense enough to check this by closing the weather door and top of the companion, and there I stood, confounded, horrified, dulled, so that I was like an idiot, I may say, by the dreadful darkness, unable to see anything but the white water, and hearkening to the shrieks of the invisible men which rose with an edge that made the bellowing of the canvas and the thundering of the bursting surges a maddening and distracting uproar indeed.

Whilst I stood thus, some one in the blackness on the starboard hand cried out my name.

"Who is that ?" I shouted.

"Me—Tripshore, sir.   For the Lord's sake, stretch along and give me hold of your hand.   I'm drowning down here."   I could not see him, but I was visible to him in the faint haze of light that came up out of the companion.   Rejoiced to hear his voice, I swung myself out on to the deck, and grasping the companion with my left hand, I threw my legs wide apart and leaned down with my right arm outstretched.

"Do you see me ?" I cried.

"Ay, sir—keep so a minute," he answered, and presently I felt him seize my hand.

Now that he was close, I could see his outline, but not his face.   The deck sloped like the side of a steep hill, it was slippery as ice with the wet, and cataracts of water were incessantly rushing down it from over the bulwarks.   The poor fellow could give me no help, and I had to drag him up, which, by a desperate effort and putting forth my whole strength and will, I managed to do, swinging him round into the companion, where he lay a while on one knee, with his hand on the handrail and his head resting on his arm, quite spent and very nearly drowned.

All this while I heard no sounds in the cabin, and the men's voices on deck were stilled. The yacht lay dead on her side. Once only, and shortly after she had heeled over hard fast aground, a sea raised and bumped her, and I heard the crash of timber aloft, and the sound of a mighty fall, but it was too dark to see what spar had gone ; and after that the schooner lay quiet, with the sea breaking against her port side, and shooting high into the air over her, as was to be known by the rattling of the sheets of water when they fell into the boiling whiteness to leeward.

I said to Tripshore, "Have you your senses ? "

" I'm better," he answered. " There's an ocean of water in the lee scuppers, and I was drowning in it. I feel full o' water. If I could be sick it 'ud relieve me."

" Where are the men ? "

" Most of 'em drowned, I fear. They got away with the long-boat."

" What time is it ? "

" About half-past four."

"Oh, my God ! " I cried. " If the daylight would only come, that we might see where we are ! "

As I said this I heard Sir Mordaunt calling my name. I slid down the steps, and, turning round, found one of the cabin lamps brightly burning, and the whole party, everybody who belonged to our end of the vessel, standing at the table, which alone prevented them from slipping down the cabin floor. Sir Mordaunt grasped his wife round the waist with his right arm, and with the other held Miss Tuke by the wrist. Mrs. Stretton and Carey clung to each other, and Norie stood beside them. Full of hurrying horror as that time was, I could yet find a moment to wonder at the supernatural calmness of Lady Brookes. She was as white as marble, but I could not question that she had her senses ; and though she may not have known that any instant the yacht might crumble to pieces under our feet, yet she surely comprehended that our peril was of the direst kind, that we were shipwrecked, lying broken and storm-swept upon some nameless reef, amid the blackness of a howling night.

Both Mrs. Stretton's and Miss Tuke's faces wore rather an expression of consternation than horror. Now and then Carey uttered a low moan—every time the water thundered on the deck she made that noise—otherwise no sound came from the women.   Their silence indeed was almost shocking to me.   In Lady Brookes I should have foretold a behavior so different, so distracting, that her rigid posture and stony face smote me like a prophesy of immediate death.   It seemed to take all hope of life away, as if the bitterness of death had passed from her and the others, and they were waiting to die.

"What has happened, Walton ? " said the baronet, in a strong thick voice.

"The yacht is on her beam-ends ashore," I replied.   "Purchase's reckoning is diabolically wrong.   I always feared so—yet I had hoped to escape this."

"What are we to do?" he said.

When he said this they all fixed their eyes upon me, with a dreadful eagerness in their expression—heart-moving beyond endurance, indeed, owing to their silence.   I gulped down a sob, and struggling to master my voice, I answered, "We can do nothing until daylight comes.   It draws on for five o'clock, and we shall have the dawn shortly.   Let us pray God that the vessel will hold together—I think she will.   She is strong, and can stand this buffeting unless she bumps."

"She is motionless," exclaimed Norie, in a broken voice.   "I have not felt her bump for some time."

"Is there no way of finding out where we are ? " cried Miss Tuke, wildly and suddenly.   "Can we not get help from the shore ? "

"It is as black as ink on deck," I replied.   "There are no lights—there is no land to be seen."

"Oh, the water—the water !   Listen to it ! " shrieked Carey, cowering, and looking around her with eyes brilliant with terror.

A heavy sea had broken over the vessel and poured over the deck above us, and a bright flood came bursting and smoking down the companion ladder.

Lady Brookes threw her arms up, and Sir Mordaunt pressed her fiercely to him ; but she remained silent as a statue.

I called to Tripshore to close the companion and come down. I reckoned that if any of the crew were alive they would be in the forecastle.   Be that as it was, we could not let the cabin be drowned.   Already the water was as high as the starboard lockers, and the cabin was small enough to be quickly flooded.

Tripshore descended with a faltering motion.   No one but

myself had known he was on the top of the steps. His clothes were streaming, his sou'-wester had been washed off his head, and his hair was pasted on his forehead, throwing out his bleached face, and making him look more like a corpse than a man. There stood a decanter of brandy on one of the swinging trays, and with the utmost difficulty I managed to seize it and gave it to Tripshore, bidding him put his lips to it and swallow a dram. In truth, numbed and confounded as my mind was by the sudden horror of our condition, I yet preserved sufficient presence of mind to foresee a vital value in this sailor if the wreck held together until the daylight, and that our lives might depend upon my recovering him from his half-drowned state.

I gathered hope when I found the yacht lying immovable. That she was bilged, I knew by the slow rise of the water to leeward in the cabin ; but, as I say, that rise was slow, and much of the water that was there had come down the companion ; and I guessed if the leak did not drain in faster than it now did, it would be a good bit past daylight before the water came high enough to drive us out of the cabin.*

The worst and most dreadful part was the heavy concussions of the seas which struck the windward side of the schooner, and kept her trembling like a railway carriage swiftly drawn. After every blow there would be a pause, and then down would come the water in tons weight, smashing upon the deck overhead, and washing in a loud roar over the bulwarks on the other side. Every instant I expected to see the companion carried away, or the skylight dashed in. But, mercifully for us, these fixtures stood, so nobly and stoutly built was that vessel down to the meanest of her appointments.

What our position was at this time I will leave you to imagine. The heel of the yacht was certainly not less than fifty, ay, and maybe more than fifty, degrees. The swinging trays lay with their lee rims hard against the upper deck. So acute was the slope, that nothing but the interposition of the table prevented us from falling headlong down the incline. In the light of the lamp we stood looking at one another, all in silence, save but for the occasional screams or moans of alarm which broke from Carey, and once or twice from Miss Tuke, though never from Lady Brookes, when a wave beat upon the deck, and ran snarling and hissing away, like a score of disappointed wild beasts. I shall never

---

* The hold was no doubt full of water, and the draining into the cabin was through the cabin floor.

forget the expression of anguish in Sir Mordaunt's face. I can
recall no hint of fear in it.   It was bitter grief and horror, as if
he were to blame for the frightful peril that with amazing swift-
ness had confronted the motionless, staring woman he clutched
to his heart.

As for *her*, her passivity was as though a miracle had been
wrought.   I thanked God for it, for I knew how the agony of
that time would have been heightened by her screams and terror.   Yet it was wonderful that she, whom a thunder-storm had
driven into hysterics, and who had fainted over the narrative
of a disaster, should be standing there now as if all sensibility
had fallen dead in her.   Perhaps, indeed, this may have been
the case.   Her aspect was one of petrifaction, or, it might be
that her senses were paralyzed by the first alarm, and were
unable to take in the full meaning of our situation.   She often
turned her glittering eyes on me, and stared as though she beheld an apparition.   It was a positive relief to see her toss her
hands when the water above boomed thunderously.   Suddenly
Tripshore made a movement.

"Where are you going?" I asked sharply.

"To see if anything can be done for our lives," he answered.

"Stay where you are!" I cried.   "If you show your head
above the companion you'll be washed overboard; and I won't
have the doors opened.   When the dawn comes you'll see it on
that skylight.   What *can* be done now, man?   It's pitch-dark
still.   Could we see to launch a boat?   Would those breaking
seas allow us to enter a boat?   Stay where you are, I say.
Here, at least, we have a refuge."

"Can nothing be done?" exclaimed Miss Tuke, with a
dreadful note of despair in her voice.

"Yes, yes," I answered.   "Everything that can be done
shall be done.   But it will be madness to leave this cabin until
the dawn comes, to let us know where we are and what we can
do."

"Have you no rockets to send up?" cried Mrs. Stretton.

"They'll be drowned by this time, sir," said Tripshore, addressing me.   "They're in the forepeak.   There'll be no getting
at 'em."

"They would not help us," I said.   "They would not show
in this mist; though could we come at them we might fire them
through the companion."

"I'll try and get 'em, if you like," said Tripshore; "but

unless yon bulkhead can be broke through, I shall have to go on deck to get down the fore hatch."

"No, don't risk that," exclaimed Sir Mordaunt. "The dawn will be here soon. Mr. Walton is right; we can do nothing in this blackness."

Nothing; nor did I regret the want of the rockets, for from the first I never doubted that we were aground upon one of the hundreds of the Bahama shoals, miles out of sight of inhabited land, and that there was no eye but God's to mark our signal of distress, though we should make a blaze as big as a burning city.

The steady posture of the yacht, and my confidence in her strength, kept my heart up; and I endeavored to cheer my companions by pointing out that the wind might drop with the rising sun, and that, though we had lost one boat, we had two others large enough to contain us all. Likewise, that we need not doubt of being able to make our way to one of the numerous islands which lay scattered broadcast upon these seas, where we should get the relief we stood in need of.

Sir Mordaunt asked Tripshore where the rest of the crew were. The man answered that he feared some of them were drowned, but he could not say for certain : he supposed those who lived were sheltering themselves in the forecastle.

I was sorry he answered the question in that way. His reply was a dreadful shock to the women. His saying that he feared some of the men were drowned gave a most crushing sense of realness to our awful situation. Miss Tuke's face contracted as with an agonizing spasm, and Mrs. Stretton cried bitterly. Lady Brookes said something to her husband—I did not catch the words—and he laid her head against his shoulder, and soothed her with the most endearing gestures, at the same time looking at me with the most heart-broken expression in his eyes.

In this manner we stood waiting to see the dawn brighten upon the skylight windows, listening with terror to the weary crashing of the seas, feeling with unspeakable dismay the dreadful ocasional quivering of the hull ; and I at least scarcely daring to hope that the vessel could much longer withstand the cruel hammering of those pounding surges.

CHAPTER XIV.

THE light seemed a long while coming, but at last the dawn stood upon the skylight glass. Miss Tuke was the first to notice it. She cried out, "The morning has broken, Mr. Walton," and pointed to the skylight.

I immediately clawed my way along to the steps, and ascended them, followed by Tripshore. I opened the starboard companion door cautiously, and peered forth. The fog was all gone and the air clear, but the sky very cloudy. The light was but a glimmering gray as yet, but it broadened and sharpened quickly whilst I stood gazing, and then the whole wild picture of ruin and desolation was clear before me.

The yacht lay with her bows very high in the air, and her stern correspondingly deep, and hence it was that all the seas which struck her rolled their volumes over the quarter-deck, leaving the forecastle comparatively free ; that is to say, the falls of water there were much less frequent than they were aft, and a great deal less weighty and dangerous. A short distance away on the starboard beam trended a low line of dark shore, the full extent of which I could compass with the eye. It was, indeed, as I immediately perceived, a low, flat island, with a little space of rising land down the east quarter of it. Between the yacht and the near beach was a tract of white water, that boiled and leaped in pinnacles and spears, as you may see water play on shoals. It was like milk for whiteness, and was raging a long way both ahead and astern of the schooner, whose starboard bulwarks lay over into it, and it constantly washed in a heavy smother of froth over the rail in such a manner, that had the heel of the yacht been less sharp, the whole deck from the forehatch would have been under water. As it was, the flood stood as high as the bulwark rail, and extended as far inboard as the companion in which I stood ; and in this lake of water, which was constantly being lashed into fury by the torrents pouring over the weather side, lay four drowned men, one of whom was Purchase. The foremast was gone about ten feet above the deck, and the wreck of it lay over the side. Every movable article had been swept overboard. The boat we carried amidships was gone, and the boat that hung at the davits had been broken in halves by a blow from a sea.

This is but a cold description. But, my God! with what agony of soul did I contemplate this dreadful scene of ruin, the drowned bodies, the horrible white water utterly cutting us off from the land, and above all, the stormy look of the sky, that threatened a gale of wind!

Sir Mordaunt had left the women and crawled up the companion steps, but being unable to see, owing to Tripshore and me blocking the companion, he asked me if I could perceive land, and what our position was. I was too affected to answer him, and motioned Tripshore to descend a few steps, so as to give the baronet room to see for himself. The moment Sir Mordaunt looked at the deck and the land he uttered a bitter cry and reeled backward, and had I not thrown my arm round his neck he would have fallen to the bottom of the steps. The sight of those drowned men, his wrecked and broken yacht, and the boiling water that cut us off from the shore, nearly drove him crazy.

But whilst I was supporting him, my eye lighted on the figure of a man standing on the beach, as close to the water as the heavy breakers would permit him. He flourished his hand and shouted to us, but though I could hear his voice very faintly, his words were absolutely indistinguishable.

"Look!" I cried. "If that island is not inhabited, then yonder must be one of our men. For God's sake, Sir Mordaunt, pluck up your heart and help me to think how to act. Tripshore, come on deck! There's one of our crew ashore."

To make room for him I got upon deck, and squatted under the companion to shelter myself from the flying water.

"It's Bill Burton, I believe, or Tom Hunter—one or the other," exclaimed Tripshore. "Oh, Lord! if we could only chuck him the end of a line, he'd be able to drag us ashore."

This, maybe, was the one hint I needed to set my mind struggling. The look of the sky was a clear intimation that there must presently come such a sea that would break up and scatter the schooner, as her boats were already scattered. I sprang to my feet, and, watching my chance, crawled to the weather bulwarks, and crept along on my hands and knees until I came to the forecastle, where, as I have said, the water was not flying heavily. This did not bring me closer to the man ashore, but I could stand erect here without great peril of being swept overboard, providing I held on tightly, and so could make him see me.

He saw me the moment I stood up, as I perceived by the

manner in which he hallooed and flourished his arms. At the top of my voice I shouted to him, " Can you hear me ? "

The wind blew my voice to him, and he immediately made an affirmative gesture.

" If we can manage to send you the end of a line, look out for it, and make the end fast," I bawled.

He again raised his hand.

By this time Tripshore had joined me, and looking toward the companion, I perceived Sir Mordaunt and his wife and Norie on the steps, watching us.

"Tripshore," I cried, "we must get a rope's end ashore somehow. How is it to be done ? "

We stood looking about us in a torture of perplexity.

" If we made a line fast to the half of that boat," I said, pointing to the broken boat at the davits, "would the wind drift it ashore, think you ? "

"Ay, sir, it might—it might ! Stop ! " he shouted. " I have it ! Where's the dog ? "

"Yes ! " I cried, the full significance of his meaning flashing upon me before the words had died on his lips. " If the beast be living he may save our lives ! "

I ran my eyes eagerly over the decks, but the sea had torn up every fixture, with the exception of the companion and sky-lights, and there was not a corner where the dog could have lain hid.

" Have you seen your dog ? " I cried to Sir Mordaunt ; but at that moment a heavy sea washed over the after part of the deck, and some shrieks from the women told me that a quantity of water had filled the companion, driving down Sir Mordaunt and the others.

" If you'll look for the dog in the fo'ksle, I'll seek him in the cabin," exclaimed Tripshore.

" Pray the Lord he's not overboard ! " And as he said this he dropped on his knees and crept along under the bulwarks.

The forecastle was open. I threw my legs over, and feeling the ladder with my feet, briskly descended. But the forecastle was half full of water, and it was up to my waist when my head was on a level with the upper deck. It was wonderful that the bulkhead that separated the forecastle from the after part of the vessel stood the weight : had it given, the cabin would have been drowned at once. I knew that nothing could be alive here. I peered and peered to see if there was any one in the upper bunks, but nothing was to be seen but the water and some soaked bedclothes hanging over the edges of the upper bunks. Whatever else was there lay at the bottom, under water and out of sight.

This choking and gurgling and dark forecastle so sickened my heart, that I stood holding on to the ladder, and looking with helpless horror like a man malignantly fascinated. But a sudden twitch of the vessel shocked me into my senses again, and I scrambled on deck, so persuaded that our end was at hand, that in the torment of my mind I could have flung myself overboard, so much crueler than death was this anguish of expecting it. I was scarcely on the forecastle, however, when fresh life was given me by the sight of Tripshore approaching with the dog. He had the animal by the flesh of the neck, and came along like an animal himself, that is to say, on his knees and left hand. The water flew in sheets over him, but he escaped the terrible falls by keeping close under the bulwarks, and presently he was at my side with the dog, eagerly telling me that he had found him behind the arms-rack in the cabin.

I immediately pulled out my knife and cut away some of the thin running gear which lay across the deck ; they were sheet and jib-halliards, long and light. I knotted them together until I calculated they made a length of over sixty fathoms. I hitched one end over the dog's neck, taking care that the animal should have plenty of freedom, and yet that the hitch should not slip over his head either. He was streaming with water, and seemed to understand our peril. I patted and stroked and soothed him as best I could, pointing to the land, and bidding him swim to it, just as I would have talked to a man. The creature looked at me and whined. I patted him again, and then Tripshore helped me to raise him, and we carried him to the submerged side of the hull, walking up to our arm-pits in water, and there we flung him overboard into the whirl of froth. He sunk in the foam, and I believed that the weight of the wet rope had dragged him down ; but presently his head came up a little distance away from the yacht. He turned, and tried to regain the vessel. I shouted and pointed to the land, gesticulating furiously in that direction, as did Tripshore, both of us menacing him with our fists to drive him shoreward, and standing with the water nearly up to our throats, as I have said, but happily without danger from the toppling white seas to leeward, in consequence of the yacht's bows being hove high, and her hull sheltering the water just under her there.

14

For about a minute—to me an eternity—the dog swam round and round, and I was in the greatest terror lest the line, which I had given plenty of scope to, should foul his legs. He rose and sank upon the seas, swimming very well, and the foam blowing like drifts of snow over him. At last a sea lifted him high, with his eyes to the land, and from that moment he began steadily to make for it.

Seeing this, I told Tripshore to shout to the man on the beach to look out for the dog. The animal had a large head, and it was impossible for the man to miss seeing him. As the dog swam, I carefully threw fake after fake of line overboard, giving abundance of slack, that the animal might be as little hampered as possible. The set of the tide—which I knew to be rising by feeling the twitching of the vessel—carried the dog somewhat to the westward ; but the strong wind blowing in a contrary direction greatly diminished the influence of the tide upon the brave brute, and with a transport of delight I beheld him slowly and surely approach the land whilst the man on the beach encouraged him by smacking his knee and waving his arm.

In about ten minutes after having been thrown overboard, the dog was among the breakers. Had he been a man swimming for his life, this would have been the most desperate part of the undertaking. But I did not fear for the dog. I knew his great muscular power, and that his long narrow body would not be greatly affected by the recoil of the breakers. And I was right ; for presently I saw him flung up on top of a running sea, and as it broke upon the beach the dog sprang out of the foam and ran to the man, and lay down at his feet.

I now told Tripshore to look about him and select the stoutest rope he could find and bend it on to the line, and tell the man to haul it ashore. He guessed my scheme, as, indeed, any sailor would, and fell to work with great energy and smartness, Whilst he cleared away the biggest rope he could come at, I crept along under the bulwarks, and, watching my opportunity, made a dash for the companion, and swung myself into it before the sea could strike me.

The water was rising in the cabin fast and in the lee side of it, it lay like a lake. Sir Mordaunt and the others stood at the foot of the steps. I told them that the forecastle was the safest place now, that very little water was coming over there, that the dog had reached the shore with the line, and that under God's providence I was sure we should be able to save our lives.

" But you must come along to the forecastle at once," said I. "The tide is rising, and the wind is increasing, and you may feel the vessel stirring with every blow. Sir Mordaunt, I will take your wife and Carey. You will take your niece. Norie will bring Mrs. Stretton."

So saying, I took Lady Brookes's hand and helped her up the steps, calling to Carey to follow. I left them standing in the companion whilst I crawled up the deck to a belaying-pin that was just abreast of the hatch, over which I hitched a rope, so that the end came to the companion. With this we should be able to drag ourselves up under the shelter of the bulwarks. How full of peril this job of getting up those decks to the bulwarks was I hardly know how to express ; for it is impossible in words to put before you the picture of those slippery inclined planks, and the incessant gushing and high leaping of solid bodies of green water over the after portion of the devoted hull, so that the foaming of the seas over the bulwarks as much resembled a river flooding a dam, and tumbling into a sheet of froth into a lower reach, as anything I can liken it to. Yet owing to the acute inclination of the hull, the bulwarks so overhung the deck that the pouring water left a clear space immediately under them. To reach this clear space was now our business. I grasped Lady Brookes firmly around the waist, and seized the rope, but found I had not the strength to drag our united weight up by one hand. A sharp wrench of the vessel, accompanied by the grinding and cracking sounds of breaking timber, struck through me like a wound in the side. I shouted to Tripshore to come and help me, whereupon he dropped the rope that he was clearing away from the raffle, and crawled aft. I told him to station himself at the belaying-pin and haul the women up as I made them fast. Indeed, there was no other way of managing that business. I passed the end of the rope round Lady Brookes's waist, and bidding her have no fear, launched her up to the deck as far as my arms could thrust her, and Tripshore hauled her up alongside of him, and so got her under the bulwark.

In this fashion we placed the other women under that shelter, though a sea dashed Carey down and nearly drowned her as Tripshore was dragging her up ; and then telling the baronet and Norie to imitate my behavior, I pulled myself up the deck, and with Tripshore's assistance got the women forward, where we were joined by Sir Mordaunt and the doctor.

It was now very evident, from the increasing oscillation of

the yacht and the grinding of her bottom upon the reef, that the tide was making fast. There was a great weight in the wind too, and I knew that the seas would grow bigger with the flood. I told my companions to hold fast to the ringbolts and cleats, or whatever else their hands could come at, and squat low out of the way of the rushing and shooting waters, and then fell to work with Tripshore to clear away the rope I wanted to stretch to the shore.

As well as my eye could measure the distance, the beach was about fifty fathoms away. All between was the broken, white water, in which no boat could have lived an instant, even had we had a boat to launch. Apparently the reef we had struck on was a shelf that would be dry in smooth water at low tide. The yacht had struck it bow on and run up it, then swung broadside round, leaving the forepart of her high.

The instant we had cleared away the rope, we bent the end of it on to the shore line, and signaled to the man to haul in. This he did, and when the end came to his hand I bawled to him to make it securely fast. There were some dwarf trees a short distance up the beach, and he carried the end of the rope to one of them and fastened it. Could I have seen any hand-spikes laying about, I should have carried our end of the rope to the forecastle capstan and got a strain upon it; but not being able to use the capstan, all of us men tailed on to the rope, and with our united weight tautened it considerably.

"Now, Tripshore," said I, " I shall rig up a sliding bowline-on-the-bite on this rope, but it'll want two hauling lines—one to drag the bowline ashore, and the other to drag it back again. Can you reach the land by that warp?"

He looked at it, and said, " Yes, sir."

" If you don't feel strong enough for the job, don't attempt it. I'll try. But if you have the strength, you'll be the likelier man."

" I'll do it," he repeated, and pulled off his coat.

With feverish haste I cleared away another length of thin line and hitched the end round his waist ; and in a moment he went over the bows, laid hold of the warp, and traveled along it hand over fist. It wanted a real sailor with a lion's heart in him to adventure such an exploit—a man used to hanging on by his eyelids, and with fingers like fish-hooks. The rope curved into a bight under his weight, and the white seas leaped and snapped at his feet, and sometimes buried him in foam as high as his waist. I watched him without a wink of the eye.

" Foot by foot he went along the rope."--Page 213.

Recalling my thoughts at that time, I may realize now the frightful intensity of my stare. I hardly seemed to breathe. Quite mechanically I let the line slip overboard, as, foot by foot, he went along, making the warp jump with his jerks as one hand passed the other. One hundred yards seem but a short span ; yet it made a fearfully long journey for that heroic man, and nothing but a brain of iron could have endured the sight of the furious, broken, tumbling water below. I say honestly, such was the condition of my nerves, that I do not doubt, had I been in Tripshore's place, I should have let go, through inability to stand the sight of the giddy, sickening spectacle of whirling, flashing, torrent-like play of foaming waters over which he was passing.

Foot by foot he went along the rope. When near the breakers he paused, and my heart seemed to stop beating. Half his body—nay, the whole, indeed—would be swept by those rushing and shattering acclivities, and this appeared to be in his mind, or perhaps he was taking breath for the dreadful encounter. He began to move again. Nine or ten times did his hands pass and repass each other, and then a tall breaker took him and swept him right along the warp. It passed, and he swung back like a pendulum, and again proceeded. But the recoil of the same sea hove him along the warp again, and again he swung heavily. I prayed aloud to God to give him strength. Thrice was he beaten in that manner, and each time left him swinging nearer the shore. The fourth time he let go, and vanished in the send of a breaker as it swelled in fury up the beach. The man who had been standing watching him darted toward the spot where he had disappeared, and plunged up to his middle in the water. Immediately after the form of Tripshore emerged, and both men ran up the beach.

Sir Mordaunt had watched this noble struggle as well as I, but Norie and the women sat crouched under the bulwarks, resembling bundles of clothes, never once uttering a sound. Indeed, Lady Brookes kept her eyes closed, and her arms hanging inertly down, and her white face made her look dead.

When I saw that Tripshore was safe, I seized a piece of stout rope, and knotted it into the bowline that is used at sea for slinging men. This done, I hitched it with a large eye upon the warp, so that it should slide easily, and attached the end of the line that Tripshore had carried ashore with him to it. I also bent on to it a similar line, the end of which was to be retained on board ; and all this being accomplished with the mad headlong haste that a man will make who works for his life, I went to Lady Brookes and took her arm, and speaking of the bowline as a noose, that she might understand me, I told her to make haste and get into it, that Tripshore and the other man might pull her ashore.

She opened her eyes and got up, being, indeed, compelled to rise by the force I was obliged to exert ; but when she saw what she was to do, she uttered a terrific shriek, and ran to her husband and clung to him.

I saw a dreadful difficulty here, and something to cruelly heighten the horrors of our position. But the yacht was beginning to bump heavily, and the seas which washed the after part of her in floods were threatening to sweep the forecastle.

" If her life is to be saved, she *must* do it ! " I shouted to Sir Mordaunt. " The vessel is breaking up. If there is any delay we must all perish. For God's sake, for all our sakes, steel your heart to her cries, and help me to get her into that sling."

Made desperate by the peril of delay I grasped the poor woman as I said this, but though the baronet did his best to assist me, he seemed crushed, broken down, without strength ; and never shall I forget his face as I dragged his shrieking wife into the bows of the yacht, nor my own shame and horror of soul at the violence I was forced to exert.

She was as strong as a man. She wrestled with me, she got her hand in my hair, and most assuredly she would have overpowered me, as I was scarce able to keep my footing on the deck, had not Norie come to my help. He grasped her hands from behind, another drag brought her close to the bowline, I slipped it under her arms, and then seizing her by the waist, I lifted her bodily over the bows of the yacht, and left her dangling upon the warp.

I was nearly spent with this dreadful struggle, but yet found voice enough to shout to the men to haul in steadily and quickly. Indeed, there was no great danger. She had only to hold her mouth closed when she neared the breakers, and keep quiet, and let the men drag her. But it was impossible to give her any directions. Her screams were terrific. Hardly had the bowline been dragged a dozen feet, when she caught hold of the warp, and prevented the men from hauling her. I yelled to her to let go, but my cries were only answered by her piercing shrieks.

" What is to be done ? " I exclaimed to Sir Mordaunt, as the yacht thumped heavily on the reef, followed by a loud crash and splintering wood.

"See--she has left go! Her head has fallen on one side! Oh, great God! has the fright killed her?" he cried.

I roared to the men to drag her along quickly. The warp was slippery with the wet, and the bowline traveled like a cringle upon a greased line. Twice the breakers buried the poor creature, and then they got her ashore and threw off the bowline, which I hastily hauled aboard.

I now called to Miss Tuke, and she got up without a word, her face of a shocking whiteness, her lips so tightly compressed that they were no more than an ashen line, with a fine gleam of resolution in her eyes.

"Have no fear," I exclaimed. "Keep your mouth shut. The wash of the breakers won't hurt you then."

I passed the bowline under her arms, helped her over the bows, gave the signal to the men, and she was dragged along the warp, mute as a statue. The landing of such heroines as this was no labor. They had her ashore in less than two minutes, and though she had passed through one heavy sea, yet the moment she touched the land she waved her hand to us, and then dropped on her knees beside the prostrate and motionless figure of her aunt.

Her fine example heartened Mrs. Stretton, who was ready for the bowline before I had dragged it aboard. She threw it over her head quickly, got over the bow without help, and was presently safe on the beach.

But when it came to Carey's turn the poor girl shrieked out, and shrunk back in an agony of terror. I had so great a horror of forcing her, after my dreadful struggle with Lady Brookes, that I cried to Sir Mordaunt, "Let it be your turn, then. It will comfort your wife to have you. I will reason with Carey, and when you are gone she may follow quietly."

He knew as well as I that there was no time to be wasted, and I believe he, too, dreaded the spectacle of Carey's terror and the sound of her cries. I helped him over the bows, and whilst the men hauled him along, I seized the girl's hand and bade her mark how easy it was, how free from danger; and was thus speaking to her as tenderly and encouragingly as the state of mind I was then in would permit, when a great sea struck the yacht right amidships, and spreading like a gigantic fan, poured in a vast overwhelming deluge clean over the vessel. Nothing could have resisted that tremendous and crushing Niagara of a sea. In an instant I felt myself carried away by a force so astounding that temporarily it killed every instinct of life in me, and I don't remember that I made the least exertion to save myself, no, not by so much as extending my arms. But in the midst of the thunder of the enormous surge I could distinctly hear the rending and crashing of the yacht's hull, and knew by the sounds, as though I had seen the fabric demolished, that the schooner had gone to pieces.

When I rose to the surface of the water I found myself among a quantity of pieces of floating timber, one piece of which I seized. The waves were heights of creaming foam, and I seemed to rise and fall upon a surface of heaving, leaping, and wildly-blown snow. Being run up by a wave, I saw about a stone's throw distant the figure of Norie clasping a short spar, and quite close to me was Carey, clinging to a fragment of one of the yacht's ribs. I waited till the next sea hove me up, and then shouted to her to hold tight, and that I would endeavor to get to her; and seizing a lighter piece of wood than I had first grasped, I pointed my face toward her and struck out with my feet, exerting all my strength. The tide brought her my way, and meanwhile I was able to stem the current by help of the wind and by violently moving my legs. At last the sea swung the piece of timber to which she clung close to me, on which I grasped her arm, and seeing that the fragment that sustained her would support us both, I let go my piece of wreck and grabbed with my left hand at hers. I cried in her ear, with the hope of keeping her poor heart up, that the land was close, and that there was no fear of her sinking if she kept a good hold. Had I been alone, I cannot flatter myself that I should have exhibited anything like the spirit that was animating me now. I might have held on with a dogged madness for life, but I dare say no more than my animal instincts would have operated. The need of this helpless woman surprisingly stimulated me. She created in me, I will say, a high and honest courage. I took her by the waist, and with a jerk planted her upon the piece of timber, so that the swell of her breast stayed her, and lifted her head well above the water. The whirl of the seas swayed us round and round; sometimes our faces looked toward the land, and sometimes toward the reef where the yacht had gone to pieces, and where the water was boiling with a frightful sound. Whenever we confronted the beach I struck out with my legs. My dread and fearful expectation was that the tide, as it gained in force, would run us out to sea, in which case there would be no hope for us ; but after we had been tossing in the water for upward of a quarter of an hour, I saw from the height of a tall sea that we were steadily nearing the beach, upon which stood the people who had been saved, and I then perceived that the wind blowing with violence against the tide tended to drift us landward, whilst every sea that ran also helped us forward.

I could see nothing of Norie, and supposed he was drowned. The wind, as I had anticipated from the appearance of the sky, had risen into a gale, and the foam flew along the water like sheets of steam ; and whenever the combers whirled us with our faces to the blast, we had like to have lost our sight as well as have been suffocated by the fury with which the pitiless spray poured against us. As minute after minute went by, the agony of that struggle grew greater and greater. I do not mean that I found my strength failing me, or that my poor companion relaxed her deathlike embrace of the piece of timber that floated us. It was the wild and dashing tossing of the sea ; the hissing and deafening seething and crackling of spume in our ears ; the rush of foam over our heads when the crest of a wave broke after we had been hove to its summit ; the appalling feeling of bitterness and helplessness inspired by those mad white waters, and the insignificance of the strength we possessed to oppose them—it was these things that made that struggle the great agony it became.

But in consequence of our steady approach to the land, my spirits never utterly sank. Whenever it was in my power to do so, I called to my companion to keep up her courage, that our sufferings would soon be over, until at last we found ourselves among the breakers. I threw myself upon the woman's back, with my hands grasping the timber on either side her arms, so that my weight might keep her body pressed to the spar ; and scarcely was I so planted when a roaring sea took us and ran us toward the beach at the rate of an express train. It completely buried us, and I felt myself flying round and round in it like a wheel, frenziedly grasping the timber and feeling the woman's body under me. Oh, the sickening, swooning deathlike sensation of that rush ! the thunder of the water in the ears ! the choking, suffocating, bursting feeling in the head and breast ! It hurled us upon the beach, and flung us there with such violence that I let go, unable to keep my fists clinched. I was seized by the hair, but in an instant wrenched away and torn back into the boiling arch of the next breaker, which rolled shatteringly over me with a sound as though the earth were splitting in halves , and then I suppose my senses left me, for I have no further memory of struggling in the water.

When I recovered I found myself on my back. My senses were active at once, and I had no difficulty in recollecting what had befallen us. I sat upright, and pressing my hands to my eyes, so as to clear my sight, I looked about me.

Some twenty paces away was assembled a small group of persons. These people consisted of Miss Tuke and Mrs. Stretton, both of whom crouched over the body of Carey, and were chafing her hands, supporting her head, and the like. Near them was Norie, wringing out his coat. I was amazed to see him alive. A little beyond sat Sir Mordaunt, with his face bowed down to his knees and buried in his hands, and his back turned upon a recumbent figure, the head of which was hidden by a man's jacket. The man whom we had noticed on the beach when the dawn broke, and whom I now recognized as one of the crew named Tom Hunter, was down near the breakers, shading his eyes, and intently gazing toward the sea.

This dismal group I took in at a glance, and was beginning to count them, to see how many we were in all, when Trip-shore stepped round from behind me.

" I thought you wasn't drowned, sir," said he. "You didn't look like a drowned man. There was no good going on chafing of you. How do you feel yourself, sir?"

" I can't tell you yet, Tripshore," I answered. "Is the poor girl I came ashore with alive?"

"I don't know, sir. I've been looking at the ladies rubbing her. I think they'll pull her through."

" And Lady Brookes?" said I.

" Ah, she's dead, sir. She was dead afore Tom and I could haul her through the breakers."

I asked him to give me his hand, and then struggled on to my feet. My limbs were sound, and I suffered from no other inconvenience than a feeling of faintness and giddiness. No one noticed me until I was close to the group, and then Miss Tuke, seeing me, uttered a cry, started to her feet, and grasped my hand. Sir Mordaunt must have heard her, but he did not raise his head nor shift his posture.

"Thank God you are spared!" cried the girl, speaking wildly, like a delirious person.

"Are these all of us?" I said, motioning with my hand.

" These are all—and my aunt is dead !   Oh, Mr. Walton, my aunt is dead ! " she exclaimed.

I could make no reply.   Mrs. Stretton put out her hand for mine.   I gave it to her, and she pressed it.   She could not rise, because Carey's head lay on her lap, but the poor maid was alive, and followed me with her eyes, though she could not move for exhaustion.

I stepped over Lady Brookes's body, and lifted the jacket.   It was not necessary to look twice at her face to know that she was dead.   Her features were very calm ; death was in every line ; her eyes were open, and the expression they gave the face was like a command to keep it covered.

As I replaced the jacket softly, Sir Mordaunt turned his head. His face was dreadfully hollow, his complexion ashen, he was without coat or hat, and the strong wind having dried his hair, was blowing it wildly upon his head.   His clothes were streaming wet—as, for that matter, were mine and the others'.   He gazed at me for a while like a man struggling with his mind. Then said he, " Walton, my wife is dead.   I brought her from home to save her life, and my hope and my love have ended in that ! "   And he pointed to the body.   " Why am I spared ? I vow to God I would willingly be dead."   Thus he went on complaining and mourning until his voice died away, when he burst into tears, and turned his back upon his wife's body, and resumed his former attitude.

Bitter sad this blow was, indeed, to him and to all of us.   I looked at the body, with a dreadful remorse in my heart.   I felt as if I had killed her by that struggle on the yacht's forecastle. But it would not do to sit lamenting our misfortunes and bewailing the dead.   We were eight living men and women, castaways, and in one, at least, the instinct of life was a passion that seemed to have taken a violence from my salvation from the sea that lay boiling and roaring in front of me.   Where had we been shipwrecked ?   What was this island ?   What shelter would it offer us ?   Was help to be obtained ?   These were the questions which swarmed into my head.

There was a small piece of rising ground a short walk from where Sir Mordaunt and the others were, and I made my way to it, that I might be alone and able to reflect, and also because it was an eminence that would furnish me with some view of the island.   My movements were very languid, and my bones ached sorely ; but I was grateful to find that my limbs were sound, which seemed an incredible thing when I reflected upon the terrible violence with which I had been dashed ashore.

I gained the top of the little hill, for I may as well call it so, though it was no more than a small rise in the land, about sixteen or twenty feet above the level of the island, and stood there leaning against the wind, that was now very nearly a whole gale. I first looked toward the sea. Where the reef was the water was blowing up in clouds of smoke, as though it was really boiling, as it only seemed to be. It was the most terrific picture of commotion I had beheld for many a long year. The great Atlantic seas, reared to a vast height by the fury of the wind, came rolling along with a wild kind of majesty out of the haze of spray which narrowed the horizon to within a league ; the crests of them broke into wildernesses of shining froth as they ran ; but whenever they smote the reef, that lay in a curve trending on my right to the westward, and coiling round into the north with the conformation of the beach, they were shattered into a perfect world of snow, which again was furiously agitated, and flashed in a magnificent tumultuous play, in pyramids and cones and such shapes, until near the shore, where the shoaling ground forced the giddy tumblers into some regularity of swing, and they swept in dazzling ivory-white volumes upon the beach, filling the air with a most indescribable and soul-subduing roaring noise. A curtain of slate-colored cloud was stretched across the heavens. I shaded my eyes and gazed fixedly at the boiling on the reef, but not a vestige of the yacht was to be seen. It was an awful thing to look upon that raging water, and not be able to see the merest relic of the brave, stout, beautiful fabric that had borne us so many hundreds of miles across the breast of the deep. My heart stopped still when I thought of our preservation, and of my own especially. I had not realized the desperate and breathless and thrilling wonder of it until I stood upon this little hill and looked down at that fearful sea. It made me raise my clasped hands and turn my face up to God. It was a speechless thanksgiving, for I made no prayer beyond what was in my face that I turned up in adoration, and with a heart full of tears.

I now put my back to the wind, to survey the island. How small it was you may guess when I tell you that even from the little vantage ground I occupied I could view the sea nearly all around it. I believed at first it was the island of Little Magna, and in that faith searched and searched in the south-east for signs of the coast of the greater island of that name, but I could see nothing. I then began to think it was too small for Little Magna, nor was it conceivable that we should have been wrecked so far to the south as that island. As I might judge, the island was not above two miles from the east to the west, and a little more than a mile from north to south. It was a coral island, what is called a "cay" in those parts, almost entirely flat, with a little bay in the south-east, formed by the curvature of a piece of land that resembled in shape the hind leg of a horse when lifted. Here and there were groups of dwarf trees, nothing tropical in their appearance. About a pistol-shot from the base of the hill was a mass of stunted vegetation that ran to the right and entirely covered the limb of land. Indeed, this island was no more than a desert, inhospitable rock, scarcely more than a reef, without signs of any living creature upon it. Again and again I tried to penetrate the haze which the gale blew up out of the foaming sea, and which hung like a fog all around the horizon, in the hope of perceiving higher land, but in vain. As far as I could cast my eyes the ocean was a storming blank, and, for the solitude of it, this rock might be have been in the middle of the Great Pacific.

What was to be done? Here we were, cast away upon an island, without a boat, without any visible means of escaping ; surrounded by reefs, as was easily to be guessed from the appearance of the water, the very sight of which was like a death-warrant, since they were an assurance that no vessels would attempt the navigation of these waters, at least to approach this island near enough to see us. I battled hard with the feeling of consternation that seized me, but I could not subdue it. How were we to support life? How were the women to be sheltered? How were we to make our situation known ?

I stood staring around me, with a deep despair in my heart ; but this wore off after a little, and I then quitted the hill and walked with difficulty against the heavy wind to the beach, where Tripshore and Hunter stood looking at the sea. The crashing of the breakers and the bellowing of the gale made conversation impossible here, so I motioned to the men to accompany me to the group of trees to one of which the yacht's warp still remained attached, and here we found some shelter.

I sat down, feeling very weak and trembling, and then seeing Mrs. Stretton and Miss Tuke looking our way, I invited

them by a gesture to this shelter.   Mrs. Stretton helped Carey
to rise, and I was heartily rejoiced to see the poor girl capable
of walking.   Miss Tuke put her arm around her uncle's neck,
and spoke to him.   He looked in our direction, and then at
the body of his wife, as though he would not leave it ; but on
Norie speaking to him, he rose and came to us, helped along
by Norie and his niece.

I did not know until afterward that my poor friend had been
very nearly drowned when the yacht went to pieces.   He was
midway along the rope when the vessel broke up, and the warp
dropping into the sea, he fell with it, and had to be dragged
ashore through the breakers.   As I looked at him, and noted
his hollow face, and his hair wildly blowing, and his long
beard scattering like smoke upon his shirt-front, and his knees
feebly yielding to his weight as he slowly advanced, leaning
forward to the gale, I thought of him as he stood to receive me
at the *Lady Maud's* side in Southampton Water—how full of life
and health he was then ; how hopefully he looked forward to
this summer cruise ; how proudly he conducted me over
his vessel, and I recalled his tenderness and anxiety for his
wife.   There *she* lay, cold and senseless as the coral strand
upon which the breakers were roaring in thunder.   Her time
had come, and she was at rest.   But her motionless figure,
painfully hidden by the rough jacket which Hunter had taken
off his back to lay over her, was a most dreadful object for us
in our distracted and miserable condition to have full in our
sight ; and when I looked from it to the halting figure of the
husband as he came along, I was moved to a degree I have no
words to express.

They led him to where I was seated, and he sank down
upon the ground.   The others drew near, some of them sat,
some stood.   I broke the silence by saying :—

"There are eight of us living, and we must go to work now
and think how we may prolong our lives, and ultimately save
ourselves.   I have been trying to discover other land near us,
but the weather is too thick to see any distance.   Tripshore—
Tom Hunter—have you any notion what part of the Bahamas
this is ? "

They both answered no.

" Let the island be what it will," I continued, " we cannot be
far from inhabited land.   We may take hope from that," said I,
addressing the women.

"We ought to look for water, sir," exclaimed Tripshore.

" Yes," cried Norie, eagerly. "I am thirsty to death. The salt water I swallowed has left me intolerably parched."

"Will you help Tripshore to seek for water?" I asked.

"Willingly—but where are we to look for it?" he replied, casting his eyes about.

"Everywhere," said Tripshore, bluntly.

"Try for a natural well, first," said I. "If that can't be found, there's a stretch of sand yonder. Dig into it with your hands, or with anything you can find knocking about, and you may come to fresh water."

"I have read that fresh water may be found sometimes by digging in the sand," exclaimed Sir Mordaunt, in a feeble voice.

"Come, sir," said Tripshore to Norie ; and the two men marched off.

They had scarcely left us when I caught sight of what looked like a stretch of canvas, resembling an immense .mass of seaweed, coiling over with the bend and fall of the breakers. It washed up the beach, but was swept back again, but I saw it would be stranded presently. It at once occurred to me that if we could secure that canvas we should be able to rig up a very tolerable shelter ; whereupon I called Hunter's attention to it, and told him to come with me and endeavor to drag the sail up the beach out of the breakers. He ran down to the beach before me, being much sounder and more active than I ; and watching his chance as the canvas was swept up, and the fore part of it stranded, he plunged as high as his knees into the whirl of recoiling foam, and grasped the sail. By this time I had reached his side. We hauled together, and every breaker helping us, we managed to drag the sail out of the water. It proved to be the schooner's main-gaff-topsail. It had most of its gear attached to it, particularly a length of halyards. We waited whilst the water drained out of it, and then seizing it afresh we dragged it toward the trees.

Sir Mordaunt had gone back to the body of his wife, and sat crouched alongside of it, exposed to the strong wind. This made me see the necessity of burying the body as soon as possible. But first it was necessary to furnish the women with some kind of shelter. So having got the sail among the trees we fell to work, Miss Tuke and Mrs. Stretton lending a hand. Hunter had a clasp-knife in his pocket, and with this we cut away the gear, and divided it into lengths to serve as lanyards. These lanyards we hitched to the bolt-rope by making holes in the canvas, and then selecting a couple of trees for stanchions, we rigged up a kind of tent, the windward side only (as the wind then blew) being protected, for the sail was not big enough to furnish us with four walls as well as a roof.

Rude and imperfect as this contrivance was, however, yet no sooner were the women inside it than they felt the comfort of it. Had we been in dry clothes the wind might have seemed warm enough, but our garments being soaked to the skin gave the gale an edge of chilliness that kept the flesh shuddering. Hence this shelter from the wind was a very great comfort indeed. It took us but a short while to rig up the sail, nor could the wind demolish it, thanks to the trees, which broke the force of the gale, and supplied us with uprights as strong as rocks. When our work was completed I went to Sir Mordaunt, and by exerting a gentle force obliged him to come with me. I led him into a corner of the tent, and made him sit upon the grass, that was coarse and thick, but stunted like the trees, as if the blowing of spray from the beach had checked its growth without killing it. I then whispered to Miss Tuke that we were going to remove the body of Lady Brookes, and begged her to stand in front of her uncle, under any pretense she could invent, so that he might not see what we were about.

"Are you going to bury her?" she exclaimed, with a look of mingled fright and grief.

"No, not before I consult Norie," I replied. "But we *must* remove the body out of the husband's sight. Pray conceal us, as I suggest, and talk to him. We shall not be long."

So saying, I quitted the tent, and motioning to Hunter, I told him to help me carry the body around the bend of the little hill, where it would be hidden, and where it might lie until we could manage to bury it. Approaching the body, we raised it reverently. The wet clothes made it a great weight, and, besides, she had been a fine, well-made woman, as I have told you. I took the arms, letting the head lie against my breast, and as we raised her I looked at the tent, and saw Miss Tuke and Mrs. Stretton both standing in front of Sir Mordaunt, and effectually concealing us. But after we had advanced a few paces, a violent gust of wind blew the jacket away and left the face exposed. Hunter had his back upon it, and was spared the sight, but I had it all the way, for I could not re-cover the face without laying the body down, which I would not do, lest Sir Mordaunt should catch sight of us, and follow.

We went round the base of the hill, and put the body down upon some grass at the margin of a stretch of deep and impervious bush, resembling the growths in Australia in respect of density, the greater portion of which was as high as my waist, though here and there it stood above my head. We laid the body down here, I say, and Hunter went back for the jacket, with which we covered the face, placing two stones upon the arms, to prevent the jacket from blowing away ; and, this done, I ascended the bit of a hill, to look for Norie and Tripshore.

I saw them, when I had mounted a few feet, about a quarter of a mile distant, coming our way very quickly, and skirting the shrubbery, that extended, with a very clean, well-defined edge, athwart the island, as far as the horse-limb curve of land, as though human hands had planted it.

I shouted to them, and Tripshore waved his hand, and when they were within hearing distance the man holloaed out, "We have found water, sir ! "

This was a joyful piece of news. It made my heart flutter, and filled me with as deep a transport as even the intelligence that help was coming could have done.

" They have found water ! " I bawled to Hunter, who stood at some distance from me.

He cried back, "Thanks to the Lord for it, sir ! We should all have been mad for a drink presently."

I then joined him, and whilst we stood waiting for the others, I asked him, having had no opportunity to do so before, how he had managed to save his life, and what had become of the other men. His story was very short and simple. When the yacht struck, all of the crew who were below rushed on deck. Pitch-dark as it was, a number of men groped their way to what I have already called the long-boat. They managed to get her over, but how he could not explain, beyond implying that they worked like fiends in their terror, and launched her, he believed, by sheer force of muscle. Nobody thought of anything but saving his life. The belief was that the yacht would clear the reef and founder in the deep water beyond. (Note.— They believed it was a reef because they could not see the least signs of land.) Hunter knew that some men were drowning in the water to leeward of the deck, by the bubbling cries which came out of the darkness that way, but it was impossible to help them. When the boat was over, they could see her plainly enough upon the foam, and the men jumped for her,

15

some missing her, and vanishing alongside. Hunter jumped
and reached her, but he could not tell me how many souls
were in her : she was about half full, he thought. But scarcely
had they shoved clear of the vessel when a sea took and
capsized the boat, and then what followed was just a dream to
him. He, being a good swimmer, struck out, not knowing
where he was going, for he could see nothing but the white
water ; but after battling, he knew not how long, he was
caught by the breakers and flung ashore, where he lay motionless, and almost lifeless, for a spell. When the dawn came he
found himself alone, and the yacht on her beam ends on
the reef, with the sea bursting in clouds over her after-deck.
He saw me standing in the companion, and then Tripshore,
but he did not believe there were any more people alive until
he saw the rest of our party crowd into the bows. It was he,
he said, who caught me by the hair when the breakers had
flung me along ; but he could not keep hold, and the water
swept me back again. The next time he caught me by the arm
and held me until the breaker had spent itself, and then
dragged me high and dry. Carey, he added, owed her life to
Tripshore, who watched for her as he (Hunter) had watched
for me, and managed to get her ashore the first time the sea
threw her up. Hunter saved Norie in the same way, "and it
was wonderful," said he, "how quiet the doctor" (for so Norie
was called by the men) "took his bath. I lugged him out, and
he was as fresh as a man swimming for to please himself.
But Lady Brookes's gell was all but gone, sir. She were black
in the face, and not a stir in her when Mr. Tripshore brought
her out o' the wash yonder."

Norie and Tripshore now joined us. I at once inquired
about the water.

"It's t'other side of the island, past them mangrove bushes,"
answered Tripshore, coming close to me, and pointing. "It's
a made well, not a nat'ral one, an' it's in the sand. A couple
o' casks, perhaps three, have been sunk, one atop of the other,
and the one atop has been left standing as high as this," says
he, holding his hand about two feet above the ground, "to
prevent the sand from filling it up."

"Does it look a recent job?" I asked anxiously.

"There's no telling, sir," he replied. "I take it to be the
work of one of the wrecking vessels which used to knock about
among these islands."

"If that be so, then there are vessels which touch here," I

exclaimed, with a swell of hope and elation in my heart. "Is the water good?"*

"It's rain-water," answered Norie; "but good enough. It has quenched my thirst, which was just maddening."

"How did you get at it?" I asked.

"I dipped with my shoe," he answered, for he had on a pair of low shoes. Then grasping my arm, he pointed to the grass alongside the bushes, and exclaimed, "What is that? Is that Lady Brookes's body?"

I told him it was, and explained my reason for bringing it to that place. He went to it, and lifted up the jacket, and took a long look at the face, and then coming back, he said, "It will be best to bury her at once, Walton. It shocks me to think of her lying so."

"I was only waiting for you to see her," said I. "But how can we bury her?" and turning to Hunter, I said, "Could you scoop up a grave for that body in the sand, with your hands?"

He answered yes; it would be no trouble, he thought.

Upon this I asked Norie to help him carry the body round to the east side of the hill, where there was a stretch of sand, and where they could inter the corpse without being seen by Sir Mordaunt and the women. Norie answered that he would take care the body was properly buried; and after waiting until they had carried it to the spot I had indicated, I called to Tripshore, whom I required to pilot us to the well, and returned to the little tent.

As I walked, I glanced my eye along the beach, and noticed that several portions of wreckage were already thrown up; and numerous black fragments were to be seen amid the white swirl, vanishing and reappearing amid the roaring folds of the breakers and the further surges. But my thirst was too troublesome to suffer me to examine and secure the articles which the sea had washed ashore.

I entered the little tent briskly, and said, in as cheerful a voice as I could command, that a well of fresh water had been found, and I asked them to walk with me across the island to drink. Miss Tuke and Mrs. Stretton, who were seated near Sir Mordaunt, instantly got up, and Carey made an effort to rise.

---

* I have since ascertained that it was the practice of the small wrecking vessels which resorted to these islands to sink casks in the sand in order to obtain water. These casks were to be found in North Cat Cay, Sandy Cay, and many other islets on and in the neighborhood of the peak Bahama Bank.

I told Tripshore to support her, and then extended my hand to the baronet, who reared himself with great difficulty and labor.

"Thank Heaven that water has been found," said he, in a voice so unlike his familiar tone, that had I not seen his lips move, I should not have believed it his. "God has not wholly forsaken us."

"Lean upon me," said I. "The distance is not great. We may think it advisable by-and-by to shift our quarters to the other side of the island. But first let us see what those breakers will give us of the wreck.

Mrs. Stretton and Miss Tuke walked first, followed by Carey, supported by Tripshore. The mastiff followed in our wake. It was hard for Carey to have to walk to the well, but we had no vessel in which to bring water to her. When Sir Mordaunt, leaning on my arm, stepped forth from the trees, he looked and looked, and then stopped, and gripping me tightly, said, in a kind of gasp, "Where is Agnes ? Where is the body ? What have you done with it, Walton ?"

"Oh, my dear friend," I answered, wrung to the very soul by the misery in his voice, "in the name of God, believe that what we do, we do for your sake."

He sobbed convulsively, but with dry eyes, and then muttering, "God's will be done ! God's will be done !" which he repeated several times, he said no more, and we slowly followed the others.

To take his mind away from his grief, and to give him some hope too, I spoke about the well that Norie and Tripshore had discovered ; how its existence proved that the island had been visited ; and how, therefore, we need not despair of suffering a long captivity in this desolate spot of land. He did not, however, seem to heed me, but walked with his eyes fixed on the ground, and very often he weighed so heavily on my arm that I had some ado to bear up under him.

It still blew a heavy gale of wind, and the sea was shrouded with the haze of the flying spray. Away to the west of the island, the sea was running in enormous surges, and the roaring of the surf upon the beach on that side of the island was like a continuous roll of thunder, and the wind was full of a fine salt rain. The sky was one great cloud. I cannot express how desolate this shadow made the whole scene of snow-white storming ocean, and this little flat island, with its chilling and stunted herbage, and its groups of dwarf trees here and there, leaning all of them somewhat to the south-east, as though inclined by some strong prevailing wind. One gleam of sunshine, one flash of the glorious tropical luminary, would have cheered our hearts ; but it was our fate that the terrible disaster that had overtaken us should be attended with many circumstances of horror. The very heavens scowled upon us, and the air howled with the maledictions of the pitiless gale.

The spot where the well was sunk was within a mile of the tent. The land, as I had said, was nearly entirely flat, and the greater portion of it, beyond the coral sand, covered with grass, which was rank and long only among the bushes and under the trees. Walking was very easy. Here and there the ground was encumbered with knobs or projections of porous rock, as though the soil that covered the island was not everywhere deep enough to conceal its structure. As we advanced, a frigate pelican soared into the air, and struggled a minute or so with the gale, then dropped, and disappeared behind the bushes on the right. This was the only living thing I had yet seen on the island.

Tripshore led us straight to the well, which I found sunk in the sand about a hundred paces above high-water mark. It was constructed just as he had described. First, the sand had been dug out until fresh water was reached ; then a cask with the ends knocked out had been sunk in the hole, and another cask placed on this, so as to raise a kind of coamings above the sand, to prevent the well from filling.

I bent my head over, and saw the water within reach of my arm, looking black, and my face reflected in it. We all stood around, and I said, " What shall we use for a dipper?"

Tripshore answered, " Mr. Norie used his shoe, sir."

" None of us wear shoes," said I, casting my eyes about, " so we shall have to use a boot." And I was going to remove one of mine, when Mrs. Stretton whipped off hers and handed it to me. We were too thirsty for ceremony, so I took the boot, filled it with water, and gave it to Miss Tuke, saying that it was not the first time in history that a woman's shoe had served for a drinking cup. She passed it to Carey, who drank greedily. I filled the boot again and again, until we had all appeased our thirst. It was the salt water that had parched us, and Sir Mordaunt and Carey drank as if they could not quench their thirst.

Our situation came home to me with dreadful force whilst I stood watching them drink. Even had we all been men, the contrast of our lot now, greedily swallowing rain water from a boot, standing—with white faces and wet clothes, some of us half dressed and with uncovered heads—round that sunk cask, miserable shipwrecked people, imprisoned by a raging sea, with no prospect of relief before us that the most hopeful mind could imagine ; I say, even had we all been men, the contrast of our lot now with what it was aboard the *Lady Maud*, that luxurious floating home, with its hundred elegances and comforts, would have made a bitter thought.   But that contrast was tenfold heightened by the presence of the women, and especially by Miss Tuke.   If I was not in love with her, I will not say I was far off from loving her ; and so soft was my heart for her, that I could not look at her sweet face without a degree of tenderness and grief that almost shames me to recall when I remember how much sympathy I had for her in comparison with what I had for the others, whose distress and sufferings were surely as great.   Both she and Mrs. Stretton were fully dressed, having had time to clothe themselves whilst waiting for daylight in the *Lady Maud's* cabin.   Carey was the worst off, having lost her hat and shawl in the water, and her dress being torn by the sea, as a squall splits a sail.

It worried me so much to see my poor friend without a coat, that I pulled off mine and begged him to wear it.   He tried to get it on, but he was so much taller than I, and his shoulders proportionately broad. that it would not fit him.   I wondered that he should have left the yacht, half dressed, in that way, but I afterward remembered that he had thrown off his coat before being hauled ashore.

All having drank, I held the boot full of water to the dog, who lapped it furiously, and when the noble animal had had enough, I dried the boot somewhat by swinging it to and fro. But it was no better than a piece of brown paper; so I sat down and pulled off my own boots, gave one of them to Mrs. Stretton to slip on, and thrusting the other into my pocket offered Sir Mordaunt my arm, saying that the grass was as soft as a carpet, and that my socks would dry the quicker for being uncovered.

These are but trivial things to relate, but it is such things as these which make up the story of shipwreck.   I never hear now of a yachting party sailing away on an ocean cruise but that I wonder if they imagine what shipwreck means, what being cast away, stripped of every luxury they have been used to, forced to confront the naked heavens without a shelter to protect them from the roasting sun or the blinding rain or the furious gale, signify ? Death is not the worst part of the horrors of such an experience. You hear of protracted anguish ending in madness ; you hear of starvation terminating in cannibalism ; you hear of hardships and physical suffering converting the comeliest man into such an object of horror, that those whom God sends to succor him at last recoil with affright from the monstrous and unnatural appearance. To be shipwrecked is a terrible thing indeed ; how terrible, no man can tell save he who has suffered it.

On our return we met Hunter going to the well for a drink. He asked me the road. I pointed to the well, and told him he would have to make a cup of his hands or use his boot.

"Where is Norie ?" Sir Mordaunt asked me ; and I thought he seemed to notice for the first time that Norie and Hunter had not accompanied us to the well. I made some answer, I forget what. He looked at me eagerly, and with great trouble in his eyes, but asked no more questions.

On our arrival at the tent Mrs. Stretton gave me back my boot ; but I was not afraid of bare feet, so I sat down and pulled off my socks and rolled up my trousers, saying with a laugh that I should not be afraid of spoiling my boots now. We found Norie in the tent, sitting, and leaning his head on his arm. He looked as if all the hope had been crushed out of him. He was like a prisoner in a cell, haggard and shocked, and full of amazement and fear. He glanced from one to the other of us as we entered, and cried, " Don't let any one of you be alone if you can help it ! You cannot guess what solitude is here ! I have had about five minutes of it, and feel as if another five minutes would drive me out of my mind. The wind howls horribly through these trees ! And, my God ! did ever any sea roar like yonder waves ? "

" Pray don't afflict us with reflections of that kind, Norie," I exclaimed warmly. " Give Sir Mordaunt your place there, and come you along to the beach with Tripshore and me, and lend us a hand to collect the things which have been washed ashore."

He jumped up ; but as he did so Sir Mordaunt gave a little cry. I looked at him, and saw that his eyes were fixed upon the jacket that had covered the face of his wife. Norie had brought it away, and had been lying on it.

" Where is her body ? " asked the baronet, addressing Norie.

It was idle to keep the matter from him, so, meeting the doctor's glance, I dropped my head.

"We have buried her," said Norie.

"It was my wish," said I, seizing Sir Mordaunt's hand.

"Oh, but without a prayer—without one last look!" he cried, in a quivering voice.

"Don't say without a prayer," exclaimed Norie. "The seaman who helped me will tell you differently."

Sir Mordaunt took his hand from mine to cover his face, on which Mrs. Stretton and Miss Tuke went to him and began to comfort him, talking as gentle as pitying women can to a man in grief. They could do better than I or Norie. I therefore beckoned to the doctor, and we trudged down to the beach, where Tripshore was bending over some object that had been thrown up by the waves.

"For heaven's sake, Norie," said I, as we went along, "don't indulge in any dismal reflections before the women. Keep up their hearts if you can. Bad as our lot is, it might be worse. This island is *terra firma*, anyway. We have found water, and now we must look for something to eat. It is much too soon to cave in, man. You ought to know that."

"Ay," he exclaimed. "But to be alone for even five minutes after burying that poor woman. I thought my hospital work had cured me of all weakness; but the sweat poured from me when I put the body in the sand, dressed as it was, Walton! God preserve me! It seemed frightfully heartless to cover the face that I knew so well with the sand!"

He shuddered violently, and I own I shuddered too. He was fresh from a sad and shocking job indeed, and I was sorry I had spoken to him so warmly in the tent.

"But I *did* offer up a prayer, Walton," he added, with a singular and affecting simplicity of manner. "It was no falsehood I told Sir Mordaunt. I made a little prayer whilst Hunter filled up the hole we had scooped out."

By this time we were close to Tripshore.

"What have you there?" I called to him.

He shouted back, for the roar of the surf was deafening. "The carpenter's chest, sir."

This indeed it was. It was fitted with a shelf midway the height inside. All the tools which had been on top of this shelf were gone; but on dragging up the shelf, which lay jammed in the box like a cork in the neck of a bottle, we found the bottom full of nails of all sorts, some half as long as my arm, together with a saw, a chopper, fashioned to serve as a hammer too, and three sailors' sheath-knives.

"We shall find these things useful," said I, "so let us drag this chest clear of all risk from the breakers."

We laid hold of it and hauled it up the beach, then returned, and in ten minutes' time collected the following articles :—

The tell-tale compass, with a portion of the beam to which it had been screwed; two wooden cases, presently to be opened; a small cask, very heavy; a large kettle, with the lid gone and the spout warped; three spare sails; and a mass of the yacht's planks and timbers. We saved all the wood we could find, with the idea of building a hut for the women to lie in that night. We searched the beach, down into the very fork of the tiny bay in the south-east corner, where the water was tolerably smooth, owing to the shelter of the limb of land I have described, and found a quantity of timber, but nothing more to our purpose.

On opening the head of the cask, I found to my joy that it was full of salt beef, and, what was equally gladdening, the two cases contained each of them three dozens of tins of different kinds of preserved meats, which had been shipped for cabin use. This you may be sure we reckoned a noble discovery, for here was food ready cooked for us to eat. Forthwith we laid hold of the cases and carried them up to the tent.

" Here are the materials for two, and perhaps three, meals a day for nine days," I cried, addressing the inmates generally, "allowing each person a tin. Tripshore, go and fetch those sailors' knives. We shall all feel the better for a breakfast."

The man brought the knives, and we opened a couple of the tins, using a piece of deck-plank for a table. I divided the contents of the first tin into eight portions, and I made the same division of the meat in the second tin. Had we had bread or biscuit, or anything of that kind to eat with this preserved food, the portions would have made a fair meal. As it was, each person's share could be dispatched in a few bites. But I would not open any more tins at that sitting. I had only to consider how absolutely destitute was this island of all sustenance fit for human beings, and how days and nights might pass without bringing us any help to understand the preciousness of the food that had been cast up by the sea. Not one of our little company but appreciated my reason for opening no more tins ; but the dread of giving expression to that reason was too great to suffer any of them to speak of it.

As the piece of plank went around, with the eight portions

upon it, each one took his or her share, and Hunter, arriving at that moment from the well, took his ; and there we sat, the eight of us, close packed together under the sail.

Suddenly Miss Tuke said, "You have forgotten the dog, Mr. Walton."

I looked around, and saw the poor fellow lying on the grass, watching us eating with a passionate longing eye. I jumped up and ran down to the cask of beef and cut off a hunch of meat, which I threw to the dog. He wagged his tail, and thanked me in his dumb way, and was presently happy, gnawing upon the piece of junk.

The gale still stormed violently over the island, and the sky resembled a vast sheet of lead, with a kind of brown smoke like scud driving along under it, and scattering, just as smoke scatters, as it went. We were close to the sea, and had the roar of the surf in our ears. The gloom of the heavens and the bellowing and crashing of the sea would have been depressing even had all been well with us. The trees made a shadow, and the sail stretched over us deepened it, and in this shadow we sat, holding our little portions of preserved meat in our fingers, and all of us, acting upon my advice, eating very slowly ; for I remembered a sailor who had been adrift for a week in an open boat telling me that by munching and munching the tiny piece of ship's bread that he was allowed twice a day, by keeping it in his mouth, and then swallowing it slowly, he made it appease his hunger, whereas when he ate it hastily it left him still famine-stricken.

Never did shipwreck create a more dismal group of human beings than we looked as we sat peering at one another in the gloom under the sail. Nor, in my opinion, did life ever establish a sharper contrast in so short a time. You are affected when a poor, hungry, shabby man is pointed out to you as one who so many years ago possessed a fortune and lived in grand style. But here were we, who only a few short hours ago enjoyed all the luxuries of a superbly appointed yacht, flung half-naked upon a desolate island, forced to squat and eat our food like savages, treasuring that poor food and valuing it at a price which the whole of the island made of gold would not have paid for ; and already having proved that we had gauged deep all the horror and wretchedness of shipwreck by the exultation which the discovery of a little well of rain-water had inspired in us !

It was distracting to sit still and think upon our misfortunes.

I got up from the grass and looked at the sea, to find out if any more wreckage had come ashore ; and then addressing Tripshore and Hunter, I said that we were well into the day, and ought to go to work at once, and rig up a better habitation than the one over us, whilst we had the light. Yonder was plenty of wood, and we had a saw, a hammer, abundance of nails, and sailcloth. But first, on which side of the island should we construct the hut? Here, among the trees and near the beach, where we should see all that came ashore from the wreck? or over there among that clump of trees to the left of the bush, where we should be within three minutes' walk of the well?

Hunter was for crossing the island, Tripshore for stopping where we were. I asked Sir Mordaunt, who said he was for stopping ; so that decided us. He wanted to come out and help us, but I swore I would not lift a finger if he quitted the shelter, as he was in no condition to work ; and, moreover, I said there were enough of us and to spare.

So we left him with the women, and the four of us, that is, Norie, the seamen, and I, went down to the beach and brought up the fragments of wreck to the trees, where we presently had a great pile of deck-planking, and portions of the skin of the vessel, and other parts of her ; for she had gone to pieces, I may say, as a house falls in. She had been ground into fragments by the great sea that had beaten her down upon the jagged, iron-hard reef. We then brought the tool-chest along, and set to work to nail the wreckage to the trees. This took us a long time, for we had but one hammer ; but happily some of the deck-planking had been thrown up in middling big pieces —that is, there would be three or four planks nailed together— and this enabled us to push forward with our job.

It did us good to work. It kept us from pining and brooding over our troubles ; and the baronet and the women watched us from the shelter of their tent—for, as I have said, it was open on both sides, and the trees we selected as uprights for our hut were to the right. We had no means of keeping a reckoning of time. I was the only one of the party who had a watch, and it had stopped when I was in the water. We had no sun to guess the hour by ; but I supposed it would be about three o'clock by the time we had fairly framed in a group of trees, forming an inclosure that might be nearly twelve feet by twelve feet.

We broke off when we had got so far, and sent Hunter with

the kettle to the well, and divided the contents of another tin of meat ; but neither Miss Tuke nor Mrs. Stretton would take their portions. They said they were not hungry, that they could not eat, so I laid their shares aside ; and the filled kettle—for it was a large vessel—serving us to a good drink all round, we fell to work with renewed energy to roof in our strange structure with the sails. This was not an easy task, for the trees in the middle of the hut were in the way. However, we managed it by cutting the cloths so as to let the trees come into them. One sail was enough to make a roof. It was, indeed, a spare fore-topsail,* and by means of lanyards we triced it as taut as a drum. To make the shelter more complete, we passed another sail round the hut outside as far as it would stretch. We then unbent the sail that had served us as a tent, and that by this time was thoroughly dry, and spread it over the floor of the hut as a carpet. And not yet satisfied, I made Tripshore help me to cut up the remaining sail, which we nailed to the trees inside in such a manner that one part of the interior was entirely screened. This space I meant for the women to sleep in.

We had scarcely finished, and were looking about us to see what more could be done, when the interior of our little shelter grew bright, and stepping outside, I saw the sun flashing with a watery-reddish brilliance in the west. The great leaden cloud that had heavily overhung us all day was broken up into masses of dark vapor, which were solemnly journeying across the sky, and here and there among them were glimpses of misty blue. The horizon was clear, the gale had broken and was falling, but the ocean was still a wild, tumultuous, leaping, and rushing surface, of a silver and splendid brilliancy of creaming white under the sun, and from the reef to the beach the water resembled hurling volumes of snow.

That beam of reddish sunshine fell upon my heart like a blessing. I stood with clasped hands gazing at it with a rapture I have no words for, and presently turning to call the others, I found them all looking—ay, the very dog stood there looking at the sun. The glorious light sparkled in the eyes of the women, and I saw Ada Tuke gazing with such an expression in her face as a shipwrecked sailor wears when he watches a vessel coming his way.

"Praise God for that encouragement !" I cried, pointing to the sun. "It is meant to give us hope."

* The *Lady Maud's* sail-locker was in her fore-peak.

"There's another cask come ashore, sir !" shouted Tripshore, and he and I and Hunter dashed down to the beach.

I overhauled the marks upon it, and sung out, "It's either brandy or sherry ! Roll it up, boys, to the hut, and we'll test it there."

It was full, and we had a hard job to get it along. Sir Mordaunt said it was sherry ; but, valuable as it was, I would have given twenty such casks for one of biscuit.

I felt greatly fatigued after the hard work, and harder excitement and emotions of the day, and went to rest myself in the hut. Carey lay dozing on the sail. Sir Mordaunt joined me, leaving the others outside. The sight of the sun and the breaking clouds had heartened my poor friend somewhat. There was a little more life in him, I mean, and his heart seemed a bit eased of that oppression of grief which had been in his face during the day.

He came and sat down alongside of me, and clasping my hand, looked at me without speaking for some moments.

"Oh, Walton," he presently exclaimed. "This is a bitter and cruel termination of our cruise. My conscience accuses me as the author of all this misery. It was my blind confidence in Purchase that has led to this."

"Nay, don't fret over these matters," said I. "What we have to do is to get away from this island."

"All this privation," he continued, "ay, months of exile and suffering here, I could have borne without a murmur, if my poor wife had been preserved. But to think of her being dead—killed, indeed, by those very efforts I had made to restore her to health——" He broke off, and lifted up his hands with a gesture of speechless grief.

I said all that I could to soothe him, and talked to some purpose, for he calmed down after a little, and when I spoke of our situation he listened attentively. I told him I could not imagine upon what part of the Bahamas we were wrecked. "There can be no doubt whatever," said I, "that Purchase was miles out of his reckoning—I mean without reference to his false estimate of our drift to the westward. Unhappily, I have no knowledge of these seas, but I know that some of the larger islands are populated, and I do not suppose that we can be very far distant from one of the inhabited islands."

"But what means have we of leaving this place?" said he. "We have no boat. I see no chance of deliverance unless a vessel should come near."

"That is certainly our outlook at the present moment," I replied; "but we need not despair. You may read of extraordinary things having been done by people in our position; and some among us, Sir Mordaunt, are not men to sit down and wait for an opportunity to come."

"God knows, Walton, what we should have done without you," said he; and he was proceeding, when I stopped him by saying that before it fell dark I would ascend the little hill and have a look around for land. He said he would go too; he had not seen the island, and would like to view it from that point.

"Let us all go," said I; "for one may have sharper eyes than the rest."

So we left the hut, and I asked Miss Tuke and Mrs. Stretton to join us. I also called to Norie and the seamen, and the whole company of us started for the hill, leaving Carey dozing in the hut, and the dog to keep watch beside her.

(Note here, that Mrs. Stretton's boot that we had used as a cup being still wet, she put on my boot for this walk; and I took notice of the very elegant shape of her foot as she leaned against a tree in order to put on the boot.)

I walked in advance with Miss Tuke, and though the road was a short one, we managed to say a great deal. She spoke of her aunt, and asked where she was buried. On my telling her, she exclaimed, "I believe she would not have lived many hours on this island. The grief and terror would have killed her. She could not endure pain or hardship. And perhaps she may prove to be the luckiest of us all," she added, in a tremulous voice.

"Don't talk like that yet," said I. "There are too many chances in our favor to make such fancies reasonable. Besides, you are our heroine. We all look up to you when our spirits are low."

She shook her head at this.

"I wish I could see you in comfortable dry clothes," said I. "If we could only manage to make a fire, we would soon dry our clothes."

"Don't think of me more than of yourself and the others," she answered. "Of all of us, poor Mrs. Stretton is most to be pitied. This is her second shipwreck in a very short time, and when I recall what she went through on that half-sunk wreck, I cannot help thinking that we are very well off."

"That's well said."

"She is a most gentle, womanly creature," she continued. "I am sure her sympathy soothed Uncle Mordaunt. Each of them has been similarly bereaved, and what she said to him carried a weight that no words of mine could have taken."

We gained the top of the little hill. The windward sky was clearing fast, and the blue of it was growing pure. No more than a fresh breeze was now blowing, and I reckoned that it would all be gone by sunset. The circumference of the deep lay open to us, saving one small part blocked out by trees in the northwest. We searched the circle narrowly, but, good as my sight was, I at all events could see nothing.

"How far should we be able to see from this height, sir?" inquired Hunter.

"About fourteen or fifteen miles in clear weather," I answered.

"Isn't that land out there?" exclaimed Mrs. Stretton, crossing to my side, and pointing into the west, a little to the right of the track of the sun.

I gazed and gazed. Suddenly Miss Tuke cried, "Yes! there is a little film there—a tiny blue shadow—I see it plainly."

"Right you are, Miss," said Tripshore. "There it is, Mr. Walton!"

I thought I saw it, but when I shut my eyes to clear them, and looked again, it was gone. None of the rest of our party could see the tiny shadow, which made those who saw it wonder, for they said it stood there plain enough. I took for granted that it was land, and asked Tripshore if his memory carried the chart sharply enough to recall what island would have land bearing west from it, visible, say, about twenty miles? He puzzled and reflected, and knit his brows, but the poor fellow could not remember. Indeed, it was not a thing to be guessed. If you look at the Bahama Islands, you will see how crowded the chart is with rocks and cays and reefs and islets, similar to the one on which we had been cast. It was idle to recall Purchase's reckoning, for I knew that we were much further to the west than that, and much further to the south too, I was sure. But there was no use speculating upon that shadow which Miss Tuke and the other two saw. If it were land, we should never be able to find out what land it was by guessing. Elsewhere the horizon was quite bare.

"But so much the better," said I, gazing into the east; "for if that water out yonder is clear, surely there will be vessels traversing it, bound to or from Providence Channel or the Florida and North Carolina coasts to the West India Islands. Don't you think so, Tripshore?"

"I do, sir. Anyhow, the chance is good enough to make a lookout a necessity. If we could make a flare, something might come of it when it falls dark."

"But how are we to get a light?" I asked. "Who has any matches?"

The men felt about their pockets, but to no purpose. Sailors seldom carry lights ; the galley-fire is their lucifer-match. We all searched, but none of us had any matches, nor the means of procuring fire.

"Something to make fire may come ashore in the night," said Hunter. "There's no use despairin'."

Still it was terribly vexing to be without fire. There were many reasons why a flare would have been good for us. We could have dried our clothes ; we could have cooked the salt beef in the kettle ; it would have made a cheerful light, too, something to keep watch by ; above all, we should never be able to guess what it would be doing for us—what passing distant vessel it might attract, that would lay-to and wait for the morning, to run down to us, the mere dream of which would have acted like a cordial upon our spirits. The want of fire was the harder to bear because the bush promised excellent fuel, and with our knives we could have gathered enough to last us through the night. Norie spoke of rubbing sticks together. I told him that read very well in books, that no doubt there were savage tribes who got fire in that way, though they must be artists to do it, and have the right kind of wood, too.

"But you might try it, if you will, Norie," said I.

(He did try that same night. He got a couple of pieces of wood, and rubbed until the sweat ran down him like water. But so far from catching fire, the wood was scarcely warm, though he had worked like a horse.)

After lingering a while on the hill, looking at the sea, and watching the red sunlight wax and wane as the clouds rolled over the setting orb, we went slowly toward the hut.

I was determined to do my best to keep up the spirits of the people, and made some of them smile by suggesting that we should take a drink of the sherry out of the kettle.

"It's too good to dip a boot into," said I. "Besides, I

couldn't fancy sherry out of a boot—not even out of Mrs. Stretton's boot, small as it is."

"But you won't dip that great black kettle into the wine?" said Miss Tuke, with a laugh, that made us all seem to forget our troubles for the moment.

"No ; but if we could manage to bale some of it into the kettle," I answered, "we could each of us take a pull at the spout."

Here Hunter walked off to the beach, to look, as I suppose, for any articles that might have come ashore. I told Tripshore to open a couple of tins of meat, whilst I and Norie worked at the cask of wine with the hatchet ; and whilst we were full of this business, comes back Hunter with a big shell in his hand, and gives it to me with a face of triumph.

"There's a baler for ye, sir—the biggest I could find in this light," says he. "Mr. Tripshore, there's a box away down in the cove" (meaning the little creek at the end of the beach). "Will you come along and help to bring it up?"

"Save all that you can," said I ; and away went the two men.

Having got the head of the wine-cask open, I dipped the shell into the sherry, and handed it to Mrs. Stretton. It held near upon a wine-glass. It was better than drinking out of the kettle, and I admired Hunter's readiness. Pretty it was to see the women drinking the wine from the shell, that was deeper than an oyster shell, yet of that shape, thickly ribbed, and each rib defined by a red line. I filled the shell for Carey, and then handed it to the baronet, to help himself and pass it on, whilst I divided the meat into portions, as before.

It was a wretched meal, not enough for us by I know not how much ; and I bitterly deplored the want of a little biscuit to distribute with it, or such fruit as any man might have hoped to find on a tropical island, where there was soil enough to give life to bushes and trees.

I felt desperately low-spirited whilst dividing the poor repast. I kept on thinking, "What in God's name shall .we do if we are not succored before our slender provisions are exhausted?" But the arrival of Tripshore and Hunter with the box took me away from these melancholy thoughts, and I went out to inspect this new acquisition. As I approached it, Tripshore sidled up to me, and whispered in my ear, "There's two dead bodies come ashore, sir. One's the cook, and t'other's poor Jim Wilkinson. Better say nothen about it. Me and Tom'll steal away presently, and bury 'em."

16

I nodded, and began to handle the box.

"Why, Carey, is not this yours?" exclaimed Miss Tuke.

The girl looked, and said yes, it was her box.

"It is locked," said I.   "Have you the key?"

She fumbled in her pocket, or rather in the hole where the pocket should have been ; but, alas ! the sea had torn that convenience away.

"You can break it open, sir," said the poor girl, simply. "I know what's in it."

I broke the lock with the chopper, and told her to explore the contents, as for all we knew it might contain something that should prove of great value to us.   She came readily, and kneeled down, and began to take the articles out of the box, whilst we stood around.   The hope I had that among the contents there might be a box of matches was soon dashed.   The box, though well made, and a good box of its kind, was full of water, and the things lay soaking in it, like clothes in a washtub.   Among the contents I remember were an old-fashioned Prayer-book, a work-box completely fitted, some dresses, a hat, some under-linen, a pair of boots, a bundle of letters, which flaked away in Carey's hand when she fished them up, and the sight of which made her cry bitterly.   We stretched the wearing apparel upon the grass to dry, and then, whilst the others went to get their mouthful of supper, I cut off another piece of junk for the dog, and got the kettle ready for Hunter to fill it when he had done his meal.

CHAPTER XV.

By this time the sun was very low, the wind almost gone, the sea rapidly calming, and every promise of a fine bright night in the sky.   After Hunter returned with the kettle from the well, he followed Tripshore down into the creek, where they buried the two bodies in the sand.   Before they came back the sun had vanished, and the night had closed upon the sea ; but happily for us, who were without artificial light, there was a bright moon in the southwest which, though only half the orb was visible, flashed a silver glory upon the water, and was strong enough to give sharp black shadows to the trees.

When Tripshore returned, he held out some object to me,

which, on first viewing it in his hands, I had taken to be a piece
of spar ; but it proved to be one of the telescopes belonging to
the *Lady Maud*, the one that had stood on brackets in the after-
companion. He whispered to me that he had found it close
against the body of Jim Wilkinson.

This was a grand discovery, though its most significant value
did not immediately occur to me. All that I thought of was
how useful it would be to search the horizon with, and examine
the coast, which Mrs. Stretton was the first to see. I called to
Sir Mordaunt that Tripshore had found one of the telescopes,
and everybody came running to look at it, whilst I sat down to
unscrew the lenses and dry them ; which done, I pointed the
glass at the moon, and was overjoyed to discover that the sea
had done no injury whatever to the telescope.

"Can you see through it all right, sir?" inquired Tripshore.

" Ay," said I. " Look for yourself."

But, instead of putting the glass to his eye, he stood like a
man musing, and then said, "Can't ye guess a fine use for this
glass, Mr. Walton, in the day-time, when the sky's clear?"

"What do you mean, Tripshore?" said I.

"Why," said he, "here's a toobe full o' burning glasses.
When the sun's up you'll want no lucifer-matches. You'll get
fire and to spare with e'er a one of them magnifiers."

I had not thought of this ; but it made the glass so precious
that, in my delight at possessing it, I grasped Tripshore by the
hand, and gripped it—rather too cordially, I remember, for
when I let go, the poor fellow turned his back upon me, in
order to chafe away the pain of the squeeze.

But the dew was falling very heavily, and the night air had
that peculiar chilliness which any man who knows those latitudes will recall. Our damp clothes rendered us very sensitive
to the swift change of temperature. I advised Sir Mordaunt
and the women to enter the hut, and take their rest for the
night. But first the baronet asked us to join him in a prayer.
We readily assented, and knelt in a circle, Sir Mordaunt kneeling in the midst of us. Of all moving moments, I never experienced the like of that short time in which we knelt, whilst
my poor friend prayed aloud. Our knowing the agony of mind
his wife's death caused him, made us find such a pathos in
every tone of his, as none of us could hear without dim eyes.
He struggled hard to steady his voice whilst he offered up
thanks for our merciful salvation, and implored God's continued
protection of the lives He had preserved. But he would pray

for his wife too, which taxed him beyond endurance, for he utterly broke down at that part of his prayer, and sobbed so lamentably that it seemed he must break his heart.

When he had recovered his composure, I urged the women to withdraw to their part of the hut, and gave them some pieces of canvas to use for coverlets. I then rolled up a short breadth of the side of the sail that we had spread upon the grass to serve as a pillow, and made Sir Mordaunt put his head upon it, and when he was laid down I covered his shoulders with Hunter's jacket—I mean the jacket that had covered his wife's face. Norie lay down beside him, and the dog crouched at their feet.

It was quite dark in the hut, but the white sail spread in the bottom of it made a kind of glimmer, and helped us somewhat. I went into the open with the two seamen, and though I was reluctant to keep them standing and talking after the sufferings and labor of the day, I could not forbear to call a council of them now that all was still, and the peace and the radiance of the night upon us, the wind gone, and nothing to distract our minds from close contemplation of our position.

First, I told them that it was necessary we should keep watch. Although we had no means of signaling a passing vessel, yet it would be a thousand pities if one should pass when we were asleep. For what we desired to know was, was this part of the sea navigable, and did vessels ever traverse it within sight of the island? If we could be sure on this head our hopes would gain strength, and we should have good reason for making a smoke in the day and burning a flare at night.

"Ay, sir, a lookout must be kept," said Tripshore.

"There are three of us," said I.

"But how'll the man on duty know when his watch is up?" inquired Hunter.

This was a poser; for, as I have told you, we were without the means of calculating the passage of time. At last I said—

"We must do the best we can by guessing. The moon will help us for a spell. If we make a three hours' watch, each man will get some hours' rest. We must reckon how the time goes as best we can."

They were very willing, they said; and so that matter was settled, and it was agreed that I should keep the first lookout.

"And now," said I, "how are we to get away from this island? Our stock of food is very small, though more may wash ashore. But let as much as may come, it will not last eight men and women long ; and we are bound to starve if we stop here."

"There's only one thing to be done," said Hunter. "We must turn to and build a raft—something that'll float—with a life-line around it, and likewise a mast. We must make the best job we can—something that'll steer—and one or two of us 'll have to go adrift in it, and take our chance of bein' picked up, and getting the wessel as picks us up to call for the others."

I shook my head. "If," said I, "we could be sure that the land some of you have seen was inhabited, why then, though it should be fifty miles distant, one or two of us as you may, Hunter, might venture for it on a raft. But to risk our lives, merely to be stranded on such another rock as this, would be a mad thing. You'll get no raft to do more than swoosh along straight with the wind, and I see no good to come of going adrift, with the certain chance of being blown away to sea, and either foundering or dying of want."

"You're right, sir," said Tripshore, gravely. "A raft 'ud be sartin death, Tom."

"But it's sartin death if we stop here, too ! " exclaimed Hunter. "Though a raft 'ud give us a poor chance, it 'ud still be a chance ; but this blooming island gives us no chance at all."

"Why not rig up a raft—a dummy—a small 'un with a mast and sail, and a board at the masthead wrote on to signify that there are eight shipwrecked persons aboard this island, and send it adrift, with the chance of some wessel overhauling it ? " exclaimed Tripshore.

The idea was original and striking. I said at once—

"Yes, we can do that. It shall be our first job in the morning. With a cloth or two of canvas set square on a well-stayed mast, a raft is bound to blow along ; and if our chance lies in her being seen by a vessel, then she'll answer our purpose better than if she were manned, for she'll risk no lives."

Hunter turned his head, and, looking toward the beach, said, in a low voice, "Would it be a bad job to lash one of them dead bodies in the sand yonder to it ? She'd make a likelier arrand for us with a body aboard than if she went naked. A ship 'ud stop if they sighted a body, but if they saw northen on the raft, maybe they'd pass on without heeding the board at the masthead."

The suggestion offended me for a moment, but only for a moment. What Hunter had said was perfectly true. A body on the raft would twenty-fold increase our chance, by inducing a vessel to approach it ; whereas, if the people of the vessel saw only a bare raft, they might pass on. What would it matter to the dead, whether he was left in the sand there, or sent adrift to find a grave in the bottom of the deep? Life was dearer to us than sentiment. We must be succored or we must perish. A dead man would make a ghastly messenger, but we should send him forth in God's name ; and whether he should be swept away or be encountered by a ship, he was sure of ultimately finding a resting place in the sea.

We stood talking briskly a full ten minutes over this scheme, and then, there being nothing more to say, I told the men to turn in, but first to take a sup of sherry. This they did, and entered the hut, and I was left alone.

As I had foreseen, the wind died away with the sun, I could feel only the lightest current of air. Here and there a white cloud floated, scarcely moving athwart the stars, and some of them carrying delicate and phantom-like rainbows in the parts they turned to the moon. Some of the stars were very large and beautiful, and the deep, unspeakable, blue-black depths of the heavens seemed tremulous with the incessant showering of meteors. There was still a heavy swell rolling along the path of the vanished gale, and as these majestic and foamless coils of ebony water passed under the moon, they flashed into mountains of quicksilver. The reef hindered the run of these rollers on our side of the island, but there was surf enough along the beach to fill the night with a most lamentable moaning noise. It was as though the sea in mockery gave our misery a voice. It was a most depressing sound to stand and idly listen to, and cruelly brought home to me our desolate condition, and our lonely and helpless plight in the midst of this dark water, with its sullen rollers and its lamenting voice wailing close at our ears.

As I looked at the moon and the peaceful sky, I thought with bitterness that had such a night as this come to us twenty-four hours sooner, the *Lady Maud* would still have been afloat. I pictured how her decks would have shown, and imagined Lady Brookes in her invalid's chair near the skylight, and Ada Tuke flitting from one side of the deck to the other in the moonlight, and Sir Mordaunt pacing and fro, and so on and so on. I say I stood dreaming forth a whole picture of the schooner as she would have appeared on such a night as this, until I broke away with a shudder from the dreadful contrast of our position, and walked down to the beach, in the hope of distracting my mind in a hunt after more relics of the wreck.

The tide was lower by many feet down the beach, and though I could not see the reef on which the yacht had struck, yet I guessed, by the play of white water there, that when the sea was calm at low tide the reef would be visible. There was a dark object almost abreast of the hut upon the gleaming coral sand, and on approaching it I discovered it to be a full cask, but what it contained I could not tell. There could be no doubt, however, from its appearance, that it held provisions of some sort, so I set to work to clear away the sand that buried it by about a foot and a half, and tumbling it on its bilge, I managed to roll it some distance above high-water mark, where it would be safe from the sea.

I returned again close to the surf, and slowly followed the line of it as it trended away to the northeast, and then into the south-east, where it terminated in the bight of the limb of land. The moon shone brilliantly, and I could see very plainly. Presently, and at about three hundred paces from the spot where I had found the cask, I saw a square black object in the water, which covered and exposed it as the rollers came in and ran back. I was much puzzled to know what it could be, until, after looking for some time, I perceived that it was the yacht's piano.

A little further on was a pile of fragments of timber high and dry ; and just beyond again was a spare fore-topmast, and the yacht's fore-top-gallant and topsail yards, the sails bent and the gaskets holding tight. These, it will be remembered, had been sent down during the gale. I thought that we might come to require those spars, but they were too heavy for me to drag up the beach ; so, after having carried a quantity of timber up the shore, I went to the trees where the hut stood, and hauled in the line by which Sir Mordaunt and the others had been dragged from the yacht, and which had parted close to the vessel when she went to pieces. With this end of stuff I returned to the spars, hitched the line round them, and made the end fast up the beach, so that the tide should not carry them away.

All this was very hard work, but not to be neglected. I was tired, and was going to sit down, when I spied a dead body on the sand about fifty yards this side of where the beach terminated in the creek. It lay on its back, with its arms out, and its head on its right shoulder, in the very posture of a crucified figure. I recognized it as a man named Martin Jewell, a young man, in life fresh-faced and smiling, and a very willing sailor. He looked to be asleep, so easy was the appearance of his face in the moonlight, though his eyes were open. I know not why his quiet look should have made me think this dead man frightful; but I should have been less shocked and scared had he presented the usual dreadful appearance of the drowned. May be, it was my knowing him to be stone dead, and his looking lifelike and sleeping, that made me recoil and tremble. And you must add the surroundings, too : the breezeless atmosphere, the moaning of the sea, the steady white fires of the moon upon the water, the swell sparkling like silver as it ran across the wake of the orb, the large stars looking down, with the shining dust of meteors quivering and fading among them. I say, figure this scene, and then think of the stirless dead body lying like a dreaming man, looking straight up at the sky, as though he followed the flight of his spirit.

I shook off the feelings which possessed me, and fetching a piece of jagged plank from the pile beyond, I dug a hole in the sand, which occupied me about ten minutes; but when I tried to put down the outstretched arms of the body, I found they would not yield. So I had to dig afresh and turn out two grooves, if I may so say, to receive the arms ; and then I laid him in his grave, in the very posture in which he had died, with his arms stretched above his head, and so covered him over.

This miserable and sad duty discharged, I walked languidly toward the hillock, meaning to rest on top of it, where I should command the sea. Having reached the summit, I threw myself down and ran my eye over the sea ; but though there had been a ship a mile off in the south or west, I believe I should not have seen her, owing to the confusing light of the moon and the play of the swell, that perplexed the eye with alternations of radiance and shadow. I carefully looked along the horizon, but could see nothing but the sea and the stars in the north and east, and the flashing moonlight in the other quarters. Here I sat for hard upon half an hour, when, feeling drowsy, and afraid of falling asleep, which would have been a bad thing for me in the heavy dew, I got up and walked across the top of the little hill, as far as the incline that faced in the direction of the well.

Whilst I stood looking toward the sea in the north, my eye was caught by an object at the bottom of the declivity

"I found my friend on his knees beside his wife's grave."—Page 249.

close against the bushes. I could just make out, after peering a bit, that it was a human figure, and that it excitedly moved its arms, which were white. I recollected that Lady Brookes was buried in that place, and I frankly confess that for a moment or two I was possessed by a weak and idle consternation, and stared like a fascinated man. But unless it were a ghost, it must be one of our people, so putting my hand to the side of my mouth I called out, "Who is that there?"

No answer being returned, I called again, and went down the hill.

"It is I, Walton," said a voice that I recognized as Sir Mordaunt's.

I hastened forward, and found my poor friend on his knees beside his wife's grave.

"I could not rest without offering up a prayer over her," said he.

"But for God's sake, take care of your own health," said I. "The dew falls like rain, and you are in your shirt-sleeves."

He repeated that he could not rest until he had prayed over her.

"But we can hold a service to-morrow," I exclaimed. "We have a Prayer-book."

"Ay," said he; "but think of her lying in this unconsecrated grave. Don't reproach me, Walton. She was very dear to me. I have lost her forever."

I grasped his hand and pressed it, meaning by that silent token to let him know there was no reproach, but rather the deepest pity and sorrow, in my heart. Nevertheless, I would not let him go until I had made him rise, and then, when he was on his feet, gradually led him toward the hut; for, not to speak only of the danger to which he exposed himself by remaining half-clothed in the damp night air, there was something in his manner that made me resolute to get him away from the grave.

I said again that we would hold a service over his wife's remains in the morning, and then I inquired how he had found out where she lay buried.

He answered that he had asked Norie, when I was at work on the beach, and he had told him. He then wished to know if it was possible to preserve her body, so that, should we ever get away from the island, he might be able to have her remains conveyed to England. To soothe him, I said there was wood enough to build a coffin, which we would set about after we had completed a certain project that I would explain the meaning of in the morning. And so I got him into the hut and made him lie down, and went to the door and stood there a while.

I could not hear the women, but the deep breathing of Norie and the weary seamen made a moving sound, and, combined with the moan of the chafing sea, affected me in a manner I cannot express. I could trace the outlines of their bodies upon the white sail, and they lay as still as ever did that dead sailor I had buried.

My mind went to the women then, and I thought of Ada Tuke lying in her damp clothes, and the poor widow who in a few brief days had gauged the very lowest depths of human distress, and the girl whose life I had under God been the means of preserving. Great heaven ! What a bitter weary watch was that I kept ! What a panorama of wild ocean scenes and desolate death was my mind !

When I believed that Sir Mordaunt was asleep, I fell on my knees, and lifting up my face, prayed, with an anguish of soul I shall never forget in this life, that help might come to us, and that we might not be left to perish miserably on this lonely, unfruitful and wave-beaten rock. So passed the time until I believed my three hours expired. I then went softly into the hut, but had to gently feel over the bodies of the sleepers before I could distinguish Tripshore. I shook him, and he started up, on which I instantly spoke to him, that he might recollect himself, and went into the moonlight where he could see me ; and then telling him what I had done, and bidding him keep a lookout for ships, and to seek for any wreckage that might be serviceable to us on the beach, I laid myself down in his place, and fell into a deep and dreamless sleep.

CHAPTER XVI.

I AWOKE very much refreshed, and found the sunshine pouring strongly into the hut, and myself alone. I got up and went out, and saw Sir Mordaunt leaning against one of the trees to the right of the hut, watching the rest of the party, who were variously employed about the beach. We shook hands warmly, and I asked him how he did. He told me that he had slept well and felt heartier, and he certainly looked so.

I judged by the sun that the morning was not far advanced, for which I was very thankful, as there was a great deal to be done that day. The first thing that took my eye was a fire burning at the foot of the little hill facing the sea. A number of pieces of rock had been piled into a square, and the fire made up in it. There was a quantity of brushwood in heaps near the fire, and Norie, coming at that moment with a bundle of the wood, and flinging it down, made me see how he was employing himself. The smoke of the fire went up in a straight line, for there was not a breath of air. The sea lay like oil slowly waving. It was of a most deep and beautiful blue beyond the reef, though the cloudless sky was a light silvery azure. The water broke in long flashing ripples on the reef, and rolled up the beach in little breakers.

Tripshore and Hunter were busy among a quantity of wreckage, a good portion of which had been collected whilst I was asleep. About a stone's throw from where I stood were Mrs. Stretton and Ada Tuke, the former kneeling, but what doing I could not perceive. Beyond them was Carey, spreading some wearing apparel in the sun.

Having exchanged a few words with Sir Mordaunt I walked over to the ladies, and then saw what they were about. A deck plank lay upon the sand, and upon it Mrs. Stretton was chopping up some beef-fat out of the cask. A flour-cask stood alongside, and, on looking at it I perceived it was the cask I had found during my watch. After exchanging greetings, and hearing they had slept well and felt well, I expressed my happiness that we should have found the cask of flour.

"The salt water has got to the outer portions of it," said Mrs. Stretton ; "but the flour is dry in the middle. I believe by mixing both parts, and kneading them well with fresh water, we shall not notice the salt when we have baked them in cakes with this fat."

She kept on mincing the fat whilst she spoke, and Miss Tuke stood by, waiting to help her to make the cakes. I was heartily pleased to see them busy, for there is no antidote like work for melancholy.

I called to Tripshore to tell me where the telescope was, and ascended the hill with it. The moment I pointed it in the quarter where the others had seen the shadow on the preceding day, I saw the land ; but I could make nothing of it beyond observing that it was full twenty miles distant, and either a mere rock or else a hill on an island, the lower portions of which were invisible. I carefully searched the rest of the horizon, but could discover nothing, and came back again to the point of land. I struggled with my memory to fashion a mental picture of the Bahamas. My having studied the chart so closely on board the yacht helped me a great deal ; but though I figured all the larger islands, such as Abaco, San Salvador, Eleuthera, and the islands as low as the Caicos Passage, yet I could not even faintly recall the bearings of the islets and cays. Nor, indeed, would it have served me had I been able to do so ; for I had no idea of our latitude and longitude, and no means of determining our position. Yet in spite of this I kept on conjecturing and wondering, and asking myself if that land could really be one of the greater and inhabited islands, and whether in that hope would it be wise to venture for it on a raft.

But the idea of a raft recalled our project of the preceding night—a good idea, it seemed to me, and full of promise. So I shut up the glass, and joined Tripshore and Hunter, who, as I have said, were at work among the wreckage, selecting wood for the raft. As I advanced toward them I caught sight of a strange looking object, resembling a big capsized tub, about fifty yards away in the direction of the wreck. I went to see what it was, and to my astonishment and delight found it a great turtle, weighing, as I should have supposed from the appearance of it, not less than four hundred pounds. It was on its back, and alive. I was thunderstruck at first, and then filled with joy. This, to be sure, was one of the months in which the turtle on calm moonlight nights comes up the shore, and lays its eggs in the sand. I might fairly suppose that since one was here others were about, so that the idea of our perishing for want of food need no longer haunt me.

I rejoined the men, and asked which of them had caught the turtle.

" It was me, sir," says Tripshore. "Half an hour after you had gone into the hut, I see that chap come up out o' the water. He made me look at him by hissing. He was like a small steam-engine slowly coming along out o' the sea. I stood stock still till he was well ashore, then picks up a piece o' timber and gets to leeward of him, and shoving the timber under him, I worked and sweated until I managed to heave him over on his back. But, Lord, the weight of him !"

"He's full of soup and meat," said I, "and his shell should

serve as a tank.   And now, my lads, what do you find handy among this raffle?"

"All that we want, sir," responded Hunter.

This was evident, for there was a great quantity of timber, and some of it in big pieces.   Among the stuff were the spars I had secured over night.   The men had dragged them ashore, unbent the sails, and snugged away the running gear that had been attached to the canvas.   I saw, however, that if we were to get our raft afloat after we had built it, we must construct it down in the bight of land where the water was smooth ; and explaining this to the men, we set to work to convey the material to that place.   This took us an hour ; but at the end of that time we had lashed and nailed three large pieces of timber into the form of a triangle for the foundations of the raft, and we had got this afloat in the smooth water, when Norie shouted to us that the cakes were baked.

We thereupon quitted our work, and after cooling our faces in the salt water we walked to the hut, where we found the rest of the party waiting for us to come.

There stood eight brown cakes smelling very good indeed, upon a plank.   I opened two tins of meat, and divided the contents.   We then poured some sherry into the water in the kettle, and breakfast was ready.   But first, Sir Mordaunt asked us to join him in a prayer, which was the wish of us all ; so we knelt, whilst he prayed aloud, putting up such a petition as I need not repeat the language of, though any man who can imagine himself in our situation will understand its character.

This done, we fell to our repast, the dog getting his bit of salt meat as usual.   I praised the cakes highly. To be sure they were a bit salt, but not disagreeably so.

"Pity some 'baccy don't come ashore, sir," said Tripshore, with a languishing look at the sea.

That was my want too.   One of the hardships of those hard times was the being without tobacco.   I sat next to Sir Mordaunt, and whilst we were breakfasting he asked me what scheme I and the seamen were carrying out.   I told him what our idea was, and he and the others seemed greatly struck by it.

"It's a fine notion," said Norie.   "There's every chance of the raft being sighted. Can you carve letters upon wood, Walton?"

"I have never tried," said I.   "But I dare say I can."

"Let me have that job," he exclaimed.   "I can carve letters very well.   Tell me what to say, and after breakfast I'll set to work."

I proposed an inscription, and asked if it would do.   There was a short debate, but nobody seemed able to improve upon it, and so my suggestion was adopted.   Norie drew a pencil from his pocket, and scribbled down the words on the deck-plank.   I then in a low voice told Sir Mordaunt that we meant to lash a dead body to the raft, and explained our reason.   The idea shocked him just as it had shocked me, but his judgment promptly appreciated the value of the scheme.

"We'll say nothing to the women about that part," said I. "They must be drawn aside whilst we make the body fast."

"But they will see it as the raft floats away," said he.

"Why, perhaps they will," I answered; "but distance will soften the horror."

Here Tripshore jumped up.   "Me and Tom's all ready, sir." I rose too, but the baronet put his hand on my arm.

"Pray let's have the service we spoke of," he exclaimed, with a most imploring face.

I could not resist his appeal, precious as the time was.   Turning to the men, I said—

"Sir Mordaunt wishes us to join him in a funeral service over poor Lady Brookes's remains.   We owe it to her memory, my lads, and to our affection for the kind and large-hearted gentleman, whose loss is the cruelest a man can bear."

Tripshore looked willing at once; but Hunter, a rough-fibered man, seemed impatient, though he said nothing.   I took up Carey's prayer-book, of which the print was not illegible, though parts of it were a good deal smeared through the soaking salt water, and giving the baronet my arm, we stepped into the sunshine, followed by the others, and walked to the place where Lady Brookes lay buried.   The sand was heaped where the body was, which enabled us to form a circle round the grave.   Sir Mordaunt read the service himself.   He pronounced the words firmly, but with a most affecting spirit of devotion, omitting certain solemn parts, which would have been superfluous under the circumstances.   I feared he would have broken down before he got to the end, but he struggled on manfully, though several times when he raised his face, I saw the tears on his cheeks.   I cannot conceive a more pathetic figure than he made.   Bare-headed, in his shirt-sleeves, his long beard accentuating his haggard features, his humid eyes, his hands grasping the prayer-book often thrown up in

an imploring gesture when he removed his gaze from the page
to fix it upon the bright blue sky—I say it would have melted
an iron heart to have seen him. And into this service there
entered an element—of horror shall I call it?—that would be
absent from the usual ceremony. I mean we could not think
of the poor body lying at our feet without reflecting that there
she was, dressed as in life, uncoffined, separated from us by a
thin layer of sand, such as a breeze of wind might easily scatter, and leave her exposed in her dreadful lonesomeness. When
I remembered her terrors, the fright the thunderstorm had
caused her, swooning away because she had not the nerve to
hear of the sufferings a fellow-creature—one of her own sex
too—had endured, I thought, " Great God! could she but see
herself now !"

When the service was over, the two seamen and I went
back to the raft, leaving the baronet and the women at the
grave, and Norie to carve the letters and mind the fire, which I
told him to feed with damp stuff, to raise a thick smoke. I
have said that we had already laid the foundations of the raft
in the form of a triangle. I recommended this shape because
it gave a kind of bows to the raft, and I believed that by affixing a broad plank of wood as an immovable rudder at the
broad end, the thing would blow along steadily. We had
plenty of nails and spikes, and the frame of the raft being afloat,
we soon decked it. Of course the work was extravagantly
rough, but that we cared nothing about, providing we made it
strong enough to hold. The raft being completed, we set to
work to rig her. We took the yacht's fore-top-gallant yard and
securely nailed it to the best and lightest piece of stuff we could
come at to serve as a yard. To this we bent the top-gallant
sail, and all three of us buckling to it, stepped the yard that
was to serve as a mast into a crevice in the middle of the raft,
where we securely wedged, and then stayed it.

Although this description may run glibly, the job was a hard
one, because our tools were few, and little to the purpose.
The morning passed quickly whilst we were at work, and in
the middle of it a pleasant breeze sprang up in the northwest,
and kept the sea shivering as though the sunlight flashed in a
mighty field of diamonds. It carried the smoke of the fire
across the water in steel-blue coils, which looked to be leagues
long, and which I was forever breaking off my work to glance
at.

We had scarcely set the mast up on the raft and secured it,

when Norie, accompanied by Miss Tuke, came down to us, carrying a piece of deck-plank.

"Here's the inscription," said he, looking well pleased with his work ; and he put the board down on the sand, that we might see it. The letters were bold, well cut, and each as long as my thumb. The inscription ran thus—

JULY—, 18— "LADY MAUD" WRECKED ON A BAHAMA CAY. EIGHT SURVIVORS. SAVE US.

There were a great many letters in this, and I was astonished at the rapidity and accuracy with which they had been carved.

"It would have taken me two days," I said, "and then perhaps no one would be able to read it."

I gave the board to Tripshore, who nailed it at the masthead by standing on Hunter's shoulders.

"Why couldn't you build a raft big enough to carry us all away, Mr. Walton?" said Miss Tuke.

"We mustn't venture it yet," I replied. "Nothing but the certainty of perishing here should make us face the peril of going afloat on a raft."

"But is it likely," said she, "that we should be on the water long without meeting a ship?"

"Ah!" I replied, "if I could foretell that, I should know what to do."

"We cannot go on stopping here," she exclaimed piteously, clasping her hands.

"No ; and we don't intend to stop," said I. "Look at the noble signal that smoke is making as it stretches across the ocean. Who knows but that at this very moment it may be seen, and help coming? And see that message," I added, pointing to the board the men were affixing to the masthead of the raft, "which will shortly be afloat, and which, for all we can tell, may be the means of delivering us from this island before another day is passed. Don't lose heart," said I, tenderly, taking her hand and looking earnestly at her. "Your courage has been our mainstay all through. Don't fail us when we most want you."

She colored up a little and averted her face, but made no reply. I beckoned to Norie, and, drawing him aside, told him in a few words what we were about to do, and begged him to go to Sir Mordaunt and ask him to draw the women into the hut, or keep them apart from us and out of sight until we had done. He walked off, and in a minute or two Sir Mordaunt called Miss Tuke, who left us. Presently I saw

the baronet, leaning on his niece's arm, and accompanied
by Mrs. Stretton and Carey, move slowly toward the interior
of the island, as if he had a mind to see the place ; and the
moment they disappeared we set to work.

The rigidity of the body I had buried on the preceding night
determined me not to disturb it.   I explained this to the seamen, and Tripshore said he believed that poor Jim Wilkinson
would make the best body for our purpose.   The two corpses
had been buried above high-water mark, and the places where
they lay were distinguishable by the appearance of the sand
there.   But the men could not remember in which of the graves
Wilkinson's body was, and therefore we had to clear away the
sand to find it out.

Every nerve, every fiber in my body seemed to shrivel and
shrink up at the bare contemplation of exposing the poor fellows' remains, but I would not suffer my inward loathing and
horror to master me.   I was persuaded that the raft, if sighted,
would serve our purpose more effectually if it carried a dead
body than if it went bare ; and the needs of eight human lives
in dire peril, and without any prospect of preservation if help
was not summoned, determined me to persevere in our scheme.

Tripshore was deadly pale, and worked with a dogged resolution, as if, like me, he would not permit his feelings to
master him.   Hunter showed no emotion at all.   Happily,
the first grave we uncovered contained Wilkinson's body.   We
raised it, and dusted the sand from its face, and carried it to
the raft.   I should have been willing to let it lie on its back,
with a piece of canvas over its face ; but Hunter, with whom
this scheme had originated, said—

"No, no, sir; let's do the job thoroughly.   He must be
fixed sitting upright, and then they'll think him alive, and bear
down.   If they see him on his back, they'll say, 'Oh, he's
dead,' and sail away."

I could not deny that he was right, so we set the body up
with its back to the mast, and lashed it in that posture ; but
so dreadful an object did it look, that I was oppressed with a
deadly giddiness and sickness after we had completed the
loathsome business, and had to sit for a while and keep my
eyes closed.

Nothing now remained to be done but to make the clews of
the sail fast and send the raft adrift.   The first was easy
enough, but the other very difficult, for, calm as it was, the
ground swell betwixt the beach and the reef was tolerably heavy,

17

and would quickly drive the raft ashore and strand her if we did not mind. To guard against this, we carried a line round the mast, keeping both ends in our hands, and arming ourselves with pieces of timber to shove her clear, we scrambled across the limb of land, and reached the extreme point of it, where we hauled upon the line and brought the raft abreast. Then, unreeving the line, we went into the water as high as our waists, and by dint of shoving got the raft clear, when her sail at once caught the wind and away she crawled, dead to leeward, but very steadily, the long rudder-like board astern of her heading her perfectly straight, and the dead body sitting in the shadow of the sail like a living man.

We scrambled back again to the beach, and mounted the hill to watch her, Norie joining us, and bringing the telescope with him. Sir Mordaunt and the women were coming slowly along from the west side of the island, but observing me to motion and point, they hurried their pace : but before they reached the hut they stopped and stood looking at the raft, that would be visible to them from that point. I saw Miss Tuke turn to her uncle, and then point to us and then at the raft, clearly astonished at the sight of the man on board, and wondering who it could be. Norie, before joining us, had hove a quantity of damp brushwood on to the fire, that sent up a dense column of smoke that arched over into a beautiful bend when it reached a short height, and went blowing along the sea, casting a long black shadow upon the water, in the very middle of which the raft crawled steadily forward, like a cart going along a straight road. The shadow on her made her an extraordinary clear figure against the blue water and the sky of the horizon. I was sure that no ship, keeping anything like a good lookout, could miss her ; and as she went further and further away, and became smaller upon the flashing waters of the southeast, I felt a new stirring of life in me : hope grew buoyant, and for a little time at least I was more light-hearted than I had been, ay, ever since that gale had burst upon the *Lady Maud*, and driven us in darkness into these dangerous waters.

The three of us who had built that raft stood watching her until she was a mere speck in the wake of the smoke Then muttering an earnest prayer to God that she might effect our purpose, I went down the hill, the seamen following me.

Catching sight of the turtle as I walked, I told Hunter to kill it : first, because I knew it is a cruel thing to keep those

animals long on their backs ; and secondly, because its meat
would save the other provisions, and be a relish for us, who
Heaven knows, stood in need of any comfort in that way that
we could come at.   I was in no mood to watch him destroy
the creature, so I walked over to the trees under whose shadow
Sir Mordaunt and the others were resting themselves.   On
my drawing near, Miss Tuke asked me eagerly who the person was that had gone away in the raft.   I was obliged to
tell her, but I did so with reluctance and a kind of shame.

" Was he *dead* ?" she exclaimed, in a thrilling whisper,
and grasping Mrs. Stretton's hand.

I exactly explained our motive, but the shocked expression
lingered long in her face.

I was worn out and overcome with the heat, and threw myself down upon the grass.   Seeing my exhaustion, Mrs. Stretton filled a shell with sherry and water, and I swallowed the
draught gratefully.   She then came and sat by my side.   I had
had little to say to her since we had been cast ashore, and
small leisure to observe her closely.   She had removed her hat,
one that Miss Tuke had given her, and which the sea had
soaked without tearing from her head—I say, she had removed
her hat when under the trees, and her thick, black beautiful
hair had come away from its fastenings, and hung about her
in a manner that gave a peculiar power and a wild kind of
spirit to her dark, handsome, and uncommon face.

" You bear your sufferings with admirable courage," said I.
" Hard as our plight is, your trials have been so heavily in excess of ours, that I can only admire and wonder at your fortitude and patience."

" It will not do to look back," she answered.   " We might
humbly wish that God's hand had fallen less heavily upon your
poor friend, Mr. Walton."

" I hope," said I—we spoke in a low voice that could not
be overheard—" that Miss Tuke does not think me wicked in
helping to send a poor dead man in quest of succor.   Heaven
knows, whatever I have done I have done for the best."

" Oh, be sure we all believe that," said she, with a note of
rich, and tender gratitude in her voice.   And after a short
silence, she asked, " Do you think we shall ever get away from
this island ? "

" Yes," I replied ; for whether I thought so or not, the
proper answer to her question was yes.

" Sir Mordaunt frets cruelly over his wife," she continued.

"It is breaking his heart, I believe, to think of her lying in the sand there in the condition in which she was buried. He told me you had promised to get the men to make a coffin for her. Cannot that be done?"

"Yes," said I. "I had forgotten. After dinner it shall be done. And by the look of the sun it seems about time that we got our midday meal. How many cakes did you bake?"

"Enough for dinner and supper," she replied.

"Then let us get dinner now," said I; for by this time Hunter had done his business with the turtle, and with the help of Tripshore had dragged the great creature up to the hut.

As there was nothing else cooked but the meat in the tins, we had some of that; but in order to save the slender stock, I asked Mrs. Stretton and Miss Tuke to devote themselves that afternoon to boiling some of the salt beef in the kettle—the only cooking utensil we possessed—and I likewise requested Norie to cut up the turtle for salting and drying. I then in a low voice told Sir Mordaunt that I had not forgotten my promise, and that I would set to work after dinner to build a coffin for his wife's remains. He pressed my hand in silence.

It was a bitter thing to look at our miserable repast, and round upon our rude hut, and recall the *Lady Maud's* sumptuous cabin and plentiful good fare. Only a painter could give you any idea of the interior the hut presented, and of our appearance as we sat, or stood, eating with our fingers. No one who has not suffered in that way can imagine what it is for the civilized instincts to find themselves abruptly and helplessly plunged into a state of pure barbarism. The women used the knives when eating, and managed with less discomfort now that they had the little cakes as platters for their portions of preserved meat; but we males had to eat like monkeys, that is, there was nothing for it but to use our fingers for forks, and to Sir Mordaunt, who was a most fastidious man in his habits, this trifling hardship was a sterner grievance than the being without a bed, or the having no coat nor hat to cover him.

We made in that hut a complete picture of a shipwrecked party. Sir Mordaunt, as I say, was without coat or hat; I was in my bare feet; Norie had not yet manufactured the extraordinary cap from a piece of canvas that he afterward wore. Though the sun had dried our clothes, yet the salt water had given them a most beggarly aspect, more especially the women's. Then, as we had built the hut among the trees, we had the trunks of some of them standing among us and crowding the interior. Happily the grass made the ground a soft lodging ; but taken altogether, the sail as a carpet, the yacht's timbers nailed roughly to the trees, the trees in the midst of the hut, coupled with our melancholy figures, one lying, another standing, a third squatting, produced one of the wildest and most striking pictures that can be conceived.

" I wonder," says Norie, filling the shell with water from the kettle, and eyeing it with an air of rueful wonder, "I wonder," says he, "if such a calamity as this ever befell a yachting party before."

"It may well have happened," said I.

"And it may happen again, sir," said Tripshore.

"If ever our misfortunes come to be known," exclaimed Sir Mordaunt, "they should make yacht-owners who undertake long cruises very cautious in their selection of skippers. And yet, Walton, as you know, I had the fullest confidence in Purchase. I never for a moment doubted that he was a first-rate navigator."

Tripshore looked at me.

"How long will it take the raft to get into the track of ships ? " asked Miss Tuke.

This question started us on a new conjecture ; but it was quite impossible to arrive at any conclusion, simply because we had no notion in what part of the Bahamas this island lay.

"If only the chart of these islands had been washed ashore," said I, "we should be able to form some idea how far distant the nearest inhabited land is by giving this rock a theoretical position. The only islands I can remember as inhabited are New Providence, Abaco, Andros, and Inagua. Of course there are others, but my memory does not carry them. Yet even the islands I name run from the high north away south as far as the Windward Passage ; consequently this cay cannot be very far from *one* of them. But how does that one bear? How far is it? How are we to reach it ? "

"That's it, sir," answered Hunter. "If them questions could be answered there'd be no call to worrit ourselves long."

"Suppose a ship sights the raft, what will she do ? " asked Mrs. Stretton.

"Why, mum," replied Tripshore, "if her skipper has eddication enough to read the board, and has a mind to help us, he'll carry the board along with him to the port he puts into, and give information there, and a wessel will be sent to look for us.

Or if he's bound on a long woyage, then I suppose he'd speak the first ship he met, and give her the news, who'd report the wreck on her arrival. That would be about it, sir, I think?" said he to me.

I answered yes, though if a government ship encountered the raft, she would probably start in quest of us at once. "But," said I, in a hopeful voice, "be the vessel that sights the raft what she will, help is sure to come;" and so speaking, I went out of the hut, calling to Tripshore and Hunter to follow me.

When I had them alone, I explained Sir Mordaunt's wish; and fancying that Hunter hung back from the job, as one that seemed to him of a sentimental kind and not to refer to our present needs, nor to our prospects, I added that the baronet was sure to gratefully remember their action in this matter should we come to be rescued, and that they knew he was rich enough to make his gratitude a thing worth earning.

Tripshore stood in no need of an incentive of this kind, but it put a heartiness into Hunter, who said "he was always agreeable to turn to and oblige people, more 'specially when they was his boss, a; he still reckoned Sir Mordaunt to be; though he believed that when sailors was cast away, as he was, the law left it to their own hoption whether they should continue as men, or be their own masters."

It was a dreadful dismal job for persons in our situation to fall to. Nothing but my affection for, and my sympathy with, Sir Mordaunt could have induced me to take a part in such work. We managed it by collecting a quantity of deck-planks, and nailing them together into a kind of long box. We worked close beside the grave, in the shadow of the hill. Indeed, out of that shadow we should not have been able to lift our hands, for the sun was fierce enough to roast us alive, and the gay wind that was blowing did not in the least degree qualify that scorching and blinding effulgence. In this tropical fiery splendor the coral sand tortured the eye that rested even an instant upon its glaring surface, whilst the sea in the south was a great tremulous blaze that seemed to fill the whole of that quarter with a fog of silver-white glory, so that the horizon all that way was as completely shut out as if a body of vapor had rolled down over it. Nevertheless, we worked very steadily; and, indeed, there was not much to be done, seeing that we did not stop to make the coffin sightly, but just nailed the boards roughly together, so that the poor remains could lie in the sand in a condition to be removed whenever the time arrived.

None of the others came near us. Norie tended the fire, but stopped short at that point. They all knew what we were doing, that we were engaged upon a solemn and dreadful task not proper to intrude on.

I dare say we were an hour and a half in making that coffin, such as it was ; but when it was finished, the worst part remained. If it had been a hard trial to me to exhume the sailor's corpse, I know no words to express my horror at having to lift up Lady Brookes's body from the sand. Yet I dared not say I would not help the men, lest they should turn and refuse to go on.

No doubt I made more of it than I should under other circumstances. My nerves were unstrung by the trials and scenes and hardships we had gone through. Though I had been rendered somewhat buoyant in spirits by the raft going adrift, yet it was no more than a little fickle gleam of the sunshine of hope on my mind. It was clouded again, and my heart dark. Besides, it was a mighty trial to look upon a human face coming blindly up out of the sand—a face whose lineaments would reflect the horror that they excited in the imagination. Above all, was it a mighty trial to look upon a face I had known in life, whose lustrous eyes had often met mine, whose voice I seemed to hear if I did but strain my fancy—to look, I say, upon that familiar face appearing amid the sand, as the seamen carefully scratched about with their hands, disclosing first one part, and then another of the body, until, my God ! she lay there, a fully dressed woman, with her eyes blind with sand, and her hands by her side, and the rings sparkling from her fingers !

I asked Hunter to remove the rings. He pulled, but they would not come away.

"No matter," said I. "Lift her gently, men, and lay her in the coffin."

This was done, and the coffin boarded up. We all three then went to work to deepen the grave, and having buried the coffin, left the dismal place.

This job had heavily depressed me. We were red-hot with the heat and the toil, and went for a drink. But, in compliance with my wish, Miss Tuke and Mrs. Stretton had taken the kettle to boil some salt beef, and so to slack our thirst we had to walk across the island in the broiling sun to the well. This was very annoying, yet excepting that kettle, we had nothing in which we could store water.*

As we went to the well, I told Hunter to go to work presently, and clean the flesh out of the shell of the turtle, and then the shell would serve us for a tank. It was too great a tax, I said, to be obliged to cross the island every time we wanted a drink.

After reaching the well and quenching our thirst, we stood a while looking away into the sea in the north. This side of the island was very flat, and yielded us but a narrow horizon. I saw the white ribs of a reef glancing in the dark blue water about a mile away in the northwest, and beyond that was a shadow upon the sea that looked like the eddies formed by a tide running over the shallow surface of another reef.

"Can we be among the shoals to the westward of Long Island?" said I, remembering on a sudden the swarm of little cays and reefs marked upon the chart over against that piece of land. "If so," I added, with a feeling of despair in me that I could not check, "I can't see how on earth we are to be rescued unless we make shift to get away on a raft, and leave the rest to Providence. No vessel is likely to come near these waters. The proper channels will be leagues away on either side."

"The water looks open enough out yonder," replied Tripshore, pointing into the northeast. "If we be in the midst of them shoals you speak of they'd be showing all around."

"What part of these cussed islands, we're cast away on, I don't know," said Hunter ; "but whatever may be your determination, Mr. Walton, mine's this : I'm not going to sit down on this here rock and wait for something to happen. I don't say northen 'll come of that there raft we sent adrift this morning ; but meanwhiles there's wood enough left to build a machine that'll float two men. I'm agreeable to go to work upon it, and when it's built, if no one else 'll join, then, if you'll give me three days' allowance o' wittles, I'll put off alone and see what's to be found. Ye'll be discovering soon that it'll be better to take your chance o' drowning than stopping here."

"I don't see my way to that—" said I.

"But I do," he interrupted.

____

* We had the beef cask, but it was full of meat, and we dared not remove the junk from the brine in the cask, lest it should putrefy. We also had the sherry cask, but at that time we thought the wine too precious to let run.

" Because," I continued, determined not to notice the man's mutinous manner, "we cannot construct a raft that will not be absolutely at the mercy of the wind. If we could reckon upon a north or an east wind blowing steadily for a week or so, then, indeed, our raft might drift to some inhabited shore. But the chances are almost all against us. The first bit of sea that got up would sweep us off the raft like chaff. Or we might be blown into the Atlantic without sighting a vessel, and wretchedly perish there."

" But what's to be done, then?" he asked fiercely. "Are we to stick here till we rot?"

"We must wait a little," I answered. "Give that raft we have sent adrift a chance. Or that smoke we are making may be seen. Some safer means of escape than a raft may offer If nothing turns up, then we must come to your remedy."

He muttered something under his breath, turned on his heel, and walked off, and he sullenly kept in advance of us the whole way across the island.

As we rounded the bushes which brought us within view of the place where Lady Brookes lay buried, I saw Sir Mordaunt at work upon the grave. I left Tripshore and went to him, and on drawing near I perceived that he was framing the grave with pieces of rock. He took my hand in both his and pressed it affectionately, and thanked me for having carried out his wishes. I asked him how he knew we had completed the task, as no one had approached us whilst we were at work.

"Norie," said he, "caught sight of you lowering the coffin, and came and told me."

"That is hard work for you," said I, pointing to the pieces of rock he had collected.

"I wish to know where she lies," he answered. "The wind and rain would soon level a mound of sand, but these stones will remain ; and I have asked Norie to nail two pieces of wood into the shape of a cross, and carve her name upon it, and the date of her death, and then we will set up the cross securely at the head there."

It was an affecting thing to see him at this work. I thought he looked ill and worn, and his attire, and long beard, and humid eyes, and his slow movements, all combined to make the picture a pathetic one. I stood in silence, wondering at the tenderness of this gentleman for the memory of a woman whose character in life was even less lovable than I have thought right to describe it ; and at the unselfishness of his nature, that left him heart enough, in the midst of our distress, hardships, and anxiety, to do all the honor that love could suggest to the poor creature who lay under the sand. To me, I own, all this seemed an idle duty. Had our escape been sure, no matter how long delayed, I might have understood the baronet's anxiety to preserve his wife's remains, that they could be removed hereafter. But, so far as we then knew, we ourselves were as people in the very valley of the shadow of death. One by one we might drop away before help reached us, if ever help should come; and the state of mind which these thoughts induced made me behold but little of worth in the devoted memory that was influencing Sir Mordaunt.

However, I had the decency to keep my ideas to myself, nor at such a moment at least would I intrude upon him the fears which at that time oppressed me. I told him if he would leave the building of the grave to me, I would take care it was properly done, and the cross firmly erected. It was not fit work for him, I said.

"No, no!" he exclaimed. "This is my share. I could not assist in the other part. I had not courage even to approach and watch you. But this is strictly my duty—my religious duty. Do not offer to help me, Walton. It will soothe me to look back and recall this labor."

As this was his wish, I said no more, and went to the hut to rest a while. I noticed Hunter on the beach, standing near the remains of the wreckage there, and looking about him, as I supposed, to see if anything more had come ashore. Norie was helping Mrs. Stretton to cook the beef and keep the fire going; but I presumed they had not been there long, and that they would not stop there long, for the heat of the sun and the fire together was not to be borne. Under the trees, and to the right of the hut, was Tripshore, operating upon the turtle, Carey looking on. I had given this job to Hunter, but it did not signify who performed it, and if Hunter was searching the beach he was well employed.

Inside the hut I found Miss Tuke kneeling on the sail, making cakes. Her sleeves were rolled above her elbows, her hair was rough, yet I never admired her more than I did then, and I thought it impossible that any posture should suit her better. I sat down near the plank on which she was molding the cakes and told her what we had been doing, and how I had left her uncle employed.

"He thinks of nothing else," she answered mournfully.

" He seems to forget that we are shipwrecked, and may never escape from this dreadful island."

" On the contrary," said I, " he is acting precisely as a man would who firmly believes that we shall escape. He begged me to make the coffin, and is himself making the grave, in the full conviction that he will come or send for his wife's remains for burial in England."

" But *how* are we to get away?" said she, pausing in her work, and looking me full in the face.

I could only repeat what I had said before—that we must hope the smoke of the fire would be seen, or the raft with our message upon it encountered.

" It will not take us long to burn all the bushes on the island," said she; "and then how shall we be able to make a fire? And how many days will you grant before supposing that the raft has disappeared without any ship having seen it?"

"What *can* we do if we are forbidden even to hope?" I replied, tormented by these questions, which only too accurately interpreted my own feelings. "The bushes were not all burnt yet, and the raft has been gone only four or five hours. We must be patient, and have faith in God's goodness. Who knows what a day may unfold?"

She had too brave a soul to go on murmuring, yet it was clear that she understood our situation as accurately as I, and that she could not look away from the immediate present without her heart fainting in her.

" If the worst comes to pass," said I; " if, after waiting, we see no prospect of relief; then, before our food fails us, we must turn to and pull this hut down, and make as big and strong a raft as we can manage. But that alternative, as I have told the others, is so full of danger, that before adopting it our extremity should be greater than it is, and our patience all gone."

As I said this, Hunter put his head into the hut, and said there was a wooden case come ashore. It was too large for him to carry alone. He wanted to know where Tripshore was.

" I'll give you a hand," said I, jumping up; and I followed him to the beach.

It was a large, white wood square box, and glanced among the ripples which rolled up the beach. It lay close to where we had launched the raft. We waded into the water, and hoisted it out of the sand, and conveyed it to the hut, where we pried open the lid, and came to a casing of tin. This we cut, and found the case full of biscuits, which had been perfectly protected from the water by the tin casing.

I called to Miss Tuke to come and look, and told her that every discovery of this kind improved our chances of escape, by enabling us to give the raft more time to do its work.

"I for one shan't stop for that, Mr. Walton!" exclaimed Hunter. "I've been overhauling that wreckage down there, and there's stuff enough for my purpose."

"What do you mean to do?" I asked.

"Build a kind of catamaran," he replied, "and take my chances alone, if nobody'll come with me."

"You can do as you please," said I, noticing the obstinate look in the man's face; "nobody will stop you. You're a sailor, and don't require any one to point out the risks you'll run."

Just then Mrs. Stretton and Norie arrived, the latter sweating under the kettle, that was full of salt meat, from which the steam was soaring in clouds. Tripshore, hearing our voices, also came round to where we stood, and listened, with the gleaming knife with which he was operating on the turtle forking out of his hand.

"All hands being here, saving Sir Mordaunt," said Hunter, folding his arms and looking around him, "I'll put my case. Here we are, imprisoned on an island. Where it is, no one knows. Two blessed days we've been here, and ne'er a sail have we seen. My belief is, that if we was to stop here twelve months we'd see northen go by. What have we got to wait for then? The raft that's gone adrift *may* do some good— I was willin' enough to lend a hand to build it—but it may come to northen; and are we goin' to keep all on waiting and waiting, when maybe, that raft's gone to pieces? What I'm goin' to do is to build a sort of houtrigging machine as 'll not capsize, and light enough for a man to shove along. If nobody 'll come in it, I'll go alone. If I'm picked up, good; the vessel as picks me up 'll come for the others; and if I'm washed overboard and drowned, well, I'd as lief rot in the sea as rot here."

"Let him do it," cried Norie, eagerly looking at me. "It's a chance, at all events."

"Hunter is his own master," I replied. "He knows the risks, and that the odds against him are ninety-nine in a hundred."

"D—n the odds!" shouted the man angrily. "What are the odds here? They're *all* agin us. You know that, Mr. Walton." Turning to Tripshore, he said, "Will you give me a hand to build the thing I want?"

"Ay," said the others, "I'll give you a hand, Tom; but it'll be helping you to build your coffin, my lad."

"Well, when you're ready, come," exclaimed Hunter. "There's a spell o' daylight left yet."

So saying, he walked hastily toward the wreckage, from which he had already selected a portion of the material he required. When he was out of hearing, Miss Tuke said:

"Why are you opposed to his scheme, Mr. Walton?"

"I am not opposed to it, I am indifferent," I answered. "I should favor it if the chance of the man losing his life was not, as I believe it is, equal to a dead certainty."

"But he may sight a ship, and be the means of sending help to us," exclaimed Norie.

"Yes, he may—he may—and he mayn't!" I replied bitterly. "If there's any good in a raft at all, then the raft we sent away this morning should answer our end. If the thing is seen, the dead messenger abroad will not appeal less forcibly than a living man. If it is not seen there is no life to be lost, no long hours of torment to be endured."

"But something must be done—some effort must be made," said Norie, in a low voice.

"My God!" I cried, "have we been idle? What more could we have done? Tell me what to do—give me an idea. If practicable, it shall be executed to the letter. But don't force us to throw away our lives in a senseless effort to preserve them."

"Tom means to go," said Tripshore, who stood by; "and he'll have his way. Only he shouldn't be let to use up all the nails, Mr. Walton. We may come to want 'em ourselves."

"Go you and help him, Tripshore, as you promised," said I; "but keep an eye upon the nails too, for as you say, we may want them, though I hope not."

For, here let me repeat that the idea of the eight, or, if Hunter would not stay, the seven of us, committing ourselves to the sea in such a raft as we should be able to construct, was intolerable to me. Of all marine fabrics, the raft has been the theater of the worst sufferings. At the very best it is but a clumsy platform at the mercy of the winds and surges. A very light sea will set it awash, so that you may reckon upon sitting

up to your hips in water nearly all the time you are aboard.
It needed no very vigorous imagination to conceive what our
situation would be in a seaway, the water pouring in coils over
the level stage, that would swing to the surges like an ill-
balanced kite, our bodies soaked to the skin, our provisions
washed away or spoiled.   It was not to be expected that Norie
and the women could realize all that was meant by the proposal to leave the island on a raft ; but to me it offered itself
as a dreadful alternative, and though life was as dear to me as it
was to the others, I felt that it would be a wiser resolve to stick
to the island, and trust to God's mercy for a rescue, and if no
succor came, then to die on dry land, than launch ourselves
upon the sea in a raft and take the risk of courting in that way
all those dreadful sufferings, that protracted anguish, and that
final extinction, which make some of the naval records the
ghastliest and most terrible literature in the world.

CHAPTER XVII.

It was hard to tell the hour by the look of the sun, but I
guessed it to be about four o'clock.   I sat down on the grass
near the hut, with my back against a tree, whilst Mrs. Stretton
and Carey hung up the pieces of beef which had been cooked,
and Miss Tuke finished her job of cake-making.   The fire had
waned ; but though we should not let it expire, it was impossible
without incessant and painful labor to keep it throwing
up a heavy smoke.   Only a very thin trail of smoke went up
now.

I asked myself, Even should the densest smoke we could get
out of the bush be seen, would its meaning be understood ?
Would it not be thought the smoke of a steamer?   Or if guessed
to come from this rock, the smoke of a fire lighted by some
persons who had landed on a short visit?

These were crushing thoughts, for, as you know, we had but
two chances—the smoke and the raft ; and if we gave up the
smoke as hopeless, we had nothing left but the raft, which
might prove useless too, and what then was to be done ?

My dejection was so great for a time, that a feeling of utter
indifference stole over me.   I thought to myself, Well, if God
has deserted us, what is the good of our striving ?   If we are
sentenced to perish here, why chafe our hearts into rags with

thoughts of how to get away? Every mortal creature has his appointed time, and if ours has arrived, let us not make ten thousand deaths of it by our fears and recoilings and our madness to escape it.

The breeze that had been blowing all day had fallen somewhat, and was now a gentle wind. The sun was still high, and the water on fire under it. It seemed cruelly hard that we should have this fine weather now when it was of no use, when had it come earlier it would have saved us from this dreadful fate, by enabling us to ascertain our whereabouts, and to steer the yacht accordingly. I looked at the reef where she had gone to pieces, and at the water beyond, but could see no fragment of her. There was a very slight swell rolling in from the sea, and the reef gleamed in it as the water rose and fell, and every now and then there would be a sudden beautiful play of foam, which glistened in a hundred tints in the sunshine, like the sparkling of light in trembling dewdrops.

All the while I looked I was saying to myself, " In what part of the Bahamas is this island? What land is that visible from the hill-top there? Is it possible that no vessel ever traverses those leagues of dark blue sea away yonder, near enough for her people to see our signal, or for us to spy her canvas or the smoke from her funnel? In this age, when all the oceans are crowded with shipping, it seemed scarcely conceivable that our fate should have thrown us upon an island in unnavigable waters. Remembering my passing mood at that time, I can understand those fits of sullenness and of ferocity which have possessed the shipwrecked mariner as hope dies in his breast.

I sat watching the two seamen collecting the materials for a small raft on the beach with a dull, unconcerned eye. I had never felt so hopeless before; but, thank God, the depression was but transient.

I had been resting and musing in this way for some time, when Sir Mordaunt came from his wife's grave, where he had been toiling since we had buried the coffin. His appearance it was that rallied me, by making me feel ashamed of the selfish character of my despair in the face of such an affliction as had come upon him. He walked very slowly, and showed many symptoms of great physical distress. I met him, and gave him my arm. He leaned upon me wearily, but said nothing until he had seated himself.

" Have you finished your task? " said I.

" Yes," he replied. " I can do no more. I have covered the

grave with stones, and to-morrow, I trust, Norie will have completed the cross he promised to make and inscribe.   I knew
the labor would soothe me, Walton.   Now that I have marked
her resting-place with my own hands, my mind is calmer than
it was."

"I, hope you will not expose yourself again to the sun," said
I, "nor attempt any more hard work."

"Ah, I am too old for hard work, " said he, with a sad smile,
laying his hand on mine.   "And surely, Walton, shipwreck
ages a man's heart terribly.   Who could imagine that our cruise
would end in this way? Yet you all seem to bear up well.
Where are the others?   Where is Ada?"

"In the hut with Norie.   The other women will, I expect,
be at work on the turtle."

"And what is Tripshore about?"

I explained, believing that he would take my view of Hunter's
scheme; but instead, he exclaimed, " Why, the man is a brave
fellow to venture it.   Do you say he will go alone?"

"Who would accompany him?"

"Yes, indeed; but that leaves him so much the braver.   Do
you know, he may fall in with a vessel, or manage to reach
some inhabited coast.   It will help our chance, Walton."

He was eager and restless on a sudden.   He looked with
animated eyes across the sea, and clasped and unlocked his
hands.

"Yes," he repeated, "it will help our chances.   Life is still
precious, Walton.   It would be a dreadful thing to die on this
island—no living creature left to tell the world what has become
of us.   Some effort must be made."

I knew that as well as he.   However, it would have been
cruel to extinguish the hope, and, I may say, the new spirit
which my explanation of Hunter's scheme had kindled in him,
by representing its idleness.   Indeed, I was heartily glad to see
him waking up out of his grief, and taking an interest in our
distressful position, and admitting the preciousness of life.
His misery had been dangerously numbing his mind, and had
he continued much longer in that mental condition, I have no
doubt that he would have fallen melancholy mad.   This quick-
ening in him therefore gave me real pleasure, and I applauded
myself for my good sense in carrying out his wishes with respect
to his wife's interment, and in not hindering him by officious
friendship from doing his part.   The mind knows its own
burdens best, and how to vent itself; and certainly one way of

lightening melancholy is to let it expand itself in forms of its own choosing.

After Tripshore and Hunter had been working for an hour down in the creek, whither they had carried the stuff for the raft, they came up to the hut for their supper. It was time for that meal, as we could guess more by our appetites than by the sun : and as we had a mind to treat ourselves to a change of food, we set a piece of boiled beef upon the deck-plank, and each person helped himself to a biscuit.

It was easy to see how greatly Sir Mordaunt and the others were taken by Hunter's scheme, by the way they regarded him. They eyed him as if he was a hero. Almost as soon as he presented himself he was asked by Sir Mordaunt what progress he had made with his raft.

"Why, sir," he answered, "I hope by noon to-morrow to have put this beast of an island a long way astern."

"You have great resolution and courage," exclaimed Sir Mordaunt. "I pray that God may protect and guide you."

"He won't guide us here," answered Hunter, bluntly ; "and protection'll be of no use if we're not to get away. As well be drowned, I say, as become a skeleton on a island. I know this, sir—I've got northen to do but to keep all on steering west, and I'm bound to come right."

"Wind and weather permitting," said Tripshore.

"Northen'll divart me," said Hunter sullenly. "Right or wrong, when that raft's built, I'm off."

He devoured his allowance of food rapidly, wild with impatience to fall to his work again. Tripshore, noticing the general sympathy with the man's scheme, made haste to finish his supper, so that the others might not think he was reluctant to assist his mate. I kept silent, resolved to say nothing more on the subject.

As Hunter was leaving the hut, he said to me, "I suppose you'll let me have the compass, sir ?"

"It is Sir Mordaunt's property," I answered.

"Certainly you may have it," exclaimed the baronet.

"Remember," said I, "should we ultimately have to betake ourselves to a raft, we shall want that compass, to know in what direction we drift."

"But what raft do ye mean to build ?" inquired Hunter. "Where's the wood ? It'll be pretty nigh all used up by the time I'm done."

"There's plenty here," said I, pointing to the hut.

18

"Oh, I forgot that," said he.

"Let him have the compass, Walton," cried Norie.

"Yes, if he goes alone he should be furnished with every requirement our miserable stock will yield," said Sir Mordaunt. "Hunter risks his life for us, remember, Walton."

"He knows," said I, "that my objections are not made to defeat his wishes, but to protect ourselves, and him too, for the matter of that."

The man without answering, walked swiftly away, Tripshore following leisurely. It was not very pleasant for me to look round, and to see on the faces of our little company that they considered my timidity was trying to deprive them of a chance of escape. Yet I could not mistake their manner. I would particularly refer to Miss Tuke and Mrs. Stretton and Norie. This touched me to the quick. Was it not to my interest as much as to theirs that Hunter should venture his life, if he chose, to find us help? I objected to his enterprise because I could not endure that the man should sacrifice his life to no purpose ; and also because it seemed an unmanly thing to let him go forth alone into the great sea upon a little raft, though any one of us who had offered to accompany him would, in my opinion, have acted with criminal folly.

Depressed by the behavior of my companions, and greatly vexed by it—for I could put my hand on my breast and say with an honest heart that I had done my best for them all and would strive to do more if time were given me—I took the glass and walked to the hill, partly to search the sea, and partly that I might be alone.

As I passed the fire, I stopped to throw some wood upon it. It was nearly out, but the wood soon kindled, and sent up a volume of smoke the twigs and stems of the bushes being almost as dry as dead wood, whereas the leaves, being green, damped the blaze, and made a smoke like one of those burning heaps of leaves and stubble and rubbish which you have seen in fields. The sun was still very hot, but it was westering fast and its noontide fierceness was gone. The first thing I noticed on reaching the top of the hill was Lady Brookes's grave. Sir Mordaunt must have worked very hard, and I wondered where he had found all the stones and pieces of rock he had piled upon it. He had raised them very near as high as a man's waist. There was no fear of that grave being missed, should the baronet ever be able to send for the poor lady's remains.

I sat down on top of the hill, with my knees up in front of

me, upon which I rested the telescope. The gentle wind that
was blowing was very sweet, though warm, and greatly qualified the heat of the sunlight. As I gazed around me, I thought,
What a little bit of an island is this! What a speck upon the
mighty Atlantic, whose vast waters washed the eastern heavens,
and interposed nearly fourthous and miles of ocean betwixt us
and home! I searched the horizon all that way, wondering,
since the atmosphere was so clear, whether there would be land
in sight; but I could see nothing that looked like land, nor any
appearance of a vessel. All that was visible upon the water
were the reefs I have before described, with here and there a
shadow, that might well have passed for the reflection of a
cloud, had the sky not been clear, but which I could not doubt
would be a shoal.

I then brought the telescope to bear upon the south and west,
and scanned those quarters very closely and narrowly. Nothing rewarded my search beyond the point of land we had before
descried. I tried hard to determine its features, but it was too
far off: it was not more, indeed, than a faint blue cloud in
appearance.

I put the glass down, and, folding my arms, looked idly and
listlessly about me, with something of that vacancy of soul that
had been in me a short time before. The two men were hard
at work in the creek. They had made great progress with the
raft, which consisted of several planks nailed to short beams;
and they had contrived a sort of box amidships, like an open
companion hatchway, meant, I suppose for Hunter to sit and
paddle in. There was a certain cleverness in the form of the
raft, and for fishing, or for making short excursions, or even
for venturing for the distant glimpse of land, it would have
been a very valuable thing on a fine smooth day; but literally
to go to sea in, it looked to me as worthless as a single plank,
and I was more than ever persuaded that the man would be
acting like a madman to quit the island on so frail and dangerous a contrivance.

The rest of the party had come out of the hut, and were sitting under the trees, which were, I believe, stunted brasilleto.
There they could see the men working, and yet be in the shade.
They made a sad group for me to watch. It was a cruel situation for women to be in, more particularly for a delicate girl
like Miss Tuke, who had been flung on a sudden from the luxury of a fine yacht into a state of absolute homelessness, beg-
gary, and harsh privation, backed and darkened by the shadow

of terrible death. Grievous was it, too, to look at Mrs. Stretton, and think that we had saved her from one desperate peril, only to plunge her into an even worse form of suffering ; for suffering is to be measured by time. Another day might have terminated her anguish on the wreck ; but who could guess how long our present imprisonment was to last, and how much misery we should have to endure before we were visited by death or succored by human hands?

My eyes, quitting my poor companions, wandered over the reef on which we had struck, and which from this height I could clearly see gleaming in the crystalline blue water. Only three of the bodies of the crew had come ashore, and I supposed that the others had been washed by the current away to sea. Thither also, no doubt, had gone the spars of the yacht and the other floating portions, and may be most of those stores which would have been so precious to us in our destitution.

I imagined there was a trickle of tide setting to the westward now, and I was letting my eye run that way, when I caught sight of a black object in the water, about three-quarters of a mile distant from the westernmost point of the reef.

I believed at first that it was a shark, but it looked too big for a shark. I snatched up the glass and pointed it. The instant the object entered the field of the lenses I perceived that it was a boat bottom up.

I would not credit my eyes at first, and continued looking and looking until it was impossible for me to doubt that the object was a boat, with her keel just above the water, and portions of her bottom glancing in the delicate swell.

I was so agitated, that I trembled as though a wintry blast had struck me ; my heart seemed to stop beating, and I felt as if about to faint ; a cold perspiration covered my forehead ; involuntarily my hands clinched themselves until my fingernails cut into the palm. I closed my eyes tight, to clear the brain, and I held them closed for some moments, after which I pointed the glass and looked again ; and being now quite sure, I sprang to my feet and hallooed to the men in the creek with all my might. They dropped their work, affrighted by my voice, and stared. I put my hand to my mouth and bawled, ''There's a boat, bottom up, out yonder ! Come up here and look at her !'' And I stood pointing in so wild an attitude that they might well have imagined I had taken leave of my senses. However, they instantly came running to the hill, and the others, who had heard my cry, came running too, all save Sir Mordaunt, who half rose, but sank back again.

Tripshore was the first to reach me. I gave him the glass, and pointed to the boat. Instantly he cried, "Ay, it's a boat! It must be the yacht's boat; her that the men launched, and that drowned them."

"What is it?" shouted Hunter, rushing up to us.

"Look, Tom! Isn't that the yacht's boat there?" exclaimed Tripshore.

He peered, and uttered a loud cry. "Yes, yes! that's her! that's the boat we launched, and that capsized with us. For the Lord's sake, Mr. Tripshore, let's go and secure her."

By this time the others had arrived, and a whole volley of questions was let fly at me. They thought it was a ship I had seen. But I had now recovered my composure; and after briefly answering their questions, and giving them the telescope, to look at the boat for themselves, I turned to Tripshore and Hunter.

"Is your raft ready to go afloat?" I asked.

"She'll swim as she is," answered Hunter, in a voice full of uncontrollable excitement.

"Will she carry you both?"

"Both?" he replied. "Ay, four of us."

"You'll want a couple of paddles," said I. "That boat is within a mile, and by paddling you'll fetch her easily."

"A couple of planks 'll do for paddles, Tom," exclaimed Tripshore.

"Come along!" shouted the other.

"Take a tow-line with you!" I bawled after them, as they dashed down the hill.

Two were enough to launch the raft, and as they were both seamen they knew what to do. Though I had pulled myself together again, my heart beat strongly. That boat, unless damaged beyond all possibility of repair, might save our lives. If she were indeed the boat that the yacht carried amidships, then she would be big enough to receive the whole of us. And never had I seen the hand of God plainer in any circumstance than in this; Hunter's raft, against the building of which I had put my face, lay almost ready to shove off in, so that we should be able to get the boat at once and save precious time, and be beforehand with the darkness, or with any wind that might come with the darkness.

Seeing the baronet wave his hand to us, I asked Mrs. Stretton to go to him, and tell him that the yacht's boat was there, and that the men were about to bring her in. She went at once, whilst the rest of us stayed on the hill-top to watch the boat and the movements of the men.

As I have said, the frame of the raft was finished, and indeed, this was not a job that need have been long in doing, for the planks and pieces of timber were all ready there. The size of the raft was not bigger than the top of a dinner table, and there were two of them to put it together. Yet it was very nearly half an hour before they got away in the raft, in spite of Hunter having told me that she would swim as she was ; the cause of the delay being they had nothing to serve them for paddles but planks, which they had to taper with the chopper at one end, in order to grasp them. In all this time, however, the boat barely drifted a hundred yards to the westward, showing the languor of the tide and its direction at that time. Yet my impatience was so great that it was a positive torture. I would not shout to the men, for I could see they were doing their best ; yet it would have eased me to stand and roar, for I was mad to secure the boat, and every minute that passed seemed to my crazy anxiety like the moldering away of our chance.

I was greatly tormented also by Norie's questions. He would ask me first one thing, then another ; was miserably importunate ; one moment wringing his hands, and saying the men would lose the boat ; then shouting that the boat had vanished, and begging me for the love of God to look for her, and tell him if I could see her ; and then, when I had pointed her out, raving again at the men's slowness. Miss Tuke hardly spoke ; but her excitement and anxiety were fully as great as mine and Norie's. Her eyes were on fire, and yet she was mortally pale ; her bosom panted as though she was fresh from a race, and once she caught Carey's arm and held it, as though she were about to sink down. The sun stood over the point of reef where the yacht had beaten, in the southwest sky, and the heavens being cloudless, the sea within the compass of the reflection of the luminary was like a sheet of flashing gold.

It was impossible to look at it ; it was nearly as blinding as the sun himself. Fortunately the boat was to the eastward of that splendor, where the water was dark blue, beautifully pure in tint, and that which helped me to keep the boat in sight was the light swell, that would heave it up an instant and expose a portion of its streaming frame, which the sunshine touched and set on fire, so that at such moments the brilliant reflection in the wet planks might have passed for a sunbright star shining in the soft deep azure of the ocean.

At last the raft was ready. Hunter got into the box amidships, that was big enough for one only, and Tripshore sat just before it, his legs under him, like a tailor. Both men kept their faces forward. They paddled nimbly, and though the raft was not more shapely than a stage that a carpenter works upon over a ship's side, they managed to impel it at a fair pace. They had to come down the creek, and strike the sea at the opening between the beach and the reef; but the water was very smooth, there was scarcely any tide, and in five minutes they were clear of the reef, and propelling the raft very steadily toward the boat.

I ran down the hill to the beach to watch them from that point, and the others you may be sure followed me. I found that I could see the boat as plainly from the beach as from the hill, and perceived that the men had it in sight too, by the steadiness with which they aimed the raft at it. We all stood in a breathless state, watching the strange figure of that raft, and the sparkle of the paddles as the men flourished them. Our lives might depend upon the amazing discovery of that boat, that veritable godsend, which lay floating there, and the one passionate thought in me now was, will she be in a fit state to carry us?

Nimbly as the men plied their paddles, the raft took a desperate long time in reaching the boat. I knew that not only by my impatience, but by the passage of the magnificent flood of light upon the sea. Even when the raft seemed quite close to the boat, she was still a good distance off, and I waited and waited to see the flash of the little paddles cease, until I believed the men would go on paddling forever.

But even so weary a waiting must come to an end at last. The paddles were dropped, and keeping my eye at the glass, I perceived the men lean over and endeavor to right the boat. Three times they tried, each time depressing the keel to the water's edge, but no further; but the fourth time they succeeded; and then, instead of her keel, I saw the gunwales of the boat, like a black line upon the blue.

I now supposed they would make the line fast, and begin to tow her; instead of which they fell to bailing her out, one with his boots and the other with his cap. This would be a tedious process; but on reflection I judged they would not be able to tow the boat full of water, for the raft was hard enough to propel alone. I watched the bailing with a feeling of passionate expectation. If the boat was injured, the water would flow into her as fast as they threw it out ; if uninjured, her gunwales would rise. I explained this to Miss Tuke and Norie, and we watched the boat as persons standing upon a gallows might watch for the messenger who is coming with a reprieve, but who may come too late.

At last I clearly perceived that the gunwales rose. I could not be deceived. The telescope was a good one : when I had first looked at the boat after they had righted her, her gunwales only made a thin line, and now they were showing to the height of three or four inches. By this I knew that if the boat leaked at all, the leak would be a trifling one, to yield to such bailing as that ; and in a transport of delight I shouted out that the boat was sound ! that our deliverance was at hand ! and ran to Sir Mordaunt, pointing to the boat, and calling that our deliverance was at hand ! He was too much affected to speak ; he got up, and stood looking. I gave him the glass, and asked him to judge for himself how the boat grew up out of the water. He rested the telescope on my shoulder, and I felt the tube trembling in his grasp. He peered, and exclaimed, "There can be no question that she is the *Lady Maud's* boat, Walton. I see the gilt stripe round her."

"She must be the boat that the men launched," I answered, "and that capsized with them. She must therefore have been floating about here ever since, and it is wonderful that we have not seen her before."

"She was our biggest boat ! "

"Certainly she was ! " I cried. "She will carry us all ! We have but to rig and stock her with provisions and water, and sail away in her."

"Ah ! " he said, in a trembling voice, "God has watched over us ! "

I felt that as profoundly as he, and could have fallen on my knees. It was as though a miracle had been wrought, to find that boat there close to the island, manifestly uninjured by the heavy seas which the gale had raised, drifting into our sight in time to stop Hunter from risking his life on his miserable raft, and at the very moment when our prospects looked utterly dark and hopeless.

The men gave over bailing after they had been at that work about three-quarters of an hour. The line of immersion indicated that there was still water in the boat, but she showed a good side, and was no longer the drowned thing she had been. The sinking of the sun had warned them to stop bailing ; it was approaching the horizon, and there would be no twilight to help us when it was gone. They kept their places in the boat, and took the raft in tow, and by leaning over the side managed to paddle the boat along as fast again as they could have urged the raft. Indeed, they were not above twenty minutes in performing the journey. We stood on the beach to receive them, and when they were within earshot we all of us cheered and cried to them. They answered our shouts heartily ; and so, paddling the boat around the point of reef, they brought her to the entrance of the creek and came ashore, bringing with them the end of the tow-line.

It would have moved you, I am sure, to have seen us shaking hands with the two men. We crowded round them, and only let them go because they said they were wild with thirst. Norie and I then waded into the water, and, laying hold of the boat's gunwale, looked into her. There was not more than a foot of water in her, and this being as bright as glass, I could clearly see that her bottom was perfectly sound. Indeed, I could not perceive that she had sustained any injury, unless I except the loss of her rudder and her amidship thwart, that was started on the port side.

I called to Sir Mordaunt : " She is an old friend, and you were not mistaken. Here is the name *Lady Maud* in black and white "—pointing to the stern.

In truth she might well have been called the yacht's longboat, for, when on the chocks just abaft the foremast, she had the look of a long-boat, with her square stern, plump sides, and motherly beam. Her brass rowlocks hung by their lanyards ; her rudder was, as I have said, gone, but the gudgeons were standing—that is, the eyes on which the rudder had been hung.

To secure her for the night, Norie and I hauled her to the head of the creek, which brought her close to the beach.

"There is nothing the matter with her," said I to Tripshore, as he and Hunter rejoined us.

" Nothing, praise the Lord," he replied.

" She'll want a new rudder," said I, " and we must rig her. But that is easily done. To-morrow morning we'll set to work and give her an outfit."

" Will she carry us all ? " asked Miss Tuke.

"Ay, miss, and half as many again," answered Hunter.

"That fore-tops'l yard there, Mr. Walton, will be the very thing for a mast. Pity we sent away the top-gallant-yard in the raft this morning, sir."

"Oh, we'll find something to bend a sail to," said I ; glad to find that the man's mutinous manner had left him, and that he talked with his old civility.

As we strolled slowly back to the hut the sun sank, and so magnificent was the sight of the huge red and flashing luminary, poised like a vast wheel of fire upon the polished red water, that we all stopped to look at it, and kept silence as the orb gradually drew down. For a few minutes after it was gone, the sky in the west seemed as though a great city was burning out of sight under it, so terribly splendid was the crimson glare upon the heavens. But this awful and majestic light faded fast, sea and sky took a kind of yellow color, and then they became gray, and quickly changed into darkness, and night came upon us with a single stride, with a bright moon overhead, and the water in the north full of starlight.

The discovery and possession of our boat had put us all into fine spirits. Instead of entering the hut, we seated ourselves upon the coral sand at the top of the beach, and clear of the grass, that soon began to sparkle in the moonshine with the dew. The air was moist, but it was deliciously cool, and it was pleasanter to sit in the light of the bland and beautiful planet than in the dark hut ; and, moreover, there was something finely in harmony with our hopeful and grateful spirits in the peace of the sea, with the darkness and the stars in the north and east, and the flood of moonlight in the south, and in the soft creaming of the little breakers and the distant melodious wash of the swell over the line of reef.

We sat talking of our chances of escape, and in what direction we should steer the boat. I told them a story of three sailors who had sailed a smaller boat than ours over two thousand miles of sea, and related some of the hardships they had endured ; how they never despaired, but manfully struggled on and on ; until, after many days, and after they had measured the amazing distance of two thousand miles, they were picked up by a brig, and safely landed in England.

Then we talked over the provisioning of the boat. Miss Tuke asked how we should be able to carry water to drink.

"In the beef cask," said I. "We will test it. If it leaks, we must endeavor to make it tight."

"There's the sherry cask," said Tripshore.

"I know," I replied; "but we will carry the sherry with us, if the other cask will hold water."

"How much will it hold?" asked Sir Mordaunt.

"Between twenty and thirty gallons, I should say," I replied.

"And how long will that quantity last?" inquired Norie.

"Why," said I, "don't you see, Norie, that must depend upon how much we use. Twenty-five gallons will be two hundred pints. There are eight of us, and even a liberal allowance would give us a fortnight's supply."

"We could sail across the Gulf in that time," exclaimed Mrs. Stretton.

"Norie," said Sir Mordaunt, leaning toward the doctor, and speaking softly, though I heard him, "before we quit the island you will keep your promise?"

"I will set about it in the morning," responded Norie.

I knew this referred to the cross that Sir Mordaunt wished to erect over his wife's grave. Hearing what had been said, I remarked that, as there would be a deal of work to be done in the morning, it would be wise to settle the programme at once.

"You, Norie," said I, "will carry out Sir Mordaunt's wishes. That will be your part, and we shall expect nothing else from you. You and I, Tripshore, will fit and rig the boat. Hunter, you will help Mrs. Stretton and Miss Tuke to empty the beef cask, and then test it, and if it leaks, you must turn to and make it tight—if you can; and if you can't, then we must capsize the sherry and use that cask. Mrs. Stretton, you will cook more beef after breakfast, so that we can ship a fair supply; and, indeed, you and Miss Tuke and Carey will see to the provisions, for when Hunter is done with the cask, he'll join us at the boat. Is my programme to your liking?"

They all said yes, it would do very well.

"But what is my work?" said Sir Mordaunt.

"Why," said I, "you can act as overseer, and take care that there is no skulking among us."

My poor friend probably felt that this was about as much as he could do, for though he begged a little to be made practically useful, he gave over his entreaties very soon.

For nearly an hour we remained talking in this manner; but now the dew was falling like rain, and I advised the ladies to withdraw to the hut.

"Let us thank God, before we retire, for the mercy and goodness He has shown us this day," said Sir Mordaunt.

So we all knelt down upon the sand in the moonlight, whilst
the baronet prayed aloud; and when our thanksgiving was
over we shook hands, and all of our company, except the
seamen and I, withdrew to the hut.

"We had better keep watch as we did last night, my lads,"
said I.

"Ay, ay," they answered.

We debated, and then settled that Tripshore should stand
the first watch, Hunter the second, and I the last.

"Is it worth while keeping the fire in?" asked Tripshore.

"No," I replied, "I am satisfied that no vessel approaches
these waters, and a fire is useless. The weather looks settled;
we shall have the sun in the morning, and then we can
light the fire. Keep your eye on the boat, Tripshore,
and keep watch for any more wreckage that may come
ashore."

So saying I went to the hut, followed by Hunter, and dragging up a bit of the sail, so as to make a pillow, I put down
my head, and was soon fast asleep.

CHAPTER XVIII.

I was awakened by Hunter. It was quite dark, for the moon
had gone. I rose and went into the open air, and found the
sky cloudless as I had left it, and the stars shining brightly.
Some of the stars upon the horizon were so large and clear
that they looked like the riding-lamps of ships lying close off
shore, or light-house lamps. There was breeze enough to keep
the water shivering, and the temperature was as chilly as an
October night in England.

After a while I felt the darkness and the silence very oppressive. The sea made a peculiar moaning noise at the other side
of the island, and the wind murmured with a complaining note
among the trees where the hut stood. I felt then, as I had
often felt before when on board ship, that at sea loneliness is
never a keener sense than on a quiet, fine night. Wrapped in
shadow, the deep is a mystery, and the glorious stars, instead
of cheering, chill the mind by their measureless distance, and

by the soul-subduing wonder of the black and spacious heights they illustrate.

Along the beach where the breakers ran were thin lines of blue fire, and beyond, again, the phosphorus flashed and faded in the invisible swell as it coiled noiselessly along the ebony surface of the water. However, I fixed my thoughts upon the work that the sun would rise upon, and whilst I moved to and fro, plotting and planning and thinking over our wants when in the boat, and on what course I should steer her, the east grew pale, and very quickly the dawn came. In that ashen light the sea and the island and the gray heaven of fainting stars made an indescribably melancholy spectacle. But soon the east became of a delicate rose-color, that swiftly brightened into a radiant pink ; and then, as with a bound, the sun soared out of the sea, the heavens grew blue, the water sparkled like silver, and another brilliant, beautiful tropical day was born.

My spirits revived with the sun, and after glancing at the boat to see that she was all right, and running my eye over the beach to observe if any more wreckage had washed up, I set to work to collect a quantity of brushwood, and piling a portion of it in the fireplace that had been built, I unscrewed one of the magnifying lenses in the telescope, and very soon had a blaze. Then, to economize time, I went down to the boat, taking with me the shells we had used as drinking vessels, and bailed her out. When she was dry I thoroughly overhauled her, and found her perfectly sound, with those exceptions I have elsewhere mentioned. I returned to the beach, and having selected a piece of planking fit to serve for a rudder, I fetched the chopper and a knife, and fell blithely to work to fashion a rudder. This, to be sure, was a very trifling job, and I had finished it, and was turning over the spikes in the carpenter's chest, to select a couple of them to bend into pintles, when Tripshore and Hunter came out of the hut, and before they reached me all the others appeared.

Hunter had forgotten what his work was, and when I reminded him, he at once returned to the hut and set to work to empty the beef-cask.

Tripshore and I then started upon rigging the boat. First we carried the topsail-yard down to her, fitted it with stays, and shaped one end of it with the chopper, so as to step it. The yard-arm sheave-hole was the very thing for halyards, and happily plenty of gear had washed ashore with the sails and yards to serve us with material for stays and rigging. When we stepped the yard we found it suited the boat to a hair. We securely set it up, meaning to rig the boat with a single lug, which having regard to the hoist of her mast, would be sail enough, and returned to the wreckage on the beach, to choose a piece of timber that we could split, and then fish the pieces, to form a gaff or yard.

However, feeling very hungry, we knocked off before tackling this job, and went up to the hut for breakfast. I shook hands with Sir Mordaunt and the ladies, and looking about me, asked where Hunter was.

"Why," said the baronet, " he has rolled the beef-cask to the well, to test it by filling it."

"Couldn't he have done that with salt water?" I asked.

" He asked me to explain," continued the baronet. " He said that after washing the salt out of the cask he would fill it. If it didn't leak, then, by lashing a couple of planks or spars, one on each side, to it, you and Norie and he and Tripshore could carry the cask full of water across the island, which would save the delay and labor of going to and fro to fill it with the kettle. If, on the other hand, it leaked, then he said he could repair it as well there as here."

"The man's no fool," said I. "That notion of carrying the cask full, direct from the well, shows forethought, for it certainly would take us all day, journeying to and fro, to fill it with the kettle. But how is he going to fill it? He's left the kettle behind." And I pointed to the kettle, that stood near the hut.

" He emptied Carey's work-box, saying that would do to bail out the water from the well."

I burst into a laugh. "After that," said I, " who will doubt that necessity is the mother of invention?"

As I said this I caught sight of Hunter coming round by the bushes. He was purple in the face with heat, and flourished the work-box as he came.

"Well, Hunter," I cried, "how have you got on, my man?"

"The cask's sound," he replied. "It's full o' water, and don't drain a drop."

"Capital!" I exclaimed.

" There'll be northen to do," said he, "but to lash a piece o' timber on either side, and bring the cask along, full, as it is. And the supporters 'll do to fix it in the boat with; ye'll have to keep it end up, and a few planks and a piece o' sailcloth 'll save it from slopping."

We all heartily praised his foresight.   I asked Mrs. Stretton
if we could have breakfast.

"Yes," she answered, in her simple way, and her fine, rich
voice.   "That kettle is full of turtle, Mr. Walton, ready to
eat."

But before breaking our fast we knelt down, to offer up
thanks to God for his merciful protection.   I make no excuse
for recording these prayers.   They cheered us greatly.   They
reminded us of the Friend to whom we had been taught all
our lives that no appeal is ever made in vain.   They made us
look up and feel that, desolate, shipwrecked, destitute as we
were, yet with God to help us we should be as strong, our
prospects as bright and sure, as though we were in a situation
to supply all the means necessary to liberate us from this imprisonment.   I particularly noticed that none of us were more
earnest at these times than Tripshore.   He had been an ocean
sailor, and in spite of landsmen's theories about Jack, I never
knew a real sailor—I mean a genuine seaman, who has knocked
about in big ships and looked danger in the eye, and knows
the sea as a child knows its mother's face—who had not a
veneration for God in his soul, who had not in his heart all the
makings of an honest religious man, no matter how he covered
up his instincts and assumed the indifference which he dropped
when alone, or when a call was made upon his inner nature.

We made a good breakfast, for the turtle was excellent eating, though for salt we had nothing better than the brine in
which the beef was pickled.   We wanted water, however, and
drew lots who should fill the kettle.   It fell to Norie, who
trudged off cheerfully, and was back before we had finished
our meal.

If I was sure of finding no other audience than sailors, I
would go closely into the preparations we made for leaving
the island ; but landsmen cannot follow sea terms, and there
is no other language in which a man can write about the sea
than the language sailors themselves use.

As regards the rigging of the boat, we had pretty well all
we wanted to our hands.   Hunter joined us, having done with
his cask, and before the sun had reached the meridian we had
fitted the boat with a rudder and tiller, shaped some planks
into the likeness of oars, fashioned a yard and bent a sail to
it, and knocked the started thwart into its place.

This brought us to the dinner hour, and when we went to
the hut to get something to eat, I found that Mrs. Stretton had

cooked several pieces of beef, and that Miss Tuke and Carey had, between them, packed the biscuits in the maid's box, and stored all the best of the flour in the tinned-meat cases, which receptacles were compact, and to our purpose. I forgot Norie's share until we had done dinner, when Sir Mordaunt, taking my arm, led me round to the side of the hill, where I saw a rude cross firmly set up over the grave, and upon the cross-piece, in bold letters, "Agnes Brookes," with the date of her death. I put my hand upon the cross, and found it as firm as a tree.

"Norie has done his work very well," said I.

" He has, and I am deeply obliged to him," replied Sir Mordaunt. "The task has occupied him the whole morning. It was tedious work. He was forced to use a piece of rock for a hammer, as the chopper was constantly in use among you on the beach. I shall quit this island with a very different heart from what I should have left it had we sailed away and left her lying as she was first buried, without a stone to mark her grave."

He spoke with the tears coursing down his cheeks, and grasping my hand, he thanked me for the sympathy I had shown him, and the readiness with which I had complied with his wishes.

I left him whilst he knelt down to say a short prayer, for the time of our embarkation was close at hand, and I hoped to have put the island out of sight before the sun was gone. I called to Norie and the men, and told them that our next business was to go across the island and fetch the beef-cask. They were ready to accompany me ; so arming ourselves with some seizings and a couple of pieces of timber, we marched across the island to the well.

We found the cask standing full of water as Hunter had left it. It was as tight as a shell, and on tasting the water I perceived that Hunter had carefully cleansed the cask of the salt. We lashed the pieces of timber to it, and the four of us stooping at once, we got the bars upon our shoulders and raised the cask, and away we went with it, keeping step, and presently landed the cask on the beach close to the boat.

But after we had put the cask down, and I had looked from it to the boat, I found myself glancing at the sherry-cask under the trees. It was a smaller cask by several gallons, but much stronger, and fitter for the storage of water.

"I doubt," said I to the others, " if there'll be room in the boat for both casks. Yonder cask should hold as much water as we are likely to need."

"I have been thinking of that too, sir," said Tripshore. "The little 'un 'll be the better cask for us."

Both Hunter and Norie were of the same opinion.

"Then," said I, "I'll tell you what we'll do. This rain-water is not over-sweet: we'll leave about a third of the sherry in the cask there, and fill it up with water, and that will make a refreshing drink."

This was thought a good notion: so we went to work and let run about two-thirds of the sherry, filled up the cask with water, and fitting in the head of it, which had been knocked out, got the cask into the boat, and securely lashed it amidship. We then brought down all the provisions we meant to take with us: fixed the little tell-tale compass to the after-thwart, put the telescope into the boat, took in some cloths of canvas to serve as a spare sail, and all being ready, we hauled the boat round to a point where the woman could step aboard.

CHAPTER XIX.

It was about two o'clock in the afternoon, the sun fiercely hot, and a little breeze blowing from the eastward. After the women were in, we put the dog aboard, and then the rest of us entered. I had been greatly afraid that all this freight would sink the boat very deep; but when we were all in I was rejoiced to perceive that, in consequence of the boat's beam, the point of immersion was not so high by a streak as I had feared.

I took the tiller, and on either side of me sat Miss Tuke and Mrs. Stretton. Sir Mordaunt sat next his niece and Norie next the widow. Carey occupied a thwart just abaft the mast. The dog was in the bows, and the men forward, working the paddles to bring us clear of the reef.

In this manner we went along until we had got the westernmost point of the reef under our stern. The men then threw in their paddles and hoisted the sail. There was a pleasant little breeze, as I have said, and the moment the boat felt the pressure, she began to run, making a pretty tinkling sound of water along her sides, and leaving two thin lines of foam and bubbles astern of her, and rolling over the swell very buoyantly.

19

I had made up my mind at starting to try for the land that was in sight, and accordingly headed the boat for the direction in which it bore, steering by the compass, for the land was invisible from the level of the water. I then asked Norie to lend me his pencil, and being without paper, drew a rude chart upon the after-thwart ; that is, I made a mark to signify the island we were leaving, and set down N. E. S. and W., around it, according to the indication of the compass.

Miss Tuke asked me what I was doing.

"We shall require to know the bearings of the island we were wrecked on," I replied ; "for unless we get them it will be a thousand to one if ever we shall be able to recover the remains of Lady Brookes."

Sir Mordaunt instantly pricked up his ears.

"How will that help us, Walton ?" he asked eagerly.

"If I mark off our courses," I replied, "then, should we be picked up by a vessel, or make inhabited land, we shall be able to calculate by the latitude and longitude of the vessel, or the land, whereabouts our island is. Of course we cannot hope to be quite accurate, because we shall have to guess our rate of sailing. But we shall be sufficiently near the mark to render the search for the island easy to any vessel you`may send for the coffin."

He was much touched by this proof of my anxiety to help the wish that lay so close to his heart. But Sir Mordaunt Brookes was a man for whom I had a sincere affection, and there was little, indeed, I would not have done to serve him.

After I had made my scrawl on the thwart, we sat all of us for a while in silence, looking at the receding island and the passing water. It was a most perfect tropical day, both sea and sky of a dark, unspeakably pure azure, and wind enough to propel the boat along at about four land-miles an hour: But the sun was terribly fierce, and scarcely endurable. Sir Mordaunt wore Tripshore's hat, and Tripshore had on a woman's straw hat that had come ashore in Carey's box. Norie had twisted a kind of turban cap for himself out of a piece of canvas, and was the best off of us all, as the stuff was white, and kept his head cool. But to sit in that boat without any protection, for the sun was almost directly overhead, was like leaving ourselves to be slowly roasted alive ; and unable to stand the heat any longer, I called Hunter and Tripshore aft, to spread the spare sail as an awning, which, after some trouble, they succeeded in doing, by setting up a couple of paddles as stanchions, and making the clews of the sail fast to them.

This shade afforded us indescribable relief, and helped us to pluck up our spirits, which really swooned in us with the heat.

" Look what a little bit of rock that island ! " exclaimed Miss Tuke, pointing astern. " What a hard destiny, that with all this wide sea around us, we should have struck upon that tiny spot ! "

" Ah," said Sir Mordaunt, " but it would have been a harder destiny had we struck without being able to land upon it."

" Are you pretty comfortable, Mrs. Stretton ? " said I, turning to the poor woman by my side, who sat with her hands on her lap, and her fine eyes fixed upon the sea.

" Yes, thank you, Mr Walton," she answered. " Will you let me ask, if the island you are aiming for is not inhabited, how you will steer ? "

" To the southward and eastward," I said ; " because we were bound to be well to the north when we struck, and by steering south and east we can hardly fail, even if we miss the populated islands, to drive into the channels where we shall encounter ships."

" Which channel do you suppose will be the nearest ? " asked Norie.

" I wish I knew. I have the names of three channels in my head— Crooked Island Passage, Mariguana Passage, and the Caico Passage—but how they bear, and which one is nearest, I have no more idea than that dog. "

" By heading as you propose, Walton," said Sir Mordaunt, " is there not a chance of your missing the land, or drifting out of the track of ships ? "

" No," said I, " because by so steering we're bound, if we keep going on long enough, to run down one of the West India Islands."

Foot by foot as we went, the island we were quitting grew smaller and smaller, and its features became indistinguishable in a kind of a hazy yellow. The land for which we were try-ing was visible over our bows, but it was still too far off to make sure of, even with the glass, though my belief was, after a long inspection of it, that it was no more than a cay, similar to the one we had left, but bolder and larger.

Such minute objects as those two specks of land presented heightened rather than impaired our sense of the vast surface of water on which we floated. In such weather as this we

were no doubt as safe in that boat as if we had been aboard a
thousand-ton ship ; and yet it was impossible to cast our eyes
upon the water within a few inches of the gunwale, and then
follow the mighty space of gleaming blue to where it met the
heavens, without a shudder at the nearness of the great deep.
I remember saying to Tripshore, who sat forward, I could not
imagine that these wide waters were never traversed by vessels.

"But, sir," said he, "if, as you have all along reckoned,
we're in the thick of the Bahama clusters, there's ne'er a vessel
as 'ud have any business here."

This was true, and very soon after he had made that answer,
the reason why this sea was desolate was vigorously brought
home to me by an exclamation from Hunter, who had been
hanging his head over the side : for looking to see what had
made him call out, I found that the boat was at that moment
gliding over a reef that might have been one or ten fathoms below us, for aught I could tell, though it seemed to be within
arm's length, so exquisitely transparent was the blue water.
The reef was white and gleamed like silver set in dark blue
glass.   It was evidently very precipitous, and no more than a
narrow shelf, for when we had passed it by a boat's length we
could see nothing but the fathomless blue under the side.   In
the course of time that submerged reef would raise its head and
become an island, with trees and vegetation.   It was wonderful to see land, so to speak, in the very making of it.

The sun was fast approaching the sea by the time we had
neared the island we were heading for ; but long since we had
discovered with the help of the glass that it was no more than
a cay, uninhabited, with a high rise of land, hard upon forty
feet tall, at the northernmost point of it.   We could see the
sandy beach and the flat land stretching from the foot of the
rise, covered with brushwood and trees ; and what was more,
we could perceive the water all round it studded with reefs,
upon which the swell broke in flashing floods of foam, that
were blood-red in the rich evening sunshine.

"There's no use going any nearer," said I.

"No, sir, we're near enough," cried Tripshore.   "Any one
of them reefs would rip the bottom of this boat out of her."

Without another word I eased off the sheet and put the helm
up, and presently we had the island on our quarter, and the sun
beyond, a great red shield going down without a cloud, and
the water beneath it a sheet of molten gold, the extremity of
which seemed to touch our boat's side.

Whilst daylight remained we served out supper. We also took down the sail we had used as an awning, and spread it at the bottom of the boat, for the women to lie on when they felt disposed to sleep. Before I ate my allowance of food I gave the tiller to Norie, and stood up against the mast with the glass, with which, taking advantage of the singular brightness and clearness of the atmosphere at this hour of sundown, I carefully swept the water line, but failed to detect any other object than the island astern and a fragment of the island we had quitted quivering on the horizon in the northeast. The others watched me eagerly as I ran the glass round the sea, but nothing was said when I exclaimed that there was no vessel to be seen. Indeed, if I could judge their feelings by mine. they were too deeply glad to be in this boat, and sailing away from the island, to find a cause in the vacant sea-line for worrying their hearts. Only a few hours ago our prospects were horribly dark. We were, so to say, locked up on a desolate rock. In their misery and abandonment my companions had sanctioned Hunter's mad scheme ; and now here we were in a brave stout boat, a beautiful heaven above us ; we were well stocked with provisions, and in respect of accommodation, not much more inconvenienced than in the hut.

We watched in silence the going down of the sun. It was a noble sight, and full of unspeakable pathos to people in our situation, and to the half-despondent, half-hopeful temper we were then in. The breeze followed us, and the sun was on our right. I wondered when that sun set again where we should be. It had shone that day over our beloved country, it had looked upon dear friends and dear scenes, and now it was going down upon our little boat a speck, unseen by any eye but God's, upon the golden surface of this glorified western ocean. I believe all our thoughts ran somewhat in this way, for, as I have said, none of us spoke whilst the orb was sinking. Even the two seamen looked toward it in rapt postures, and when the last flashing fragment of it vanished, we all drew a deep breath and turned to gaze at one another, and I observed that Mrs. Stretton was crying, but very silently, and in a way that made us see that any notice taken of her would pain her.

"We shall have the moon with us for the greater part of the night," said I ; "and that beautiful sky cannot deceive us. It is full of good promise."

"How fast are we sailing, Mr. Walton ?" asked Miss Tuke.

I answered about three and a half miles an hour.

"How short the twilight is !" cried Norie. "Look behind you, Walton. The sky is full of stars. The darkness in the east and that brightness in the west give you night and day side by side."

"Couldn't you spin a yarn, Mr. Walton?" said Tripshore. " There's northen like stories and songs to keep the heart up."

" But our hearts are not down, Tripshore," I replied. "Our chances are too good for that. Can you sing ?"

"A trifle," he said. " But if it's to be singing, I'd rather not be first."

"Well, I'll break ground by telling an adventure," said I ; "and when I'm done you'll give us a song."

" Right, sir."

I reflected a bit, and then spun them a yarn about an adventure I met with at a little Chinese village up the Yellow River. Three or four of us, being ashore, had missed our way, and coming to this village, endeavored to obtain beds for the night, but were everywhere repulsed. Being determined not to lie in the fields, we forcibly took possession of a little house, and went to bed in it. In the middle of the night I and one of my companions, who lay with me on the top of a mattress, felt it moving, and getting up and tumbling it over, we found the owner of the house and his wife under it, half dead with fear and suffocation.

When we dragged them out, they made such a noise that a crowd of the villagers came to the house. We feared for our lives, but there was no light, and we had to grope our way. I missed the way, and coming to a door, opened it, and put out my hand to feel, and stroked my fingers down a Chinaman's face, the door I had opened being a cupboard, and the man in it, hiding there in terror of us. I made them laugh with my description of the horror I felt when I stroked down this naked face. I took it to be a dead man, but not being sure, half closed the door to prevent him coming out and felt for him again, till I came to his bit of a nose, which I pulled until he screeched out, on which I scrambled across the room, and coming to a door, made out of the house by a back way, and ran for my life.

This story put Norie in mind of a hospital adventure, and when he was done Tripshore sang. He had a strong voice and a correct ear, and his song was a sailor's song, the melody of which was the windlass chorus, "Across the Western ' Ocean." Hunter and I knew the air, and guessing at the words, we helped Tripshore by joining in at the end of every verse.

By this time the night was all about us, the moon brightly shining, and the great stars flaking the sea with their rickling silver. These crystalline reflections were made exceedingly beautiful by the play of the phosphorus in the sea. The mysterious fires rolled with the swell, and resembled puffs of green steam. The water broken by the boat's stem tinkled through our voices like the bubbling of a fountain, but so strongly phosphorescent was the sea, that our wake was a line of fire : and when Miss Tuke leaned over to look at it, I saw it shining in her eyes and shimmering upon her face, as though phosphorous had been rubbed over her skin.

Our story-telling and singing not only killed the time, but did us good by distracting our thoughts from our position. I kept the ball spinning as long as I could, and then we fell into a general conversation, in the midst of which, and whilst the seamen in the forward part of the boat were arguing upon the bearings of the island we had left, and whilst Norie, who had taken a seat next to Miss Tuke, was talking with her in low tones, I found myself asking Mrs. Stretton what would be her plans when she arrived at Kingston.

"I hardly know, Mr. Walton. I feel like an ocean stray. Besides, I may not be able to get to Kingston, for, should we be picked up by a vessel, we can scarcely suppose that she will be bound to that place."

"Have you no friends in Ireland ?" I asked.

"Yes, but they are poor. They will be able to do nothing for me."

"You have other friends who are not poor," said Sir Mordaunt, gently. "Your future need give you no anxiety."

She held her peace, perhaps scarcely understanding him. But I did. Indeed, I had all along suspected that if our lives were preserved my great-hearted friend would stand by this poor woman whom he had been instrumental in rescuing from a horrible death.

I thought the hour would now be about nine, or even later, and counselled the women to lie down and take rest whilst the boat ran quietly. There was room for all three of them to lie upon the sail in the bottom of the boat, and as Miss Tuke hung back, I got Carey to set the example. She crouched down and got under the thwarts, and when she had stretched herself along the sail she said she was very comfortable. Then Mrs.

Stretton lay down, and, after a little persuasion from her uncle, Miss Tuke crept under the thwarts. So there were the three of them, snug enough. The end of the sail rolled up furnished them with a pillow, and the other end was turned over them. The thwarts overshadowing their faces, protected them from the moonlight and the dew.

As for us men, there was nothing for it but to sleep as we could. The seamen and I divided ourselves into watches, as we had done on the island, it being arranged that I should steer and keep a lookout for the first two hours. These fellows made no trouble about sleeping. Tripshore put his back against the mast, folded his arms, dropped his head, and was asleep in a few moments. Hunter was bothered at first to pose himself comfortably. He tried first one place, then another, until at last he hit upon a posture that pleased him—in the eyes, with his face looking aft, and the dog bolstering him on the right side, and in a short time he was as motionless as the other.

But neither Sir Mordaunt nor Norie could go to sleep for some time, though the doctor closed his eyes and kept his head hung. Sir Mordaunt, indeed, did not try to sleep for a while, but sat close against me, speaking in whispers. We had much to talk about—our cruise, our shipwreck, Lady Brookes's death, our present position, and our chances of preservation. At last weariness mastered him, his voice failed him, and he began to nod, and soon, by his regular breathing, I knew he was asleep.

The breeze held steady ; a little more weight had come into it before Sir Mordaunt fell asleep, and the sail pulled well. The narrow furrows of the sea ran in short flashes of foam and broke up the starlight in the water, but gave instead a brilliant surface of phosphoric radiance. On our starboard beam the ocean was a tremulous field of moonlight, but the horizon in the north was very dark, though the luster of the moon made the sky pale to a long distance beyond the zenith. The water seethed at the boat's stem, and the sobbing sounds caused by the eddies in the wake were very mournful for me, a solitary listener, to hearken to. Indeed, it was a solemn time. It was not only the thoughts of the narrow planks which lay between us and eternity, nor the speculation as to the future, that was forever active in me. It was the being surrounded by sleepers ; it was looking into the bottom of the boat and seeing the glimmering faces of the women in the darkness there ; on one side of me the baronet, with the moonlight shining on his hollow countenance, in which all the anguish of the past few days

had left an imprint cruelly visible, even in that colorless light ;
on the other side Norie, who had met misfortune as a gallant
man should, helping us all as heartily as was in his power,
peacefully resting, with his chin upon his breast and his arm
hanging idly down ; and forward the figures of the two men
and the dog, dark as bronze statues, and as motionless. I say
it was the looking first at those silent and unconscious beings
and then away at the leagues of sea, and the serene stars, and
the silver moon, poised in the silvery blue ether, that made
this watch of mine as solemn to me as a long prayer. The sense
of loneliness no pen could express. The slumber of the people
about me heightened it. Now and again one would mutter
softly ; once there came a laugh from the bottom of the boat ;
frequently I would hear a deep sigh, that sounded above the
mild complaining of the wind in the sail and the delicate hissing of the passing water.

Again and again I stood up to search the water, and shortly
before I called Tripshore I thought I saw a darkness on the sky
over the starboard bow ; but when I pointed the telescope at it
I could see the stars there shining down to the very level of
the deep.

But the bright moon was very comforting. It enabled me
to see all my companions, and to command a wide expanse of
water, which was like giving the soul breathing room, for nothing is more terrible than darkness to persons placed as we
were. It seems to cloak and muffle up the instincts, and fold
up the spirit as though it were death's mantle. Besides, I
could watch the compass, and know how we were heading.

I held my place longer than two hours, as I believe, wishing
Tripshore to get all the refreshment he could out of his spell of
sleep ; but I grew so drowsy at last that, lest I should uncon-
sciously fall asleep myself, I was forced to arouse him. I had
to awaken Norie, to hold the tiller, whilst I went forward to
call Tripshore, not choosing to sing out to him and disturb
the others. But before doing this I made a calculation of the
distance run since we had left the island, and scribbled the
figures down on the thwart.

At the first touch the seaman started up. I whispered to him
that his watch had come round ; and then telling him to keep
the boat dead as she was going, to look smartly about for ships,
and to call me if the wind drew ahead or the weather changed,
I took his place, and speedily fell asleep.

CHAPTER XX.

When I opened my eyes again, the dawn was just breaking, and I discovered, to my wonder, that I had slept right through the night. No one had aroused me. My limbs were as stiff as broomsticks, from having been kept in one posture for so many hours, and my clothes were saturated with dew. I gaped with something of astonishment at the scene of sky and ocean, for it was not easy to immediately realize our position. And then again the sight my eyes encountered was very striking for a man whose senses were struggling out of the cocoon of sleep to behold ; for the dawn in the east lay in the sky like a sheet of delicately green glass, faintly illuminated at the water line, and melting into blackness as it approached the zenith. But the rest of the heavens were wrapped in night, and the sea was of a pitchy black, even under the dawn, which made the horizon stand out against it with fearful distinctness.

But, even as my eye rested on that strange, cold, pallid green light, it changed its color into primrose, the sky brightened into sapphire and gold, and the sun showed his flaming head.

Hunter was at the helm, and Tripshore asleep in the bows of the boat, but the sun woke him up ; and as I sat rubbing my legs, to get the blood to circulate, and looking around me, Sir Mordaunt called good-morning to me, and then Norie ; and glancing at the bottom of the boat, I perceived that everybody was awake.

I scrambled off my perch and helped the women on to their feet, and was glad to learn that they had all managed to get some sleep. Then, taking the glass, I planted my back against the mast and searched the sea, that was now brightly illuminated by the soaring sun, but to no purpose : there was nothing to be seen.

The breeze that was propelling us when I fell asleep still blew, the water was smooth, and the morning had broken with a cloudless sky. Both Hunter and Tripshore told me there had been no change of wind or weather in their watches, and when therefore I made a calculation to jot down upon the thwart, I reckoned that we could not have run less than forty miles from the time of our leaving the island.

"It is impossible," I exclaimed, "that we can go on sailing very much longer without sighting land. That we have not made land sooner, I can only account for by supposing that the island on which we were wrecked must be lying further to the eastward than we have imagined."

"In that case ought we not to steer more to the westward Walton ?" asked Sir Mordaunt.

"I hardly think so," I replied. "Our object is to meet with ships, and not to box ourselves up among a mass of reefs and cays and uninhabited islands."

"Is the compass right, sir, d'ye think?" inquired Hunter.

"Yes," I said, "judging from the bearings of the stars, and the rise and set of the sun."

"Oh, Mr Walton," cried Miss Tuke, "I hope we shall not have to pass another night in this boat !"

"Courage, Ada, courage !" exclaimed the baronet. " See what a beautiful day has come. Let us think of ourselves as a pleasure party blown out to sea further than we intended to go. There is no danger ; a little patience, my love, and all will be well ; " and he looked at her, lightly shaking his head, and smiling mournfully.

I glanced at her, to see how she bore all this hard usage of the sea. Her roughened hair, her pale face full of deep anxiety and grief, her apparel creased and defaced by the wet and the wear and tear of shipwreck, did not in my sight, at all events, in the least degree impair her beauty. Indeed, I could not help thinking that all this disorder of attire, and the wild sparkle in her pretty eyes, and the restlessness of her movements and glances, gave her charms a character that accentuated them with a fresh and fascinating picturesqueness. Norie appeared to share in this opinion, for he would frequently look at her with fervent admiration.

Mrs. Stretton, on the other hand, was much more passive. She gazed dreamily at us with her fine dark eyes as we conversed, yet was always quick to give a smile to any of us who met her glance. She had a rougher appearance than Miss Tuke, owing to her black hair, which, as I have elsewhere said, was remarkably abundant. and hard to stow away without combs and hairpins and such things. She too was very pale, but her lips were red and healthy, and her eyes clear and shining.

Of the women, indeed, Carey endured these trials the worst. She had been a plump, piquante little woman aboard the *Lady Maud ;* but now her cheeks were fallen in, her eyes sunk and the hollows dark, her lips pale and dry and tremulous, and the expression of her face was haggard, like that of a sick person. I should have supposed that a woman in her station of life would have borne hardship very much more stubbornly than Miss Tuke. But the truth is, and most men's experience confirms it, the more thoroughbred a woman is, the more effectually can she cope with and support trouble. I would rather any day be in peril with a lady, with no experience whatever of hardships, than with a woman of mean extraction, who has had to rough it, who has had to work, and who therefore, you might imagine, would be a great help in time of danger, or when hearty activity or the negative virtue of fortitude was wanted.*

Carey's box, that had already done service as a bailer, was now used as a washbasin. I filled it with salt water, and the women refreshed themselves by bathing their hands and faces. We men cooled ourselves by splashing up the water over the side. This done, I served out some salt beef and biscuit.

I had taken Hunter's place, and was steering the boat, eating with one hand and balancing the tiller with the other. The seamen were forward, Hunter feeding the dog. I was pointing to the figures I had scribbled upon the thwart, and Sir Mordaunt was calculating with me the distance we had traversed, when I was startled by a vehement cry from Tripshore, and, raising my eyes, I saw him standing with his arm around the mast, and pointing to the sea over our bows.

"Sail ho!" he yelled.

At this magic sound the whole of us sprang to our feet as one person. The sun being well on the left of us, the horizon ahead was beautifully clear and the sea a soft violet, and upon it, quite visible to the naked eye, was a speck of white.

I snatched up the glass and pointed it.

"Yes," I cried, "it is a sail!"

Miss Tuke clapped her hands, and gave a loud hysterical laugh.

"Which way is she standing, sir?" shouted Tripshore.

"I can't tell you yet," I replied. "She will be a square-rigged vessel I believe, for what is showing of her canvas is square."

---

* Lady Brookes's behavior may be quoted against me, but it will be remembered that she was an invalid.

"Let me look at her," exclaimed Sir Mordaunt, in a voice quivering with excitement.

I gave him the glass. He crossed over to the mast, to rest the telescope against it, and took a long, long look, but could make no more of the object than I.

"But it *is* a sail, uncle?" cried Miss Tuke.

"Certainly it is," he replied; "but it is impossible to tell which way she is going."

The glass was passed from hand to hand.

"Let us finish our breakfast," said I, sitting down again. "Though that vessel should pass without noticing us, it is enough that we have seen her to prove that we are in navigable waters at last. There will be other vessels about, though we should miss yonder one; be sure of that."

They all seated themselves except Tripshore, who had the glass, and kept it fixed on that small white spot; but though Sir Mordaunt and Miss Tuke pretended to eat, I saw that the sight of that sail had taken away their appetite. They could not remove their eyes from the horizon where that gleaming speck was.

I dare say my own emotions were not less strong than theirs, but I perceived the need of assuming an unconcerned demeanor, so that, if the vessel passed away from us, I should be able with a good face to say that her disappearance signified no more than another spell of patience for us, and that other sails would be showing before sundown. Nevertheless, I was looking, too, all the time, at that distant sail, and every moment growing more and more puzzled by its steadiness and appearance.

"If yonder is a ship," I exclaimed at last, "she is bound to be coming or going our way. We are heading a steady course, and should have noticed by this time if she is crossing our hawse. But she's mighty slow if she's coming our way, and if she is steering as we are, what manner of vessel must she be to let a boat like this overhaul her?"

"What do you make of her, Tripshore?" called out Sir Mordaunt.

"Why, sir," he answered, "it looks to me as though that bit of white is the main-royal or topgallant-s'l of a ship heading south."

"But do we rise it?" I asked.

"No, sir. All that it does is to grow bigger, without rising," he answered.

I told him to pass me the glass, and I took another steady look.

The object was unquestionably a ship's sail—apparently, as Tripshore had said, the main-royal of a ship ; it was square, and white as silver ; it was certainly bigger too than it was when I had first looked at it, which struck me as most extraordinary, for the enlargement of the sail proved that we were approaching it, and I could not conceive how it was that other portions of the vessel did not show themselves.

"No use speculating," said I ; "we must wait and see."

There was a light swell rolling up from the westward, that made the water look like a waving sheet of dark blue shot-silk ; the sea was crisped with little foamy ripples, which ran along with us ; but the sun had gathered its fires fast, and was pouring them fiercely down upon our unsheltered bodies ; whilst the atmosphere seemed almost breezeless, in cousequence of our being dead before the wind. At intervals a number of flying fish would spark out of the melting glass-like blue of the water and scatter in prismatic flashes. A frigate-bird came up out of the north and hovered at a height of about thirty feet over the boat balancing itself on its exquisitely graceful wings for a minute or so and then fled and vanished like a beam of light. But we took no notice of these things nor of the stinging heat of the sun, our thoughts being chained to that sail ahead, that was slowly enlarging its form, but never rising, so as to exhibit other sails, beneath it.

"That's no ship, sir," said Hunter, breaking a long silence.

"It looks like a small lugger-rigged boat," exclaimed Sir Mordaunt.

"It certainly is not a ship," said I.

We waited and watched. The sail was a most clear object now, and with the naked eye we could see that it was well on this side the horizon—indeed, the blue water-line rose beyond it.

On a sudden Tripshore let drop the glass to his side, and, looking around, motioned to me with his head. I quitted the helm, and clambered over to where he stood.

"Look ! " said he, in a low voice, with a note of horror in it. " You may see what it is now."

His manner startled me. I took the glass hurriedly, and leveled it.

"My God ! " I cried, "what a meeting ! "

It was the raft we had sent adrift on the preceding day ! The sail was full, the strange machine was swarming along steadily, at the masthead was the piece of inscribed plank, forming a cross upon the water, and with his back to the mast sat the dead messenger.

My blood ran cold. It was a dreadful object to encounter upon that lonely sea. And now that it was come, the disappointment stung me like the very fang of death. I looked round upon my companions, with a hopeless face.

" What is it ? " cried Miss Tuke, instantly remarking my looks.

" The raft we sent afloat yesterday," I answered.

She hid her face in her hands. Sir Mordaunt sat looking at the thing, with stony eyes, but neither he nor Mrs. Stretton nor Carey made any observation. The raft was right ahead, and in a short time we should be up with it. To us, who knew what its freight was, it was bad enough to have even the sail of it in sight ; but to come in eyeshot of the corpse, that would by this time be a most loathsome object, was a thing that would have been unendurable to our shaken and agitated weary hearts. Interpreting my companions' thoughts by my own, I returned to the helm, and headed the boat into the west. This brought the wind abeam ; the little craft felt the increased pressure and buzzed along sharply, riding over the swell, that was now dead ahead, like a cork.

I whispered to the baronet that the corpse would have been too shocking an object for the women to see.

"Yes," he answered, under his breath ; " and for us too. I could not have borne it. But I hope, now that the raft can no longer serve our purpose, it may speedily go to pieces. The inscription will set people hunting for us."

"If we are rescued, the news will soon get about," I answered.

We drew rapidly away from the forlorn and dismal fabric, yet it excited a fascination that constrained me to keep on stealing glances at it. The condition of mind to which our shipwreck had reduced me was well qualified to furnish a wild and ghastly significance to that dead seaman sailing along out there. I could not dispossess my imagination of the idea that he was following me with his eyes, and I figured a kind of blind upbraiding in them for leaving him in that mocking, unconsecrated plight. I had the face before me as I had seen it when we sent the raft adrift. It was a dreadful memory to come into my mind at such a time, and a foolish disposition to shed tears assured me of what I had not before suspected, that our hardships and anxieties had lamentably reduced my strength, and that, if we continued in this state much longer, those weakly women there would be able to boast of much more physical stamina than I.

I believe this very thought was in my head when I was aroused from the miserable reverie into which I had sunk by Hunter's shouting, "Sail ho !" at the very top of his voice. I started up savagely, maddened for the moment by the fear of another disappointment. The man was pointing into the northwest, and Mrs. Stretton and Miss Tuke, clinging to each other, looked wildly in that direction, whilst Sir Mordaunt and Norie stood peering, with their hands shading their eyes.

" Do you see her, sir? " shouted Hunter. " It's no raft this time ! See how she rises !"

I looked, and saw a sail—this time no raft indeed, as Hunter had said, but a vessel swiftly rearing her white canvas above the blue, inch by inch, foot by foot, so that, watching her with the glass, I saw her fore course come up until the arching foot of it was exposed, and then the glimmering top of the black hull quivered in the refractive light upon the water-line.

She was heading dead for us. Until we were sure of this, no one spoke ; but when I cried out the news, Tripshore and Hunter and Norie uttered a loud hurrah ! Miss Tuke clasped her hands above her head, and gave a long, mad laugh ; Mrs. Stretton sobbed as if her heart would break ; Carey fell a dancing in the bottom of the boat ; and Sir Mordaunt threw his arms round my neck, and, with his head lying on my shoulder, breathed like a dying man.

I broke away from my poor friend, and bawled to Hunter to lower the sail and stop the boat's way ; and, whipping a handkerchief out of Norie's pocket, I fastened it to one of the paddles, and bade Tripshore stand up in the bows of the boat and wave the signal.

The vessel came down upon us fast. What her rig was I could not yet see. She had a main skysail set, and a coil of foam sparkled at her glossy sides, and ran up the sea behind her in a flashing white line. We had cheered, and given way to the passion of excitement and rapture that the sight of her had kindled in us ; but we grew silent very soon, and watched her coming breathlessly. I knew her people could not fail to see us. But would they heave to? Would they attempt our rescue? We had to find that out, and the waiting was such mental agony as there are no words to convey any idea of.

One of the most moving memories which my heart carries of our shipwreck, is the faces of my companions turned toward the approaching vessel. Expectation had so wrought upon their lineaments, as to harden them into the severity and immobility of marble; they looked to have been petrified at the very moment when their staring eyes, their parted lips, the forward posture of their heads, showed that the hope and the fear in them were at their greatest height.

Suddenly Tripshore turned his gaping face aft, and cried, in a hoarse voice of triumph, "She'll heave-to, sir!" And, as he said this, the vessel, with her mainsail hanging in the leech-lines and her skysail halyards let go, slightly shifted her helm, and went past us at a distance of about five times her own length, drawing out as she passed into a small handsome bark of about three hundred and fifty tons, with a clipper bow and elliptical stern, a low freeboard, and a white netting round her short raised after-deck. From this point, that was apparently the roof of a deck-cabin, several men were watching us, and forward a small crowd of heads overhung the bulwarks. As soon as she was to leeward of us, she put her helm down, swung her foreyards, and lay hove-to.

"Out with your paddles, men!" I shouted; and, in a fury of impatience, Tripshore and Hunter threw over the rude oars, and the boat went slowly toward the bark. As we approached, we were hailed by one of the men on the poop.

"Boat ahoy! What boat is that?"

I was overjoyed to be addressed in English, for I had feared from the appearance of the vessel that she was a foreigner. I put my hand to the side of my mouth, and shouted back—

"We are the survivors of the passengers and crew of the schooner-yacht *Lady Maud*, that was lost four days since, on a cay about sixty miles distant from here. We have been adrift since yesterday. Will you take us on board?"

He waved his hand, and answered, "Yes, yes; come alongside. But is that another boat out there?" pointing in the direction where we had last seen the raft.

"No," I cried. "I will explain what that is when we get aboard."

A rope was flung to us, the gangway unshipped, and some steps thrown over. All hands had assembled to see us arrive. The first to be handed up was Miss Tuke; she was followed by Mrs. Stretton and Carey; then went Sir Mordaunt and Norie, the rest of us following with the dog. On gaining the deck a giddiness seized me, and I had to keep fast hold of the arm of the man who had helped me up the steps, to save myself from falling. It was, in truth, the effect of a wild hurry of conflicting emotions; but a short stern struggle subdued the

20

sensation, and glancing around at the men, who were staring at the women and ourselves with open mouths, I asked for the captain.

"I'm the master, sir," said a quiet-looking, sunburnt man, who stood close to the gangway.

I grasped his hand and shook it, and then, without further preface, I told him our story, briefly indeed, though I gave him all the facts.

"Well, sir," said he, when I had done, glancing at Sir Mordaunt very respectfully, "you've had a hard time of it, and I'm glad to have come across you. This bark is the *Princess Louise* from New Providence to Porto Rico. I hope Porto Rico isn't out of your way?"

"No," I answered. "We should be able to get to Europe from Porto Rico without trouble."

"Certainly," said he. "But we sighted a small boat out yonder. Does she belong to your people?"

I told him that she was a raft we had sent adrift from the island, with a board at the masthead inscribed with the circumstances of our shipwreck; but I said nothing about the dead man on it. I then begged him to tell us what reckoning his vessel was now in, explaining that Sir Mordaunt Brookes was anxious to have the bearings of the rock on which we had been wrecked, that he might recover the remains of his wife for interment in England.

"Can you give me your course, and distance run?" said he.

I answered that it was jotted down on the after-thwart in the boat. He at once went over the side into the boat, entered the figures in a pocket-book, and returned.

"We'll get the bearings of your island fast enough presently," said he. "That's a good boat of yours—too good to send adrift. Here, Mr. Swift," he sung out to a man I afterward learnt was his chief mate, "get that boat cleared out, will you, and slung aboard. You can stow her on the booms. And swing the fore-yards as soon as that job's done. Bo'sun, take charge of these two men"—indicating Tripshore and Hunter—"and see that they get something to eat at once. Will you follow me, ladies and gentlemen?"

He led the way into the cabin or deck-house. We hobbled after him, for, owing to our confinement in the boat and the want of space to stretch our limbs, we had some ado to work our legs properly. The cabin was a very plain interior, with a table amidships, flanked by hair sofas, and a row of five small berths on the port side.   We sat down, not because we were weary, but because we found exercise an awkward and inconvenient effort.   The captain, whose name was Broach, went to the cabin door and bawled to he steward, who was among the men on deck, to put some beef and biscuit and claret upon the table.   He then entered his berth, and returned with a large chart of the Bahamas and West India islands, which I saw Sir Mordaunt devouring with his eyes, proving where his heart was.

·'Yesterday," said Captain Broach, "we were in such and such a position, and our position now would be here," said he, putting his finger on the chart.   "You say you have been running fifty miles to the south'ard and east'ard."   He measured the distance, and exclaimed, "Here you are ; here are two cays. It is one of these, gentlemen."

"It will be the one to the norrard," said I.

"Then," said he, writing down the position of the island on a piece of paper and handing it to the baronet, "this will be the latitude and longitude of it, sir."

I reflected, and then addressing Sir Mordaunt, "Those bearings," said I, prove that Purchase was heavily out in his latitude *as well* as his longitude."

He motioned, with an imploring gesture.   "For God's sake, don't recall the man !" said he.   "I desire," he continued, turning to the skipper, " that you will look upon us as passengers, for whose accommodation and entertainment you will charge as you think proper ; though," he said, extending his hand for the other to shake, and speaking with great emotion, "no recompense we can make you will express our gratitude for the prompt and generous help you have given us."

"Say nothing about it, sir," answered the skipper, in a blunt, sailorly way.   " It seems hard that shipwreck should befall gentlemen like you, to whom the sea is no business ; and I am very sorry indeed for the ladies "—giving them a low bow. " Now, steward, bear a hand with the grub, man !   Shove it on the table, *can't* ye ? "

We had not long before eaten our breakfast in the boat, and even had we not already broken our fast, I questioned whether the emotions which kept our hearts hammering in our breasts would have left us any appetite for the victuals on the table. But Captain Broach begged us so heartily to eat, that we made a show of munching just to please him.   He said he had but the cabins we saw.   One of them was his, and the next one the mate's, and the third abutting on that the second mate's and the carpenter's. "But," said he, "if you don't mind a squeeze, I think we can manage. The ladies will have that cabin "—pointing. "There are two bunks in it, and we can lay a mattress on the deck." And then he arranged for me to share the mate's cabin, Norie the second mate's, and Sir Mordaunt would have a cabin to himself.

This was a very good arrangement, and so the matter was settled.

We then inquired how long it would take to reach Porto Rico.

" I give the *Louise* four days," he answered, " reckoning fine weather and breezes after this pattern. When I tell you that we left New Providence the day before yesterday at six o'clock in the evening, you'll believe the bark has got heels."

He sat talking with us, asking questions, and, with every answer we made him, growing more and more respectful. He told Sir Mordaunt that he would find no difficulty in chartering a small vessel to fetch Lady Brookes's body ; indeed, he said, it would give him pleasure to see to that himself, for he knew a man at San Juan who owned a trading sloop, a fast vessel, that would not keep Sir Mordaunt waiting. He also told us that steamers from Liverpool, Southampton, Spain, and the United States touched at Porto Rico—how often he could not say, but often enough to serve our end.

" And now," said he, "there's Mr. Swift and myself—I'll say nothing about the second mate—plain sailors, with kits not good enough for a man to go to Court in ; but such as our togs are, gentlemen, you're heartily welcome to the loan of them till you can get better. I'm only sorry," addressing Miss Tuke, "that we can't accommodate you ladies in that way. But we're all men aboard the *Louise,* and so you'll please take that as our excuse."

He called the steward, to see to our cabins and supply our wants, and, bestowing a regular all-round bow upon us, he went on deck, where we could hear the men singing out as they braced round the yards and got way upon the bark.

My story is as good as ended. You have had our shipwreck, and now our rescue. But there still remains a short length of line to coil down, and I may as well leave the yarn clean and ship-shape.

Imagine that two days have passed. In that time we have

slept well, eaten well, pulled ourselves together. We have all of us knelt down in the cabin, and offered up hearty and earnest thanks to Almighty God for His merciful preservation of us; and now we are looking about us with tranquil hearts, which have already grown used to this new condition of life, waiting with patience for the hour when the cheery cry of "Land oh!" shall bring us within reach of the scores of things our destitute condition demands; now and again talking of the dead; of the yacht, that the sea had scattered as the wind scatters chaff; and of our sufferings and anxieties and painful struggles on the little island. The weather remained beautiful—a constant wind blowing, though shifting occasionally to the northward, and then hauling back again to the eastward, the sea calm and frosty with the breaking heads of the tiny surges, and a heaven of stainless, glorious, tropical blue.

It was the night of the second day, dating from our rescue. I had been conversing with Mrs. Stretton and Mr. Swift, the chief mate of the *Princess Louise*, who, it turned out, had known Captain Stretton and the vessel he commanded. In another part of the deck were Norie and Miss Tuke and her uncle. The moon was standing over the sea, shedding little or no radiance upon the sky, but whitening the water under it with lines of light which looked like silver serpents, as the swaying of the swell and the fluttering of the ripples kept them moving.

I left Mrs. Stretton and the mate, and walked to the end of the short poop. The wheel was just under me, and the figure of the fellow who grasped it was so motionless, that he and the wheel and yellow binnacle card were more like a painting than real things. I stood drawing at a cigar, enjoying the tobacco with unspeakable relish after my long-enforced abstinence, and contemplating the beautiful dreamlike picture of the bark lifting her heights of glimmering canvas into the dark air, blotting out a whole heaven of stars with her dim and ghostly cloths, amid the hollows of which, and among the delicate gear and rigging, the soft tropical breeze was whispering in notes that sounded like faint and distant voices singing. The eastern sky was glorious with stars, of such magnitude and beauty as you never behold in our northern climes, with a fine sharp whiteness, though here and there the smaller stars shown in delicate blues and in rose color, like the reflection of a bright flame in highly polished metal. It was a night for solitude. The seething of the thin line of foam at the vessel's sides, the occasional clank of the wheel-chains, the mysterious song of the wind up in the darkness among the pallid sails there, the leagues of black water, the star-laden sky, and the moon clothing with the beauty of her soft, white, misty light a large circumference of the dark heavens, combined to produce a deep sense of peace in the heart, not without melancholy, but infinitely soothing, and to make one almost dread the intrusion of commonplace sounds.

My thoughts were full of the past, and let me say of the future likewise. A low, soft, girlish laugh from the group at the other end of the deck had set my fancy rambling, and in the short time I was permitted to stand there musing, the thoughts which swept through my mind—a commingling of shipwreck and ocean perils, and of fancies very much nearer heaven than any the deep could yield me—made a wild and singular panorama of visions.

But my reverie was interrupted by Sir Mordaunt coming up to me. He stood at a little distance, peering, as if he was not sure, and then said, " Is that you, Walton ? "

"Yes," I answered.

"What a perfect night, is it not ? " he exclaimed. " It makes our shipwreck seem no more than a dream. We might still be on board the poor *Lady Maud*, and all the anguish we have suffered and escaped, a nightmare."

" We are lucky," said I, " to have fallen into such kind hands. But I am rather puzzled to know what I shall do when we reach Porto Rico. Is there a consul there ? "

"Oh," said he, "I have arranged with Captain Broach to obtain the funds we shall require. Don't let that trouble you."

"And Mrs. Stretton ? Shall you send her to Kingston ? "

"I will wait till I am ashore, to talk to her. I have a scheme —but I am not yet resolved. She shall find me her friend. She is strangely mixed up in the cruelest experience that ever befell me, and the sufferings she has passed through give her the strongest claims upon my sympathy. By the way," he continued, "I have a piece of news for you. It scarcely took me by surprise. Norie has proposed to Ada, and she has accepted him."

"Indeed ! "

" I say I am not surprised, because I knew all along that he admired her. But I did not know that she was in love with him. Did you ? "

" No."

" At the beginning of our cruise, don't you remember that she used to snub him ? "

I said nothing.

"But," he said, "I am sure he will make her happy.   I shall be glad to see her settled.   I had hoped to have her as a companion, now that I am alone," said he, in a shaky voice, "but a husband is better than an uncle for a girl, and I cannot question, from her manner of speaking to me just now, that she is really attached to the doctor."

I kept my voice very well, and I am sure that he had no suspicion of the truth.   Between that girl and me there had been little passages full of encouragement on her part.   I held my peace while Sir Mordaunt talked on, coming presently to his wife, and speaking of her with tears in his voice, if not in his eyes.   Then, taking my chance, I crossed over to where Miss Tuke and Norie were standing, looking at the waning moon—a blushing emblem of my own idle dream—and addressing the girl with as much cordiality as I could infuse into my manner, I said that Sir Mordaunt had told me of her engagement, and that I would not lose a minute in offering her and Norie my sincere congratulations.

"Thank you very much, Mr. Walton," said she ; and Norie added that he felt sure that the news would give me pleasure.

And so ended a little business that everybody will smile at but I.   But I relate it, because I doubt if the story of my shipwreck would be quite complete without it.

I put on a wooden face for the rest of the time, determined that Miss Tuke at all events should not suppose I considered myself jilted.   But this matter hastened my departure for San Juan, where we arrived in due course.   Sir Mordaunt begged me to stay until his wife's remains had been removed, and then accompany him and the others to Europe ; but I told him I was anxious to get home, and an opportunity for leaving Porto Rico occurring three days after our arrival, I took leave of my companions, bidding poor Mrs. Stretton a tender farewell, in the full belief that I should never see her again.

Two months after my return to England, I received a long letter from Sir Mordaunt.   He told me that he had brought his wife's remains with him, and that they were now interred in the family vault at ——.   Also (I should perhaps be surprised to hear), Mrs. Stretton had consented to come and take charge of his establishment, as housekeeper.   He asked me to spend a fortnight with him, but I had other engagements, and could not get away.

Not very long after the receipt of this letter, came an invitation to attend Ada Tuke's marriage. I could not go, though I would gladly have been present, if only to sustain the character of indifference I had assumed. However, I took care to call upon the bride and her husband on their return from abroad when passing through London, and, time being on my side, my impersonation could not have been better had my indifference been honest ; and I was sure the bride went away convinced that any suspicions she might have had that I had been fond of her were altogether unfounded. Norie is now in a practice in a town in the north of England,.and I believe doing very well. Sir Mordaunt gave his niece five thousand pounds and a house of furniture, and I don't doubt they needed all they can get, for the little Nories threaten to make a big family.

I often visited Sir Mordaunt, and when I first went down to his house I was pleased to find Tripshore installed there as a sort of all-round man, having no special duties, but lending a hand generally.   He told me that Tom Hunter had left San Juan, before the others, with a present from Sir Mordaunt of fifty pounds in his pocket, but what had become of him he did not know.   Tripshore and the noble dog who had saved our lives were great friends, and always together, I heard.   The fine animal knew me at once and it curiously delighted me to be remembered by him.

On every occasion of my visit to —— I had the pleasure of shaking Mrs. Stretton by the hand and complimenting her on her looks.   The baronet would tell me that she managed his household capitally, and that if she left him he would miss her as he would his right hand.   His references to the late Lady Brookes gradually grew less frequent, whilst his praise of the shipwrecked widow improved in strength and quality ; so that, exactly three years from the date of his arrival in England, I was not surprised to get a letter from him, in which he said that Mrs. Stretton had become Lady Brookes.

THE END.

9 780992 523459